Druid Quest: Magics Heir, Book One

G. L. CRAMB

MAGPIE PUBLISHING

Prologue

Ètœn Bearheart has been in the saddle from sunrise to dusk, near to twelve turns of a sand-glass. Near now to his journey's end, a destination he alone knows, not Druid, nor Aeglèsia. Their wish, not his, for he carries a burden not at all certain he can bear.

He has sworn an Oath on all that he holds dear, and Ètœn Bearheart would be ever faithful to his word and loyal to a fault as his heart beat steadfast and true to his name. He will keep his Oath to any end, even as he will forever hold his deep feelings for the woman to whom he has sworn it.

From crushing waves of the Great Eastern Sea crashing against granite cliffs upon which the Druid's Keep stood, to the foothills of the Shadow Mountains, braced against the Great Western Sea, he has traversed the very breadth of Aeryth. Having left sparse-of-tree slopes and grassy knolls betwixt high rocky mountains, arriving now to a land of thick forest, rivers, and lush mountainsides. Here is a land more akin to Ètœn's childhood homestead, both being the smallest of villages, and a place of relative solitude, with abundant wildlife in the surrounding countryside. Using mostly trappers' and traders' trails, he's shunned contact with Mid Realm folk for the near three full moons it has taken him in his travel. Here he will feel, in most part, safe for a time.

He has chosen his destination for the reasons stated, but also, because loyal friends of like mind and history call it home. They had themselves, a'times past, parted ways with the life he is now leaving.

Though no longer garbed so, Ètœn remains an elite soldier—a warrior of greatest repute on many a field of battle. In most cities and townes across the whole of Aeryth he would be known and honored as mayhaps the Kingdom's most prolific Kingsman, a storied soldier who has brought the King's justice down upon countless enemies.

Standing a head above the tallest man he has ever met, Ètœn's shoulders are broad, his reach long and his mean and manner in battle fiercer than any tiger cat. Though he is sky-bolt quick with a broadsword, his true love remains his great bow. It had been beautifully crafted by his pæder and felt easy and right in his huge hands. But his soldier's life must be put behind him, and from this sun forth he will carry the name Bard, in lieu of Bearheart.

Though he sits upon a great and proud warhorse, the harness and saddle are homemade and of a common design, akin to any huntsman's or trapper's saddlery. Indeed, it remains the self-same that he had left his humble homestead upon, a score and five-year past. A common traveler's cloak and garment lay about his shoulders, and he wears upon his jaw and chin a growth of sandy blond curls, only somewhat trimmed. His hair a tangle of many moon's growth and with chiseled features, he has what women would certainly call a handsome countenance. He wears an easy smile and is quick to a laugh. As he gazes ahead, finally approaching the small towne's Inn, dusk is settling on this warm spring's sun. The late eve's quiet reflects his mood as it clings to and about him.

On the saddle afore him sits his burden, and takes the form of a younger-a lad not yet having reached his six-year-end. He sits cross-legged and leaning back, fast asleep against the stomach and broad chest of Ètœn... Bard.

But, to Ariastone Côeurdrægon, Ètœn's charge and only responsibility in life now, he will simply be *Da*.

1

Da's Secrets... and a Wolf Pup

His head lay still on my lap, eyes staring up at me. He'd just said something desperately important I fear, though his spoken voice remains just hollow sounds to my ears. I can't make myself understand. It must be important because he'd reached up with bloodied hand to weakly squeeze my wrist as he spoke in the muddled sounds I cannot assemble in my panic. Like his own, my hands are slippery with blood from grievous wounds all about his body.

*I sit up in a sweat, gasping for a breath and...*The sky rumbles.

A long breath drawn in now, I stare back south and westward for a moment to a bright orange and purple sky. The sun is fighting back dusk and a brewing storm. The hairs still standing on the back of my neck as the same bloody scene has rattled me thrice this past fortnight. This time, it has appeared mid-sun. Reality is dragging me back to the present now. Though, again, this vision has felt entirely real, too. I sit, reflecting on how it has found me once more. This sun has been exhausting and I'd laid back on my rock letting it's earlier heat and the warm air about me lull me into a kip.

Thundering grey-green clouds from the south begin to crowd the sky now, with the chill air pulling the sun's warmth from my rock. The wind is rustling the leaves and branches in the trees above me and the kids are bleating and growing a little more anxious. The *sight*, though startlingly real but a moment ago, is fading away. Shaking my head to clear it, I reason I'll hear Da's bell presently as he always rings it around sunset to call me to eve-meal. Plenty of times have I asked him why he still rings it sun after sun as I know when to come, but he just says the bell is an important part of our life. Giving thought to this new memory, a momentary sharp breeze envelopes me as I sit on my rock, forcing a different type of chill to run down my spine, and the other nightmarish vision dissolves completely now.

When I was a younger, he made a game of it; the bells. They held a secret code only for us. Secrets were a fun thing for a seven-year, the age at which I claimed when Da first explained his secret of the bell to me. at the time of the memory. Da would say secrets are a King's goat's whiskers, and he'd rub his chin and make a long face. I had no idea what that could mean, but it made me laugh and want to keep special secrets with him. And it made me want to rub our goat's whiskers, which I often do, to this very sun.

My mind's eye shone on the memory clear as his bell's toll, as I could hear even now, Da saying back then....

"Arias, lad, if I ring the bell but once, it's time to head in for eve-meal," he'd say. "Finish what yer up to and come home. Wash yerself up at the well and come in, to the table.... If it tolls twice, it means we have guests. Come on straight away then, wash up and be on yer best behavior."

And finally, Da would say, "If I ring the bell three times... Now listen to me, Arias, 'cause this is the most important bell tollin' part of the secret. If I ring the bell three times, no matter where ye be, run like a deer to the Frost-Cellar and hide down below, and stay there 'till I come and get ye. When I come get ye, ye'll know it's me by my speaking the pass-word."

"The pass-word? What's the pass-word, Da?

"Why, it would be *Pickles,* o'course!" And his face would brighten noticeably, a smile spreading, whilst mine remained scrunched and rather confused.

"And that's the special secret of the bell, Arias. It's our secret alone. Not for friends, not for anybody but us, do ye understand?"

"Da?" I had asked. "I like our secret code with the bell, but I don't get why I should hide in the Frost Cellar if I hear three bells. It's cold there!?"

This giant of a man just stood, looming over me with sparkling eyes and shaking his finger, then drawing his thumb back to pointing at his broad chest. "That's my secret, lad. I'll not tell ye why till I come to get ye from the Frost-Cellar."

He wouldn't respond any more about the three bells, no matter how many times I'd ask, and so it stuck with me. But when he would a'times mention it to *me.* I'd say, "Da, I'm seven... Or, I'm nine... 'course I remember. It's our secret Da, I wouldn't forget our secret or our secret password – *pickles!*" And I'd laugh, having learned since that pickles were his most favorite treat.

Now well past my sixteen-year-end, Da still rings the bell, once for eve-meal and twice for when Moor or Widow Grayce comes by. He's never rung three times, so I've never learned his secret about that. But nobody except Da would ever find me if I hid in the Frost-Cellar, it being our other real secret. Nobody knows about the Frost-Cellar and to good reason, Da explained.

My thoughts spill back to the present for a moment as the sky rumbles a little bit more. The kids scamper about me, but Bane keeps them close. Sitting atop my rock, we were not too far from where I'd found the kids. And though a ways away from the cottage, I'd hear Da's bell as it sounded across the vale. We were pretty much alone out here, living about half a morn's ride from the nearest towne that folk call Middenvale. Alone, 'cept for Widow Grayce who lived just a small piece down the road towards towne. She said she liked it out here in the quiets, with forest and stream nearby. And she was not your typical woman in any case. She could take down a deer at fifty paces with a bow. Easy and sure as the wind.

I'd seen her do it one day near this very edge of the forest. Afterwards, she saw me watching her from my stone perch and just waved. I wondered how she could see me here, tucked past the edge of the forest inside the tree line at such a distance. A different kind of woman than the ladies in towne; sure certain. She would wear tanned-hide britches as well when she hunted. All the women in towne wear linen skirts and dresses of a sort. Da and her get on really well, too. So, it's not bad having a neighbor like Grayce.

About the Frost-Cellar. See, Da and I didn't need much from towne most fortnights, for life as such. But Da would visit people in towne, drink ale at the Inn's tavern, and he always liked to help people. That being so, we went into towne on a regular basis. And the Frost-Cellar played a part in that. It had some special properties that were quite useful for trading in towne. And only Da and I knew where it lay hidden. And hidden it surely is. Da first took me there as a seven-year, leaving me sweating and exhausted from a trek that took us crisscrossing game trails that only Da could follow. Concealed in plain sight up in the hills, just a small piece off the main fur trader's trail, you wouldn't easily find it. To peer straight at it with the eyes of a falcon you still wouldn't see the fold in the stone rock wall. Still, the entrance opened as wide as Da and almost as tall. It lay disguised, sideways on a tall, sheer rock face of a hill.

When we went in that first time, the cold turned my hike-sweaty skin near to ice. A chilly cloud formed as I breathed out and Da laughed aloud to see the wonder on my face. Da laid a torch he had pulled down from a bracket on the wall at the entrance. Already soaked with lantern oil, the flick of his flint on his blade and he sparked a flame to the torch. We'd entered a cavernous room where Da had stacked burlap bags of vegetables from our gardens and slaughtered game meat and beef and pork hung on great hooks about us. I stood in wonder surveying the cave that lay well hidden in plain sight.

Da explained that the cool kept the meats and vegetables near fresh so we could eat them well into the winter. Stocking the Frost-Cellar with Da became a regular chore after that. We took little chance and were always ever so vigilant to see that nobody ever followed us to the Frost-Cellar. Though hidden, it wasn't far from the trader's trail and they always were a curious sort. This way it remained a secret. But there was something even more special about the Frost-Cellar. Da led me past the shelves and hanging meats and barrels to the back wall, into the shadows and deeper still into the chill. Again, akin to the outer entrance, there is an unseen fold in the rock wall and Da led me around it.

There appeared afore us a stair hewn into the rock and winding down. Making our way downward, after about five or six steps we came to a landing with a few barrels sitting in an alcove. The stair here, turned roundabout and back and we descended a few steps more. Of a sudden, the sound of trickling water met my ears. Still further down, we entered another cavern. The cold here chilled deep, like the coldest winter winds slapping me in the face, and contrary to what one would think, there was light in this room.

Two bored holes in the ceiling, letting sunlight in from far above. Along one wall ran a steady stream of ice-cold water from a hole about Da's height in that wall. The water trickled down into a stone trough that stood about knee-high and ran along the side wall. I ran my fingers through crystal clear and icy water. From the other end of the trough, the stream escaped out into another hole where the wall met an all stone floor and disappeared to places unknown. Da put the torch in a bracket in the stairwell. The sunlight kept the room well-lit, streaming from the holes in the ceiling above. My voice echoed over and over as I finally spoke and Da laughed heartily to my Oohs and Ahhs of the echoing sound. It made me laugh. This, of course, made the echoing that much more extreme and it was too hard for a seven-year-ender to settle down, so we laughed yet more, for just the fun of it, as my breath rose in a billowing frost. Chilly-bumps raced up my arms.

Alas, that cold brought me shivering back to my senses. I settled to a point to where Da could explain this wonder. He couldn't explain the cold exactly, but to say an ancient mægic must be involved. This made my eyes widen and pull in a cold breath 'cause some of Da's tales were about ancient mægics. Those were the tales that held a seven-year-end captive. He did, however, tell me why the cold was very useful to us.

"Do you see, the boxes sunk in the stone floor about you?"

And I did. There were maybe a dozen large holes placed around the room, some with what appeared to be oaken boxes laid within the holes and were filled with winter ice. And yet the heat of summer lay just outside.

"Da! This is where you get the ice we take on down into towne and to the Inn."

Another of Da's secrets revealed! As far back as I can recall, four times in a fortnight, Da would wake me afore dawn, load me on the bench on our wagon and take me into towne. The wagon is always full with covered bundles in the back, wrapped in stiff leather. The large box shaped bundles were cold to the touch. After the ride into towne, Da would pull round back of the Inn, unwrap what turned out to be huge blocks of ice, and he would use great metal tongs to pick up the ice blocks and carry them down into the cellar under the Inn. Then we'd go up into the kitchens above and eat a grand morn-meal prepared special by Mãam Bergierre, as the Innkeeper thanked Da. He'd always slap down a few coin in front of Da, as well. Master Bergierre would often say Da was the reason the Inn was always so popular with folk in summer. Da would say Mãam Bergierre's cooking had more to do with it. Mãam Bergierre would of course hear this and give him back a wide smile and we always got the biggest portions on our plates.

The memory fell away as flashes of thundering sky-bolts lit up the entire and ever darkening-grey sky as multiplying storm clouds rolled over the setting sun to the west. A gust of the gathering winds threatened to blow me from my perch on the rock, the kids bleated the louder for it and even young Bane howled. I love a good storm.

As if to a cue, Da's Bell rang a clear, crisp toll across the valley. Picking up the kids, who were shaking now, I snuggled each under an arm and slid from my rock perch on sure feet, landing upon the forest floor in a swirl of autumn windblown leaves. Starting home at a trot, Bane followed, nipping at my heels. I made it my personal game to arrive home afore the sky opened up and soaked me to the bone. I am quick, always have been. Da always said I move as fast and silent as a deer chased by a mountain cat.

Past sixteen-year-end now, and mostly past my growth spurt, I remained more than a head shorter than Da still and nowhere near as large. My defining characteristics are probably my eyes. They are a sparkling gold circling around a silver gray that sometimes appears emerald or even lavender in the right light. There is never a person that does not glance twice at them whenever I first make eye contact. My hair, a mousey brown, has unruly streaks of blond that won't be tamed. I let it grow long as it hides one of my more embarrassing features. Da insisted hiding them unwarranted, as I should take pride in all that I am, but the unusual pointed curl to my upper ears did nothing for my ego. When somebody would look into my eyes and note their unusual color, it would a'times be followed by an exclamation of awe. But should they notice my ears, I most often heard a curt 'Oh'.

Though fairly tall to my peers, I would be oft described as wiry with knotted muscles, to Da's huge brawn and bulk. My hands and fingers were unusually long. In spite of my height, where Da had to duck under every door lintel, I remained a hand short of reaching them. Da stood as wide as an ox and as strong as one as well. He has arms thicker than my legs and legs of a size to match no other. I am strong from chore and work about the homestead and Da's friend Moor named me lithe and quick. He insisted this would serve me better than being a mountain of a man like Da. I guess I took after my mœther's bloodline.

On days that Da would leave me to my own doings, which happened more often as I grow older, I sometimes run the entire day, hardly stopping at all, traveling through the forest up into the high hills surrounding our homestead and exploring the countryside. I would chase deer and outrun bear and climb rock outcroppings and run all the way home as well. When Da would ask about my day, I'd tell him the fish were jumping clear out of the water at Moon Lake. His face in wonder, he'd admit a long hard two day's trek to the lake for him when pushed hard. I'd reached it and returned in a day hardly winded.

Reaching the homestead just as the clouds are beginning to release their torrents of stinging rain, I drop the kids in the barn and quickly, washing up at the pump, make my way to the cottage porch and door just afore the downpour. The door squeaks on worn hinges as I enter, Lilit's and Jilly's heads popping up from their cozy blanket in the cottage corner and turn to me.

Stew with mutton from the towne butcher make the eve-meal tonight. This is a treat because Da doesn't keep sheep, and we don't have it regularly. The smells of carrots, tubers, and onions in thick gravy waft about the cottage and make my mouth near to drooling. Da serves the stew in a bread trencher that he fresh baked in his homemade stone oven.

Hot, it's hot! But it is delicious and eases the hunger, sure certain. Having not eaten since morn-meal, and that being only a rasher or two of bacon and a tater slathered in cheese and butter, I'd grown hungry during the hunt for the lost kids. I tell Da where I'd finally found them.

"They were getting trouble from a large, black buck-snake not too far from my rock perch. 'Twas as long as my leg."

"The wolf pup just snagged that snake up back of its head and with a quick whip in his jaws, he put an end to the threat and made lunch of it." My hands mimicking the wolf pup's actions.

"He's a wild and growing pup," Da declares and his eyebrow raises, "and I still wonder about him."

What Da means is that Bane sure certain is no ordinary dog. Being, Da said when we found him, not a dog pup nor coyote nor any type of dingo at all. He is, in fact, a wolf.

When we found him a fortnight back, Da had peered with his head slowly nodding side-a-side into Bane's copper and gold speckled eyes. Bane lay weak and caught in a trader's iron coon trap and securely staked to the ground.

"If I wasn't sure they had gone extinct from this world, I'd say he was a Mountain Dread pup."

As he had approached the pup to pull the trap open, the bedraggled and bloodied young wolf rose up on three legs, bared its teeth, raised his hackles and stared down Da, daring him to come near at his own peril. Now, this was completely foreign to me, as I'd never seen any animal react this way to Da. You see, Da is known as the animal whisperer to all in and around Middenvale. People bring their wild mares and oxen and dogs to Da for taming and training. I'd seen Da stare down a young grizzly or a mountain cat and they'd turned and sulked away. He'd have a stallion trained in a fortnight when its owner couldn't even approach it afore he started. Animals just instinctively take to Da and he to them. He has empathy for all creatures and they just naturally trust him.

When the pup reacted this way to Da, he'd said, "I'll most like need to put him down, Arias. I'll not be able to help him even if I get him free from the trap."

"Da," I insisted. "There has to be another way!"

Determined it not to be so, I approached the wolf pup myself.

Drawing near slowly, I kept my eyes still, gazing deep into his. Of a sudden, as if by mægic, the pup's growl ceased. His lips closed over his teeth and his tail raised in response to my approach. Reaching out, I slowly offered my hand palm down, as Da had taught me. The pup sniffed, then licked my fingers. Next, I rubbed and scratched behind his ear. He responded with a contented growl deep in his throat. Da stared incredulously at this but proceeded to pull the trap jaws apart and remove the pup's damaged leg as I ministered to his ears and he wiggled under my scratching hand.

"I'll be damned," whispered Da. "He certainly can't be a Mountain Dread after all."

While I held the pup, Da wrapped his damaged leg and then made a sling for me to carry him in. He lifted his muzzle to lick the underside of my chin. I would need to carry him as he would not abide Da getting too close. I cupped my hand while Da poured some water into it and the pup eagerly lapped it up. He shortly settled down into the sling Da had fashioned for him and fell asleep against my chest, comforted by my heartbeat, Da said.

"I've never seen a creature act like he did to you, Da," I said quizzically.

Da just chuckled and said, "Mayhaps he thinks me the trapper who set the trap. And I've never seen a creature of the wild react in such a way as that pup did to ye, lad. It's a wolf and a wild untamed creature of this forest here. We will repair its hindquarters and be able to set him free again in a fortnight's time. Though he be just a pup, he's got some meat on his bones and should be able to fend for himself when his leg is whole again."

And so, we headed back to the cottage with the wolf pup in a sling and sound asleep.

"So, what is a Mountain Dread, Da? And why are they all extinct?" I queried on our trip back.

"'Twas a story my Da told me as a younger, and he'd tell me tales like I do ye," his voice quiet and pensive as he glanced again at the pup in its sling at my chest while we walked.

Though I know most could be naught but tall tales, I always love to hear Da's stories of soldiers' adventures in the world. They are full of action and travels and sometimes battles. Da always has a moral or truth to his tales. He tells them many eves sitting at the hearth fire. Hearing that his Da did the same for him just made a kind of sense.

As we continued our trek back to the cottage, Da elaborated. "My Da told me many tales about creatures, as he knew I had a love for that sort of story. He once told me a tale of a fierce wolf that lived as a lone traveling creature, not like your typical wolf, that moves in packs like a gray or a timber."

I checked on the young wolf pup who now appeared to be faring well. He even wagged his tail a bit.

"This wolf," Da said, "stood as tall as a grown man's chest and was no animal's equal, not even a full-grown grizzly because it was so fierce a predator. So much so that a great King of old sent hunters and soldiers abroad into the mountains that were its natural habitat to wipe it from this world. The pelts from this wolf were made to be the most desired form of garment for lords and the like. In the years that followed, they were hunted 'til no more could be found."

I found this a deeply disturbing thing and told Da so. He nodded in agreement.

"But why would you say this pup could be such an animal?" I queried, glancing at it again.

"Because of the eyes, ya see," Da explained. "Da said the Dread had fierce eyes. Not like wolves' eyes at all. In fact, more like a cat's eyes. Eyes of copper speckled in gold, and I've never seen their like in any other creature. But the pup has 'em, just as my Da described. The tale went that the wolf's hide did not have the value unless accompanied by the creature's eyes. And then the hide would fetch twenty gold pieces. A fortune for a hunter or trapper."

Da said that as many or more hunters and trappers paid a higher price—their life, with no gold in return. 'Cause the Dread is a keen hunter as well, and the hunter, a'times, became the hunted.

We made our way back to the cottage, and Da worked his healing mægic on the pup's hindquarters. The pup slept that first night at the foot of my cot. I fed him and he followed me around tight to my leg with a limp like a domestic dog pup, much to the amazement of Da. After a ha'fortnight, the pup's leg being well on the mend, he still followed me about as I did my chores around the homestead. Da would watch close, as he worried we'd come up short a chicken or goat if he didn't. But the pup, though he stared intently at the farm animals, never harmed them. To be fair, the animals would not stay long around me anyway with the young wolf nearby.

"Pup, you are the *bane* of the barn and pasture here abouts, I'd say. And Da is mighty wary."

After a time I found myself calling him Bane.

But when I went out at the end of the day to round up the livestock to the barn, the pup somehow realized what I was about and started herding the creatures back and to me. Goats and cows alike moved swiftly home to the barn under Bane's direction, making the chore so much easier on me. At the end of the day, Da would throw a piece of chicken or some fatty bacon to the pup and he'd take it and drag it a distance away and dine on it.

After eve-meal one night, Da said time had come to take the pup (I'd named him but didn't tell Da, only using the name when not around him) and release him back into the forest. Bane had become familiar with Da by now and no longer growled in his presence, but still ever calm only around me. Da just shook his head and wondered at this.

So, on the morrow's morn, a fortnight and seven after saving Bane from the trap, we headed out for a long trek towards the distant mountains. We had our packs and Da his bow. We expected to be gone a while.

We hiked for three suns with Bane following me, the wolf becoming ever more interested in the scents and the creatures of the forest. We soon realized we had no need to feed him anymore as he would wander off, track a rabbit or other small creature of the forest, and find his own meals. Come the fourth day, we had made the foothills of the western range of the Shadow Mountains. Bane clearly felt very much at home here. As I woke next morn, I noted that he was on full alert as he stared into the dim, morn-lit forest about us. Da and I observed him in wonder for his steely intent on something in the distance. His ears went on alert and with a twist of his head he straightened and headed out after some prey that was deemed most important to him.

As soon as Bane left, Da started breaking down the camp.

"What Da, no morn-meal?"

"No, Arias. Yer pup is very intent on tracking some prey just now. It would be a very good time to head back, mayhaps at a good clip. That pup has taken to ye in a strong way, and very much beyond his native instincts."

"And I him. But you are right, Da. This is his natural home. I will surely miss him, though you have the right of it. Let's be off then." Resigned to the reality, I helped Da break camp.

Da paused and peered deep into my eyes. I'm sure he knew that I had indeed formed an unnatural attachment to the wolf pup.

We set off after making our packs, making good time back towards the cottage, but my thoughts were on Bane the whole trip.

As we arrived home from our trip returning Bane to the wild, we noted Grayce just heading out from the homestead. She had milked the cows and tended the livestock for us these past few days.

"Grayce, are ye off? Won't you stay and share some venison stew with yer favorite men?"

"You surely are my favorite men and aye, I'd love to share that game with you."

Da had shot a large doe on our return trip, his bow ever true. The field dressed deer lay upon Bregoe's back.

"You've had some strange company about while you've been gone."

Her gaze went to the great oak standing next to the barn. Hundreds of huge ravens filled every branch of the Oak, seeming to stare at us even as we stared back. A shiver raced down my back. Of a sudden they all fluttered about and cawed a moment en masse.

"An omen, mayhaps," was all that Da said to the matter. I stood a moment and stared in wonder.

He and Grayce started off in different directions, each with few words as they began eve-meal preparations.

"Arias, some carrots, onions, and tubers from the garden, if you please, young man." Grayce motioned to the garden. "I'll prepare the stock, Ètœn"

"Good then, I'll prepare the meat."

With some butchering and seasoning and celery,onion, and root vegetables added, Da and Widow Grayce had a stew boiling in no time. Da brought a large skin of homemade ale out of the cottage cellar. The three of us gathered in the shade of a giant saw-tooth oak and sat in chairs Da had crafted for the purpose. We raised a toast. Da allowed me an ale now and then since I'd reached my sixteen-year-end.

With Da and Widow Grayce starting a conversation that had nothing to do with me. I immersed myself in a daydream of Bane. He had caught his young elk somehow, easily four times his height. With his muzzle around its neck, he shook his head in a vicious jerk and the elk dies with a snap under his young paws. In the distance, mayhaps twenty paces away, two full-size wolves regarded him but didn't approach. A mountain cat cried out from a rock even further out. Bane stared up at the cat and then returned to his prey. It had been a three-day hunt for him. It seemed too real to be a daydream to me.

"Back to the routine tomorrow, Arias. Grayce tells me that our Innkeeper, Master Bergierre is hungry for a wagon full of ice. He's out and his patrons have taken note."

We were sitting about our small table in the cottage.Our bellies were full, and the scent of stew lingered about the kitchen. Glancing out the window, I watched as the sun creeped down into the treetops.

"So, I'm back to school then, unless you have another chore for me in towne."

"Nay, lad, you've been away from yer schoolin' far too long as it be. It's more important than any chore I can give ye there," Da said as he stood and stretched An audible crack emitted from the back of his neck.

"I wonder if I can borrow Arias from you, Ètœn. The past two days I've noticed some scrambling and squeaking under my floorboards. It sounds like something bigger than a mouse, and the cat won't have anything to do with whatever it is. The space is a bit cramped for one my age."

"What say you, Arias?" Da asked as he cleared the plates and pot from the table.

"Of course, I can leave out early on morrow's morn, and you can pick me up on the way into towne."

Widow Grayce headed out after our early eve-meal, and Da returned to the cottage and sat down at the table to assess our ha'fortnight past. Then, though near to worn out, but too early to head off to bed, Da rose and retrieved my leatherworking tools and set them upon the table.

"Idle hands are a dæmon's tools," Da proclaimed as he sat back down across from me. Twas one of the many sayings that Da sprang on me from time a'time.

"Arias, you get started back on your pack, and I'll see to the horses."

The straps on mine and Da's packs were uncomfortable and constantly needed rearranging on the hike. I'd been working on an idea to add in an entirely new concept for carrying my pack. I sewed a panel of elk hide equal to the width of the back of the pack in place behind it. This being of the thicker stock of mountain elk's skin, and trimmed and attached to the side of the pack that laid against my back and extended up past the top of the pack the length of my torso and shoulders. I cut a large hole in the panel to where my head would slide through and cut the front into a triangular-shape, wider at the shoulders and then to a hands width at my waistline. I then folded this last portion back onto itself, so thus a loop at the bottom was formed. Then from the pack on either side, I sewed a wide belt to pass through the loop in the front and which could be secured at my side. I had been at this for a couple of hours when Da returned and inspected my handiwork.

"Arias, lad, you've got a life in the Saddlery if you ever decide. Many a time as a soldier, I woulda liked to have been carrying such a pack as this," he exclaimed. "I have a suggestion or two if you'll hear it though."

"Sure, Da," I said with pride as he admired my work. "I would always consider the advice of an old soldier." Winking at the man I admire most in life. I would be glad I'd heeded his offered advice, in the suns to come.

2

Middenvale and Schoolroom Studies

I awoke on the morrow's morn and my internal biological clock had worked for me in its flawless manner. Da brought the wagon filled with ice a little later. So, after morn chores, I set out on foot toward Grayce's homestead.

Da was already leaving for the Frost-Cellar. He had harnessed Bregœ, his stallion of twenty-some-year. The same stallion Da had arrived to Middenvale on, more than eleven years past. Bregœ, being unhappy to be left out of Da's excursions of late, insisted he come. Even if harnessed to a wagon, he remained a proud horse from a great line of warhorses and stood 21-hands-tall. A Silver gelding bred for strength, stamina, and intelligence, he would let nobody but Da ride nor harness him. Though getting old, the horse's love for Da was still palpable, and he made it known that he would not be left behind on our trips into towne.

Myself, I set off at a strong pace with the shoulder bag, contemplating finishing my pack and incorporating Da's new suggestions. Arriving at the Widow Grayce's homestead at dawn, I knocked to make her aware that I had arrived.

"Good morn to you, Arias. Thanks so much for helping me out." Grayce's front door swung to with a small bang as she stepped out on the porch to greet me.

"I'm always glad to help, Grayce. Just point me in the right direction, and I'll get started."

She leaned forward and pointed left down the side of the house.

"The noise is coming from near the chimney, I believe."

"I'll start there then."

I removed my shoulder bag, pulled my dirk and walked down around to the chimney side of the cottage. I followed a typical foundation made up of fieldstone that was mortared and grouted into a number of piers to hold the wood timbers off the ground at about knee height. Using flint and steel, I lit a small torch to take with me under the house. With dirk in one hand and the torch in the other, I dropped to my knees into soft, thick grass and then onto my stomach and proceeded to shimmy and crawl between the stone piers and under the house.

Something tittered as I approached the chimney. Afore me lay a nearly decapitated and quite venomous rock snake. Its body lay still behind its nearly severed head. It lay in a death grip inside the mouth of a long and furry rodent-sized creature with an equally long and furry tail. The rodent also quite still and quite dead from the viper's earlier bite.

As I peered past the two carcasses and into a hole alongside the chimney, four tiny red eyes stared back at me in the torch light. I could easily have used my dagger to end the nuisance critters, but something stayed my hand. Da had always taught me to respect all creatures and to kill only in defense or for food. These little ones' mum had just recently died in a fierce battle with a highly venomous snake to protect them. Sheathing the dagger and placing the small torch some distance away, I slowly extended my hand to the edge of the hole. I calmly stared into their hidey hole. I waited patiently, then remarkably, after a good while passed, one of the little furions ventured out and sniffed at my hand. It returned my gaze with tiny golden eyes. Eventually, it just climbed into my palm and curled up. His brœther or sister followed immediately and squeezed in next to her sibling.

Softly closing my hand about them, I snuffed out the torch in the soil and slowly shimmied my way out from under the house.

Grayce awaited me as I crawled out, and she appeared somewhat amazed at what I held afore her. Shuffling in piles scattered about her porch, she soon offered up a small basket, and the two furry creatures were placed within.

I returned under the house to retrieve the remainder of the snake and the critters' mum so as not to leave a lingering odor under the cottage. That work done, I sat upon the edge of Grayce's porch, playing with my new furion friends.

Shortly afterward, Da arrived with the wagon pulled by Bregœ and full of wrapped block ice. He chuckled at the tale and the new pets. Grayce rewarded us with rashers of bacon and scrambled eggs. After a very quick morn-meal, we mounted the wagon with the basket holding my new pets on the seat next to me. They were treated to scrambled eggs and some milk from Grayce as well. They gobbled down the eggs and immediately curled up into the straw that had been placed in the basket with them.

I had two new pets to name.

Our time in towne was that of a usual sun.

Da had taught me reading and writing from an early age. I remember as an eight year-ender he would read to me from the few books he kept at the homestead. He would show me the pictures in his books about herbs and plants and when we would hike he would show me those same plants out in the forest. He would show me the written words for the words we spoke, and it wasn't long afore I could read on my own.

Da arranged for apprenticeships in towne and at the Mills, and he had a friend who would come by and train me as well. He proclaimed that these were all skills that I would need and would prepare me for when I struck out on my own. This part I did not understand as I had no desire to leave our homestead. I reckoned I was living life in a fine fashion already with plenty of adventures in the forests and mountains near and about. But I did not complain as I had a strong curiosity and loved the learning of it all.

Betwixt Mæster Cræbbe's schoolhouse lessons of maths and cyphering, geography and histories of the realm, there was also Da's lessons of herb and animal lore. Mæster Cræbbe seemed to me a man who knew most anything. Da told me he had studied with the greatest of mæsters in a far away city called Esperance and that he had a neck chain with batches of learning hanging on a hook in the cubby at the schoolhouse where he hung his cloak. Like Da, his tales of the histories of Aeryth kept me riveted to my seat. I felt quite brilliant each sun after a lesson from him. But Da told me that book learning was not enough. And so, he arranged apprenticeships and physical training for me. I loved it all.

My first apprenticeship was with Effie, the towne healer. I had even helped her birth a baby. She taught me to have no shame in knowing the male and female body (though back at fourteen-year I would have confessed a preference to studying a female body).

As fate would have it, Da started discussing these very things. "Virtue and morals and the fairer sex" is what he called them. To his credit, he never dodged a question. We spoke of a male's manhood, which he referred to as "his hunk" and at which Effie's eyes went wide and laughed with abandon to hear. She explained to me the proper terms, of course, but Da's mind remained set on his own language for his parts and pieces. He explained it was normal to have thoughts of woman folk but I should remain wary of their wiles and ways (to which Effie laughed even harder), and that it was normal for a man's hunk to grow stiff and hard. Effie explained the body mechanics of the condition, and though I understood, her explanation did not help the cause and effect. I remained happy to understand the condition was normal, if no less embarrassing. I learned being a healer's assistant did not help in all things. It did assure me that indeed I was thus a man, as I had personally experienced this feeling ofttimes at this point.

In the end, Da made it clear as to how a man should respect a woman and treat her kind and to give aid and comfort as they might need. He said it was a man's duty to protect a woman as they were weaker in constitution and in need of such. I thought of Grayce and how she could handle a bow or knife on a hunt and decided that some woman would need less protection than others.

These lessons had been reinforced in me at fifteen-year, when one day, after leaving the schoolhouse and venturing for a rare idle afternoon in towne, I passed an alleyway beside the butcher shop. I heard a scuffling and a sharp but muffled yell.

Peering down to the far end of the alleyway and into the shadows, there stood Brüsson, the butcher's son, and Dulchè from my class. Her given name Dulcinẽa, though her friends called her Dulchè..

Brüsson had her pushed up against the wall with one hand against her mouth and the other at her bosom. Anger struck me of a sudden as I could see him clearly taking advantage of his strength against her, while she stood struggling against his efforts. He was near fifteen-stone and a head taller than I and twenty-four-year, and she was not ten-stone, near to my height, and seventeen-year.

"Yea there, Brüsson." I began walking towards the two of them.

"Be off, lad, or I warrant you'll be nursing a broken limb."

I kept walking towards him as he pushed Dulchè behind him and turned back towards me with a sneer. A misfortune to him, for by that time he found his reaction to be a bit late. Four-year of hand-and-hand battle training with Moor had prepared me for just this type of encounter. Recalling it now, it was amazing to even myself. Near to instinct alone, a sky-bolt quick strike with my leg sent my heel into his left knee, and as he screamed in pain and collapsed to his damaged leg, I swept my elbow, with the momentum of my body behind it, in a pummeling blow to the side of his head. He fell, senseless against the shop wall. He tried to rise to his feet, but only wobbled to then fro and once again slid to the ground with his back to the wall and a glassy haze about his eyes.

Stepping forward, I took Dulchè's hand and led her speechless out from the alleyway. We walked over to a small area near the schoolhouse, it having been set aside for the youngers to play. The area empty now, I sat with her on a large boulder.

"I'm sorry that muttonhead was hurting you, Dulchè. It was not right." Her bright blue eyes were brimming with moisture. She bit her lower lip and stared at me.

"My Pa likes that Brüsson, and likes that he asks after me because he is the butcher's son. He reckons that he would make a good son-by-law. But I detest him because he is just like Pa," she hissed.

I stared back, taken unawares by her statement.

"Your Da puts his hands to you in harm?" I queried, aghast.

"Nay not me…. Well, sometimes when he's in his cups, but more to mum. She takes his wrath, I think, to save me and my sister the bruises. Sometimes I think he does it because mum gave him no sons. Mum seems to be bruised all the time, but she hides it from us." A tear found its way to her cheek, now. As I pondered what she said, she asked me, "Why did you do that Arias? We hardly know one t'other."

"How could I not? It was wrong what he was doing."

"Thank you," she said warmly and leaned into me, her arms about mine.

Her soft bosom pressed against my arm, and my heart beat so hard then that I would swear I could hear it.

"I must go. Pa will be angry if I am late to eve-meal." She rose and hurried off, but not afore pausing and gazing to me with a smile.

I met Da back at the Inn shortly after, and I told him of Dulchè and my violence with Brüsson. He listened intently while I even told him all that Dulchè had said afterwards. When we finished our meal, he placed his large hand to my shoulder, and looking me eye-to-eye he said, "I'm mighty proud of ye, lad. Ye did right innit."

"Yea Da, but I felt I had no choice but to hurt the meathead."

"Sometimes, it's what must be done for justice, lad. Cleanup about yerself and see to loading the wagon, will ye? I have one more errand afore we leave out this evening."

When we headed out for the Homestead, I left feeling good about myself, not least as I had done right with Moor's training.

My lessons and learning under Mãamel Bræder entailed more than just healing. She taught me to stretch my body through different exercises that she called 'Chẽ-Song.' Besides showing me that a woman's body could indeed be quite lithe and beautiful, it taught me control of my own. But her most important lesson trained me to calm my mind and body. I learned to sit as in a trance, lowering my heartbeat and emptying my mind to refresh my thoughts, body, and spirit. This she called reaching my *Calming*. In this she proclaimed me her best student. I admit to being quite good at it, though I never saw her with any other students so mayhaps my competition being scarce and few, made an easy target met.

I one day asked her where she had learned her craft and all these other skills. She spoke to me of growing up on an Island to the South of the Mainland of Aeryth and across a great bay where her teacher hailed as a great Sjaman among the people there. I found the island as the Wilden Isle on maps, but she knew it as Hermitẽae, the Isle of Healing. Her Mæster there a very old and wise healer who taught her his craft.

"Mayhaps, one day you will travel about all of Aeryth, Arias, and even travel to Hermitẽae. If you do, I hope that you will find Sjaman Hestorae and show him that I have had an apprentice of which I am quite proud," she said, laying her hand upon my shoulder, and making me flush red in the face.

3

Training with Moor and Da

Aside from my apprenticing and schooling in towne, my training with Moor started when I made my eleven-year-end. I met him the sun following Da's eleven-year-ender gifting to me, and in a manner of speaking, could be said to be part of it. Da had gifted me my Schäaken board and pieces that year and explained to me after he'd presented it, "Arias lad, in proper trainin' there is the mental, the physical, and the spiritual. I'm hoping this board will teach you a bit of the mental part of it."

He touched the side of his head. I scratched mine.

"But there be four parts to that as well. There be the book learnin' part as ye are getting at the schoolhouse with Mæster Ræbben, and the doin' part, as you'll get from 'prenticing out to Mãamel Bræder the healer, and the Miller and the Saddleryman and Argo the Smithy. Then there be this board here that I've gifted ye and will be playin'. That'll be the logic and the thoughtful part." He gestured to my new Schäaken board that I began standing the pieces upon.

"And finally, there is a mind toughness to it all. I'm spectin' a man from my soldierin' time to be calling in a sun or two. And he'll be trainin' ye on both the brain strength as well as the body strength that ye'll need to be learnin' as you're coming of an age."

"Four parts of this and three parts of that— it sounds more like maths, Da!"

My mind wasn't having it. Mayhaps my mind was having a weak sun of it.

"Da, I understand the book learning and appreciating all of it, but I can't figure the meaning of the brain toughness part," I admitted.

"Aye, lad, well that can be the most gruelin' part of it to learn. It means learnin' to conquer yer fears, I reckon. Stand your ground no matter the consequences and ye knowin' it's goin' to be hard on ye," Da tried to explain. "It's hard to explain but that's why there'll be the teachin' of it. And Moor will have the way of it. You'll be seein' soon enough."

Sure certain, Da's friend Moor arrived on the morrow's morn just after sunrise, and he did a lot of hugging and backslapping and the such with Da. Though a small man compared to Da, he held his ground to the backslapping and that alone said a great deal about him. To my thinking, he had a peculiar way of dressing, though. His clothes were all grey. A great cloak of grey, tunic and trousers of grey and even grey boots. I did not say anything about this to him.

Da introduced us as we sat for a morn-meal of eggs, honey buttered bread and rashers of bacon. Moor tucked into it with gusto, leaning back on two legs of the chair, crumbs falling about as he finished off the last butter and honey biscuit. Da said my first real day of training would start even now and I was to do as Moor told me.

Moor eyed me head-to-toe, and slapping crumbs from his hands, fell back forward on his chair, said "Let's run."

I knew I could do that.

So, we ran. Moor didn't talk, he just set a pace and expected me to keep with him. When he reached the forest, I was glad as the running would be easier there than in the tall grasses of the pastures that dragged at our ankles. Except that Moor didn't make it so. He took paths over logs and streams and even high boulders I needed to climb. And he near never stopped. We ran until the sun climbed to its highest, just pausing briefly at streams to quench our thirst. We barely had time to catch a breath and he would be off again without speaking a word.

After a while, I could not keep up any longer and I slowly fell behind, but would not stop. The woods were familiar hereabouts, and I knew he was headed back to the cottage. But after a time, I saw him no more as my running became more to a jog. Moor did not wait on me.

When I finally made the cottage, Moor and Da were finishing the eve-meal and both were looking fresh and reminiscing about this and that. Da had me wash, and he fixed me a trencher of stew. I wolfed it down. Moor went out to sleep in the barn loft that night, and I was glad to get to my cot.

"Arias, lad, fancy learnin' to play a round of Schäaken?" Da pointed to the board and pieces.

"Nay Da, if it is all the same to you," I simply said. He could see the exhaustion in my face, no doubt.

"On morrow's eve then," he said, squeezing my shoulder and sending me on my way.

Moor stayed at our homestead for two fortnight that first trip. Each morn's sunrise, after I finished my homestead chores, we ran. The first few morns were brutal. My body became too stiff for me to even move. But as I loosened up a bit, by chores' end, I would be ready to go again. And we did. We ran every morn. At dawn we would start and by highest sun, we were still not done. Moor never said anything during our runs but would sometimes query me afterwards.

"Did you see the snow owl watching us as we passed? That rattler eye-ing us close at the great dead oak, 'twas within striking distance when we passed, were you aware?"

"Nay, I did not see it. Was it really so close to strike?" I'd honestly answer.

I would do all I could just to keep pace with him. But, if he'd seen these things, why had not I? I found myself paying closer attention on our runs, determined to be able to answer his queries on our return. After a fortnight, able to keep more apace and no longer sore as I rose at sunrise, I found myself taking note of our surroundings while running. One morn I said as much and Moor just smiled. He picked up a long branch that Da had apparently stripped and planed mostly smooth.

"This is a Bo-stick. When you learn to carry it, I'll train you to use it." He tossed it to me. He said nothing more and started our run with a Bo-stick of his own in his hands. The

stick was not light and it was as tall as I was. I almost did myself grave bodily harm as we ran carrying them. In the forest, I nearly knocked myself out. I took many blows to my body as the stick would hit trees as I ran by. It would hit a branch or tree trunk and swing back to bash me in the leg or body or head. Ahead of me, Moor had no such problems. I observed how he carried it and tried hard to mirror his moves.

My stamina increased and I learned to wield the Bo-stick most effectively. Moor's training continued over the years. We trained with more than just the Bo-stick, but it is what we concentrated most on. We also trained on what he called Hæ-Kæ-Dœ, which were tumbling and striking techniques that kept an opponent off balance and easily disarmed and disabled. When Moor showed up at our homestead, mayhaps three times in a year's passing, he would stay two fortnights or more and we would train. When he was not with us, Da would become my training opponent.

When I passed my thirteen-year-end, Da crafted a wooden training opponent for me. He took a log the length of a grown man's torso and augured a hole through it at shoulder height. He pounded a thick branch through it to play as arms. Finally, he fashioned legs into it in a like manner. Moor painted red spots upon it as targets. At knees, hips, shoulders, ribs and head, he marked it. I would use tumbling and striking techniques to land blows only at the painted target points. Each morn I would do a training routine upon the log man. As I became more adept at this, Moor again changed the rules.

At fourteen-year-end, Da and Moor crafted a second log man and hung them each from a long Elven-vine rope from a high timber beam within the barn. First, Moor let swing the log man and instructed me to strike the target spots as it swung fore and back. When I had mastered this, they would swing the two log men at and across each other's path. Moor taught me to use Hæ-Kæ-Dœ tumbles to move within the log man arcs and still be able to strike only the target spots.

With time I conquered this as well even though I was left bruised and beaten. I found that if I used Mãamel Bræder's Chẽ-Song and *Calming* lessons, I could reach a state of immense concentration. In the *Calm*, I was able to sense the log swinging motion behind as well as afore me, and my strikes became more accurate. After I started using this method, Moor stared in amazement and proclaimed me the best fighter he'd ever trained and mayhaps the best he had ever faced. He asked me what had changed.

"How is it you've increased your swiftness, and accuracy so suddenly?"

"I've added Mãamel Bræder's Chẽ-Song and *Calming* methods afore I start. I find I can transition into the state almost immediately after many suns of practice with her. The log men appear to swing in a slower motion, and I can sense them at all times."

"Ho, Arias, please show me. And I hope this old hound can learn a new trick."

"Ètœn did not say that his Effie had taught you such a thing. I've heard tales of a technique such as this, but I've never known anyone who could instruct me. In this, Arias, the student has become the Mæster. To think, here she has been all along," sighed Moor.

Also adept at throwing blades, Moor made this a part of my instruction as well. He would shout, throw his blade into a knot of a tree, with me matching his throw—all as we ran. Da was also an excellent thrower and when Moor was not with us, Da would do the schooling. He had noted me becoming more proficient at using my left hand and arm as well as my right and had me depend more on my left at sixteen-year. He would use the swinging log man and had me target with the Bo-stick in my right hand and throw to a target with my left.

When Moor was not with us, Da would help me train in other ways as well. When we did not visit towne, my lessons were what oft times occupied my sun after morn chores. I would run for a good while and return to more training with Da. This had become my regimen, and I came to anticipate and relish the challenge that Da and Moor had put upon me.

Da was a master bowman, and though I had not a mighty bow such as Da's, I have had a strong and stout hunting bow from age thirteen-year onward. Da has taught me to train my eye with my hand, and he has made me build my strength to the task by having me do naught but draw and hold the heavy bow and keep it taut till my arm shook violently with the strain of it. And, like Moor, he has me repeat and repeat. With time and practice, and Mãamel Bræder's Chẽ-Song techniques of concentration, I became able to hold as long as Da. This is a great accomplishment, if you could see the strength of Da.

"'Tis good…. You are learning a bit," said Da. "But this is just the first part."

Then, likened to Moor, Da would add a challenge.

"Ye must be swift as well as strong with the bow, lad, to catch your target afore it moves or bolts and might ofttimes catch you unawares," he would say.

Besides training with the bow, Da took up my schooling with a short sword as well. We didn't actually use real short swords though—my training consisted of use of wooden short swords. Da taught me to move both defensively and in offense as well. He showed me feints and double feints and then triple feints. He taught me to read my opponent's eyes, not his hands. He'd be hard and relentless on me, leaving me bruised and exhausted. But I took Moor's advice to heart as well and used my quickness and the concentration Mãamel Bræder's Chẽ-Song had taught me. With it, I now could hold my own and even strike back sometimes at Da's relentless attacks. As I grew into my fifteen and sixteen-year, I found that they would train me in earnest, with Mãamel Bræder having to come to our aid with her healing craft. Early on, she spent most of her time with me, but as I grew stronger and quicker, Da and Moor suffered as well. They smiled when this happened in some dark glee, I thought.

By my sixteen-year Da said, "Ye grow more quick and stronger every meet, Arias. I believe even now you can stand up to most any and the best among the King's soldiers."

Pride did fill me to hear this from Da. But still, he did not lessen our drills.

My horsemanship had improved enormously since Da had gifted me my horse, Paint. He was a formidable mount, but he also had become a strong creature friend. I'd come to distinguish a difference betwixt my human friends and my creature friends. Though there were exceptions in both cases, on the whole my connections with my human friends was foremost a connection based on strictly spoken communication, whereas with my creature friends, a very strong empathetic and emotional bond is clearly most strongly present. I could clearly sense their feelings and wants and they, even more so, knew mine.

From the very first moment I came in contact with Paint on my fifteen-year-end, I sensed his inner strength and rebellious nature. This horse had a most independent soul even as I fancied I did. Da taught me methods of training my new horse, and Paint learned quickly. He was of bloodlines that had produced Da's great warhorse, Bregœ, after all. The mare he sprang from was likewise a strong filly from the southern reaches. But more than that, Paint seemed to want to please me. I took great pleasure in letting him run of his own free will. Many a time I would give him rein and let him carry me where he might, reveling in his power and spirit as we would travel on unexpected paths and open pastures.

Riding atop Paint became a natural thing to me, and unlike my first attempts to hold a bow and loose an arrow upon a horse, Paint and I rode together with ease. He would anticipate my needs and even help me to my task. As such, my skills with training atop Paint became an easier task. A quick whistle and Paint would come, and he would learn most any task I set to him with an ease about it, learning most things in but one attempt.

As I neared my sixteen year-end, Da and I would oft hunt together, we also would spend time apart. I would travel further into the forest and mountains, sometimes being gone for three or four suns at a time either hunting, fishing, or just adventuring. I also practiced diligently and regularly all the lessons from Moor, Da, and Mãamel Bræder. I was not really aware of my life being anything out of the ordinary, though my towne friends did nothing of the like. I lived the life of a retired soldier's son and thought this a normal thing. I often thought my towne friends led frightfully docile and boring lives with little contact with wilderness and adventuring, but I imagined that my life not so unusual to families that lived in other homesteads such as ours. Mayhaps, I was wrong.

4

Giftings from Da

I recall my first significant year-end gifting came at my nine-year-end. Midyear, when the big storms typically come to our homestead, I had learned the reason Da had dragged the Ænt-wood log to the top of Fork-Rock. Oft-times climbing the hill sized boulder to study Da's log, I would a'times lean against it as I read the books I'd borrow from the schoolhouse.

Da's Ænt-wood log had been hauled all the way from Moon Lake. I practiced my reading out where no animals came bothering me and I had plenty of light. The Ænt-wood log was a curious thing. A deep walnut color with streaks of blonde throughout, the log didn't have the appearance of wood at all. It had no bark and was as hard as rock. I tried carving into it a'times, but my sharpest blade left nary a scratch. Da said the tree it came from had likely died hundreds of years ago and the species no longer existed alive in any forest. He said legend and lore held that the tree was a 'sentient' tree from back when mægic still existed in the world. Travelers could leave messages by thinking or speaking at the tree as they would pass, and the message would be passed to the right traveler as they in turn would pass by. What a brilliant thing that would be, sure certain.

That summer I also learned why Da put the log atop Fork-Rock. Many a time when thundering storms rolled across our homestead, Da would step out under the back eaves and stare up at the Ænt-wood log. Then, one day, there came a strong storm. Winds were howling and the animals were more than a little restive in the barn. The grey-green clouds were roiling, and flashes filled the entire orange and grey sky. After a time, the thundering clouds were clearly over the cottage. I knew Da would be up on the roof come morn fixing the tiles.

And then it happened.

Our house rattled and there came a thundering and a boom near akin to the Sky-stone crashing at Moon Lake. I jumped and drew a great breath. Da just stood with a wide smile across his face. I went to the window to spy why he smiled and saw that the Ænt-wood log was no more! I could not understand why Da would smile as a Sky-bolt had just shattered the Ænt-wood log.

In the coming two fortnights, Da did a strange thing. He worked each day and well into the night in his barn workshop. And stranger still, he kept the door shut tight and would not allow me in.

He had me do my chores and some of his as well. We ate tuber, carrot, and onion stew most days as he did not hunt. I would snare a waterfowl on occasion, and he would smile at my cleverness and add it to the stew or spit roast it. Most suns during this time, he simply left me to my own devices. Some suns I would go to Grayce's and get a good meal in return for some simple chores.

It came to be a full moon and a fortnight later, and one eve I was out at the chop block. I had snared a large waterfowl and it would make Da proud if I chopped its head and gutted it, I thought. I would pull its feathers and butcher it myself for the roast. But I didn't get that far. Using Da's double bladed dirk- sure certain much too large for a nine-years sized hand- My eyes went wide as the blade slid easily through the fowl's neck... then through my left hand taking my littlest finger with it. I didn't feel a thing with the blade being so sharp. But when I saw it my eyes went wide, and I screamed, "Daaa" at the top of my lungs.

The barn door quickly slid open and Da came to me, straightaway. He assessed the situation, grabbed my wrist, squeezed my finger tight, and carried me into the cottage. He cleaned the cut as I stared in disbelief at my missing finger. Da pulled a covered cup from the high cupboard and opened its lid. With his finger, he reached in and scooped an unguent out and smeared it all about my hand where my finger once sat. With a paring knife from the counter, he trimmed some jagged skin from my finger and squeezed it tight once again. The balm he used both stemmed the bleeding and made my hand go numb. He then calmly proceeded to sew the gap where my finger once lay. He then folded the remaining skin over and stitched it closed.

I said nothing.

He said nothing.

I never pulled away or otherwise impeded his work. Da finished and I promptly fell into a deep sleep. After a bit, I sat up with a start. I groaned and examined my hand which was bandaged and was throbbing, and it hit me that it really wasn't a bad dream.

"Would ye be ready to eat some roast fowl? I've beans and tubers, as well."

Life went on.

Though they happened at each year's end, thirteen-year-end had brought my most special gifting of all. Da brought me to Argo's Smithy. This day Da shared with me his secret of the Ænt-wood log and his three-fortnight of nonstop working in his shop in the barn. Placed on a work table in the middle of the Smithy lay a long object—nearly as long as I was tall and covered with a leather wrap. Afore he let me uncover it though, he told me the story of the Ænt-wood log.

"Arias, when we found the Ænt-wood tree up at Moon Lake, I told ye me Da had carved me own bow from Ænt-wood and that made it me most prized possession," Da began.

"Yea, Da, I remember. Have you made me a bow?" anticipation clear in my voice.

With a twinkle in his eye, he ignored my question.

"After me Da gave me my bow, he taught me about Ænt-wood. You saw that it was hard as rock and no knife, nor saw, nor axe will make nary a mark or dent in the wood, this is true. 'Cept in two manners as he knew," he elaborated. Argo leaned back against his shop's work-table, listening to Da as well.

I knew not to interrupt at this point as Da was clearly in storytelling mode, and no rushing would get me closer to revealing my year-end gifting. So, being the wiser lad that he'd said I had become this year, I encouraged him to continue. "Tell me Da, what you mean about the Ænt-wood?"

"I drew the Ænt-wood log up to the top of Fork-Rock and waited. Patience it took, though me hands were aching to work it. I didn't know if me Da had been telling me just a story, ye see. Sky-bolts he said, will let ye work the Ænt-wood best." He inhaled, pausing and tapping his fingers against his thigh before he added, "And then it happened, by putting the Ænt-wood log to the highest point at homestead, the storm's Sky-bolt was made to strike it. And when it did the log splintered into many pieces. Some were long and tall pieces, and some were smaller, and this gave me what I needed. Ye see, this is one way to make the Ænt-wood become more like other woods for a time. For three fortnight after the fierce strike from the Sky-bolt, I was able to carve the special wood. In those suns, I worked the Ænt-wood. I made the hilts for yer knives, the board and pieces for the Schäaken game and a few other pieces as well."

Hearing Da recite his tale, I now understood that the year-end giftings from Da were indeed special and unique.

"The time ye can work the wood does not last and by the time ye cut yer finger from yer hand, I could work the Ænt-wood no more. The many pieces became as if they were rock once more," he said. "But, there is more to this story and why we are here now with my good friend Argo.

"Arias, lad, the Sky-stone we found all those years past plays a part in this as well. Using forge and smelting fires, Argo is able to separate the metals from the slag of the Sky-stone. The metals he tirelessly forged and folded and strengthened in. The properties of the metal when folded and pounded together has made the best blade known to either of us and are what your dirk and throw-knife are made from."

Aghast that Da and Argo would do such things for me, I leaned against the table, humbled at Da's words. Finally, I came to my senses and rose to shake Argo's large hand profusely.

"It has been my pleasure to work these new and marvelous metals for you." His voice filled the space, always deep, melodic, and more suited to chanteur than a smithy. "And Ètœn has gifted me a bit of the metal for my own purposes as well. And now, Arias lad, we've outdone ourselves in this new project. Go ahead then and uncover your year-end gifting."

Making my way slowly to the worktable, I pulled away the leather wrap.

Wonderment.

"My Drægon's tooth—oh, and is that the Drægon's Firestone as well, Da?"

"Aye. And a little something more of you as well." He pointed to the center of the Bo.

In front of me lay a staff near as long as I was tall. The Bo lay there dark with blonde layering and smooth as river stone. At one end, the top I suspected, was the white 'Drægon's tooth' I'd found on Moon Lake beach and on the other end it held the long ruby 'Drægon's Firestone.' It was the very one I brought out from within the cleft of the boulder struck and split by the mighty Sky-stone. The walking stick held the natural curves, knots, and bumps of a stout branch, and in the exact center of the staff sat what appeared to be a piece of shining ivory embedded into the wood itself. Just below the Drægon's tooth on one end and below the Drægon's Firestone on the other end were a few elaborately carved runes. Da said they were from an old chest a friend had given him to hold valuables. He had always fancied the runes upon the box.

With pride, I'd never afore seen in Da, he explained how he and Argo had made the staff. "Though Moor and I have been training you to use a fighting staff, to this point you have not had the real thing. This is called a Bojutsu staff, or 'Bo,' and is truly both a staff and a mighty fighting weapon."

I gasped and touched the staff lightly with my fingers.

"In its making, the only other way that the Ænt-wood can be bent to yer will, is what Argo and I have done for this year-end's gifting," he said, placing his great hands upon my shoulders from behind. "Argo set up the tools as we needed. He built a jig to hold the staff tight and sit centered over his smelting flame. As ye know, yer Drægon's tooth and the Drægon's Firestone were shaped each a bit like a dagger, if-fin' ye will. This gave me the idea of embedding the stones directly into the Bo-staff at each end. They are each pointed to one end and as long as me hand, or near about. Anyways, Argo got the smelting fire roaring with two spikes in it with the center of the stick about three hands above it, and with the spikes white-hot at their heads, me and Argo pushed the spikes into each end at the same time. I'd swear the

Ænt-wood screamed as we pushed, and the staff split into three fingers at each end. Then we each stabbed yer Drægon's tooth and Drægon's fire into the split ends. While this was a happenin', just as I thought it might, the center of the stick above the smelting fire opened in a crack, and I placed a piece of your finger bone—the one that ye cut clean off yer hand—and stuck it right in the crack. Argo picked up the staff and put it into his water trough. The staff likened to take life! It grabbed them Drægon's stones and yer finger bone and squeezed them tight into itself to become part of the wood, I reckon. And now you can clearly see bits of the Drægon's tooth, Drægon Firestone, and your finger bone through the cracks."

It lay there, smooth, varnished, and all about finished to a fine sheen, but Da said they didn't do any of that. It was just finished that way when the firing and dousing was done.

I was astounded that Da would give me such a thing. He but claimed the stones and the bone were already mine, and he and Argo just fancied it up a bit. I knew "fancied it up" meant hours of carving in his shop, and my eyes watered a bit at the wonder of Da's affection for me to have done it at all. And the finger bone, likened to what his Da did for him with his bow.

"Well then go ahead, lad." Da prodded me. "It's yer gifting. Go ahead and pick it up."

They had to almost force me to pick it up, and when I did, I almost immediately dropped it. As I gripped it again and tighter about its center to lift it off Argo's worktable, my whole body warmed from my head to toes. The heat radiated from where my hand grasped the Bo, and I swear the Drægon Stones glowed a little. Raising the staff, it immediately felt like an extension of my own body, truly a part of me.

"Da." I looked straight to his eye. "What did it feel like when you lifted your bow for the first time?" He said not a word, but something in his eyes answered my question.

My fourteen-year-end gifting reflected more about training in the art of soldiering as that was what Da knew best from his life. He gifted me a short sword. But again, no ordinary short sword. Argo had forged the blade in manner and fashion to my dirk and throwing knife with a double edge and a Drægon likeness etched into the center valley of the blade. The length along it's edge measured the same as my arm, from shoulder to wrist, and it's breadth, no more than a hand's width. The edges were honed to a sharpness that would cut a ripe tomato and yet did not nick nor dent or ever lose its edge. It seemed I used the whetstone just for the practice of it. A deadly weapon; sure certain.

My fifteen-year-end gifting was a compass and crafted of the moon metal. Argo had fashioned for it a chain that I could attach to my belt or place around my neck. It too had an intricate Drægon motif on the back etched upon the surface by Argo in the likeness designed by Da. Da tutored me on its use. He lessoned me in reading maps and travelling afar. I knew not why he felt I should understand such things, but ne'er-the-lesser fascinating to me. The compass held a special mægic all its own.

On my sixteen-year-end, Da had spent the previous two days in towne without me, and when he announced his arrival back home, I came round front from the barn to meet him. There, tethered to the rear of the wagon stood a marvelous horse. It was a sixteen-hand Paint of black-and-white.

I slowly approached the skittish colt. As Da had taught me, I kept eye to eye and bowed my head ever slightly to him as I approached. At first, he balked, but I kept calm, and with a confident gaze upon him, he soon started to settle. Approaching yet closer... as with Bane, I found a connection with the beast somehow. I leaned forward and touched my forehead to his and then reached up to rub his head between his ears. A contented whinny was my reward, and his whole body shivered as he relaxed. I knew then that training would come easy with him. Da nodded in appreciation of what I had done and explained that the colt's sire was Bregœ.

Paint, as I immediately named him, turned out to be a very intelligent horse, and Da taught me the methods to train him in the likes of Bregœ. I was becoming an animal whisperer in my own right.

5

𝕭lackbird

"The Fates be damned"

The birds are back. First it was the hundreds of them in the great oak when we returned from delivering Arias' wolf pup back to the wild, seven moons past. A mountain dread wolf, no the lesser. I took it for the evil omen that it was. Then, as I lay my haälberd down upon the rock after my routine, just now, a raven of tremendous size alights upon it. Sitting, staring back at me, and unmoving...still and intent. Now, a murder of the black-as-night birds is causing a rucus in the air over Grayce's homestead. They are heading this way, ahead of a brewing storm. This sun. Now.

Walking to the back porch of our cottage, I tug on my bell's braided cord with a frayed end. Something I've done, if once, then three thousands of times. But this time is different. I pull the cord not once, nor twice, but thrice. It rings out clear, three times. The first time I have ever rung it such, as the meaning is dire.

Argo has helped me fashion a lethal haälberd of exceptional balance and weight. 'Tis my new favorite weapon for closer combat and when Arias is not about, I continue my practice with it. When Moor has been here, he has helped me train with it in the barn and amongst the swinging logmen.

Effie and Moor have helped me with Arias' *calming* technique, and I find it a remarkable tool. It has been a priority for me ever and since Arias has told me of his dream, and I recognized it for what it was...he's had a vision, even as his grand-sire is known for. It gives me some hope though, as Arias is alive in the dream...he must stay that way.

Returning to the haälberd, I find the Raven has left it to join its murder in the branches of the great oak. I retrieve the weapon and stand ready now. *Waiting.*

Something about this sun is not sitting well with me. The upset in my stomach had left no room for a morn-meal. I woke well afore sunrise to the *memory* of a nightmare I hadn't experienced in several moons. It had haunted me for a full moon. But even the memory of the dream remains disturbing and all-consuming to me. After experiencing the same, all too realistic, nightmarish vision a half dozen times back then, I had been re-lieved when it no longer returned. I had forgotten – until this morn. Morn chores could not dispel or allay it. even now the fine hairs on my neck and arms stood to end.

I've been foraging in the forest for shrooms and herbs we do not have in our garden. I've done this same thing countless times past. The clouds are grey with their undersides a sickly green. A storm appears imminent. Da has promised a grand meal of sorts as he is expecting Moor tomorrow's eve and has invited Grayce and Effie and Argo also. It is just a single sun till my seventeen-year-ender and the meal he is planning will be to its honor. Even though it is a bit past high-sun, from the skies you cannot imagine it so. Thick clouds have buried the sun, and the forest has gone quiet. I hear now what I have never in all my years heard afore. The home bell is tolling clear and ever distinct, *three* times.

I jump with a start. Rising up, my heart has taken on a beat as loud as thunder in my chest. First, I'm wondering if I had heard wrong, for it was not the time of sun to hear any bell ringing. I'm certain that I have not. In years past, I might have thought it a game, devised by Da for my year-ender celebration. But near to seventeen, I hold little doubt this is not the case. I drop my harvested foodstuffs and pick up my bow. This does not seem right.... *This is not right!* Da's secret of the bells is forefront to my thoughts but running away to the Frost-Cellar is not even an option to my mind.

Over the past year since I'd finished it, I wear my pack at all times when I am away from the cottage. I carry my bow and my short sword which is sheathed against my back as well. I don't run to the Frost-Cellar as he had once charged me to do. I am no longer a younger of seven or eight year. I will not run and hide.

Instead, I run towards home. *An inner urgency propels me.*

Sprinting to the edge of the tree line, I stop to catch my breath and stare down from the high point at the edge of our pasture. Da is in front of the cottage with his newly forged haälberd in his hands. *This is wrong.* It is his weapon of choice beyond his bow. He and Argo had crafted it this year past from a pole he'd kept for himself from the Ænt-wood and Sky-stone metal. *These are not friends.* A disturbing thought struck, just now. They had started it's crafting after I had told Da about my dream.

Da holds the axe head to the ground as he faces twelve mounted men in matching burgundy tunics and dark gray capes. A uniform of a sort, it is clear. There is a sigil woven into the leather breastplate. One of the mounted men is yelling at Da. *I must do something!* These men hold their hands to the pommels of their long swords. Three others hold cross bows to their sides. *Could there be bolts already loaded to them?*

Da must have seen me as his head is turning slightly towards me. He turns back to the man who is yelling, answering him with words I cannot hear. This man sits on the saddle of a mighty warhorse near to the size of Bregœ. Even at this distance, I note a scar running from his ear to his chin.

Of a sudden, Scarface yells an order. Four men drop from their horses to the ground. Each draws his broadsword. These soldiers move with a trained precision I've never seen afore. They move forward to attack Da.

I jump from the tree line and yell, "Nay!"

Scarface turns my way. Da does not. He is a man possessed and in chaotic motion. Scarface barks another command and two of the riders are suddenly headed my way at a gallop. Da is swinging his halberd. Three of the men are already crumpled to the ground as two more spring from their mounts and pull their swords.

"Pickles, go! Bregœ, to him!" Da's voice booms and he gives a great whistle.

I hesitate no more and begin to run towards Da, watching as the three with crossbows loose their bolts. Da has finished the fourth and fifth attacker with one swing that first hit one swordsman straight on and then another in a powerful upswing. He sweeps through broad swords and nearly decapitates the fifth man. I am amazed at the brutal deftness with which he defends... and kills. But two of the crossbow bolts have struck him. The crossbowmen drop their weapons and leap from their horses to draw their swords as well, even as Da runs another enemy through the heart.

The two dispatched to me are nearing as I continue my sprint to Da. Da goes down on one knee. One bolt has stricken him high in his chest and another lay embedded in his thigh. Bregœ comes thundering past me and strikes with hooves high, one of the charging horses. He canons into the great horse from the front and side in a bone-crushing crash. A roar arises as the horses meet. The second rider, unable to stop, collides with the first rider and Bregœ, to his deadly fate. He is thrown from his mount. An audible crack can be heard as his head hits the ground.

The first rider has somehow managed a swinging dismount with his short sword drawn. His steed is limping back and away. Bregœ keeps the swordsman fighting for his life as he remains a flurry of anger in motion, kicking in all directions, and his jaws snapping afore him.

I continue my race towards Da.

Da has risen. Despite his wounds, he charges the three bowmen as they are pulling their swords. Two never finish drawing them from their scabbards as the curved blade of Da's haälberd, swinging in a mighty arc, strikes straight across their necks. He stops the weapon's forward momentum, and with a twist of his body thrusts the spearhead of the haälberd into the chest of the third bowman.

I am nearly there, but for all my speed, I cannot reach him in time.

"Da! Behind you!"

Scarface has dismounted and is coming at Da from behind with a short sword. *Coward!* The blade enters into Da's left side just below his ribs. Da roars. He swings back to his right with the tail end of his haälberd in a tremendous thrust that takes Scarface directly in the front of his neck and lifts him off the ground. He flies backward and to the ground.

I reach Da just as he too collapses. Falling to my knees, *I hold Da's head to my lap.*

Blood covers everything. It is pooling under Da from the sword thrust to his back. The crossbow bolt to his chest is too close to his heart. The bolt to his thigh continues to literally pump blood from his body as I watch.

What should I do? *Fear. Anger. Hate.* Raw emotion is welling within me.

How can I save him? I have to save him.

Da opens his eyes and whispers to me, "Kingsmen, Arias. You must find the Druid now. Frost-Cellar. Pickles." Then, of all things, he chuckles and tries to smile. *Confusion.*

He draws an agonized breath, pained and tattered, his eyes glazing over now. I know in that moment that Da will not see me again. There is nothing

I could do to keep him. I sit silent with his head in my lap for a short time, all thought beyond me. My eyes stay dry, even as my heart pounds with aching grief.

Finally, I rise to stand above the carnage. I lift my bow and pull my short sword from my pack, walking now, around to each of the soldiers. These Kingsmen. *Anger. Hate.* Da had said in his tales that the King's sigil is a great black raven over a gilded häalberd. *But these men are no longer a threat.* There are ten men down, here and about Da, and it is clear that they will not be getting up. Each wears a thick leather cuirass with the King's sigil embossed upon the breastwear.

Behind me comes a pained whinny and a great snort. Bregœ. My heart is breaking, but I am moving on with the force of necessity and a surge within me that, Mãamel Bræder had once explained, comes with one's fear, a trauma, or extreme emotional exertion.

Bregœ is clearly suffering, and there are still two more soldiers I need to check on. I glance to the homestead trail thinking of Grayce and something catches my eye as all these happenings are being processed in my overtaxed mind. I find that my eyesight sometimes becomes clearer to great distances when I am excited or stressed, and I spy another soldier at the tree line, not eighty paces out.

Another Kingsman.

I stare right at him and start running towards him, nocking an arrow and stopping just to loose it. He remains still, watching only, as I continue towards him. Finally, as my arrow strikes a tree nearby to him, he reigns his horse, turns, and gallops away.

I will not be able to catch him.

I run back to Bregœ. He is thrashing about in severe pain caused by two broken legs—one his hind leg. A shortsword has pierced his belly. But these soldiers about the great aged warhorse, like the others, are not going to rise again. One lays with his head clear around behind him. The other is crushed and smashed and lays in a heap. Bregœ lays next to him, occasionally still thrashing. I pull my dirk and kneel. With a sigh, I take Bregœ's great head into my hands and stare into his eyes. He huffs and whinnies and then becomes very still and relaxed. In a quick and deliberate motion, I thrust my long dagger up through the underside of the majestic steed's jaw and into his brain to relieve his pain forever.

6

A Stone Barrow... No Requiem

Resigned that I can do nothing more for Bregœ, I turn back towards where Da lays. Of a sudden, the sky is now turning ever darker and is nearly black as the sound of hundreds of cawing ravens assault my ears. They are descending upon the carnage in front of the cottage where great buzzards have already landed. A great sickening wrenches at my stomach. My heart wails.

I run towards Da's body, not willing to let the carrion birds desecrate his remains. But as I approach, the most amazing sight presents itself. A score of ravens, maybe more, have formed a circle around Da's body. Even as great vultures approach, the ravens beat them back. All the other bodies are being decimated by the carrion birds. But the great black birds keep vigil in a wide circle around Da. Not a single predator or scavenger bird comes near. As I walk over, the ravens part afore me, and I approach unmolested to him.

The other horses had panicked—either from the scent of blood or the myraid of ravens, I am not sure which—and stand well away. With great effort, I pull Da's body away from the carnage and lay him down, covering his body with a great canvas tarp from the barn.

Looking around at the maelstrom and chaos of the carrions attack of the dead about in the yard, I fear delaying my next task, so I hitch one of our burden horses to a buckboard and bring it over to Da's body. I somehow manage to get Da's great body atop the wagon's backbed. I use the wagon to take him to the great oak behind the barn. With a weighty determination, I dig and dig. Da's grave.

Sweating from exertion so that no further thought can invade, I place Da into it with as much care as I can manage. Across his body, I lay his great bow and to his right, the haälberd.

I bury him. A simple barrow under the great Oak.

I cover the grave with large stones as well. At its head, I fashion large stones, an "E" and a "B"

Ètœn Bard.

I walk over and all but collapse against the great oak and sit there numb and silent. I shake uncontrollably, but I manage to pull myself into my *Calming* and let the nothingness embrace me. I do not want to wake from it. Time passes and as I emerge from the *Calming* it is near to dusk. Life must resume.

Around me, the murder of ravens is feasting, and with them, the other great carrion birds are helping to rid the land of the treacherous Kingsmen who have taken Da from me. They work tirelessly as the skies clear. A full moon rises, and a myriad of stars appear. Plenty of light for their feast of the dead.

After a time, I make my way over to our cottage. Mine now, I guess. I enter and do not bother with the fire. With deadened heart and fatigue beyond measure—from the grief and numbness within—I collapse onto my cot to sleep, despite the eerie sounds of cawing ravens and the screeches of the other carrion birds. The furions are huddled in a quivering bundle in the corner. fearful of the sounds they hear without. I feel them joining alongside me on the cot. I know they are disturbed by the scent of blood all about me, but they do not leave me.

I awake with a start, afore the morn's sun breaks upon the horizon. With Da's last words crystal clear in my mind, I set a fire going in the fire-box and wash at the sink basin. I dress and exit the cottage. I milk our two cows, muck the stables, and put the goats, horses, and cattle to pasture. I set them out the rear doors of the barn and furthest away from the carnage near the front of the cottage, where many carrion birds keep up their feast. These are the every-sun things I did throughout my life with Da. They give me little comfort.

The huge ravens, however, have all retreated to the great oaks branches that overlook Da's grave.

I saddle Paint and don my pack with Lilit and Jilly aboard for the ride. They have scurried from their second home under the cottage to join me. They do not want to be left here amongst our raven guests; I am sure. I will deal with them upon my return. I head out to the Frost-Cellar, Da's final words again surfacing in my mind.

It isn't a long trip since I am riding Paint. I dismount and enter the top cavern of the Frost-Cellar quickly, pulling the torch from its bracket and lighting it. It strikes me now, our secret from long ago and its meaning, and the meaning of Da's password as well.

Da had known that one day, what had happened would come to pass. I don't understand the why of it, however. Da must have been made a wanted man by some lord who insisted he had been wronged and petitioned the King to serve justice. But I have known him always to be only the most honest and honorable of men. This scenario, therefore, makes no sense to me. But these thoughts will have to wait, for Da wanted me here for a rea-son. Da's special password holds the key.

I have always thought Da's special password a joke, as his favorite treat was pickles, and we always have plenty on hand. In fact, the largest bar-rel in all the Frost-Cellar holds just that, pickles. Da's garden has always grown cucumbers. It was the first thing he planted of all his vegetables each spring. As he harvested his cucumbers, he prepared and pickled a good portion of this special crop. Da would have his cucumbers mixed with greens, onions, and tomatoes with vinegar and oil mixed atop. But the special treat remained always the pickled variety. He often said he rated taverns not only by the quality of their ale, but by their pickles. It bringst a great smile to my face even now as I think it.

I hold the lit torch above and in front of me and proceed to the back of the top cavern. The answer is not here. I make my way past the hanging meats and rolls of cheeses in niches in the cave's walls and back to the hidden passage and the stair to the Frost-Cellar below. I do not need to go all the way to the bottom of the stair into the icy Frost-Cellar itself. The landing at the turn of the stair will be far enough. There sit a few barrels of varying sizes holding things Da wanted to stay cool, such as ales and ciders for the most part. And in the biggest barrel amongst these are pickles. A large wood burned 'P' is prominently displayed upon the side of the barrel. I have seen and opened this barrel many a time, so I know Da was not meaning me to do that.

With the torch afore me, something else about the alcove becomes apparent. The barrels are stacked against a slatted wood wall of a sort. As I hold the torch near to it, I can see betwixt the wooden slats that the alcove actually continues deeper behind it.

Muscling the pickle barrel aside, I find the wall in truth opens as a hinged door that swings inward to hide the hinges of it. For all the times I have been here, I have never afore noticed. I find the hidden latch and push the squeaky door open. I step into an even deeper alcove. It extends near three-paces deep, and the ceiling here is tall enough that I can stand upright. As I shine my torch, I find four items in the alcove afore me. The first that catches my eye is an intricately carved bow, then a small chest, a rolled leather secured with an elven-vine cord, and a small wooden box of a size that would fit upon my lap. I swing the torch about the space but can find nothing more.

I remove these items from the alcove and onto the landing in front of the barrels, and pul the door shut once again and secure it. I gather the bow, chest, box, and parchment, and I carry the items out of the cave to examine them in the light of the sun. I make to secure them upon Paint's back, noting as Ido that the bow's intricate carving is of a scaled serpent. A fiercely carved head that clearly represents the head of the mythic Drægon as it sits atop the bow's upper limb—a theme I've seen afore. The lower limb of the bow carries the remarkable likeness of the spiked tail of a Drægon. There can be no doubt that I have found my seventeen-year-end gifting from Da. Another piece of my finger resides within the grip.

Afore I head back to the cottage, something niggles at my brain. I pause for a minute to cypher what it could be. Then a dawning comes. Da had expected Moor and Grayce and Mãamel Bræder to come calling to the homestead today. Then, like a huge stone, the ache fills my heart again, but the practical side of my brain also comes upon me. Going back into the Frost-Cellar I gather into sacks the meats, cheeses, and vegetables for the makings of a few meals. As a last thought, I bring a small barrel of Da's special ale. I think to lift some cups to his life and memory and try drowning out other thoughts I am having just now.

With the added burdens secured atop Paint, I trudge back to the cottage, leading him. Lilit and Jilly scurry from my pack and climb atop Paint. He has become accustomed to the furions racing to and fro upon his back and pays their scurrying and play no mind. But they do none of that this day, sensing as they always do, my state of mind.

Stocked and packed, we approach the cottage through the open grasses of the pastures and as we do, I spy Moor standing at Da's grave and witness his shoulders slumping as I'd never seen afore. The hundreds of coal black ravens have retreated to branches of the great oak under which he lay. It appears just as it did when we returned from our trip to release Bane back to the wild. I recall that Da had called it an 'omen.' I reckon he had been right. The ravens now hold vigil over his grave barrow, and it has become a great, black oak silhouetted against the sky. All but a few of the buzzards and carrion birds have left from their gruesome task of clearing the blight. There is more, but mayhaps they've eaten their fill. The flies and insects are still at work.

Moor turns to face me as I approach, moisture in the bottom of his deep blue eyes. Gazing past him to the east, I hear and then see a gray speckled mare with Grayce astride. Her mare, of a sudden, bucks a bit, and I can reason why as the odors have probably wafted to them by now. Grayce notes us and kicks her mount into a gallop, heading our way.

She reins in her horse and fairly leaps to the ground. Her eyes immediately go to the grave, and then back to me.

"Oh, Arias," is all she says and pulls me into a hard hug. Her body shakes with a sob.

To battle the deep despondency and despair that grips my heart, I reach for normalcy.

"Grayce, I've just come back from the Frost-Cellar. I have two sacks of meats and vegetables and the like. Can you mayhaps start our meal? Mãamel Bræder is expected by mid-sun."

Her eyes widen and new moisture pools in her eyes as she thinks, I realize, of the coming of Da's Effie.

"And Moor, I'd like to speak with you about some things. Will you help me dispose of... this carnage? It's man's work and nothing Grayce and Mãamel Bræder need to see. We can discuss what has happened after, when Mãamel Bræder and Argo have arrived," I continued in a soft voice, breaking a bit.

"Aye, Arias, but I see Argo arriving now. He will give us a hand."

Grayce takes the two sacks, stopping to glance a moment at all that lay about and peeking back and up into the branches filled with Ravens, black as night. She hurries then into the cottage.

I receive furtive glances from both Moor and Argo as we go about the ugly and grueling task of loading in a wagon what remains of the Kingsmen's corpses, but they ask no questions as we work. We transport them to a depression in a rock-strewn clearing a good bit clear of the cottage. There, we drag branches, kindling, and small logs into the makeshift fire pit. Dousing some lantern oil amongst the bodies and branches, we light a pyre. The flames soon rise close to the height of the surrounding trees for a bit and burn on hot and hard for a while more.

A few of the soldiers' steeds are still wandering close by and have even joined our own burden horses in the pasture. Moor rounds them up, removes their saddles, and brings the saddlery and bags to the fire. Argo and I round up the weapons from the bloodied battlefield and bring them as well. We do all this with few words and no explanations. It is though they don't need to hear from me at all. We feed the fire some more with any wood readily available, and then we three return to the cottage.

We are finishing up at the outside well and trying to remove any traces of our morns travails as Effie arrives in her buckboard wagon. Meeting her, I solemnly guide her over to Da's grave. Her eyes grow wide at the site, and she falls to her knees and wails. A sudden chill breeze flows about us and the hundreds of ravens flutter upon the branches above, but they make no other sound.

Grayce comes running from the cottage and straight to her. They hold each other for awhile before Grayce guides her back to the cottage. Moor, Argo, and I gather the remaining things I have brought with me from the Frost-Cellar, and we carry them into the cottage to join the women.

The time has come for me to tell the tale of events from yester's sun. I am not wholly prepared to do this, but I know his friends need to know the how of Da's fate.

7

Council of Friends

Cleaning our boots upon the edge of the cottage porch, the three of us enter to find our little table set for five. Grayce and Mãamel Bræder are filling trenchers of fresh baked bread with a rich and hearty stew. Mayhaps Grayce is trying to keep Mãamel Bræder's mind from lingering on Da's murder. But Da's death will not leave my mind for even a moment, and I think it the case for all of us. Their eyes are red, and Effie rushes to me and hugs me close. No word is spoken, and she sobs. I hold her. No tears come to my eyes though, and we release after a time.

We all sit about the small table and with an unspoken agreement, we eat the hot, rich meal in silence. I lather butter upon the warm bread trencher as I pull it apart. It is fresh from Da's stone oven. I eat like a famished nave, guilty of taking pleasure in this hearty meal, guilty of being alive and sitting here while Da lies out back of the barn beneath rock and soil. I am physically and emotionally worn. But the whole time while eating, something hard stays stuck in my throat. I can't speak if asked the simplest of questions. Moor fills our cups with Da's strong ale. I drink down two cups with the meal.

57

At the last of it, Argo and Grayce clear the table, and Moor fills our cups a third time. When Argo and Grayce return, I finally find the strength and speak.

"Da had sent me to gather shrooms and berries in the forest after the midsun meal," I begin. "He wanted them for today's meal, I suppose. And that is what I'll remember first on what has become the worst day in all of my life." Grayce places her hand on mine for a moment as they lay crossed on the table afore me. A sad glance is all I can spare without failing what I've started, so I stare back down to the table.

It comes pouring out of me in all the gruesome details. Just as I begin, Lilit and Jilly come up through their blanket in the corner of the kitchen near where we sit and curl upon my lap.

"Da's bell tolled three times in the early eve. He's never rung it three times in all these years, and it was not at a time I would expect. We had a secret from when I was even just a seven-year-end."

Around our small table, Grayce and Effie huddle close together hand in hand, their eyes already beginning to fill. Argo leans forward with hands clasped and elbows resting on the table. Moor stands leaning against the cottage's center post, which holds the loft above. His steely eyes are fixed upon mine, intent on the details of my recounting.

"If his bell tolls once, he's calling me to dinner, two if we have guests. He's never faltered in this routine in all my years that I can remember, so I always am listening for his bell. But three was to be a different kind of tolling. If I were ever to hear three bells, it meant for me to run to the Frost-Cellar, as nobody knew where it was. I was to hide there 'til Da came to fetch me, and he would say a special and secret word, so I knew it to be him, *Pickles*. Of course, I always thought it just a game, but he never struck the bell three times.… Never. *Pickles* was the special word because pickles were always special to him, is what I thought. Do you remember, Grayce, you could probably hear the bell all the way over to your homestead?"

"When out and about, I would always hear the bell each day. I found it a comforting thing, somehow," she said quietly.

Just having her say this, helps me to go on. It is a familiar feeling to me as well.

"But I didn't run to the Frost-Cellar this sun because I am no longer a lad of seven… Or eight… Or nine year. And I knew something *was not right*. I ran towards home as fast as my legs would carry me and as I burst out from the tree line and into the open pasture, I stopped cold. Twelve men on horses were all about Da, and one shouting something in such a fierce manner at him. They were all dressed in like garb."

Moor interrupts me. "Arias, you are sure there were twelve?"

"Yea, there with Da," I say. "But one more I spied, after it was all done. He sat atop his mount just outside the tree line on the Homestead Trail to the east. Later, it was, when I spied him and he turned my way. Thirteen in all."

Moor nods in a knowing manner.

I recount the gruesome details, leaving nothing out. From Da's first shout to me… to Scarface's craven strike to Da's back.

"It all happened so quick, much less than the time it took me to tell the tale to you," I state matter-of-fact. "Even as it began, I ran as quick as I could to get to him…to help against the attackers. But I was too late. I reached him only in time to hold his head in my lap and hope for help, though I knew none could come in time. Da opened his eyes and looked into mine. I could tell he was in such pain to even draw a breath. His dying words were, 'Arias, find the Druid…the Frost-Cellar, *pickles*.' And he chuckled when he said it. Of all things, he chuckled. Then a hitch caught him within his chest and his breathe caught at it. Then his eyes glazed over, and I knew it was done."

Distraught beyond measure, I can speak no more.

Effie bursts into tears in the last of the telling. Grayce hugs her. Argo and Moor sigh and slump forward. But for the sobs of Effie, silence hangs heavy about us for a further while. After a time, I speak again.

"Moor, tell me what it all means. Your brow rose as I mentioned the other rider. You know something, and it is time for the telling of your part of the tale." I stare at him.

The others turn to him as well.

After a time, he nods and leans forward and away from the post to finally say, "I know some of it, but not all." Taking a chair, he swings it about, sitting astride it with its back forward and his arms crossed about its top rail. We hear the calls from the ravens outside.

Effie's sobs lessen now, and all attention turns to him.

"You've heard his tales as you grew from a young lad, Arias." He takes a deep breath.

All eyes are on him now, especially Effie's.

"You may have thought them a soldier's tall tales and fantasies. I assure you anything he told you was indeed all true."

My eyes widen and I say, "But surely not."

"Aye, Arias, he told me he was telling you the details. And they were the tales of his life and all were true," Moor says matter-of-factly.

"Ètœn could not lie, to his fault. Mayhaps his only true one."

"Aye," they all say as one.

I am taken aback at this as Da would've been the most renowned soldier of all time.

"Aye," says Moor, apparently reading my thoughts. "He was the greatest soldier in the King's army, no one… nor ten were his match in his prime. Or even now, it would seem."

And then I think back on what I had witnessed yester's-eve.

"He saved my life once, Arias, and put my life's path onto a new direction, in the doing. You see, I was once a paid assassin and mayhaps the best at it in all of Aeryth," continues Moor. "It became, at one time, my charge to kill Ètœn and he knew it when I came for him. The details of it are no longer important, but to say he could've ended me and instead he saved me. He stayed with me afterwards and helped me survive and gain back my strength, as I was in dire condition. And over that time, we talked and then became friends after a fashion."

I hold hard to his gaze and query, "Who sent you to kill him, and why?"

"That is somebody else's tale to tell. Mayhaps this Druid he spoke of."

Thoroughly confused, I ponder at that moment, that I do not know Da at all.

Grayce speaks up. "Arias, what Moor has said is true. You see, my husband fought alongside Ètœn in the King's battles as well. He owed his life thrice over to him and called him his best friend in all this world. Alas, that soldiers' life finally took my man from me."

She lightly pulls at each of her hands with the other, a more thoughtful than nervous gesture.

I do not know what to say to this, nor all that Moor has told.

Argo picks up the tale. "Arias, I see all of this is new to you. Understand that it is as Ètœn had wanted it. He did not want you to know his true past yet. Though, if you recall his tales, you are aware of more than you realize. Even knowing it would one day catch up with him, the both of you, actually. My story is similar. I am all that he told you. But what you don't know is that the Master Smithy that I served meant to kill me for surpassing him at his craft and scheming to do just that. My brœther was a good friend of Ètœn and told all to him. Ètœn lay a rouse that led my Mæster to think me dead. Ètœn then found me a home here, so that I could continue my craft. He had saved my brœther's life twice as well."

Finally, I turn to Effie to hear if she has a further tale to tell of Da.

"I have nothing more to add to these histories, Arias. I did not even know any of this. Ètœn spoke little of his past. Though I knew he was once a soldier. I just loved him with all of my heart for what I did know of him." Her voice cracks.

I sit in silence for a time, pondering these people with tales to tell of Da, that I, in all my years of knowing him, had not a clue. I glance to Moor and Argo, then back to Moor again.

"Can you tell me then, Moor, what a Druid is and where I can find this one that Da would have me seek out?"

"Nay, Arias, I cannot tell you where to find this Druid, other than to help you with any map he may have supplied to you. Druids are only men of myth and legend to my mind. I can tell you some of what the lore tells of them, though," he elaborates.

Slumping my shoulders, I can but wrinkle my brow in confusion.

"Lore? Myths? Why would Da send me seeking after myths?" I query "Is it some code that I must decypher? Is there even such a man, this Druid?"

"They may not be only myths, Arias," remarks Effie. "Recall that I received my training from a Sjaman on the Isle of Hermætêa off the coast in the Southern Reaches. The Sjaman of the Isles had powers I've seen in no other man. It is from him that I know of the lore of the Druids. They are said to be wise and hold knowledge past all others and are said to be Seers and mayhaps even practitioners of the ancient mægics," she continues in a solemn sincerity with no evident jest. "The Sjaman spoke as if they still were of this world."

"Ancient Mægics?" I blurt incredulously.

"Aye, Arias, do not discount such a thought. As a fact, you should always keep open your mind to the unexplained. I will admit to this council that I have witnessed things that are not explainable but did ne'er-the-lesser happen," says Moor. "Mysterious and unexplainable and the most peculiar happenings... And even the King is said to be a Seer of a sort."

"My mentor explained that there were five great Mægics practiced by ancient Mæges in long past times. There is the Mægic of healing that the Sjaman of Hermætêa certainly has a great ability with and has taught me some. There were Mæges that were Seers and could tell what would or might come to pass. The third Mægic was the communing with beasts. These were Mæges that could communicate with animals and have them do their bidding. The fourth great Mægic was the power to move objects with the mind. Finally, the fifth great Mægic was the power over the elements, such as wind or fire. The Sjaman said that the Mæges that were able to master this discipline were said to be some of the strongest. The Druids were said to be either Seers or those Mæges that could lift and move objects with their mind, I believe. They were the Mæges of greatest intelligence and were revered and respected amongst others of Mægic. They were also said to be the most reclusive and the keepers of the knowledge."

It all seems but a child's fable to me.

"The Sjaman explained that some small part of these Mægics are born within the rare person even today, as it is a matter of bloodline from the original great Mæges," Effie says.

"Da certainly had a way with any beast. I've seen him calm a bear and turn it away from attacking us. And Bregœ always seemed to know what Da was thinking and feeling," I say, pondering this thought of ancient mægics. "It was eerie almost, that when Scarface sent riders after me, with just a word from Da, Bregœ charged them like the warhorses in Da's tales."

Even as I say this, a bit of a queer thing is happening. Lilit and Jilly rise up from my lap and give me a start as they jump up unto the table. They proceed to weave over and under each other and then scurry off the table and over to the box I'd retrieved from the alcove behind the pickle barrel. I had stacked the items in a corner when I returned with them from the Frost-Cellar. They are my subconscious mind, I think a'times.

I've been having a niggling thought trying to sneak into my conscious mind since we started this conversation. It is as if the two furions have picked up on it. With the unexpected behavior of my little furion friends, the thought comes clearly back to me. Da would have told me how to find this Druid. Moor spoke of a map. I do not know to what purpose, but I can only assume the Druid can tell me why Da had been killed by the Kingsmen. I rise to retrieve the objects I'd found in the Frost-Cellar this very morn and bring them back to the table to show the others.

"There is a bit more to this tale that I have yet to tell," I say to Da's – *my* – friends gathered at the table.

"Da's last words to me led me to find these items he left for me. I acted on his words this morn and returned with these items I have never seen afore," I divulge. "I've just reached my seventeen-year-end even today, and Da died just this one day short of it. Clearly, this bow is his last gifting to me. But I found these other items there as well. Mayhaps, there are some answers to be found among them."

Putting the bow aside, I untie the elven vine from the leather scroll to reveal two parchments within. The first afore me, a beautifully penned journal of a sort, proclaims myself as its intended recipient. I marvel at its intricacy. The script is flowing and quite striking.

I read aloud from the parchment.

'Ariastone Côeurdrægon, if you are reading this now, I have not survived, and I must beseech you to act on your own behalf to make every effort to seek out the Druid of Esper and known to me as Eschereon.'

Whenever Da became especially impatient with my attitude, or he imposed a special urgency upon me, he would use my true first two names to emphasize the import of all that was to come. So, his use of Ariastone Côeurdrægon therefore, is an indication of the tone of the tome afore me. He had also already mentioned a Druid named Eschereon and so I now know this Druid is indeed real and important somehow. He has a name. Da's letter continues,

'What you read below, I have not ever discussed with thee. Know that I would have done so, but was bound by a sacred Oath to refrain from telling you much that I would have preferred to teach ye of your past.

My past? I do not understand any of this. My past has always been with

Da. I recall playing with goat kids and piglets when barely able to walk. What further past could I have had? But I continue reading.

'*The same Oath even now prevents me to discuss much more. But, Arias, take heed, it will be of utmost import that ye shall seek out the Druid. He will be able to explain what I am unable to. The map will guide you to his Keep.*'

I search quickly for a map and surely as he'd spoken, I find the leather scroll that wraps the parchments is indeed a map. Scribed upon its inside surface is a map of the whole of Aeryth. It's a smaller version of the great map on the school room wall. I go back to reading, leaving the study of the map for a later time.

'*His Keep is a great way from our homestead, mayhaps several moons travel time. Ye are to make it your immediate quest. As ye read this, a grave danger lurks not too distant from ye, even now. I knew this happening could not be far off when we returned to find the ravens in the great oak. I indeed took it as an evil omen and so have I written this parchment.*

I gape in shock to the others. Grayce, of course, knew of the first appearance of the ravens as she was here when we returned after releasing Bane back into the wild. Hundreds of the large Blackbirds had perched and filled all the branches of the great Oak behind the barn, as if they were specifically awaiting our return. Even as I read this, I recall that Argo and Da started crafting his great haälberd, just a few moons after.

Pausing in the reading, I recite the tale of Bane's rescue by Da and I, and our returning him again into the forest after his healing. More so now, an additional loss beyond Da becomes evident to me. I find that though I had known him not much more than a fortnight, I missed him. There had been there, I knew, a genuine and primal connection. I return once more to the parchment.

'*Make ye all haste, Arias. Put the homestead in order and depart alone as soon as ye are able*'.

Moor nods at this and I cannot help but wonder what more he knows.

'I have attached my last testament to aid to this end. Also, ye shall have found an intricately carved box. It has not been opened these many years as a condition of my Oath, as it is to be yours alone.

Arias, lad, may destiny be kind to ye as I make my final fare-thee-wells.

With deepest devotion,

Da

I have no words.

But Moor remarks, "Arias, the men who killed Ètœn were a company of Kingsmen. They always travel in a troupe of thirteen men. In an engagement, one will always stay apart from the others. It is his charge to report back if such a thing as this has happened. Ètœn's warning is a valid one and you indeed must leave here as soon as possible. If they were charged with his killing, they may well have been charged to execute any family and witnesses as there may be as well. That sentry knows of you and another company will be dispatched to that purpose."

"But why?" I question.

"I cannot tell you the why of it, Arias, but your life is surely in great peril. You must indeed leave."

I gaze about the room and can see the tension apparent in the others now.

I turn back to the items in front of me. I recognize immediately the runes on the box as they are the exact same as those that Da had placed on my Bo-staff. Having studied them for many years now, I know them by heart. Not quite sure what gives me pause, but I decide I will not look within the box until I find myself alone later.

The other parchments are indeed Da's testament. I am determined to read it through to those gathered as they are his closest friends that I know. But afore I do, I explain that there are chores I must tend to and ask those gathered if we can wait until the morrow's morn to read through it. All are agreed as they want each, to ponder alone what has been said.

I start about my chores and Moor and Argo go about the continued business of trying to remove any evidence of yester-sun's battle. A few more of the Kingsmen's horses are found and we bring them in as well. With the promise of the feed bag we have little trouble in rounding them back to the barn.

Is this a sort of normalcy amid chaos? To my mind, Yes.

Grayce and Effie go about straightening up the cottage, it's never had so much womanly attention afore. We sit about the hearthfire that eve with no more thought of the parchment and the other items awaiting us. Moor and Argo make their beds in the loft of the barn, Effie and Grayce take Da's large bed, and I retire to my cot in the cottage loft. We will see to the remaining items on morrow's morn.

8

Testament and fare-thee-wells

Waking afore the next morn's sun, there is a chill to the air and within my bones as well. Listening intently, while lying upon my cot, birds chirp outside, and our farms burden beasts' morning noises make their way to my ears. Da's passing has left something missing within me even as life about me goes on at its usual pace.

Effie and Grayce have shared Da's bed last night and awakening to their presence in the cottage is welcome to me. As I lie there, I think more on Da's quest for me and the parchment he has left, his testament, and the unusual box. We decided that we would examine them in the light of the morn. But first, there are the homestead chores that need doing, and I desperately need to splash some cool water upon myself.

As I sit up upon my cot, ready now to greet this sun, Lilit and Jilly scramble from their corner and scurry up the loft ladder to make their way to my shoulders, nuzzling the underside of my chin as if to say their condolences once again and give comfort to me. I rise with my two friends as they remain playful. I get the hearthfire restarted and then head for the door. As I unlatch the door and open it, I am startled and then amazed. There afore me on the porch lies Bane. His sparkling golden, unnatural canine

68

eyes are focused upon me. A smile comes to me unbidden to see such a sight. Lilit and Jilly approached the young wolf excitedly as well, as they had become unlikely friends several moons past, upon his fortnight and seven recuperating with Da and I.

"Well then, you've found your way back to me. I take a great comfort in seeing you, Bane." Dropping to my knees,, I roughly grap and scratch the scruff of Bane's neck, and then hug him, as a burst of emotion threatens to engulf and overtake me. I slip past the door's threshold finally, pulling the door closed quietly, and leave my friends to sleep as I tend to the morn chores.

Argo and Moor meet me in the yard. Bane gives a low growl as they approach. Seeing this wild animal at my side, they are curious, but wary of the wolf cub as well. He has grown in the many moons since we were last together. He no longer looks the pup, and the two men are rightfully wary. But, as I interact with them, Bane relaxes and recognizes them as friends. They, in turn, calm to Bane's presence, also.

"I'd imagine there is more of your wolf tale we do not know, Arias," Moor says as he examines the wolf pup. "As you said earlier, this is a unique wolf cub at the least. And he has taken a strong fancy to you if, as you said, he was left far up the mountainside and put back into the wild."

"Yea," say I, "and an ever baffling one to me as well since I awoke this morn. If you'll both give me a hand with the morn chores, I'll tell you the longer tale."

Embracing the morns chill, we get about the work of it.

As we go about putting the livestock and horses to pasture and putting feed out and mucking out the stables, I explain to them about Bane. The blackbirds are no longer perched in the Oak, and the homestead about the cottage shows little signs of the turmoil from two suns past. Chores complete, we wash and return to the porch of the cottage, stomping the dust from our boots. We are met by Effie and Grayce and the smells of the morn-meal through the doorway behind them, sizzling upon Da's stove plate. Effie's eyes show shock at Bane's presence. Grayce, of course, knows of the wolf as Da had told her the tale, but has never beheld him. Bane stays distant from them, but I call him over and introduce them as friends, and as I did with Moor and Argo, Bane accepts them immediately, as such.

Our council of five retire to the cottage, and Bane, Lilit, and Jilly make to play about the yard. 'Tis a sight to see them at it and we all laugh. Such an astounding sight, prey and predator bounding about and playing together.

After a filling morn-meal, Da's four friends—and now mine in every true sense of the word—share Da's life and memories among us. And then, they announce that they too, have giftings for me.

"Ho, but why would you do such a thing?"

"This is why we had all meant to come to your year-end-gifting with Ètœn, Arias, as we all played a part in your teachings and trainings since such a young age, and you are now officially a man." Effie explains.

Indeed, they all had.

"I'll not deny that, and it is MY honor to have had your lessons."

Argo pulls out a chair. "Aye, so as it's your seventeen-year-end, and coming to manhood, we thought it appropriate to get you something as well."

We each take a seat around the table again, with the exception of Moor, who stands leaning against the cottage's center post betwixt us and the door but appearing especially alert and vigil.

"So then, my gifting is in two parts. One is of both Ètœn and my crafting and one I have worked for three full moons myself in the making," Argo explains.

First, he brings me a most amazing quiver of arrow, a score of them inside. I recognize Da's work immediately in the quiver itself, and the arrow shafts are fashioned from Ænt-wood. Argo had tipped each arrow with the blue hued metal from the Sky-stone and fletched each with stiffened feathers from a mountain eerie eagle. The arrows are straight and true as could be, and the quiver is made to withstand the rigors of a true Bowman. Beautiful and lethal.

The second gifting is a metal design attached on one end to a branding iron. Its pattern is made of an intricate filigree. Taking a step back from it and examining it as a whole, I clearly see it. A Drægon with fine scales and wings and talons. A most beautiful piece of work.

"Bring me your pack and vest, Arias. I've designed this to be branded upon it." Argo's pride is evident in his voice.

He places the brand into the fire as I lay out my pack and vest on the table. When the brand glows red, Argo pulls it from the fire and presses it against the breast swatch of elk hide and holds it there for a short time. When he finally removes it, the image of a fierce Drægon with wings spread has now been forever imprinted upon the leather. It is a magnificent image in keeping with his other work upon my short sword and dirk and throwing blades alike. I thank him profusely with a broad smile and a hug.

Moor says he won't present his gifting to me at this time but promises that we will talk more later as he has something he will pass to me of great importance.

Effie steps forward to the table now and gives me a shy smile. She places a rolled bundle afore me on the table. 'Tis mayhaps the size of my forearm, and aside it she places a worn pestle and mortar made in what appears to be jade with runes carved around the outside. I have seen it upon a shelf in her cottage's workroom.

"It is the same pestle and mortar gifted to me by my mentor, Arias, and it means I graduate you from apprentice to practitioner of the craft of healing. You have the skill and knowledge of a great healer even now, but just lack the practice."

I give her a halfhearted smile and turn to examine the rolled bundle that still lays afore me. When unfurled, it reveals many pockets carrying herbs and powders sealed in waterproofed pouches. I recognize them all, but she has also labeled them, ever the organized healer. Goldenseal, Sambucus, and Elderberry. Also, Osha root, Bacopa, Bladderrack, and Blessed Thistle. And tucked in pouches are Rhediola and White Willow and even a fair amount of Laudium. These are both the common and the extraordinary and are a wonder to me.

I am moved by this gesture from a mentor that has given me so much more than a healer's knowledge already.

I know that Da and Effie had a connection not wholly realized, and this gifting seems more to me than just a gift between healer and apprentice.

"I am speechless, Mãamel Bræder —"

She interrupts, "Stop ye right there, Arias. Please address me as Effie now and I'll greatly appreciate it."

"This is too generous. I know the time it must've taken, and the pestle must be priceless." I touch it hesitantly with just a graze of my index finger.

"I believe ye may be a special healer one day, Arias, and it gives me a great happiness to pass all of this to you. I have seen you with all manner of creature and man alike, and you have a natural ability I've seen in no other. My mentor would be proud of me to acknowledge this, and you," she says sincerely.

"And so, I shall accept your gift and try always to use it wisely and as you have taught me," I say in my own sincerest reply. I am truly humbled and honored both.

"Now it is my turn, Arias." Grayce clears her throat. "You've been as a son to me. You've never hesitated to help me no matter the circumstance and never with thought of coin in return. And so, I gift this that was once my husband's and may be of use to you more than me, even more so now that you are to set out on your own. My husband, Artur, was a butcher afore he became a soldier to the crown."

Moor leans, more relaxed now, against his corner post as he smokes a pipe, and the scent permeates our small cabin. Observing me, I think. Argo has poured himself an ale.

Grayce hands me a folded leather sheathing that has a good many pockets and sleeves. Unfolding the leather carry reveals all manner of blade and cutlery, just as I'd seen the towne butcher carry. The blades are honed to a fine edge, and it is clear someone has taken great care with them. A whetstone lay in a pocket of its own.

"Another gifting that is beyond me!" I exclaim as a great emotion fills me with these friends of Da's who give to me even as we mourn the loss of Da. "Enough of all of this then. Let us see what further Da had to say while I am with such friends."

There are smiles all around and a deep sadness as well.

I bring out the remaining items found in the alcove of the Frost-Cellar.

In the same flowing script as the parchment he had left for me, a testament and will now lay afore me. Spreading the rolled parchment, it amazes me that a man who spoke like a soldier, worked the land as a farmer, and trained animals as a whisperer, could have such a flowing script and eloquent speech upon a parchment to belie his spoken words. I read them.

As ye prepare to pursue the quest I have set afore thee, Arias, I would ask that you honor my last testament afore your departure.

I've always had a love for creatures and would place those about the homestead in good hands. Please deliver our bull ox to farmer Artemis, so as to be of service upon his fields, as he has returned to me these many year a crop that I might produce our homestead ale with each harvest.

I recall with pride the fine brew ale that Da used to make each year and store within the Frost-Cellar.

I would have one cow delivered to Master Slaeger, as he has, to my knowledge, honored our agreement of two-year's-past and has made a more peaceful home for his wife and daughter Dulcinẽa.

And here, I recall the trip he had made after I told him the tale of

Dulchè and the butcher's son and how her pæder showed cruel intent to-wards her mum and sister and herself. He had reformed his drinking and abusive ways once Da had discussed it with him.

All the other beasts, I would have delivered into the hands of Grayce and knowing all will be well with them. Also, show her to the Frost-Cellar to do as she will.

To Argo, a smithy of no ordinary talent, and a true friend, I would leave all that is left of the Ænt-wood and Sky-stone metal to do as he may.

To Moor, I would give into his care Bregœ, and any saddlery or weapons save my bow, as he has become as a brœther to me, and Bregœ will bear him.

I would have you lay my bow with my body if it be possible.

Arias, if you would personally deliver for me into the hands of Effie, prithee, the smaller box and let her know that it was my mœther's and her mœther afore her. She gave it on to me as a keepsake as I ventured out on my own. It has been treasured by me, as I treasure Effie. Prithee, explain to her that I would have been honored to have had her as my wife, if not for my Oath.

Effie's eyes are filled to the brink, and a tear leapt upon her cheek. I hand her the small box.

Further, under the floor plank board in the corner nearest the firebox, you will find two bags of coin. One is for yourself, Arias, and one is for Effie.

I stare over at the corner in which Lilit and Jilly have made their nest in a blanket. They rise to stand at attention, staring back at me.

"Did you know you slept upon a treasure, lassies?"

Stepping over to the corner, I stoop and prise the floorboard up and lift two heavy sacks of coin as promised. I hand one to Effie with a hug. She weeps freely now and hugs me all the tighter. After she releases me, I return to the table to finish reading the testament.

Lastly, Arias, I give unto ye unopened, as per my Oath, the final box afore ye. 'Twas entrusted to my care to be handed to ye when ye came of an age. As ye are reading this, the time of it would be now.

May a kinder destiny guide thee, Arias, know that ye have made my life a fuller one to which I hold no regrets.

Afore ye is my full wish and will and testament,

Ètœn Bard

The testament's end. Around the table, Da's friends in this world pledge to carry out his wishes. As Bregœ had died with Da, Moor suggests that he will round up the few horses that remained from the Kingsmen and will remove them to another towne distant from Middenvale so that no consequence will come to a citizen in possession of King's property.

Effie and Grayce adjourn to talk of Da, I believe, and to tend the garden and gather makings for the midsun meal. Argo and Moor step out of the cottage as well, talking amongst themselves. Bane follows them out, just to be out of doors, I am sure. I remain seated at the table and ponder the box afore me.

It is a box but a hand's-width tall and less than a forearms-width to each side. On two sides lay runes carved deep into the wood. I suspect it to be Ænt-wood as it bears a close resemblance to the wood Da had used in my year-ender giftings. The ancient symbols are the same that Da had shaped under each end of my Bo-staff. Upon the top of the box and embedded within, is a design fashioned as an eye, with many golden amber crystals formed in a circle that is the iris of the eye, and within that one band lay another equal band of the silvery glaze to make up of a group of gems. Finally, within the center sits an onyx stone with a polished sheen that has survived these many years. I at once realize that the design carried, indeed, a very close resemblance to my very own eyes.

But missing from this beautifully carved, crafted, and polished box is any latch. No lid nor hinge of any sort is visible upon it. I pull and push in all directions, unable to cypher a method to open it.

It has been quite some time, and Lilit, Jilly, and I are losing patience with our inability to fathom its secrets. I set the box aside as Grayce and Effie return to the cottage. As they join me, I suggest that I show Grayce and Effie the way to the Frost-Cellar and mayhaps bring back some meats and cheeses and other foodstuffs while we are there. They agree and we are off, me on Paint and Effie and Grayce on Da's buckboard wagon. Bane keeps an eye and the pace of us at a good distance. He will not be left behind again.

As we travel, I discuss my frustration with being unable to open the box meant to be opened by me. Effie quirks her chin towards me as if a thought had just struck her.

"I believe I've seen such a box as you are describing, Arias. Much younger and apprenticed to the Sjaman of the Isle," she remarks. "I saw him open it once. He but held it upon his lap with his hands upon each side of the box and he went into his *Calming*. The box appeared to glow and then the lid just snapped open. I did not see him push or twist anything upon the box…. amazed to see such a thing."

"Do you mean he simply meditated over it as you have taught me to do?"

Effie nods.

"It would seem there is more to the *Calming* then you trained me in, Effie." becoming comfortable with Da's familiar name for her now.

But mayhaps I will give this strange method a try later, though I cannot see how it could work so.

We arrive at the Frost-Cellar and the ladies are amazed at it all. From the hidden doorway to the frost room below, and even more so, all that Da had accumulated within it. They gather some food stuff and a block of ice from the lower cellar, and we are soon off and headed back to the homestead. When we arrive back to the homestead barn, Moor and Argo have removed the training logs from the barn ceiling beams and have likewise removed any weapons that were about. Moor insists that if, or more likely when, more Kingsmen return, the less they know of me the better. Though left unsaid up till now, it is assumed by the others that I will be departing on a quest to find the Druid that Da spoke of.

Having arrived back to the homestead, the women return to the cottage to prepare an eve-meal for us all. Half past midsun now, I resolve to try Effie's method to open the box. Gathering it to me from the cottage, I take it out to the great Oak and sit with it in my lap with my back against the trunk of the great tree.

Seated and overlooking Da's grave, I place the box in my lap. Recalling the method that Effie had taught me years afore, I slow my heartbeat, clear my mind, and breathe shallow and long. I have little sense of time when I sink into the *Calming*, but I hold an acute awareness of all things and happenings about me. I find it no different this time. My furion friends are standing on their hindquarters and intensely watching both me and the object in my lap. Bane has silently approached. He settles in with contact to me at my knees. He, too, sensed my mood and feelings and knew something to be happening, or about to in any case.

My hands lay against the side of the box. Tracing the runes and intricate carving about the sides of the box, my fingers weave with its pattern. I continue about this for some little time and, of a sudden, a warmth spreads from my hands all the way to my heart and then up into my neck and head. Even as this happens, the crystals upon the face of the box begin to glow, and the furions' and Bane's eyes flash to mine own. In a trice, the top of the box opens with a soft click.

My pulse gains its rightful place as I climb out from the *Calming,* and I peer within the small open chest. Not deep in any sense and lined in a deep purple velvet cloth, within lay but two things.

One, a small, rolled parchment, and the second a fairly large and intricately carved amulet of what appears to be simple bronze and, mayhaps, Ænt-wood as a stone's setting. The white center stone itself is opaque and flows in a rainbow of muted colors. Threaded through an eyelet at the top of the amulet appears to be a seamless piece of Elven-vine, quite pliable but strong beyond measure as is all Elven-vine. I admire the amulet for some period of time. Within the intricately carved latticework around the creamy white stone are again indecipherable runes as a setting, holding the gem. It is a remarkable piece of craftsmanship, and it seems to warm to my touch. Laying the amulet on my thigh, I turn my attention to the rolled parchment. The only other item found within the box.

Setting the box itself to the side of me. I unfurl the delicate parchment across my lap, a flowing script born of much practice is presented afore me, and words I would never have expected to read. It began:

Arias Côeurdrægon, I am your mãmere.

My mœther!

'Tis like a jolt to my body and, of a sudden, I remember myself as a boy of five years and in the soft arms of my mãmere. She smelled of lavender and lilac, and I realize immediately who she was, and her smiling in my mind's eye warms me to my soul. And then the memory becomes just that, a memory. A true memory that I always had but afore now, could not recall. I know I had truly experienced it. A sigh escapes my lips, and I turn back to the scroll. As he lies against my leg, a shiver runs down Bane's back, and Lilit and Jilly climb and settle in my lap, their tiny golden eyes gazing up into mine. Their eyes mirror my own with thoughts of a mœther lost. I read on.

If you are reading this, then you have come of age, and Ètœn Bearheart has presented to you my testament. Know this first and foremost, though you remember little of me, I have always loved you with all of my soul, and it has broken my heart to have had to send you away from me.

But your life was in the most extreme peril, and I found it to be my only choice if you were to grow to be a man. As Ètœn has, I am sure explained to you, he and you must now return to the Druid, for the Druid alone will have the answers you will seek, and further protection asides.

Prithee, wear the amulet from within the box at all times and you will have a level of protection from those who will seek after you.

May your destiny keep you safe on a road fraught with danger and heartache.

Love always,

Mãmi

I sit stunned. And her signature, Mãmi, as I read it aloud, comes to me as if from a dream, and I know it for what I always called her. I have just learned something of my mãmere. Nay, it is more. She appeared, as if by mægic, in my memory and soul, and I cannot fathom how I could have forgotten these memories. She foretold of a road to this unknown Druid, the travelling upon which will cause me both, and specifically, danger and heartache. What danger? What heartache? How could she foretell such a thing, so many years in the past? A quest it seems, ne'er-the-lesser, that I must venture onto. And she bequeaths me an amulet said to hold a *mægic* to protect me from being found by enemies. But why do I have enemies?

In but three suns, I have found myself without Da, with strong memories of a mãmere I had previously no recollection of, and apparently enemies in King's Court. Enemies apparent to my mãmere many years ago. 'Tis a world turned topsy turvy upon me.

I wonder at the change of direction my life has taken in these last few suns. And as I do, the parchment that holds my mãmere's words, of a sudden, flame a bright and blinding white and in doing so, turns to ash in my hands. I leap at the happening of it, and the furions, in turn, jump from me as I rise, my brow furled in disbelief. The amulet had fallen to the ground.

79

It is a connection to the mãmere I now remember so clearly. I reach for it and slowly place it about my neck. An uncommon warmth envelopes me as it makes contact with my skin.

My heart aches for the loss of Da, but yearns to be reunited with my mãmere. Could she be with the Druid?

Da's grave looms just paces away and even more questions stream into my consciousness. But they will need wait, it appears, at least until I find this Druid that I am fated to quest after. Taking stock of this new knowledge, I brush the dust and ashes from my tunic and trousers and taking up the *mægic* box, head back to the cottage. I stop along the way to wash up at the well, doing so to establish again a sense of connection to a past even as it unravels afore me.

I enter the cottage to the wonderful aroma of an early eve-meal prepared, and join my friends, Da's friends from an earlier time in his life, sitting and chatting about the table.

"I leave out on the morrow's morn."

We eat and speak of Da. I toss a few tidbits from the table over to Lilit and Jilly. The tales are many, and it lightens our hearts a bit. After we clear the eve-meal remnants, I proceed to quietly gather up my gear and my giftings to fill my pack and saddle bags in preparation for my travels. Afore retiring, Moor asks me to join him in the yard. We exit the cottage and step down from the porch. The gravel of the walkway crunch under our boots as the sound of the door bangs shut behind us and invades the quieter night sounds. The gravel gives way to grass as we head towards the barn and the song of crickets resume anew.

"Arias, I've known for some time that you would be traveling, as Ètœn years ago told me it was to be so. It is for that reason you have been taught and trained through the years," Moor explains. "Ètœn told me he lay under Oath to prepare you, but could not explain it to you. He swore me to an Oath to likewise not disclose it to you. I presume what you found in the box has persuaded you to proceed on the quest that he beset you?"

"It has."

"Well then, here is my gifting to you. You must put it to memory and keep it only there and I hope it will be of aid to you in future need."

With that, he presents me with a parchment that lists a number of townes, villages, cities across all of Aeryth. Beside each village and towne he has written a person's name and where they can be found within the towne. Over the next few suns, I will do as he has asked and commit each to memory.

There is little left to say among us on the morrow's morn. I gather my pack and supplies onto my own back and bedroll, tarp, and travel food in saddlebags upon Paint. My Bo-staff and new bow hang from leather strappings along the horse's flank. Amongst my pack and strapped to Paint are all of the giftings I have received over these past seven year. Short sword, throwing blade, Bo-staff and my new bow. Within my pack I have the Schäaken board and pieces Da had carved for me and all the latest giftings I had just received from my friends here at the homestead. My mãmere's box I keep within a saddlebag.

Hugs are made all around, and Grayce and Argo promise to execute Da's wishes in his testament. With my mãmere's amulet around my neck, the furions perched atop my saddle in front of me and Bane within sight, our unusual company sets out to fulfill Da's special mandate to me, to seek out this Druid.

Fare-thee-wells complete, I head east down the homestead trail where I would connect with the main travelway and from there head north away from Middenvale. Gazing back over my shoulder, I notice the four watch me as I head off. Effie is hugging herself, Grayce and Argo stand with hands upon their hips, and Moor leans into his staff eyeing me with intent. All of their faces are solemn.

9

Moon Lake Memories

As I lie in my bedroll, looking to fall asleep after my first day out from Middenvale, I find myself reminiscing about Da, his year-ender-giftings and the other things Da had done for me. Cyphering, now, that all along, he had been preparing me for this quest he had put me on.

Amongst the many things that Da did right, one thing for certain had been year-ends. I had asked him after he had gifted me the short sword on my fifteen-year-end how it was he knew what to gift me for each year-end. His eyes gazed past me to another place and time.

Then after pondering a bit, he said, "Do you know what is my most prized possession, Arias?"

I didn't have to think at all, of course. "Your bow, a-sure."

"Aye. My Da gave me that bow for me eighteen-year-end, just afore I left on me own to travel to Seas End to make me a way in life. So, I guess between yer tellin' me what yer are most needin' and me own experience, I just know."

"What do you mean, Da? I never asked for the gifts you've given, I don't think."

"Aye, ye did a'times, and fortune plays a hand innit as well.... And I'm not saying a lot of work and thought don't go along with it."

Da was sitting afore me again in my mind's eye, clear as the sun. He pondered for more than a bit, as if he were recalling to mind a fond memory. When he spoke, it took me back to the time myself.

"Arias, do you recall the trip we made together to Moon Lake when ye was just a lad of eight year?" he had finally asked.

"Yea, Da. Of course. 'Twas the first time you took me on a hunt with you. Afore, you used to leave me with Widow Grayce. I rode in front of you on Bregœ, and we camped for the first time. You let me use your flint to start the campfire, and we found those things at the lakeshore and watched and felt as the Sky-stone trembled the ground when it hit across the lake. You started telling me your tales about soldiering on that trip. Yea, Da. I remember it well, that trip."

"Well, lad, that trip was special for me as well," he began. "As a fact, all yer year-end giftings go back to that trip."

I'd stared at Da with a quizzical expression, I'm sure, as I tried to remember the trip in more detail and relate it to what he had just said.

We had traveled for five days and nights, and each day we would stop and make camp afore the sun could reach the trees. The forest teemed with wildlife. We were constantly setting birds to flight and rabbits, deer, coons running in all directions. We spent the day enjoying the creatures skittering here and there. Da said that these creatures weren't accustomed to a giant like Bregœ stomping down the trails, nor human folk like us making a fuss as we went.

And I didn't realize it at the time, but Da set up camp early so we could explore the forest. I remember moaning that my butt hurt something awful for sitting on Bregœ for hours, but Da would set up the tarp between a couple trees and tell me to collect some branches while he dug a fire pit. Afterwards, we would immediately set out and explore. The streams were teeming with fish, crayfish, turtles, and such. Da put a net in the stream, and we sat and talked about things or he'd tell me a tale. A bit later he pulled the net out of the stream, humming in satisfaction.

"Soup Makins," he declared and there would be some fish or turtle or crayfish caught in the net.

Da set two or three snares right off, as well, and showed me how to do it. At eight-year I wasn't so good at it, but proud that Da would bother to show me. And so, we had made our way high into the hills until we reached a secluded mountain lake. I asked Robiss, my schoolhouse friend, years later if he had ever been to the lake and he had no idea where I was talking about. We arrived to the lake late, and Da set up camp on the lakeshore. No breeze blew, with everything still as could be. Afore the sun went down the mountains, around the lake was purple and the sky was orange behind them. There wasn't a cloud in the sky. Later as I lay next to Da staring up, the sky was twinkling with countless stars. Too excited that night to even sleep for some reason, I pestered Da with a thousand questions and he just chuckled like he was wont to do and patiently answered. These memories I hold dear.

But the two things that made that night the most memorable were what happened a bit later. I had fallen off to sleep but awoke with a start for I don't know what reason. It slipped from my mind immediately as afore my eyes shone the biggest moon ever, hanging there in the sky just over the horizon and its twin below it spreading across the lake. With mouth agape, I elbowed Da, speechless. He rose to his elbows with a sparkle to his eye.

"Aye, lad," he whispered. "That's why I call her Moon Lake."

A spectacular wonder.

The moon that filled the lake shone brilliant, but then, as if the sight hadn't made the trip memorable enough, a tremendous loud crackle thundered in the heavens and from our right something streaked across the sky with a tail of smoke and fire, striking in a massive explosion across the lake to our left and at the shoreline. There was a resounding boom so loud my ears popped, and white fire that, from our vantage, climbed to the height of the mountains surrounding the lake. Bregœ reared up behind us as the ground shook in monstrous tremors. Da leapt up, staring first at Bregœ then at the vibrating sand at our feet and then to the steaming, hissing lake, and back again to his great stallion. Ever the practical man, he spent a great bit of time settling Bregœ. I just sat and stared in amazement. Best trip ever. In some manner, and a time later with Bregœ and Da settled, I fell asleep again. A thousand thoughts were invading my dreams.

When I woke to the morrow's morn, Da had a very uncharacteristically solemn and far-away face. But he had a fire going with the pan over it and rashers of bacon frying with some roots amongst it. He told me to do my business and wash. I jumped up and wandered to the edge of the trees and started peeing into the big green and leafy underbrush making the large leaves flap back and forth and small lizards scampered to avoid my assault. Great fun.

And then I walked over to the lake edge where the giant moon no longer resided, stripped out of my clothes, and stepped into the lake. I squealed and Da glanced up and laughed with great mirth.

"A wee bit chilly, eh lad?"

"Yea, Da. I got chitter bumps up to my neck!"

"Well, finish up and get some hot morn-meal then."

He didn't have to say it twice. Finishing quick, I made my way to the fire and tucked into my meal.

Worrying a thick piece of bacon, I asked, "Da, what happened, last night?"

"I don't know, lad, but I mean to find an answer this morn."

After morn-meal, Da and I broke down our little camp and packed everything unto a much more settled Bregœ. We followed the shoreline along the sand. A good 10 paces of beach stretched from shoreline to the trees, and extraordinary treasures littered the sand—shells and remarkable rocks and flotsam and driftwood so smooth it glistened.

Not 100 paces into our march along the Lakeside, my eye caught a stone so white against the gritty sand I had to investigate. At the same moment, Da's eye caught on to something at the tree line and headed in that direction. Investigating my white rock, I watched as dozens of little crabs popped in and out of the tiny holes in the sand about it.

Approaching the water and the white stone, something popped from the surface of the lake and startled me so that I plopped down on my butt to the beach. A blue and silver fish as big as my leg had jumped above the surface of the water to catch one of a dozen buzzing Drægonflies hovering over the water. But I had reached my white stone and it had all my attention now. I went to lift it from the sand and found I couldn't budge it all. So, I went about digging around it deeper and deeper in the sand, wriggling it as I went. As big around as my eight-year-end fist, it tapered to a point on the other end far down in the sand and it measured easily, the length of Da's huge hand.

Finally able to grab it out of the sand, I went running to Da as he stood and stared at what appeared to be just a dark brown log, but smooth, and slick with dew so that it appeared to be made of stone. He turned my way as I ran up to him with my stone.

"Ho, Arias, let me see what you found." His eyebrows arched and exclaimed I'd found a treasure.

"What do you mean?"

"You have certainly found a Drægon's tooth!" Da exclaimed incredulously.

"Oh!" and then, "Are Drægon's real?" I gulped in a breath. "But school Mæster Ræbben says there is no such thing!"

"Aye, Arias and he would be right. It may surely be a tooth or a horn of a sort. But from a large, great fish of the deep. They're found most on the shores of mountain lakes such as this. But a true find ne'er-the-lesser. They are rare and a treasure all the same."

I smiled an even bigger smile and slipped it into the shoulder bag that Da had given me to carry things.

"What did you find, Da?"

"A very special thing, lad," he said. "I found Ænt-Wood."

"We have plenty of wood at home, Da. Why would you want some old wood eaten by ants?"

Da smiled at me. "Nay, lad, not ant wood, Ænt-Wood. It is the name of a very special wood indeed. This is the very type of wood my Da made me bow with, and ye will not find any wood of this sort in all the forest around our own homestead. I'll be hoping Bregœ here can help me bring this log home."

After our discoveries, we wandered further along the beach, always headed toward where we witnessed the blaze that flashed across the sky in front of us and shook our world the previous night. Da even discovered a copse of elven-vine, a treasure unto itself he declared. As our long walk continued, mighty Bregœ became skittish, forcing Da to use his most influential whispering ways to settle his giant steed. With the sun direct over our heads and having just rounding about a boulder strewn cape in our path, we finally were approaching the site of last night's spectacle. As I walked out into the shallows to get around the boulders blocking our path, I exclaimed in astonishment, having remembered my freezing wash in the lake that very morn.

"Da! The water is hotter than the bath back home!"

"Aye," said Da and mumbled to himself as we proceeded.

And surely, we could see the hot water rising as steam in a great circle fifty paces or more out into the lake. Dead fish were floating upon the surface. Some, nearest shore, looking like they just had come from Da's stew pot. And the smell of rotten eggs, thick as gravy. I covered my face with my elbow in an attempt to stanch the odor.

"Ho, Da, what is that smell?"

"That smell be of sulfur, lad," Da said as he cocked his head.

"What is sulfur, Da?" I gasped for a clean breath of air.

Da said nothing.

Because afore us in a "V" of missing beach sat simmering a half-submerged boulder, cleaved in two. In it lay a hunk of black and blue rock the size of the smithy's largest smelting pot. The lake a few paces from the Sky-stone roiled and steamed still, and the cleft inside of the boulder that it had collided with lay in a rubble of crumbled rocks. We made our way to the beach beside the boulder, the water too hot to wade in. The trees in the small cove that we were in were burned black, back thirty paces from the face of the tree line. The ground lay charred black as well but sodden to the touch. It was as if it all had been lit afire and then doused with a bucket of water. Or, dozens upon dozens of buckets.

"Ho," says Da, "I hope the King never finds a war machine that can throw a rock such as this."

"What do you mean by that Da?" I said to him, looking puzzled. Da had never mentioned a king afore and… war? Da shrugged my questions aside and said,

"Let us go back around and set up camp, lad. Do some hunting mayhaps. I'm hungry me-self and want to ponder this strange happening. Fishing will be easy here for a fact."

Later on, Da decided to wrest free the Sky-stone. I was lifted onto Bregœ's back. Da had rigged a harness of the thickest Elven-vine he'd found in the copse on the closer side of the Sky-stone cove. Da had wound great bundles of it to take home as well.

He bade me give Bregœ a kick, and the giant horse pulled outwards towards the center of the cove, knee and then belly deep in the water, straining on the harness as Da sought to lever the Sky-stone free with a branch as thick as his arm that he had stripped and brought for the purpose. With grunts from Da and muscles I could feel rippling under me, coupled with the snorts of determination from Bregœ, the Sky-stone finally wrest free of its temporary prison within the boulder.

"Hold there, Bregœ," barked Da. "Easy now. Arias, reign in that beast of a horse back round to shore!"

Bregœ turned at my bidding and dragged the Sky-stone easily back up to shore. Da pulled me from the great horse's back. Bregœ snorted and whinnied in delight at his success. I waded over to the huge fissure in the boulder to take a look at where the Sky-stone had been prised away. I could actually walk back into the cleaved crack from which Da had pulled out his prize. As I ran my hands along each side of the rock crevice, I noticed they were as smooth as glass. But further in, I spied a large oblong rock with cracks about it and a ruby hue within it as it lay down in the fissure. I stretched to get my hand around the narrow end of it. Eventually able to worry it out with an effort, I pulled it to me and carried it out to show Da.

I found Da standing over the Sky-stone admiring this gift from the moon, as he called it. "Broke clear of the moon and fell to earth, I wager."

The Sky-stone was black all over and pitted like an orange peel only deeper, and it held within it a silver blue metal sparkling in the cracks and crevices all about it. It was an amazing thing to behold, and Da continued chortling and chuckling as he mumbled to himself.

I showed Da what I'd found back in the rent boulder, and his eyes widened once more as he scrutinized the ruby red in the cracks.

"A good find again, Arius, lad. You may have a piece of Drægon's Fire-stone in your rock," he declared.

"For never having existed," I said, "Drægons sure leave a lot of their parts lying about!"

Da broke into a belly laugh at that, which in turn made me laugh hard. I placed the Drægon's Fire-stone rock into my shoulder bag with my other treasures.

When we came back to the Ænt-wood log, Da wrapped it with a hitch and strung it to hang behind his great steed. Bregœ would have to pull it all the way home.

"Ho, Arias, we'll not be riding back to the homestead ourselves as ye can see. Are ye up for it? It'll take us the better part of a ha'fortnight to get back, I reckon."

"Yea, Da, I can run the whole way!"

Da chuckled. "That won't be necessary, lad. It'll be tough enough for Bregœ pulling this Ænt-wood log through the forest at a walking pace. Off we are then."

The trip back was slow but not totally uneventful.

There was one final and strange thing Da did when we had made it back to the homestead. About a ha'furlong from the cottage, there was a rock as wide and as tall as the cottage, which he called Fork-Rock. It had a cleft at its peak as wide as a well bucket. Cleaved in two, he said, by a sky-bolt. After unburdening Bregœ of his load, Da proceeded to tie a stone up with a medium-sized Elven-vine, and he then threw the stone with the vine trailing up and over Fork-Rock. He then hitched the Ænt-wood log to it and took Bregœ round to the other side. He tied the other end of the Elven-vine to Bregœ's harness. Slowly then, he had the horse pull the log to the top of Fork-Rock. Finally, Da climbed to the top of Fork-Rock and with a mighty grunt stood the Ænt-wood log upright in the crevice at the top. I looked up to the top of the rock and the dark shapes against the sunset. A mountain of a man that was Da and the log his height or a bit more were both silhouetted against the sunset sky behind them.

"Why did you do that, Da?"

He just laughed his laugh and said, "Let's get something to eat, lad. We have a full sun getting the livestock and gardens cleaned up on the morrow. And then we will be needing to head into towne."

Da remained an ever-moving man.

As I think back on this, I recognize that my year-end gifting's had indeed all lead back to that trip with Da.

10

I'll follow the Sun

he sun bakes my face as it stares back at me from the north and west. I've left another wooded portion of the great travelway a bit ago, and the sun has become a warm companion again. Even the sounds of the rustling leaves are absent now. The clap clop of Paint's hooves against the gravelly surface of the travelway are the only sound now. Lilit and Jilly lay on their bellies facing East and West across my saddle in front of me and are enjoying the heat of the sun on their backs. They lay fast asleep. The air these last three suns beats down upon us, so warm and dry that dust from the travelway rises up to greet me as I ride on in a stupor of sorts. 'Twas seven suns since I left my homestead in Middenvale. My ponderings of Da have shortened the time it has taken to reach this point. Behind me now are all my friends in the world and a routine life that I had grown accustomed to. My first two suns, I rode upon Paint in a fugue, not caring to even gaze about me at this new territory I've never in my life seen afore. On a quest that had been forced upon me. Delivered onto me by Da and reinforced by a parchment in a box made of Ænt-wood and carrying gifts and words from the mãmere I do not even remember but for a few glimpses in my mind. Not even that many afore reading her parchment had awakened them from deep within me.

I do remember though, in detail, all the times I'd ever spent with Da as just a small lad and riding endless suns across the saddle atop his great steed Bregœ in the same position as Lilit and Jilly occupied on my saddle now. Til that faithful sun not a fortnight past when twelve men in the garb of soldiers struck him down. But not afore he had sent to their fate those same twelve.

Da's parchment had said that should anything happen to him; I should head east on a many moons trek in search of a Druid. I do not even truly know what a Druid was. I have just come upon my seventeen-year-end, and it being nothing like I thought it would be. Seventeen-years are supposed to be men. A near overwhelming loss lay on my shoulders as I long for Da's guidance and aid more than any other time in my life. Two things I will never have again from him.

Bane appears from time a'time, weaving in and out of the tree line and now the tall grasses which crowd the travelway north. I have, as habit after these first few suns, set camp as sunset approaches. I'd do so in a clearing I would find usually some fifty paces inside the tree line. I had been warned by Moor that the travelways could be unsafe with highwaymen who prayed on the unwary wayfarer. And I remember Da's discussions with Master Bergierre, the Innkeeper in Middenvale, and the reports he'd heard more frequently of late of just such occurrences. So, the wise traveler stayed wary. Hence, I would find a clearing to set up camp nightly, there to withdraw into the saddened thoughts of Da and my world turned downside up.

A few suns back, my fourth on the travelway, I'd turned my thoughts away from my misfortune and towards my new purpose. I have Effie to thank for that. My apprenticeship with the towne's healer included lessons in training my spirit as well as healing the body. To keep myself from dwelling on Da's death, I decide to use the healer's method to put my mind in the state of the *Calming,* as Effie has taught me. These past three nights, Bane would come lie next to me, and I would place my hand into the heavy deep fur in the scruff of the wolf's neck, and it alone did help to settle my mind. But then, I let my heartbeat lower, and my breathing lessen and clear my mind of all thought, simply hearing the forest sounds in crystal clear detail. After a short time, they too fade, and I find myself just being, and somehow completely in touch and in sync with my woodland surroundings.

During the *Calming*, Bane's heartbeat pounds a rhythm to my brain. In such a state, my mind accepts what I cannot change and in the same instant analyzes circumstances more clearly, just as Effie had said that I could. After a few of these dusk time rituals, there comes a new clarity of purpose, but also unthought of questions.

Why do twelve Kingsmen (for Kingsmen they surely were, as evidenced by their sigil on garb) attack Da? And Da's secret instructions to me, so many years past, for me to seek hiding in the Frost-Cellar at the toll of three bells? Do these happenings of the last fortnight in some manner involve me? Answers clearly lie with the Druid on the far side of Aeryth. Each night as I return from my *Calming*, I become more resolved to my quest.

And then something got in the way.

Nearing dusk on this seventh sun, I take my camp deeper into the woods, as I search for a stream to refresh myself, bathe and fill my water skins. I also need to hunt for food supplies now as the trail food I had brought is nearly depleted. I set snares in the underbrush and nets in the stream and resolve to stay a sun or two here. Camped a good way from the travelway, I have found a little more permanent shelter in a great overhanging rock ledge embedded in a small hillside deep in the woods. It appears to have been used at one time as a den for wolves, mayhaps in the distant past. I have built my fire and set about putting myself into the *Calming* as I do on most eves now. Bane has found a place at my side again, and Lilit and Jilly are curled into my lap as well.

As I enter the deep *Calming*, all else fades away. I sense rather than see

Bane's ears raise, and with clarity not of my own body, I hear a cry of distress. It is as if my hearing has grown much more sensitive. I must certainly be hearing the sound through Bane's ears.

A girl's cry of distress and rough male voices along with it. I snap upright and rise to my feet. Drawing on my pack, I grab my Bo-staff and head out.

I have an immediate sense on which way to go. Moving at a strong pace I have a never wavering heading impressed within my mind.

Bane trots at my side, and I hear the furions scampering along with us. Bane and I quickly outpace the smaller creatures, but I have no intention of slowing.

The sun has dipped below the horizon by now, and I pass over a trapper's trail. We are high and headed downhill and eventually, off in the distance, I spy a campfire. It lies a few hundred paces out and in a clearing within the woods. Slowing, I silently creep towards this camp. Bane has left my side and swept around the clearing as if some eons old pack hunting instinct is guiding him. Keeping to the shadows, I draw closer to the camp until I can see that to the right of a fire and some four or five paces away, a lass lay bound with rope about her wrists and tied to a stake secured in the ground with but two paces of tether line. She lies curled as to protect her body from further harm. Her hair is long and matted, and she is bare of foot and wears naught but rags about her. She whimpers quietly.

At the fire sits a short wiry sort of man. Poorly kempt but with steely eyes, he carries a mean-looking dagger at his belt. Two rabbits are skewered and basting as he turns the spit over the fire. Four horses are tethered to a wagon across the camp from me, and a huge man near to Da's height tends to them.

"Quiet, bitch!" the steely-eyed wretch yells at the girl.

The tall guy is well muscled. He has left the horses, now, and is wandering over towards her.

"She sure is tasty morsel, Seth." His clearly lecherous expression at the bound and frightened girl on the ground makes her scramble, pulling herself as far away as possible from him.

"Away from her, ya arse!" Seth spits back. "She'll be of little profit to us if she's too beat and abused."

A third man who sits in the shadows to their left and under a blood-red hooded cloak snorts at the exchange.

"He's led around by his cockhead, that one," this third man chortles.

"And you was not, at her homestead with the farmer's woman?" The huge mountain of a man laughs.

I've had enough of such talk. Even as the fire crackles, so does my ire.

"If she's unsullied like her mama and poppa said, she be worth double the coin," says the seated weasel at the fire. "So, let her be. Come get a bite here, man. It's done."

"She's a shiverin' like a cornered coon, she is. It's likely to be that gimpy leg she's gotten since we took her," says mountain man. "Castor, like as not won't even want her."

"Leave her be, 'n come share one of these hares, we'll not be stopping again till we deliver the cargo," the weasel says. "It'll be trail biscuits and jerky for a time."

My anger boils. The heinous things they are hinting at doing to the girl is enough to call me to action. I draw my Bo-staff to me and step out of the shadows and in front of their fire. They all three startle and stare at me as if I were a Dæmon just appeared. Silence rules but for a moment and the forest's insects and the crackling of the fire are all that can be heard. An orange glow illuminates the left side of the weasel.

"I'll be relieving you of your burden, so you will not have a care about her anymore."

That stuns them for a further moment.

And then, all three of them chortle.

"And mayhaps we'll have a second parcel to be delivered for coin," the weasel states with cruel intent.

A tense silence ensues for a trice, as the girl sits up and gazes at me and then at her captors. Weasel looks me in the eye as the three of them rise to their feet, and Man Mountain and Cloaked One start to slowly circle the fire towards me. I'm a good three to four paces from them with my pack on and my Bo-staff in position as Moor had trained me. My stance is relaxed, balanced, and ready.

"Will you now, lad, ...rescue the girl, I mean?" Weasel asks with a grin as he is obviously quite sure to how this intrusion into his camp will end. Cloak begins reaching to his waist where a dagger lay sheathed, and Man Mountain stands squeezing his fists while wearing a smirk.

Moor has trained me to assess my opponents well. I reckon Cloak to be the immediate danger as he carries a dagger. I spy no weapon on Mountain Man but his fists, though they themselves are surely impressive. Weasel stands across the fire from me and though he carries a wicked dagger he would need to find his way around the fire and spits of rabbit. Man Mountain, though strong, would be slower. Cloak remains my first and foremost danger.

Weasel begins to speak again. I do not wait any longer. Feinting toward Man Mountain, I lift my Bo. Three Sky-bolt fast strikes. First, hard to Cloak's chest, then neck and finally into the center of his face as he rushes me. He crumples to the ground with a single grunt. I do not believe he will rise again.

Turning now toward Man Mountain, the Weasel screeches from across the fire.

Weasel.

I instinctively drop low as Weasel's blade flies over my head. He is more dangerous than I first anticipated. Reaching with my left hand to unsheathe my throwing blade from its place in my lower pack, I first drive the

Bo-staff with my right hand into Man Mountain's left knee. It crunches. He screams. I glance to Weasel.

Lilit has herself attached to Weasel's right ear, and Jilly has her tiny muzzle in a death grip on his left shoulder. He continues to screech and flail at the furions.

I loose my throwing blade and turn back to Man Mountain. He's fallen to his knee but begins reaching for me with a very palpable hate in his eyes.

With an instinct and reflex formed from many a day with swinging logs flying at me in the barn, I rise. Already my Bo-staff is thrusting on the upswing. Coupled with my rising momentum, the Fire-stone end of the Bo catches Man Mountain under his chin. He collapses instantly backwards to the ground.

I glance around.

Cloak will not be rising again. Weasel has my throwing blade sunk deep into his heart. Man Mountain's condition isn't readily known, but he looks to be out cold.

The girl stares about her, wide-eyed in terror. I start towards her and as I do Bane howls. The thrum of a bow string twangs simultaneously.

Hit with the force of a bull charging into my back, my body slams into a tree in front of me. The world spins as I taste blood, then all goes black.

I awake to Bane with his wet muzzle in my face and the girl screaming and pulling with all her might against her tether. My senses are slowly returning. I roll up to my knees and manage to loosen the belt on my pack, lifting it over my head and dropping it to the side. An arrow is standing out from the middle of my pack. Tasting blood, I peer over my shoulder to a Bowman laying mayhaps ten paces across the fire from me with his neck torn apart. I remember there were four horses. An almost critical mistake on my part.

When I pull Bane in a hug around his neck, the girl goes silent and wide-eyed. "Thanks for having my back, Bane."

Somehow, I manage to get my legs under me and drag my battered body toward her. My dirk slices through her bindings in a trice. I stab it into the ground beside her with a groan as I turn and back myself against the tree I'd marked with my face. The girl just stares at me. Deep sobs rack her body.

Now with the battle won, of a sudden, my body starts to shake uncontrollably. I slide down, my back against the tree trunk. I sit there trying to take stock of all that has just happened. My furion friends climb to my lap and lick at my face. They stare up with a human expression of concern for me. The shakes subsiding, I pull in deep breaths, trying to settle. Bane has laid his head in my lap. His wet muzzle is due to the Bowman's blood.

The girl settles herself a bit and stares at me with a look of awe. She's cut the bindings from her wrist with my dirk still stuck in the ground afore her. I am still shaking. A sudden groan near the fire and Bane lifts his head with a start to look towards Man Mountain.

In the next instant, the girl lunges toward Man Mountain as he tries to rise from the ground. Bane jumps to his feet, and I am attempting to as well. But the girl is already to him. She plunges my dirk to the hilt, once, twice and then thrice, leaving it embedded in his groin as he howls and she climbs atop his chest. She reaches for a large rock at their side and lifts it over her head into both her hands to bring it smashing down on Man Mountain's nose with a great force. A quite audible crunch fills the air. He stops howling, but she does not stop striking him.

I reach her and stay her arms. She looks at me, then back at him and just faints away to the ground. I ease her away from the carnage she has wrought and pull her to the fire and lay her down. Gathering a bedroll from nearby, I place it under her head. I try to bring presence of mind and assess the situation as Moor has taught me.

The sound of crickets has not resumed yet, but the horses have settled. The hares lay in the fire, burnt black.

Rising, I walk around to the men laying on the ground around the camp. They are all surely now dead. I have killed two men, and though I have a knot within my stomach, I feel they were deserving of such a fate. Bane had dispatched one in my defense and if he had not torn the man's neck apart, I surely would've been dead also. And the girl has killed the Man Mountain with a fierceness I have never seen in any person and I am certain that there remained no remorse in her action.

I am drained. Emotion for these men is stripped from me, except for a gut-wrenching knot remaining in the bottom of my stomach and a cold sweat laying on the back of my neck. I have killed two men, after all.

The girl still lay unconscious. It would be wise to remove her from the scene as soon as possible. Still, I take some time to search about the camp. One of the horses has worried himself loose and is gone. A large gray, a smaller tawny mare and a chestnut with a cream-colored mane remain tethered.

I settle the smaller chestnut and tie two sets of packs together and swing them over the horse like saddlebags. There are a few extra linens and blankets about, and I place them between the saddlebags as well. Finally, I manage to get the unconscious girl up onto the mare and secure her so as not to fall. The other two horses are let loose to their own devices.

Lilit and Jilly climb the camp wagon and hop upon the horse to settle in amongst the burden I've assembled from things about the camp. This lot would no longer be needing them. 'Tis quite dark now as the fire has gone out, but a full moon allows for good vision, even amongst the trees. The underbrush being sparse, the trek back to my camp, though a good distance, will not be too troubling.

I worry sorely for the girl as she has an infected and swollen calf. She is sweating and has a heart that is pounding hard within her chest, yet she remains unconscious. I could help her with Effie's gifted medicines, and I could better treat her at my camp near the clear running stream.

We make the camp as the moon reaches its zenith in the sky above. Lifting the girl down from the mare, I place her on some blankets within the stone ledge shelter. Taking some linens to the stream, I soak them with the clear, cool water. Returning to the girl, I clean her leg as best I can. There is an open wound upon it and an ugly pus is weeping from it. Withdrawing a tin from my healing kit and placing a salve at the open wound to draw out the pus and gore, I tightly wrap the calf with fresh linen. I spend the remainder of the night laying cool, water-soaked linens upon the girl's head to try and bring down her fever.

By morn, she appears no better. In fact, the skin of her leg bulges and squirms and is turning a sickly green. Never have I seen anything it's like when apprenticing with Effie. I feel sure that the girl cannot survive with an infection such as this.

I need to relieve the pressure building within her leg. And so, I wash and then place my dirk within the flame to clean it as only fire can, even as Effie had, afore she cut the smashed and beyond repair hand from farmer Tasson, two-years past. The girl's leg remains in an ugly state, and I wonder if I will need to sever the limb below the knee to save the life of the girl. But afore I resort to removing her leg, I think to cut open the calf and relieve the pressure of the infection. She is still out cold as I place the honed edge of the blade to the back of her calf just above the weeping wound.

I slice her leg open in a cut as long as my finger and stare as pus and mucus stream from the wound. But then I see something else. It appears to be a worm of a sort, but quite pale in hue. I grab hold of the squirming thing and start to pull it from her leg slowly. So as not to sever it in two. As long as my forearm, I pull it finally from her leg. The girl sits up wide-eyed, sees what I am about, and screams in horror. She then proceeds to fall back in a faint.

The thing has partially wrapped itself around my wrist and hand. I promptly pull it loose, throw it into the fire, and go back to working on the wound on the girl's leg. I apply pressure down her calf and express handful after handful of mucus excrement from her wound until finally blood flows freely from it. The swelling is now near gone, and the upper reaches of her leg, though red, appear tremendously better.

I carry her down to the stream, lay her next to it, and place her leg into the icy water. I take in her true condition, and it is dire at best. She is bruised over all parts of her body that shows. What I had last night taken to be dirt and grime upon her are in reality only part dirt and more bruising, old and green and still many others, fresh and blue. Her long auburn hair lay as a greasy and matted mess and her scalp red from insect bites.

Determined to put things right, I tightly bind the wound on her leg after applying a healing unguent and turn my attention to her head. As she lies there limp, I take my throwing blade and start to cut away her hair that has reached the center of her back in what were once flowing locks, I presume. I cut it back near to her head, throwing the infested mess downstream to be carried away. Then with a cold wet linen I gently rub her badly bitten and inflamed scalp. I reach back into my healer's kit and pull out another tin of a salve that Effie had used to remove lice on the unfortunate children that were affected in towne. I liberally spread it over her head and the back of her neck.

Then with a mindset determined to helping this girl, I proceed to cut away what is left of her clothing. I take in her bruised and battered naked body and nearly cry to see such harm. I retrieve my soap and spend a long, slow, but thorough job of cleaning her entire person from head to toe. She is still feverish, and I try to get some of the fresh cool water from the brook into her mouth and down her throat. She seems to respond, even in her state, and swallows some.

Her fever is still so high that I finally resolve to just immerse her whole body into the stream to let the cool water be an aid. After a time, her fever lessens a bit. I carry her back into the rock shelter and wrap, nay, swaddle her tight into a blanket and sit back to observe her.

I am exhausted, for I have not slept since the night afore last. Fatigue and trauma finally overtake my own body, and I lie down under my rock shelf abode and fall into a sound sleep even as the sun reaches its highest in the sky above.

I awake at dusk with Bane and the furions next to me and the girl, still unconscious across the shelter. I check on her and then go out to tend to Paint and the Chestnut mare. Quickly as I can, I put together a stew pot and hang it over a steady flame, hoping she will awaken so that I can get some good sustenance into her. But I also remember Effie's teachings and the wonders of the human body.

"Left to its own devices, Arias, the body is a wonder of healing onto itself. Sometimes the healer needs to know when to stand back and let a body heal of its own accord. And this goes for the mind as well. The human body is a beautiful and wondrous force of nature." She would cite cases of a man who lay unconscious for a year, simply mechanically eating when fed, but otherwise nonfunctioning and asleep, only to awaken a full year later healed from a great disease and totally aware. To his own mind, he but lay asleep half a sun.

I can attest to the beauty of the body in the case of this girl, in any matter, at least. I take to removing her bruised and battered body that remains feverish, though not as bad, and carry her down to the brook each morn, and I Remove my own tunic and trousers. I lay her within the stream bed as I sit with her head and shoulders in my lap. The water gently washes over her body and eases its stiffness for a while. And during these times, I marvel at her beautiful, though badly beaten, form.

11

Tell me Why

Awakening to the early sun filtering through the trees and into my den under the boulder, I ponder what to do for this girl. This is the second morn, and she still lays unconscious, wrapped in a blanket and lying within my shelter. My intention was for her to live, and it might be possible now that her fever has dropped some and the wound appears on the mend. Time now to do a little more for her.

While her body is healing, I set to work. As Da would oft say, "Idle hands are a dæmon's weapons." I open my bundle and pull from it a mountain elk-skin that I had used to make my pack. Dyed green, it had been further stretched, scraped, and cured to leave a soft but durable skin perfect to my purpose. I have some softened buckskin as well. I retrieve the Elven-vine thread from my sewing kit. Though I had intended to make garments for myself during my trip, clearly the girl has greater need. And so, when I'm not checking my snares or attending to Paint and the Chestnut, or cooking, I use my time to fashion green tunic and buckskin trousers for my ward.

I still carry her each morn to the stream and tend to the balming and wrapping about her wound and manage to get her to drink freshwater with the medicine Effie had gifted me for the purpose of fighting fevers. All of this time she remains steadfast asleep. As I would sit down with her in the stream, one thing I could not help but study was her bosom. I rationalized, 'twas so I could fashion her tunic to fit. As I could see and feel this girl has a softer construction than men, I decide that some added linen to the tunic would carry and cover her breast in a more comfortable manner. Certainly, I am thorough to this task, if nothing else.

Lastly, I craft a pair of boots for her. 'Tis easy to measure for them in her current state. In the meantime, I continue my routine with her and as her Healer, note marked improvement with each rising sun. On the seventh sunrise, her garments are complete. I bring the garb up to the shelter and pull the blanket from her sleeping form. And in as gentle a manner as I can manage, I dress her in the newly made tunic and trousers. They fit her well from what I can tell, and I am proud of my work. As not to aggravate her wound, I leave her boots beside her and then cover her with the blanket once again.

Come late morn, I check my snares and find I had caught a large hare. I set about making a stew in the pot I had relieved from the slavers' camp. It has been simmering for a bit as Lilit and Jilly come running to me in quite a state of excitement. The girl is up on her elbows and staring down the hill at me in a most quizzical manner.

I rise quickly, which makes her start and pull the blanket tight to her.

"Well, greetings," I say. "We've not been introduced, but you may call me Arias".

She cocks her head and just stares back at me.

"I must say, you take your sleeping quite seriously. This is the seventh sunrise since you laid your head to sleep." I smile in an effort to put her at ease. "Let me get you some water."

I make my way over to her, and I kneel to offer her some water from my water skin.

With a struggle, she works herself into a seated position, takes the skin, and gulps the water as if it would be her last.

"You should probably go a little bit easy on that," I say politely. "There is plenty more at any rate." With a shiver, her eyes lift to me.

"I had a dream that you pulled a pale worm from my leg,"

"Yea, that was quite disgusting, but it had to be done."

Her hands clench about the blankets edge.

The bottom of her eyelids fill with moisture.

"So, if that wasn't a dream, the other things that happened that night at the camp…?"

"Yea," being all that I can manage, a bit choked to see her process all that has happened.

"Seven sunrises, you say?" The words catch in her throat. She pulls the blanket up exposing her feet and legs and stare at her leg and wriggle her toes, a thoughtful expression on her face.

"It no longer hurts…." Her eyes go wide, and she stares at her arms and then her other garments. She lowers her brow and looks to me shyly. "My clothes?"

"Yes, well," I explain, "they were in a rough condition."

She runs her hands over the tunic and then down her new trousers. Her cheeks flush as she hugs herself and desperately scoots to the back face of the shelter. And then I realize her meaning.

"Oh, no." I lower my eyes. "I would never… I wouldn't… I would never hurt you."

Gently falling to my knees afore her, I lay my hands lightly on her shoulders and gaze calmly into her eyes.

"I just… I needed to get you clean, to help the healing," I explain. "You were in terrible shape. Those barbarians kept you tied like some kind of rabid creature. Your leg was infected, and the worm was eating at you from the inside. Your body was so battered and bruised."

I stop to catch my breath.

Her clenched hands relax about the blanket.

"Your hair was matted and filled with lice and other vermin."

Her breath catches in her throat and her hands reflexively go to her head. "My hair!"

"Yea, I'm sorry. All I had were my blades. No shears. It's a beautiful color. It will grow back, I promise."

Her shoulders visibly relax as tears come fully to her eyes now. "You saved my life…. Thank you."

Falling back on my heels, I offer, "Well, I also made a bit of rabbit stew with tubers. onions, and shrooms. Mayhaps some broth? If you can't stomach the bits and pieces?"

She blows out a long soft sigh, and her lips curl into a smile, warming me all over. Rising up, I fetch the bowl and spoon and return to her. I hold the bowl and spoon some broth to her lips as her hand shakes so that she cannot hold the spoon herself.

"This is heavenly. You made this yourself?" she asks. "You are a hero, and you can cook as well!"

She giggles and tears return, leaving me baffled as to what to say.

"Aye, the aftertaste has hit you now, I see."

She snorts through her tears and tries to catch the sprittle. "Thank you."

I gaze into her eyes. I am mesmerized by her voice and her shyness and just… everything. And in her weakness, she seems so strong as well. I feed her some more stew broth and she gladly accepts.

"I am so fatigued," she sighs.

"Yea. Your body is still recovering. Mayhaps you should lie back down."

She shakes her head. "You say I've slept half a fortnight, and you put me back to bed afore I finish this delicious stew you've made for me? Nay, I think I'll stay awake a while more."

"Well, then, as you are staying for noon-meal, might I inquire as to your name?"

Her emerald eyes sparkle. "Steffænie."

"Well, Steffænie, I am happy to make your acquaintance and so happy you could finally join us in a meal." I offer her my hand.

"Thank you," she repeats, accepting my hand which calms her shake a bit.

"My pleasure. But it is just a humble stew."

Feeding her a few more spoons full of broth, I make to wipe a drop caught on her chin.

Quirking her chin up, just so, "Can I ask you a question, Arias?"

I find myself ecstatic that she remembered my name for some reason.

"Most certainly," I respond. "There is nothing I would like more. You see, I've not had a decent conversation in over a fortnight. Of course, I tried with Lilit and Jilly, but their responses make no sense to me."

Again, with the cute tilt of her head and the quizzical, furrowed brow.

"Lilit, Jilly, come introduce yourself, you're being quite rude," winking at her.

Immediately, my furion friends scamper up into Steffænie's lap and start kissing her chin. A squeal of pleasure escapes her as she pets and strokes their inquiring, bobbing heads. "They are wonderful little friends, and if you don't understand them, they surely understand you!"

"So, what is your question?" I ask when the three of them finish getting acquainted.

There is a long, silent pause as she considers her question. I fear she will query me about the thugs' episode, and so am caught off-guard when she says,

"I dreamt I was burning, and the flames were washed away, and that I was floating in the air with a wonderfully cool breeze washing over me." She stares directly at me.

"Yea," the truth without hesitation. Steffænie deserves this much from me. "Most morns, your fever would peak, and I would carry you down to the stream. I would lay with you in the stream and hold your head and shoulders in my lap and let the cool stream wash over your body."

"Oh," is her only comment as a flush comes onto her face. Satisfied though, that I answered truthfully, I think.

And then she does that quirky twist of her head thing, and bites her lower lip. She scrunches her eyebrows. "And where did you find these clothes for me?"

"Yea, well that query is easy. I made them. Being left with little else to do as you weren't speaking to me," I deadpan. "Do you like them okay?"

"I... they are amazing," she exclaims. "They fit my body as if they were crafted by a royal seamstress, and they are the softest garment I have ever worn."

"High praise for my work. Thank you," neglecting to tell her that studying her form, floating in the stream afore me, had inspired me to fit every curve with care.

We but stare eye-to-eye for a moment. For her part, eyelids are drooping a bit.

"And now, though I protest the need, I do believe I'll close my eyes for a bit." With that she lays her head back on the blanket roll, asleep in but a heartbeat.

I tuck the blanket back about her and serve myself some stew, clean up about camp, and sit by her, to watch as she sleeps, and I cannot explain why.

When the sun falls midway to dusk, Steffænie wakes again with a start. Concern has marked my expression, I am sure. She tries to rise as she throws off her blanket but cannot as she is so weak. Tears of determination fill her eyes.

"Steffænie, what is the matter, let me help."

She shakes her head side-to-side. "I need to do my business."

I reply in as sincere a voice as I can project, "Then I will help you. Think of me as only a healer as that is what I am right now."

Reluctantly she lets me help her to wobbling legs, and we take a short walk. After things are sorted, she says, "We've become quite familiar in the short time we've known each other."

We return to the campfire and sit on a log facing it. She is a bit wobbly kneed at first, but determined, ne'er-the-lesser for it.

"Yea," say I. "And I am grateful as I am in need of a friend at this time."

I say this to change the direction of the conversation, but it is also a confession.

"You see," I say, peering directly into her emerald eyes. "I've lost my Da, just a fortnight past, and it is weighing heavy upon me."

And, of a sudden, we embrace and both of us weep a good long time. And I believe it is a great help to her to hear this.

I reheat the rabbit stew for dinner, and Bane joins us and I introduce Steffænie to him. He nuzzles his head into her lap and from that moment the dread wolf and the girl become fast friends. I believe Bane knows, even though we ourselves have just barely met, that I had strong feelings for this lass.

The morrow's morn dawns with a chill in the air but quickly grows warm. There are birds about and a breeze that rustles the leaves in the trees and makes for a very pleasant sun. That sun and for several following, Steffænie becomes stronger, and we walk amongst the trees and talk and become friends all the more.

One dusk, after eve-meal, she finally bursts into the tale of how she came to be with the four thugs where I had found her. I had not pressed her for the tale as I wanted that she would tell me in her own time.

She just comes over to me and sits next to me on the ground. My back is against a large log, warm in the fire glow. She leans into me, and I place my arm around her shoulders.

"It was on an evening just about this time," she starts softly, turning her head up to gaze into my eyes, seeking reassurance. I squeeze her hand. Turning back, she stares into the campfire. "We had just finished our eve-meal and were relaxing in front of the hearth."

There is a long pause here, and she squeezes my hand upon my lap.

She continues, "They kicked our door in and immediately the man they called Seth and the large one burst in. The large one, they just called him Beast. He even had to duck to get inside our cottage. Beast immediately went over to Papa, took him by one hand about his neck and threw him across the room. He beat him mercilessly and so severe as to tear the very life from him, and when mama ran and jumped on the Beast's back, he simply shook her off and threw her into a wall where she lay for a time unmoving."

I inhale, waiting for more, now squeezing her hand to encourage her to go on.

"Kattalæn and I just stayed in the corner with our heads low. Kattalæn is – was my little sister," she says, peering off into the dark for a time. "The other two entered the cottage a while later while the Beast and Seth were still rummaging through our things. Mama awakened and tended to Papa. Oh, Arias, he was hurt so bad, he could not even sit up."

My heart hurts imagining it, imagining her seeing it.

"The one in the cloak, he wore it all the time, came in carrying one of papa's small barrels of ale. He said, 'Found this in a shed out back. The farmer makes a good ale. He's got a good bit of smoked hog hanging in there too.' And then Beast says, 'Well, that's good because I'm mighty hungry from beating on that old sod, and have a thirst, too.'"

She takes a deep breath. Bane readjusts his head in her lap, and her hand goes to his fur, combing it with her fingers.

"And then Seth just snarls and says to Beast, 'Well then, take them out to the shed and lock them in and bring back one of them hams.' That's just what he did. They kept us in the shed near to half a fortnight. Papa wasn't breathing well and spitting up blood all the time…. We had food and they brought us a water bucket, but we had little taste for either. I don't think Papa even knew we were there. Mama tried to care for him as best she could."

The story grows worse, as I feared it would.

One or another of the men would come to the shed every morn, sometimes two of them. They bent her mother over her father's butchering table to have their way with her and then just tossed her aside like a ragdoll. They came for Steffænie one day, but her mum begged them not to, saying she'd never been with a man. And when he heard that, Seth would not let anybody do those things to her like her mum. He said she'd be worth more coin, unsullied. I'd heard him say the same things before I killed him.

"One day they came in, Seth and the Beast. Papa was having a better day and knew what was happening, though weak and still broken," she says. "But he saw what they were doing to mama. He tried to get up, and he yelled at them. The Beast just walked over and… he slit papa's throat without even a thought to it. Afore I could stop her, Kattalæn jumped up and ran at him and pounded him with her fists. She was but six-year, Arias, he could not have even felt it! But filled with murderous intent so that you could see it in his eyes…. He turned and with a simple swipe of his huge arm sent her across the shed, and she hit hard and fell. Her head was twisted in a bad way on her neck. Her mouth lay open and her eyes staring." Her voice catches in her throat.

The fire pops, then crackles, sending up sparks. In the distance, some creature calls out.

It takes every ounce of resolve for me to keep listening, to stay calm, to be there for her.

"Seth stared angry and yelled at the Beast. Said he'd wasted good coin, and he'd take it from his split. But Mama couldn't take any more. She gazed at me with sad eyes and then she just ran at the Beast and pulled his blade right into her belly. And then... she was gone, too." Her hand twitches in mine as she says this. "I just shut down then, Arias. No more thought. No feeling. And neither of them did bother with me then. They dragged my family out like so much pap.... out of the shed, and I don't know where they took them."

"They ate and drank themselves into their cups every night. Finally, one sun, they tied me up and threw me into the back of my family's wagon. They killed all the farm animals for the senseless evil of it. When they had finally dragged me from the shed that sun, I gazed about in a daze and found they were all dead and flies buzzing about."

Steffænie had not wept at all during the further telling, but she weeps for a good long time now that the tale is done. I think that if this is what the real world is really like, then Da was in the right raising me to be a warrior. He had raised me with compassion also, though, and I am thankful to Da for that as well. And so, I hold Steffænie to me and let her weep and grieve and know that we had done right to put an end to the bastards that night.

We stay at my campsite for the next several suns as Steffænie grows stronger. She has a resolve about her. I like being with her and she with me. We grow closer and talk of many things. Though her bruises linger, she is a strong girl and soon a great help about the camp. Amazing with any blade, she proves a remarkable camp cook as well. The suns passes quickly and Steffænie recovers, soon back to full strength. I teach her to use the bow, and she has a natural talent for it, likened to her ability with the blades. She remains steadfast to learn these things so as to never again be helpless.

After eve-meal, a fortnight and seven after she had awakened, I say to her, "Steffænie, let me take you home to settle things with your family."

She tears up, then just as quickly wipes her eyes with the back of her hands and looks to me and just nods. She tells me of the closest towne to her family homestead, and I find it on Da's map. I will find it for her.

12

Finnie

At sunrise on the morrow's morn, Steffænie and I pack up the camp that we have called home these past two fortnight and find our way back to the northern travelway that heads to Seas End. We leave some of what I'd taken from the slavers' camp and put it under our shelter ledge of rock.

I, of course, ride Paint, and Steffænie rides the Chestnut mare. She's come to calling the mare, Chessie, and we joke at the originality of our choice of names for our steeds. At times, we speak to each other about our lives as we ride, and other times we but ride in silence. Each of us reflecting inward, I guess. During one of these times, three evenings hence, we round a bend in the travelway and come upon a scene that reflects badly once again on our fellow man.

There in the travelway stands a wagon surrounded by four highwaymen. Two have dismounted and one has a knife to a man that he has pressed up against his wagon side. He appears none too happy with the man's pleading. They have not noticed us as they are intent about their business. A panicked woman, most surely the man's wife, sits upon the buckboard squeezing a young girl tight to her and pleading most desperate, "Pray, don't hurt him, take what you will and leave us."

"Aye, we will take what we want lady, and be still, iffin' you don't want a similar fate as yer man," replies one of the men still mounted. He has a long sword out on display.

"Stay here," I say quietly as I dismount, string my bow, and nock an arrow in a heartbeat. Lilit and Jilly have slithered out of their nest in my saddlebags and stand upright upon my saddle and stare about.

I stride five quiet paces forward and as the one pressing his blade against the girl's pæder's throat appears serious about acting just then, I call in a loud voice, "Nay, I would stay your hand, man."

All eyes turn to me, and I loose an arrow upon that same instant. The arrow flies true. The eyes of the man with the blade go wide as my arrow passes into his neck and lodges there. The arrow's head clearly protrudes on his neck's opposite side. Letting his blade fall from his hands, he collapses to the ground frantically grabbing at his neck.

"Ho, Pa!" the other man standing on the ground yells as he backs off a pace.

But the two on horseback turn and charge me with swords drawn. I nock and shoot a second time. One of the riders falls with my arrow in his heart. With no time to nock another as the second rider is near upon me, I need not have worried, as an arrow flies past from my right and strikes him. The highwayman drops backwise from his horse, landing hard on his head and most assuredly lies dead with a broken neck as well as an arrow to his body. I pull my short sword and bound quickly towards the fourth man. He is no more than my age and raises his hands and steps back two more paces. Fright now filles his eyes as he proceeds to wet himself. I stare at him a moment and say, "Take your boots off."

He stares dumbfounded as he shakes for a long moment. I furrow my brow, and he quickly drops to the ground and do as I demand.

"Now be off with you, and if I see you as I ride your way, you'll suffer a similar fate as your fellow thugs. Oh, drop your coin purse," I add as an afterthought.

He gets up and runs as if his life depends upon it. It does. The lady upon the wagon stares wide-eyed with her hand over her open mouth, and the man peers up from where he had slid to sit against the wagon's wheel.

Steffænie comes up to stand next to me and states, "Have no fear of us, we but have a high disdain for the likes of these."

Sneering, she walks over to the small family at the wagon and tries to comfort them as I retrieve the arrows and the highwaymen's purses. I then drag their bodies to the side of the travelway and round up the horses. I throw the saddles from their mounts into the wagon and collect the saddlebags. I lead the horses to the back of the wagon and tether them with a rope I found amongst the meager possessions in the bed of the wagon.

Thægan and Dænèa, his wife, tell of how this is the second time they have been accosted on the travelway, having been robbed of most of their possessions just a few suns prior on the west road from NewCæstle. They had little to begin with and were headed west and south to find a better life. I collect the two heaviest coin purses and hand them to the man. Then I advise him that the Smithy in the towne of Middenvale, in the direction they were headed would give him coin for the horses and saddles as well with no questions asked if he'd mentioned how he'd come by them. I also offer that it would be a good towne to settle in as the people there are good and kind and that the Innkeep and his wife mayhaps would help them to settle in.

As they start back on the travelway, I hear the young lass say to her mœther, "Did you see the Drægon on his chest? I think there is one on his sword as well!"

"Shoosh, child," her mœther quickly admonishes her.

The fierce air I had seen on Steffænie's face when I glanced to see where that second arrow had come from is gone. A resigned and faraway look replaces it now. When the wagon has finally rounded the bend, she bends over and vomits upon the travelway and rises shaking. We stay awhile seated on the side of the travelway, and she gathers Lilit and Jilly to her lap and pets them. I don't speak of it at all as we travel the rest of the way to Steffænie's homestead. I know it for something she would need to deal with in her own mind. Killing a man with knowing intent is a shock to one's body and mind, I had also discovered.

It takes us another three nights to reach our goal. Steffænie guides us the rest of the way to her home when she recognizes the area near to her homestead. We arrive at dusk there, but Steffænie will not enter the cottage and so we camp outside under a great oak.

Come sunrise, she squeezes my hand tightly as we venture into the small house. It lies broken and mostly empty inside, but she takes down from two hooks upon a wall, a woman's dress and a small child's, as well. She just sits on a rocking chair near to the hearth and holds the garments to her face, taking in their scent. I slip out of the house, leaving her there to find her peace if she is able. As I step out through the door, I am met by Bane, and we search about the homestead.

Behind the small barn, we find the remains of her family in a twisted pile. They are no longer recognizable as who they once were. It will do no good for Steffænie to see them this way. Finding a shovel in the barn, I proceed to dig three graves. Two large ones and one smaller. It takes a time and effort, but I bury Steffænie's parents and collect many large stones to place as cover over the graves. The task complete, I wash up at the well and return to the small stone and thatched cottage.

Taking Steffænie's hand, I guide her out to the graves under the great oak. She simply kneels and cries softly for a while. I do not interrupt but lay my hands upon her shoulders to let her know I am here.

Her chin falls as she gazes upon the graves. "She called me Finnie, Kattalæn did, as when she first began speaking, she could not say my full name proper. Mama and Papa took up her name for me as well after that, and I came to thinking it a fine name after all."

She rises then and faces me.

"Will you call me Finnie, Arias?"

Her emerald eyes are desperately expectant.

"I would be honored." I kiss her lightly on her forehead and pull her tightly to me. She sobs into my chest and I into her hair. I find in that moment, with Finnie in my arms, the ability to grieve a little for Da.

13

We Can Work It Out

Finnie and I stay in her family's cottage, on her family homestead for a few more suns. She is reluctant to leave immediately, so she just slowly meanders about the homestead, recalling life's memories here. The slavers had destroyed most of what had been good about it, murdering the livestock and trashing the cottage. Finnie wants to put some order back to it—she can't leave it with the villains' stain, as she refers to it. We straighten it up, trying to remove evidence of the now-dead slavers. She has found a keepsake of her little sister and her mum as well and placed them into a small leather satchel.

Finally, ready to move on a few suns later, we sit at the table that was once her family table, to discuss it. I can tell her anger for the murderers of her family still resides within her, and I want to distract her from it, I guess.

"Finnie, when I was sometimes in a melancholy—or simply bored— mood, Da would suggest a trip into the wilderness. There is great beauty and marvelous creatures to be found within the forest, and a way to find a calm after a storm with fresh beginnings there." I express this with an enthusiasm that is part for show, I'll admit. "The solace of nature can help one relax and refresh the spirit. I had a tutor, the Healer you've heard me tell of, who taught me a method to bring the spirit together with the mind and let the body heal itself in many ways. Will you come with me and I'll show you, if you'll allow it?"

"And where will I go, in the end, Arias? I have no family anymore," she chokes out, in not much more than a whisper.

"But you have, Finnie. I will be your family, and Bane and Paint and most certainly Jilly and Lilit. We will be your family, if you'll have us. I believe Lilit does prefer you over me, in any case," I say with a chuckle.

At that moment, Lilit bounds to the tabletop and throws herself into Finnie's arms and climbs to nuzzle her under the chin. Finnie laughs aloud, her face bright like I have not seen in days. Jilly joins the action, and the three of them fall to the floor in a tickling mirthful fit. Finnie finally sits up, and the two furions curl immediately to her lap. She in turn tends to the requisite rubbing and scratching of the ears and belly of the both of them.

"Aye, Arias, you are a hero to me and family as well. Take me on a holiday into the woods and teach me your ways to mend my spirit as you have mended my body," she sighs.

"If it please, call me not hero anymore, Finnie, but friend, or family, as you wish."

"But you are all of those things to me, Arias, and that cannot change, and I'll not deny it." Her eyes are now most sincere. Her tone determined.

We resolve to set out at sunrise on the morrow's morn. We make a last eve-meal in the cottage, and Finnie gathers some lavender scented candles her mum had crafted with her and Kattalæn and place them in her satchel. She spends the night in Kattalæn's cot, and I in hers. In the morn, we fry up some spiced tubers and carrots we'd found still in her mum's garden and set out shortly after. We leave the homestead off the back to the north and west and into a great stand of trees. The way is open, with little underbrush to hamper and hinder us, with game trails in abundance all about. We pass over a trapper's trail but decide to stay upon the game trails. We ride for a while and then walk a bit, letting Paint lead Finnie's pony as we take our time and just wander about. As we walk, she tells me of growing up upon her homestead, and I do the same in easy conversation. The difference being she has tales of a mum and a little sister and I, Da and Moor.

As we walk, I point out wildflowers, plants, berries, and such that Da and Effie have taught me about.

"The flower there, that is a Willerwill," I point out. "When dried and crushed with mortar and pestle, and mixed in water, it will clear an upset stomach in a turn of a sand-glass. And this root," I say as I pull on a leafy plant to expose its tuber-type root, "when mixed into an unguent, will protect a wound from infection, and fight one already there. It is what I used upon your leg."

"Will you show me how to make such things, Arias?" she queries, and I wonder if she is but humoring my enthusiasm for such things.

"If you like. Effie, my mentor, would be happy if I did. You would like her, Finnie, and she would like you as well."

Eventually, we come upon a clearing with tall waving grass and a great, broad tree upon a knoll. Seeing that, we stop for a bit, Lilit and Jilly bounding up the tree to rustle some nuts for a meal.

"Teach me your Healer's special way, Arias, I would very much like to learn it. You know, that *Calming* thing you talked about?" she says.

"This would be a perfect place, and I think it will be of value to you." Lowering myself into a sitting position, I sit facing her as she leans back against the tree, nestled betwixt two great roots exposed above the ground. Her emerald eyes lock onto mine. I speak quietly in almost a whisper to her, in a disjointed cadence as Effie had done to me my first time experiencing the *Calming*.

"Listen to… the wind as it… rustles the… branches above… us and smell the… blossoms all about… in the grass.…" I continue this for a bit until I see the telltale sign as her pupils contract and her body relaxes. "Feel the... cooling breeze as it caresses... your face... and hear your... heartbeat as it slows... and... becomes quite steady... Clear your mind of... all but the breeze... and your heartbeat... and let... the *Calming*... envelop you."

I can sense Finnie's heartbeat has slowed to a much lower pace than is common for her, and we just sit for a long spell like this, in the shade of the tree. Lilit is keeping watch above, and Bane is keeping watch along the tree line. Feeling safe and tranquil, I let the *Calming* wash over me as well.

As I gently bring Finnie back from the *Calming,* she surveys about her as if seeing things differently than when we arrived upon the knoll.

"I feel... different somehow, Arias. I see that the sun has dipped in the sky, but it seemed just a moment past that I was losing myself in your crazy, vibrant eyes. And the colors I see about me are somehow more brilliant and clearer. The breeze makes my skin tingle, and I am more aware of the sounds and scents about me." She breathes in excitedly.

"That was my first experience as well, Finnie. After a few more lessons, you will be able to bring yourself to the state on your own accord."

Finnie raises her flattened hand to eye level and holds it just so.

"Arias, this is the first moment my hand has not been shaking since those beasts attacked my family. I thank you yet again." An anger, without the fear, enters upon her face. "There is a hate for those scum within me, but there is no longer the fear to accompany it, and I can sense... I don't know? I feel freer with my other emotions as well. Does that make any sense to you, Arias?"

"Yea, Finnie, I too found there was an insight and calmness that overcame me with the experience. And decisions also came to me with more clarity. Connections between lessons in training that Da and the others had instilled upon me made more sense. All of this was atop a strange perception of better well-being. I hoped that you would experience the same," I say, breathing in deep, the air about us. "The technique does heighten my senses as well." A warm breeze rustles the leaves about the branches in the tree above, and a bird's sharp song punctuates my statement.

I stand up, wiping palms against my thighs, surveying the surroundings. Bane peers up at me, as does Finnie.

"Stay here a bit, Finnie, and I will explore more round and about. We can set up camp here if you like, and I'll visit the brook I hear over yonder way and see if I can find some fresh fish or game for an eve-meal. You'll be safe. Bane is watching over you and Lilit is up in the tree on guard as well," I assure her.

"I do feel safe, Arias, and mayhaps I can help set camp whilst you are hunting." She stands, too, shaking out some stiffness.

I find luck in my foraging and return later to an exuberant Finnie. Camp has been set up, and she has even started a fire and collected extra kindling and branches. She'd set up our tent tarp and is busy playing with Jilly and Lilit and even Bane. It does my heart good to see her eyes glimmering, and her grin I find quite contagious.

Finnie helps prepare our eve-meal and then we brush down the horses and chat casually, getting to know each and the other a little more. For my part, there is a comfort being with her that I have experienced with no other friend I have ever known, and I enjoy our time together immensely. Da's quest falls to the far reaches of my mind.

We travel over the next few suns with no destination to mind. We come across a small lake and with just a little embarrassed smirk, Finnie says we should shed our garb and experience the lake water. She does not have to ask me twice.

"I'm smelling a bit ripe," she says with an awkward grin. "And asides, you've stared at me in my nether-all for half a fortnight and kept me washed *as a proper healer would.*"

I am not opposed as Da and I would not think even twice at such an idea when we had been out on trips together. We strip ourselves of tunic and trousers and slip into the lake. She looks to me as I slip into the water. She, of course, notes my 'stuff' in a state, and says, "Oh my," then turns away and slides below the lake surface with a gasp as the water is so cool.

"I'm sorry, Finnie, but Da and Effie said it was a natural happening when a man is with a beautiful woman, and you are certainly that." But, as I slide further into the very cool lake, it, of a sudden, becomes less of a problem. Finnie's face flushes at my words, and I hope it does not bring back bad thoughts of the thugs and her helpless mœther.

I need not have worried as Bane makes a tremendous plunge betwixt us as he has decided to join the fun. Splashing hilarity follows, smelly wolf and human combined.

As we remove ourselves from the cool lake, we find some sun to bask in and the furions join us, expecting to have their bellies rubbed as they lay betwixt us.

I've been showing Finnie my snaring and trapping methods over these past few suns, and we don our tunics and trousers and go to check the traps. The forest is teeming with wildlife and we are in luck with game for our midsun-meal. We have started working about camp in a comfortable unison and make short work of tasks at hand, working so together.

Our after-high-suns are spent with bow practice or me teaching Finnie defensive moves taught to me by Moor. We also start to sewing more garments so that we will have replacement wear. My pack, when I left the homestead, and the linens we'd recovered from the slave traders' ill-gotten gains, give us material to work with. Finnie stares, amazed at the thread thin Elven-vine I have spooled in my pack kit and even that much more amazed at the dexterity with which a man can use a sewing tool.

"Idle hands are a dæmon's weapon," I spout Da's common expression. "And Da made sure mine were never idle and so I learned such things."

"I very much would have liked meeting your Da, Arias," Finnie says while masterfully working her sewing tools, eying me all the while.

Being with her fills me with a warmth, and I think she feels the same. But each night as we retire, we do so on opposite sides of the campfire, although, these past few nights I awake with her close by my side, with Lilit and Jilly tucked betwixt us.

For a fortnight, we travel to nowhere in particular, but now more north and east, so that one morn we come upon a well-traveled trappers' byway, and it rubs my mind side-aways, somehow. Trapper's byways and trails that I've known are always lightly used and little-known. The trails are more direct routes from trading posts, townes, and villages throughout Aeryth. They make travel shorter for the traders of pelts and other goods. Trappers are most often a tough and a hearty folk and do not fear highwaymen and thieves. Being so, they use these types of trails. Moor once explained to me that highwaymen frequent the main travelways, as their prey there causes them less trouble in their work. But these types of men are few and far between. So, to see a well-worn byway does not sit with my knowledge of the trade. 'Tis but an uneasiness, but there, ne'er-the-lesser.

As the travel is easiest upon this well-worn trail, I resolve we should travel upon it for a while. We encounter no one during our first sun along this trail, as I expected. But we find our journeys are less scenic and uneventful upon the byway and as that is our purpose, we venture once again into the woodlands where we find a creek to follow. Finnie becomes much more relaxed about me. And for my part, I find that saying her new name comes quite comfortably to me.

Each morn we take some time about camp doing familiar chores like tending to the horses and sharpening blades or foraging for tubers and herbs. Being with Finnie has pushed my quest to the back of my mind. I begin showing her the Chě-song that Effie has taught to me, and we make the moves of it in the early morn. She talks of her pæder and mum and little sister to me. I imagine her life quite different than mine with the three women in her family.

We continue our travels to nowhere in particular, keeping a leisurely pace and stopping for a sun or two when we find a place we are enjoying. It might be a small lake among the trees, or as this sun has led us, a small falls feeding a pond in a secluded vale thick with trees and brambles. There is a clearing nearby where the horses can pasture and so we decide to spend a few nights together here. We set our camp and the furions quickly settle in and begin to explore our little paradise.

We welcome Bane this sun as he comes into camp to let us know he is indeed still traveling with us. He keeps growing at such a pace that we can no longer call him a pup. He spends most of his time in the woods. Though I seldom see him most suns, I remain always aware of him keeping track of us, never letting us get too far from him. And though we are together less, I somehow find our bond has become even stronger. I sense him at all times, now.

As we plan to be here mayhaps half a fortnight, Finnie helps me set some snares and fishnet upstream. She has become adept at such things and enjoys the work which keeps her hands and thoughts from idleness, as it leads to unpleasant memories. We spend the time foraging and are rewarded with a wide variety of berries, tater roots, carrots, shrooms, and the like. There are herbs and even hot pepper tubers, and I continue to show Finnie the different types that she knows by name but cannot recognize amongst the forest floor plants. We find tarragon, sage, and parsley. She but shakes her head in amazement that I know such things.

It comes to pass as we are exploring, of a sudden, I put a quieting hand upon Finnie's shoulder and string my bow and nock an arrow in a trice. A fear creeps into Finnie's expression as she does not know my purpose. Unbeknownst to her, rustling and snorting sounds of a wild woodland boar have reached my ears, and it appears to be upwind of us. Finnie gives a puzzled look as she has not heard anything. I motion her to quiet and still.

My hearing is more acute than anyone I know Da and Moor would often remark about it, as they said I was better than they, and they boasted of being better than all they knew.

'Tis a small boar, as I've seen some taller than my waist on hunting outings with Da. This one is the height of my knee, and well fed. It busies itself just now, snuffling up shrooms as tasty morsels and does not see us but twenty-some paces away. Bane has left us this morn in the opposite direction, so this will be our prey alone. I intend the thought not to be competitive but only that Bane is the better hunter. With a practiced, Sky-bolt speed, I nock my arrow and send it in a thrice to its target. I love Da's last gifting to me. My aim and arrow fly true. We have but to retrieve our prize. Being a good ways from camp, I gut and clean the boar where it has been killed.

Finnie helps as well, remarkably handy with a blade as a tool. "You wield that blade with some knowledge, Finnie."

She accepts the compliment. "I'm near to my twenty-year-end, Arias, and mum and Papa would not abide an unmarried daughter that was more hinderance than a help."

I stare back, over disemboweled boar, mouth agape. A fly buzzes by, and I shut it just in time.

"You are nineteen-year?" I query. "You are too fair to be of such an age!"

She first frowns at me, which takes me aback, and then she raises her eyebrow in a bit of sinister glee.

"I'll take that as homage, Arias, but know that it is not polite to query so about a lass' age…. But it is not so with the lass' curiosity towards a man's age. So, what age have you reached, Ser?"

Startled by her question, my dirk pauses in its work.

"I had just made seventeen year-end the morn after Da died," I answer quietly.

She knows it has been just a few fortnights since and recognizes that I'd attached such a meaning to it. She diverts my attention.

"Well, curious lad, though your pretty eyes may say it, your actions belie otherwise. You act a man of many more years than your given age. And I sometimes act and mayhaps show a younger age than I am. But I wager that your shearing my long and beautiful hair of auburn may be somewhat the cause of it!" As she affixes a stare of blame with a raised eyebrow upon me for emphasis.

"And it was, I am sad to say, no thing of beauty when I relieved you of it, ratted and full of crawling nasty little creatures as it was. But I find it quite stunning now," I muse, and her face flushes as she turns away and reaches instinctively to her head.

She smiles and somehow, we become a bit closer.

Turning my attention back to our prize, I say, "You can see Finnie; our friend here has found a treasure of special shrooms of a taste we'll delight in. Mãam Bergierre at the Inn called them troofels and said the boars had a knack for snuffling them up. Let's gather as many as possible."

I set about digging them up from amongst the roots of the hazelnut tree against the brook's bank where we found the boar. I bag some nuts, asides, knowing once crushed, they'll be tasty steeped with java beans.

Finishing with our scavenging and leaving the boars innards to forest scavengers, I heave the prize to my shoulders, the boar's carcass weighing at least four stone. We then head back to camp. We will have plenty to feed us in camp for our stay at the falls pond.

As we arrive, Lilit and Jilly are upon us immediately to play as is their wont. I make Finnie enjoy herself with them as I have plenty to do to cook up our beast. She shuffles off with furions tangled in her feet and climbing to her shoulders to nip at her pretty earlobes, clearly fast friends in a short time. Mayhaps, they prefer her company to mine now. I hear her laugh from across the camp and grin in silent agreement with them.

Going about my task, first, I dig a pit, a foot-length larger than the boar on all sides. I dig the hole deep and line the bottom and sides with stones the size of my head that I have found aplenty about the area and in the stream bed downstream of the falls pond. Next, I build a roaring fire within the pit with thick logs I have found about. Throwing in a few extra stone into the middle of the fire, I feed it the rest of the morn and well into the after-highsun.

Laying out the boar carcass on a large rock next to the stream that sits about waist high, I first cut a slab of bacon from the belly of the pig. Next, I unroll Grayce's gift to me, a bundle of spices and herbs she had assembled for a traveling cook, and a set of butcher's blades. Finnie joins me, and we mix salts, pepper, and ground dried chilies. Then Finnie expertly chops some of the herbs we'd gathered as well and mixes them all with a little dried cane sugar to make a rub for the outside of the boar. We wrap the pig, skin, and all with broad leaves from a Banyun bush. I pull the extra rocks that have cooked in the pit out and place them within the boar's body cavity, and we tie everything tight with twine.

Lastly, we lower the boar into the pit, cover it with stones, and bury it with soil. Da had taught me that the pit would act as an oven for up to two suns and would cook the meat slowly. By the morrow's morn it will be done.

"For such a young lad, Arias, you are quite well accomplished in such things. I wager that someday when you've gained a few years, you'll make a lucky lass a wonderful husband." She laughs heartily and then it is my turn to turn red about the cheeks.

Our plates will be full for many suns to come when we remove the boar from the pit. But for this night we sit to an eve-meal of skewered rabbit, carrots, and troofels.

We pack the belly bacon in waterproofed skin and submerge it in the cold water of the stream to preserve it. As the moon rises, Bane has returned with a full belly. After bringing Paint and Chestnut back from pasture, our little party beds down for the night. Again, Finnie takes a spot across the fire from me with Lilit and Jilly snuggled close about her.

Come sunrise Finnie awakes with a start and lets out a blood curdling scream. Being once again next to me, I take her into my arms. She is sweating profusely and staring wide-eyed at me.

"Look to me Finnie, and use the *Calming* I've taught you," I instruct her.

She barely nods but begins the breathing exercise. She finally calms.

"I was back with the Beast and the other thugs that took me from my family, the night you rescued me," she whispers.

"I think that the night terrors will lessen if you speak of it aloud, Finnie. Effie would always advise her patients such."

"I've just recalled that night, I had previously buried it within my mind, I think. All the blood and violence. You killed two and Bane tore the neck from another." She gasps, puts her hand to her mouth, and stares at me. "Oh, Arias. The beast that raped my mum and struck my sister to her death, and Papa too—he began to move upon the ground. I panicked; you were not able to protect us. I pulled your blade from the ground afore me and… Oh, Arias what I did."

Tears pour from Finnie's eyes. Though the Man Mountain was deserving of it, she cries that she could do such a thing. I hold her tight, knowing nothing I can say will help. I carry no emotion whatsoever for the beast of a man, but my heart breaks for Finnie, yet again.

Finally, while wiping her eyes, "But how did you survive the Bowman's arrow, Ari?"

My eyebrows rise to the question, but just as much to her new name for me. A warmth envelopes me.

"Let me tell you that tale, Finnie, as it goes back to one of Da's giftings and they have saved me in different ways and more than once," and then

I tell her of the Schäaken board-game and how the Bowman's arrow had struck the board within my pack and saved me, though leaving me with a very sore back.

"I'll show you how to play it if you'd like." I say, hoping to distract her from her memories. "But first, we have some bacon to pan fry and mayhaps a tuber, smashed with some garlic. And then it will be time to pull our pig from the ground. What say you?"

She stands. "I'll gather the kindling and start a fire, you pull your bacon and slice out a few rashers of it."

And off she goes.

When she returns, it is with a strut and air of accomplishment.

"See, Ari, I found a wild-fowl's nest and pilfered four eggs, just laid this morn," she crows as she presents them proudly.

"If you'd like to bathe first in the pond, I'll cook up the bounty you've brought, and I'll bathe later," I offer.

"Nay," says she. "You smelled a bit off this sunrise as you hugged me. So, I'll prepare morn-meal and you can wash yester-sun's scent from yourself." She turns her nose up to me and cocks her head while taking up her knife.

"Well then, keep your eyes to the meal making and do not peek as I slip into my bathe," I kid.

"Ho, you are too proud of yourself. Mayhaps I was hasty in calling you a man," she says, but she cannot hide her expression as I walk away and feign a bruised ego.

I lead the horses to the clearing so they can pasture and strip off my garb, climb to the head of the falls, and dive into the pond. Bane leaps in upon me and Finnie laughs at her boys at play.

14

Kings Court

Subtle changes had taken place in King's Court. Nothing that would be noticed by the dregs on the docks or the farmers that surrounded the towne. The smithies, cobblers, bakers, and butchers would not have been aware either. The merchants and tinkers that travelled across the length and breadth of Aeryth may have had a clue, one could suppose, but the nobility and the Royals scattered about the Keeps and major estates across Aeryth were aware. The last decade found King Aegèas a more reclusive king, and his visits that bolstered their positions in Aeryth's hierarchy and politics had, to some minds, suffered. To others it had been an opportunity to grow their individual fiefdoms without interference.

Aegèas, two score year ago, was a great warrior, conqueror, and hero to the people of Aeryth. He had defeated foes from beyond the southern seas and defended his pæder's kingdom from usurpers. Those who were determined to have a centuries-old monarchy failed. For two decades after his ascension to the throne and a popular marriage to a beautiful and intelligent woman of nobility from the Southern Reaches, Aegèas governed with a strong and fair hand, and the kingdom prospered and grew under his reign and rule.

In his first decade as new King—with a new beloved king's wife, Èglæsèa, at his side—Aeryth especially prospered as lands were given in the Middle Realm to trusted nobility and those loyal subjects that helped him defend the Realm. The Kingdom grew stronger. With nobility loyal to him ever expanding into theretofore untamed lands of the Middle Realm and further even, into parts of the Southern Reaches, townes and cities grew up on new travelways throughout a growing kingdom. Aegèas and his wife travelled the lands, and they were accepted with great fanfare and love.

The king's wife gave birth to twins early on in his reign—a prince and a lass—and he was happy he had a son. The royal children grew. Aegèas' son Adrèæn began his tutelage and training, preparing him to one day succeed his pæder. Aeglèsia, the king's daughter, likewise began an education befitting royalty, though under the king's wife's purview.

Both children were striking in their appearance and demeanor from an early age. Adrèæn inherited his pæder's intelligence, though less, contemplative way. Oft times reprimanded to pay closer attention by his tutors, he proved to be a prince with a natural dexterity and strength beyond his age, and his pæder the King took great pride in him. His appearance was equally striking. His eyes were a sparkling blue and veined in gold like unto his pæder's, but his hair grew to be a soft, mousey brown with shocks of lightest blonde intermixed, like neither his pæder nor mœther.

As sparkling blue and tinted that her brœthers were, Aeglèsia's eyes were even more effervescent, if that were possible, but in the bright golden hue of her mœther but with a bright silver veining. Her hair was a match to her twin brœther's.

The king's wife made it a priority that her daughter had her own tutors, separate from her brœther's but just as revered, for Èglæsèa, the king's wife from the Southern Reaches, held steadfast and determined that her daughter was availed all the education heretofore afforded any male progeny.

It should be noted here that Èglæsèa hailed from a family of noble bloodlines from the South of Aeryth, whose royal home was made in the Keep and within the southern port city of Esperance. It was named, they say, for an Ancient Sage that had advised its line of kings for many generations. Before the war with the invaders from across the Great Southren Sea, this was also a kingdom on par with Aegèas' own and the seat of rule for all the Southern Reaches of Aeryth. The great war had taken its toll on this reigning family though, as the invasion of Aeryth had come from the South. The monarch's family was near to obliterated by the invading forces before the Mid Realm's King's son Aegèas arrived with an army and turned the tide of battle and burned the fleet of the invading enemy. The combined forces of both the Middle Realm and those that were left of the Southern Reaches and lead by Aegèas, attacked the invaders without mercy and thus vanquished them totally, with peace restored.

But the southern kingdom's reigning family had been decimated, leaving an aged King with no remaining sons to rule. An arranged marriage between Aegèas and Èglæsèa was formed to bring all of the Middle Realm and Southern Reaches together under a single reign from King's Court, with deference shown by the southern royal house. With the natural death of Aegèas' pæder, the combined kingdom had come to Aegèas.

After more than a decade of peaceful and prosperous reign, harmony within the royal family itself began changing behind closed doors. With no more great battles to be fought and Èglæsèa otherwise occupied with raising his heir, the King took to him a concubine. Èglæsèa was not overly concerned as she had her own life and priorities and having grown up within a royal family, this dalliance on her husband's part was not out of the ordinary to her.

But the King's concubine had other plans and aspirations. And so, after a dozen years into his reign, she acted on her lofty aspirations and designs upon the throne. She knew from her own noble upbringing that opportunities must sometimes be seized. Under the whisperings and devious intent of her own family and *others*, she set about a plan to poison Èglæsèa.

The plot was successful in its employ, but her greater plan would not be realized. The King discovered his concubine's betrayal and murder, albeit too late to save Èglæsèa. In his anger he had the concubine beheaded, her brœther, as well as the co-conspirator whispering in her ear. Her family was banished from King's Court and their entire land holdings forfeit as further punishment. A guilt then befell Aegèas, and as such, he turned his attentions to his daughter and took a more special interest in her. Of a sudden, threatened with such palace intrigue, he assigned his most accomplished soldier at arms to become Aeglèsia's personal guard and swore him to Oath to protect her at all costs and above all else. Aeglèsia herself realized all that had happened and became colder towards her pæder, the King.

Just as Adrèæn was of special character, so, too, was Aeglèsia. Aside from being an astute pupil of natural intelligence and a dexterity likened to her twin brœther, she had an unusual connection with creatures of all kinds. She had a horse she loved and was a natural rider. Always by her side was a great and fierce dog, and no person but close friends dared approach her without express permission. As her personal guard had a gift with creatures as well, they became close. A close friend as well as protector. He would show her the ways of creatures, and the two would often ride, upon Aeglèsia's insistence, out into the forest surrounding Kings Court.

Her most trusted confidant, however, remained her elder tutor in the histories. And they would talk well into the night about the greater realm and the histories of Aeryth. She, in this way, grew with a passion to explore the realm to her pæder, the King's, ultimate dismay.

As brœther and sister reached their eighteen-year-end, their destinies diverged yet again. And, mayhaps, the point in which the King himself took a road to a different fate as well.

Rumor had always held that Aegèas had been so successful in his early years because of a talent few knew of prior. It was thought to be one of the ancient mægics, the likes of which kings of previous generations, for a century past, had denied, outlawed, and openly opposed. It is said that Aegèas had the *Sight*. It was reasoned that he became so bold in his military campaigns because he saw success in their outcomes. This may or may not have been so, but by decree a score and ten of years ago, and but a few years after his coming to be King, practice of the ancient mægics were no longer considered a crime. The King himself took on an advisor at the time who was lauded as a Seer.

Upon his eighteen-year-end, Adrèæn was dispatched to the palace at Esperance, where his gran'sire lay gravely ill. Charged with taking control of the lesser kingdom, he became Warden of the Southern Reaches and in training to, of course, one day inherit the throne in Kings Court himself.

In Kings Court, Aeglèsia had come of an age to marry, and Aegèas had been arranging for a marriage of political convenience. But, to his further dismay, his daughter caught wind of this development and refused him. This angered Aegèas a great deal, and he insisted and soon started to become physical in his handling of his insubordinate daughter.

This led to one morn, after a few months of anger and abuse by her pæder, her visiting her truest friend and tutor.

"Mæster Escher, will you hear me?" pleaded Aeglèsia as she entered his library sanctuary.

"Oh, my dear Aeglèsia, what has happened?" He gasped out at the sight of her. "The King?"

"Yea, Mæster, and I need a friend; can you be him in my hour of greatest need?" She teared up. "I must leave and escape my pæder and his plans for me."

The Mæster knew Aeglèsia to be as strong a woman as ever he had met, and to see her this broken was beyond him.

"Aeglèsia, I did make an Oath to your mœther, and I will honor it. But we must be most cunning as to not give away our intentions."

"Mæster, how can we manage it? I refused this planned marriage by my pæder, and he has me watched day and night."

He advised, "Your first duty will be to return to the King and tell him you'll submit to his plans. But, be sure to do so reluctantly at first. It may be at least a few moons afore all preparations can be made. This will give us some grace to sort things out. I also know one other we can enlist to our purpose, as he has made a similar Oath to your mœther."

And so, they did plan and then execute their ruse. Mæster Escher had slowly emptied his library on excuse to returning to his home in the Southern Reaches as his tutoring of Aeglèsia was no longer needed. And Aeglèsia came to be allowed to ride once more with her personal guard. Her wedding was planned just a few months into the future.

Then one day, three fortnights hence, Aeglèsia had left on one of her typical forest rides and never returned. Neither did her personal guard. They did, however, meet up with the elder Mæster and proceeded to travel far to the north and east and through the Barrier Mountains. Then on to a keep not easily reached and one which most would forget they knew existed at all, once they were out of sight of it.

The King became furious to find his daughter had left him, and his own fate did seem to change that day as well. Upon that selfsame day that the King had realized his daughter had left him, he had one of his dreams. His chief advisor visited him that very next morn and proclaimed that he had a dream the night before as well. They were, on this occasion, the same *Seeing*.

In the dream, a Drægon stood glaring down from a hill with his daughter standing afore it and cradling a babe into her arms, and a clearly elder King Aegèas stood while all around him, his world was in flames.

Among Seers, it is known that one cannot see his own death, but this foretelling was distressingly clear. It was also known that *seeings* were not always what was meant to pass. Or could be ambiguous in their interpretations. One could also change this one future if he acted in a manner that would alter the primary element to prevent it. And so, from that point, King Aegèas made an Oath to himself that he would not stop until he had found his daughter and her unfaithful personal guard. For he was certain that if he did not, her heir would mean the end of his reign.

The merchants and courtiers began to notice that the King held fewer feasts and with each year, traveled less. In these past fifteen years, he was rarely seen outside the palace itself. The King increased his armies twofold and taxed his people more to cover the expense of it. He commanded that companies be trained and sent to all corners of Aeryth in search of Aeglèsia and her Kingsman guard.

Over the past few years, he commanded that all young men of age sixteen-year-end to twenty-year-end would be conscripted to his army for a term of two years. Searching now for not only his daughter and the guard, but also the heir that must exist. He knew this because as he gazed upon a looking glass each morn, the King of his dream now reflected back at him.

As Aegèas drew his army closer to him, lawlessness grew in the further reaches. But, throughout the years, he never ceased to send out his special companies, ever vigilant to find his quarry. Then one day, a lone rider appeared from the tree line on the travelway from the west, and at a gallop now on a near broken steed from the fatigue of the trip. He did not slow until he entered the west gate of Kings Court and reached the King's army stables in a cloud of dust. He slid from his sweaty and worn horse and yelled,

"Yea, Aäron, send a lad to see to my Grey. I have urgent business with the captain," barked Jæron.

"Where will I find him?"

Aäron whistled to a stable hand. "He'll be with the new recruits in the yard now."

Jæron stopped only for a cup of water at the well and hurried onto the training yard. He found Captain Hæster with a couple of eighteen year-end recruits, conscripted without choice most likely, as was the business of the King's army nowadays. He nodded and caught the captain's eye.

Approaching, the captain regarded Jæron with a wary eye and asked, "Jæron, has then Gäston and your company returned so soon? I would not have expected you back for another moon or more. And where is Ser Gäston then to give his report personally?"

"Dead, Ser," was all that Jæron would say in a low voice.

Capt. Hæster's eyes went wide. Gäston was one of his best field commanders and had trained his company to be the best in all the corps. An accident, mayhaps? It wasn't unheard of, but the appearance of Jæron suggested otherwise. His manner leaden and disheveled, he'd doubtless ridden long and hard. Clearly fatigued, he had obviously come directly to him.

"Let us retire to my office then, Jæron, and you will give me your reports."

Jæron, Hæster knew, was Ser Gäston's espy officer. His observer trained to take account of all the company's interactions and journal them for review by himself and the King's advisors if Hæster found the reports may be of interest to the King. For his companies had a special motive. They traveled throughout Aeryth, on the stated business of conscription of certain aged candidates for King's service. This was true, of course, but they also had a further purpose.

Upon entering the office, Jæron wasted no time in getting to the report.

"They are all dead to a one, Ser," he said to Capt. Hæster's astonished stare.

"We were in the farthest reaches of the West, in the foothills of the western range of the Shadow mountains, Ser, near to a small village called Middenvale. We were acting on information gained from a retired hinterland soldier who in his cups, was regaling new recruits with tales of the greatest Kingsmen he had ever fought aside. This old braggard of a soldier said he'd been told that this great Kingsman had retired in this towne of Middenvale some years back," Jæron said.

"When we made this Middenvale, Ser Gäston queried after an animal whisperer he'd heard had settled in those parts. He'd said they'd come upon a horse recently they needed breaking before they had to travel back to King's Court," he continued.

"Gäston said that he'd heard the animal whisperer may live with a healer as well."

"Nay," said the stable hand he'd been talking to. "But he lives out west near the foothills and his nearest neighbor is a Widow he's said to be dear friends with," the stable hand replied. The stableman put an end to the queries, though, putting the stable hand back to work.

"At sunset, we quartered just outside of towne for the night. Come the morrow's midsun, after queries to other townsfolk, the company set out North and then to a west track as directed by the man. There we came upon a small farm and quietly spied a small woman who clearly was not the King's daughter. We stayed in the woods to remain unseen by the woman," reported Jæron. "We returned to the track and galloped some further distance west. Then, as we rode, we heard a bell chiming three times."

The captain interrupted. "A bell?"

"Yea Ser, likened to a chime my mum would sound for eve-meal call, when younger." Hæster scooted his chair back now and rose to retrieve a bottle and two pewter mugs. Filling a few fingers in each he offered one to Jæron. They drank, eye-to-eye.

"We shortly came out from the tree line. We saw a small stone cottage and a barn just beyond. 'Twas not 100 paces from us. And Ser, there he stood. A mountain of a man and clearly fitting the description of Ètœn he, but older." Jæron paused, as if lost for a moment in the memory. "Twas as if he were expecting us, standing as he was to the side of his cottage by the well."

"Expecting you? How so?"

"He stood staring at the track as the company came from the forest. And he held a staff, a great haälberd, it turned out to be, the like I've never seen. He held it with its head to the ground, though it's axe-head shown a steely blue in the mid-sun light."

Again, Capt. Hæster nodded. "He was like no soldier I've ever known afore or since. It sounds like the man I know."

"And Ser Gäston acted as such also, Ser. He mumbled it is him indeed. The company approached him as I held back, at the tree line to observe, as ordered Ser," said Jæron, as if guilty of some transgression. Hæster looked to him and nodded.

"They approached the man and circled their horses at four paces and staggered, fore and back, so all had a view of him. Ser Gäston addressed him by name, and he did not react at all. Four dismounted. Asked about Aeglèsia and again he just stared, silent. The bowmen had loaded their bolts and the captain informed him he was under arrest for the kidnap of the King's daughter. At that moment, three things happened in a thrice, ser. A boy appeared out of the woods, mayhaps 100 paces to the Southwest. Ser Gäston immediately sent Ash and Geræld for the boy and Ètœn yelled out these exact words. '*Pickles.*' 'Go now then, lad.' And then he whistled, 'Bregœ, to him.'"

In the moment, the air in the office lay heavy and stilled. Stifled and rich with the stench of the sweat of the two men. The captain reached to scratch his stubbled cheek and chin.

Jæron continued after taking in a gargled breath. "Captain, Ser, then things happened I'd never think possible. He moved so quickly for the giant of a man that he was. Three men were falling to the ground, one nearly decapitated, and a fourth and fifth gone with two thrusts as quick as a blink. The bowmen shot their bolts immediately and they did strike the man. One to the torso and one to his leg. Captain, I diverted my eyes but for a breath it did seem, as a great warhorse plunged headlong into Ash and Geræld and they all went down. Later, Ash and Geræld did not rise. The boy was running towards the melee now."

He looked up into the stone face of his captain with sad eyes.

"Ser, in the instant I turned back, this man, in spite of two steal bolts in him, had somehow killed all the remainder of the company save Ser Gäston. As I watched, Gäston struck his short sword in the man's side and from the rear, only to be struck a heartbeat later himself with the backend of the haälberd to his neck. Thrown two paces with the force of it. Dead instantly, Ser."

The captain's lips pressed into a hard, thin line.

"I then watched as Bearheart collapsed himself, just as the boy arrived to him. As the boy held him, as a son with his pæder in such a time, I watched as Bearheart whispered his last words to him. The man, and his warhorse, killed an entire company in less time than I've taken to recite this," Jæron finished.

Capt. Hæster inspected his own fingernails for the briefest of moments before asking, "How long has it taken to return from this Middenvale, Jæron?"

"Twenty and one suns, Captain. Exactly a fortnight and seven riding hard from sunup to Sunset, Ser."

"Come, Jæron, afore you can rest, you must report this direct to the king, just as you've spoken it to me, as soon as he will hear us."

Jæron stood up, in shock. He had never been in the direct presence of the king.

With very few words spoken to his advisors, the king received the two soldiers immediately. As they entered the king's private receiving chambers, they saluted and then kneeled in front of Aegèas.

"Arise and be at your ease men, after all I was once in the field myself. Make your report so we may consider what you have to say." *It must be of some import, from the countenance of the one soldier*, Aegèas thought.

Jæron recounted all that he had told Capt. Hæster and then he stood and awaited a response.

Aegèas paced to the window, placing his fingers lightly upon its sill and gazed out.

With not a word of the men killed or the encounter itself, the Kings one question was about the boy.

"Describe this boy for me, Kingsman."

A quick pause and an almost imperceptible twist of his head as if to question the inquiry, Jæron spoke. "Sire… A tall youth, mayhaps sixteen or seventeen year. He appeared fit as he sent an arrow near to 50 paces that struck chest high in a tree trunk and not a pace from me. He then started running, swift as a deer and towards me. There was a flash about his eyes, but I remained too far off to see their color. His hair was a soft brown with shocks of blonde nearly white in evidence."

The King sighed at the hearing of this last remark and turned to glance at his most trusted advisor and seer, Mensæ. "That will be all, Kingsman. Captain, see to this man, he looks hard traveled. You will have new orders shortly."

15

Crown's Business

The Seer did not hesitate as he knew the King was sure as well. "The boy, by the Kingsman's description, coupled with the fact that he was with Ètœn Bearheart would certainly lead one to deduce that he is, in fact, Aeglèsia's son."

The King slammed his fist upon the table. He paused, settled, and rang for his steward and ordered some wine.

"Sit with me awhile, Mensæ. We have strategies to discuss," Aegèas said in a more restrained voice and looked to his Seer and advisor.

They sat, and the King remained silent for a time as their wine was served and the steward had exited the chamber. These would be discussions between Aegèas and his advisor alone.

"Is it still true that you have had no vision of my daughter in all these years Mensæ?" The King inquired. Though certain that Mensæ would never utter an untruth directly to him, he knew his advisor to be not above withholding information to serve himself best.

"Nay, Sire, none since I lay purposely upon her bed after she left, those many years ago." Mensæ stared back into the incredulous eyes of the King. Mensæ spoke carefully, and truthfully. Aegèas could not understand how his daughter could disappear so completely. Though not expressing it, Mensæ had more understanding, he thought.

"After she was *taken* from me by her traitorous personal guard and aided by the equally treasonous tutor her mœther brought from the South," the King raised his voice yet again. It was clearly a subject that irritated him. "And the deceit planned well in advance, as evidenced by the tutor's empty library and chambers. Why did we not see these things before they transpired, Mensæ? My sight has so seldom let me down."

"The sight is sometimes a fickle courtesan, Sire, as you well know," rejoined Mensæ.

"Yea, man, and she's left me to mundane dreams since that last vision of ours." The King's face was drawn as if hurt by it. Mensæ's unreadable.

"And this guardsman," the King spat. "This supposedly loyal Kingsman seeded her and Aeglèsia has produced this bastard child that the sight says will undo me!"

"The vision is twenty-year past, Sire, and we both know the sights such as these may sometimes not come to pass or are misread" Mensæ noted that the King had not forgotten. He had, in fact, been actively searching for his daughter ever since.

"Yea, if one may design against them, they may not, and that is what we shall continue to do. At least we can say that the King's justice has come to the recreant bastard Guardsman, I hope he died a painful death," Aegèas spat. "I will see my daughter's bastard son in my dungeons, alive or dead at my feet, it matters not which."

"Sire, I am hesitant and dismayed to say, but mayhaps your daughter indeed no longer lives and that is why I have not any further sight of her. Her absence from this Kingsman's tale would support such a theory," ventured Mensæ.

"Yea. And that alone would keep me from killing her bastard offspring, so I might know that truth," reflected Aegèas. "And so, let us make our plan to do just that. I shall have the captain send a company immediate on the morrow to retrieve the lad, alive if possible, but dead if needs be."

"I would counsel that you send two companies, Sire," advised the Seer.

"And why two for such a task, he's but a bastard and only a lad, to hear from the company's espy." But the King was listening.

"To approach him from both the South and East travelways, Sire. To guard against the chance that the boy could be moved. Ètœn Bearheart has remained hidden from us for twenty years and may indeed have a plan for the lad's safety should something occur, such as what did happen. As the Kingsman's tale suggested, Ètœn Bearheart still expected us, even after a score of years."

The King nodded. "Prudent advice, Mensæ. It shall be done."

"If I may, Sire, one more thing."

"Yea, Seer, I'm listening."

"Mayhaps a carrier bird to the Lord Tullamoor, as he is the closest Lord to this… Middenvale. He would be in a position to strike quickest and hold the boy until the captains can retrieve him."

"That pompous ass!" But then, said the King, "Yea, I like that idea. A test of his loyalty and a morsel I can throw him to let him perceive his importance to the realm. But tell him nothing of the true motive and reasoning for the lads capture," said Aegèas.

"Send for the Captain again, Mensæ."

The King, he sat, pensive for a while.

16

Trader's Trails and Byways

The eve times are warm and the suns warmer still. But the gentle breezes and shade amongst the trees and the cool pond that the falls emptied into make our camp an ideal retreat from the ugly of the world Finnie had experienced of late. We take time to just relax with the simple chores of camp life—brushing and caring for the horses, gathering and hunting as needed, and cooking meals and learning of each other a bit more, playing with the furions and teaching them little tricks. They are very clever and enjoy this immensely.

Finnie and I stay at the falls pond for a full fortnight. After I'd told her the tale of how Da's gift of the Schäaken board had saved my life the night I'd found her, she had me pull it out and asked me to teach her how to play. She would often finger the crack that had formed because of the arrow striking it with such force. But it remains whole and after only a dozen sessions she is becoming very adept at the game. We continue our Chẽ-Song and *Calming* routines, and she insists that we run together as Moor had taught me. We have a strengthening routine as well that Da had started with me as just a ten year-ender.

She is fascinated most with my Bo-staff and my bow, and so, I crafted her a Bo-staff of her own from a stout, straight branch of an oak. Though not fashioned in the manner that Da had crafted mine, it is straight and purposeful. She has a bow and arrows of a good-size for her frame from that same night of our meeting. We train every day. In the morns, we practice. After the morn-meal, we run, climb, and work to strengthen her in all ways. I find her especially adept at shooting a bow, and within a fortnight she can hit a swift rabbit as it runs at twenty paces. Her eye at a moving target is remarkable and I tell her so.

"Finnie, soon you will be my master at the bow. I am proud of your progress!" I compliment her. "You are clearly my best pupil."

She laughs and returns, "And what other students have you had, oh great mentor?"

"None, if you don't count Lilit and Jilly. But it is truth, Finnie. You train hard and with unmatched fierceness, which Moor has always said is most important. I could not have a more focused apprentice."

She stops what she is about and fixes me with steely emerald eyes.

"Ari, I'll never again be in a position that a man not of my choosing shall lay a hand upon me. I will not have done to me what they forced upon my mœther," she says in a most resolute tone.

I nod solemnly and rise to approach her.

"Then it is time for more of Moor's Hæ-Kæ-Dœ moves as they will serve you well if an attacker has gotten too close to you, for I would not have it so, either."

'Tis a welcome time, our fortnight at the falls… but we continue about the countryside after a while. Our lessons continue though, as we travel. We never meet a single stranger upon our trails, and life becomes routine and uneventful. This surely means a peace for Finnie. We work hard at Finnie's training, but have fun as well. We laugh at the furions' antics as I entice them to startle Finnie with a drop from a tree, or she has them unlace my boots. Bane, also, has welcomed this laughing, boisterous human lass into a close friendship and has become very protective of her—in great extent due to my feelings for her, and hence he feels the same, I somehow know.

As she lies down one night across the fire from me, I ask, "Finnie, ofttimes I wake to find you next to me at sunrise. Won't you come sleep next to me now?"

Her eyes sparkle, and I warm to the sight. "Well, it's about time you've invited me Ariastone Côeurdrægon. I'd almost given up hope that you would!"

I stare like a buck caught unaware, as I have not realized that it is my place to have asked. Life with Finnie is more complicated than I remember it being with Da.

Somehow, something has suddenly changed between us, but I shake my head in wonder as I don't know what it is. It is as if she has a secret, with me not privy to it. She brings her bedroll and snuggles close beside me with her back to me. I lay my arm across her waist and it feels different somehow, but right.

Lilit and Jilly are standing on their hindquarters staring back and forth betwixt Finnie and I and then between themselves. They squeak and chitter as if to mock me. It appears they are smiling in their own fashion afore they curl up in front of Finnie, with there no longer room betwixt us.

'Twis better than two fortnight since we have left Finnie's homestead, and one eve-meal at the campfire I broach a new subject.

"Finnie, we have wandered about for a while and we've seen ne'er a soul. Not trader nor tinker. We're carrying weapons and linens and wares we have no need for. My thought is it might be time to visit a towne or village. There we can sell these goods for coin and replenish needed supplies. What are your thoughts?"

She tightens visibly at this idea, but after a moment, she sighs and lets herself relax. A sad and pensive guise spreads upon her face.

"I suppose you have the right of it, Ari. It is time I stepped back into the real world, and that world has real people within it."

"Yea, mayhaps it will be an adventure in itself," I put forth.

"Let us find the traders trail we traveled aways back and it surely will lead us to civilization again."

On the morrow's morn, we head back south and east, knowing we will cross the trader's byway within a sun or two. Riding at our leisure, I reflect on the past two moons since I'd left out from our homestead. Much time has passed since the Kingsmen's attack of Da and the counsel with his friends and the quest he had set upon me. There has been little thought of it since coming upon Finnie that night. This has become a more pressing deed, and the quest will need wait a bit.

I ponder other things. Bane has matured to almost a wolf, full grown. His back stands to my waist, and we are attached to each other in a way I would never have thought possible.

Some eves, afore sunset, when I find myself resting, I would fall back into the *Calming* and I would find myself traveling with him as a spectator behind his eyes. I experience his hunts and feel his emotions within myself. These I know are more than just dreams. If a thought is sent to him, he would respond to it. When he would return to camp with the prey, I had *known* the kill, I could no longer doubt it.

The furions are much the same and putting travel to mind brings Paint to me most times. I wonder if it had been the same way with Da and Bregœ. He never told me such. Peeking across to Finnie as she rides beside me, her thoughts, to me, are readable from the expressions upon her face. And though I spy her in my side vision and ride a bit behind her, it seems to me she knows I was just then thinking of her as she wrinkles her nose and brow and suddenly turns back to me, her face a query.

We find the traders' byway our second eve looking and make camp not far from it for the night. Again, a discomfort and unease befalls me when I see evidence of increased travel on the trail.

"Bane, stay aware tonight, something is not right about the trail yonder," I say as we make camp.

"What is it, Ari?"

"It's just that the byway looks more traveled than I'd expect and hence a little off, to my mind. Moor has taught me to listen to my instincts and so I shall; is all there is to it."

Though I do not want to alarm her, I think it prudent to let her know my instinctual sense of it. We move around the camp quietly that eve and have but a small fire.

"Finnie, fear not," I say, reading the unease on her face. "Bane will give us fair warning if anything should come amiss."

Ne'er the lesser, it makes her care to snuggle closer to me that night, and I keep my dirk and Bo close to hand.

I wake afore the dawn and bid Bane to leave out and travel ahead of us alongside the byway. I bring up the fire and bid the furions to help find something worthy of morn-meal. They are good to the task and drag a few tubers and onions back to camp but a little time later. With morn-meal cut, fried, and left to stay warm in a pan amongst the dying embers, I sit back against a tree and put myself into the *Calming* to make contact with Bane.

He warms to my presence—he always does— and then I peer and smell out from his senses to accustom myself to his whereabouts. He is traveling north alongside the byway amongst the trees near to the tree line.

I/We hear them first and then they appear. There are two riders on stout stallions of deep brown. These are well stabled horses, and the men are suitably garbed and armed with broad swords. Not of the King's corps, but mayhaps the men of a greater Lord. *Why would they use a trader's route?*

They pass on by us/Bane not noticing us at the edge of the wood, hidden amongst the brush and shadows.

As they head south, we continue forward and north, as well. Some distance up the road, we stop again at the approach of more horses and a wagon. There are two more riders and the coachman upon the wagon. The coachman is in a simple cloak and woolen tunic and trousers. Not a Lord's corpsman then. But the horsemen are of the same livery of the earlier riders. They wear no sigil on their breast, but sure certain I am, that they must be in the employ of some lord. It appears that the first two are but scouts afore these men, and I see why when we glance upon the wagon. There is a cage with four youngers within. Lads of a dozen year and much less. Bane feels my unease and brings a low growl to his throat.

They are bedraggled and scared in appearance, and resigned in their manner, to a fate reminiscent of Finnie's on that night we had found her. I think to Bane to follow them and then remove myself. I wake from the *Calming* to Finnie eating a share of the morn-meal.

"Finnie, we must pack and move to the trail immediately," I proclaim as I startle her. But then she sees the serious look upon my face. To her credit, she starts packing her bedroll and supplies onto her chestnut, just of a sudden. I forego any food as I will not be able to eat, in any case. My mind is abuzz in preparation.

"There are four men and a wagon with a cage atop it holding four younger lads. They are of the same purpose as those who had captured you, but of a Lord's livery, I think. It makes no sense to my mind," I tell her.

Her brow wrinkles, and she asks, "How could you know such a thing? I hear nothing and you were just leaning against the tree in a *Calming.*"

She ties down supplies upon her mare. She has already saddled the chestnut.

I smother the fire, tossing the remaining food and quickly rinsing the pan in the brook alongside our camp.

"I will explain later, we must hurry. Two of the men are riding ahead of the others and I want to be on the byway to meet them. You'll stay inside the tree line with your bow at the ready in the shadows." I look to her. I see that she does not doubt any that I said, and she nods her assent to my plan.

We arrive alongside the trailway just a short time later. I show Finnie where to watch from, telling her to keep her bow at the ready and leave her horse tethered some ways back and unseen from the byway. Lilit and Jilly quickly climb the tree above Finnie and stare out to the traders' trail.

Walking Paint across the trailway, he islet to graze along and slope. I play to be arranging the saddlebags on Paint, with my pack upon my back and my Bo-staff in my hands. I can now hear the two horses approach from around a bend in the trailway just ahead.

They come around the trails bend and, of a sudden, notice me.

"Ho...lad, and who might you be, traveling upon this trailway?" One of the horsemen query as they approach to within ten paces.

I've come to the center of the trailway to meet them.

"Well met," I say, in hopes of putting them at ease. "I'm a trapper's kin, and he's bade me visit him this season and gave me a map of the trails. For myself, I would not have expected to find a Lord's corpsmen upon such a byway. Who do you serve?"

I see them clench their jaws as they glance betwixt themselves. One dismounts.

"'Tis not the business of a ruddy pup as yourself. I'll have you lay your weapon upon the ground," he says as he eyes the pommel of my short sword rising above my right shoulder. He has unsheathed his broadsword.

"I think I'll hold them to me, as it's just the same," say I, and do not reach for the short sword, but ease my stance and turn to give the swordsman a smaller target.

"Did you hear, Edrin? Come help me teach this welp a lesson. You, lad, will leave here less a limb or two," He sneers.

The second horsemen begins his dismount and I make my move.

Sky-bolt quick, I tumble forward, and coming out of the roll I sweep my Bo, first into the corpsman's knee and then with its other end a swift upward jab into his neck as I rise. My stroke hits hard, and he falls grasping for his neck, unable to catch a breath with a crushed trachia. I reckon he will not rise. The horse carrying the second dismounting corpsmen is spooked by this and bolts up, sending the rider to his arse and upon the trailway. To his credit, he rises swift and sure, unsheathing his longsword in a single motion.

The longsword is a deadly weapon and without thinking and strictly on reflex, I draw my throwing blade and loose it in an overhead motion. It flies true and pierces the guardsman's neck from the front. His eyes go wide, and he reaches for his destroyed neck, even as he slumps to his knees. All over in a thrice.

Finnie comes running to me, bow still ahand, I note. But she drops it and throws her arms into a deathly grip around my neck. She is sweating.

Hugging her back quickly, I say, direct to her ear, "Quick now, Finnie, it is not over. Take these horses back to your chestnut and tether them as I drag these two down amongst the trees. The others will be upon us soon enough."

To her credit, she does not pause, but goes about it immediately. The others will be here shortly and will be extra wary when they see me.

Sure to that thought, squeaking wheels can soon be heard shortly after I had dragged the second dead guardsman from the trailway and into the woods. I kick the loose soil of the trail over the bloodstained ground as they round the same bend. Finding me still standing in the center of the byway, the two horsemen spur their mounts and swiftly approach, wary and drawing their swords, wondering, I am sure, why their two scouts had not dispatched this problem afore them.

The coachman has immediately reined in his team, throwing the break and leaping from the buckboard while drawing a crossbow out from under the wagon seat. The soldiers dismount in unison not ten paces in front of me, glancing furtively about.

"Your comrades made the same mistake you are making," I say boldly, and they draw up short. I draw my Bo-staff about in a sure manner and it makes them pause, but only for a moment. One advances quickly, bringing his broadsword above his head and ready to strike down upon me, extreme anger upon his face.

Acting in anger, a mistake.

Bane chooses that moment to strike. He springs from the trees, and after a few quick strides and a mighty leap, reaches this first guardsman, throwing his ten-stone of claw, tooth, and knotted muscle into the guardsman unawares. I turn my attention to the other, now totally distracted swordsman. In my mind's eye, he has become the swinging logman in Da's barn, and I attack in a flurry of strikes with my Bo, which somehow glows upon both ends.

The coachman is bending to a knee taking aim at me with his crossbow. As I finish with my attacker and stand, he is about to loose his bolt, even as an arrow's shaft appears to leap from his shoulder from behind. My sight focuses where Finnie stands, feet firmly planted, some fifteen paces behind him, having just loosed her arrow. The coachman screams in pain as he falls forward, no longer able to lift his crossbow. I nod at her and she back at me.

Seeing me trot forward, short sword in hand, Finnie throws her hands forward in a gesture to stop. Her face is pleading. No more, she clearly is saying. And so, I hold up, taking the crossbow away from the wailing coachman and stand above him as Finnie approaches. I glance behind me and see the others, one his throat torn asunder by Bane and the other with a pool of crimson spreading under his head which lay strangely askew to his body.

Stepping forward, I rip Finnie's arrow from the shoulder of the coach-man. He passes out at my feet. I promptly, and not delicately, cut and pull his tunic from his torso and bind his wound with the linen of his shirt. I do not bother to treat it. I then bind his wrists with a rope that Finnie has retrieved from the wagon for that purpose. When she hands it to me, four bedraggled youngers stand behind her on the trail watching me. It remains uncommonly quiet and dreary about us as I stare back at them, the hairs on the back of my neck prickled.

"They said of the coachman, he was the kinder of this group of slavers and has tended them in a different manner," Finnie says to me, making excuse for him, I think.

I nod that I'd heard, but my anger is barely in check, and I don't want the youngers to see. "Let us retreat aways into the forest and set up camp. We can see to our new friends, and when this thug wakes there'll be a few queries of him. Mayhaps a spell in his own cage is in order."

The group behind Finnie gasps at this thought.

I load the coachman into the cage and set Finnie about driving the wagon with horses tethered behind into the woods towards the other teth-ered horses. The children ride about and upon the cage in the wagon.

Whistling to Paint and drawing a rope around the ankles of the two horsemen, their bodies are dragged further into the trees on the other side of the trail, and I relieve them of their cloaks, weapons, and purses. They will have no further need of them.

We make camp a good way into the forest and next to a small stream we have found. We tend to each of the youngers, who are bruised and battered. One of the older lads has a broken arm. They are aged from but six-year to thirteen, and the youngest, to our dismay, is indeed a little lass dressed as a boy. Finnie holds up through it all admirably and we have them all bathe and I tend to the healing part. They are cut about and bruised a good bit more. The oldest lad's arm that broke I set, splint, and wrap it tight. We then go about preparing a meal from the wagon's provisions. The guardsmen had stocked it well for their own purpose.

As we sit and eat as a group, the youngers settle and tell us their tales. As we had suspected they would be, they are indeed tragic.

The two oldest are brœthers of thirteen and eleven-year, and the other two are brœther and sister of a different family altogether. Their capture and taking is the doing of others and not the guardsmen nor coachman and of similar circumstance to Finnie's home. With the telling done, there is much hugging, and no eye is dry among us. Lilit, Jilly, and Bane are of help here as they snuggle and lick the children about their ears and face. All are afraid of Bane but the girl, who comes and hugs him and buries her head into his furry neck to licks and snuffles. She laughs at this, and it does our hearts a little good.

The coachman finally wakes to the bars from inside the cage. He is barely able to sit upright within it. I reluctantly toss him a roll and some jerky. I then give him an entire water skin and tell him he should keep water in his belly to fight the pain.... But I do not care at that moment what he does. I leave him to himself for a while. I make my rounds in the woods outside of camp touring about to set up alarms. After a turn of a sand-glass, I make my way back to the cage and take in the manner and make of the man.

"Coachman, do you have a name?" I query.

He says nothing but stares across the camp at Finnie and the children.

"You owe her your life, you know. She can hit a running hare at twenty-five paces ten for ten times. You were a still, much larger target and aiming a crossbow at a dear friend of hers."

He turns to face me. A dour and defeated look about him.

"She had other motivation to shoot you dead as well, as she was taken from her family even as these youngers were."

His eyes wide, he turns back to look at Finnie once more. Reassessing.

"On the morrow's morn, I will have some queries for you. If you try to deceive me, know that I will see through it and I will not be of the same mind as she was. Think about that tonight. But answer truthfully and I will send you off with a chance at a different life." With these last words to him, I make my way back over to Finnie and the children. When I arrive, the lad of nine-year stands.

"Thank you, Ser, for saving us. We are all very grateful. They talked of selling us as slaves. We would like to know who has saved us, how should we call you?" he asks, acting quite mature for his years.

Afore I can even begin to answer, the little lass stands quickly and points to my chest. "Benjie, silly, see his crest, he is Ser Drægonheart!"

I study my chest and the image that Argo had branded upon it. Finnie covers her mouth to hide her grin. Thinking Drægonheart is more chivalrous than Bard, I bow back to her.

"At your service, fair maiden, you speak truth from your heart," I say, to a smile upon her face, spread ear to ear. "Alas, it is time to retire as the moon has ridden high into the sky. Gather your bedrolls around the fire and let us try to get some sleep."

Not a one puts up a fight as they pull the bedrolls about themselves. Little Seri leaves an arm out to lay across Bane as he settles to her side. Finnie pulls the younger boy Benjie to her and settles in amongst them as well. Lilit and Jilly stand watch over the camp, and I tend the fire well into the night, thoughtful, to myself.

Sunrise came and with it I see an entirely different side of Finnie. She has the children washing in the stream and then helping her make a mornmeal of flat cakes and rashers of bacon. Benjie finds some berries, and Finnie finds a way to make a berry syrup for her flat cakes.

I make a plate for the coachman and after he had finished, I open the cage and direct him out and into the woods. Bane follows with a low growl every few paces to let the man know he is there. We reach the trader's trailway after a silent walk, and then I motion him to a log and have him sit. Bane passes back and forth in front of him at but a single pace and sweat forms on the coachman's brow.

"Coachman, morn has come and your fate awaits. Only two questions I will ask. No half-truths, no half answers. Tell me what you know and I will set you free," I state, matter-of-factly as I stare without blinking into his eyes. He has seen what both I and Bane are capable of.

"Your two questions are, 'What Lord?'" I spit out the last word, "Then, 'What was the children's final destination?'"

The coachman's lip quivers, and his right hand upon his knee is trembling.

"I always tried to help them and keep them safe and fed along the way, I did. I never did them any harm for my part," he begins.

"And yet your work is still evil, ne'er the lesser."

"He's taken my land for back taxes that I could never afford to pay and then I must farm it still for him, and he makes me pay for the food I produce upon it for him. We are but his slaves, in effect. I earn a few coin more for this task and no questions. I use it for my daughter and my grandsons who are but infant youngers," he mumbles, but I hear in his voice that he is truthful.

"And then, what of your grandsons, man. Do you think he would not sell them as well? Even as he would do these children, when their time comes? ... I said two questions only, you can leave this one answered only to yourself?" Sarcasm fills my words.

"He will kill me," he says, his own voice dead.

"So then, what do you owe him? And after he kills you, what of your kin?" I've struck a chord. His family, his grandsons, probably the bastard sons of the guardsmen we killed or others of the same ilk.

"Your answer, coachman." He pauses, and I do not rush him. "It is the Lord of Tullamoor, he who stands as Lord against the mountains of the Northern Reaches and of Port Tullamoor, once called Seas-End. His guardsmen patrol the city streets. It is mostly the street urchins that he catches and sells to the markets. But of late, others, and not *his* guardsmen, bring him children to sell. He asks not from where they come, as they are just a product to him, even as fruit or linens that enter his port."

The coachman shakes his head now, realizing what he is saying and the truth of it. Blood rushes to my face as I hear his tale. There are more layers upon layers to this villainy than anyone could have suspected.

"The King allows this?" I cannot keep the anger from my voice.

"Mayhaps the King does not know as he has not been seen up in the coastal cities for nigh onto fifteen years. His soldiers, though there is steady conscription hereabouts in recent years, are seldom seen either. Our old Lord, who thought more of his land's people, has died and it is his son, not thirty year, that rules now." He shakes his head again.

There is silence for a good while as I ponder this coachman's words. There is truth in his telling.

"And my second query coachman?" I at last ask, finally of a mind to hear the rest of his tale.

"I cannot say to what far end the market is, though I've gathered it is Coffs Harbour to the far south and west of all of Aeryth. But we only travel aways south past the mouth of the great Lake, to a village in the foothills of the Dryad mountains. Some are sold to work the great mines there; the others travel the river further to the south."

"And what is the name of this village upon the foothills of the Dryad mountains?"

"It is called Dæmons Due."

"An apt moniker, coachman. I think one day I shall pay this village a visit." I pull my map from my tunic and place it afore him.

"This is a map of most all of the traveled traders' byways."

He looks at me in a new light. "Whomever gifted you this map was a well-traveled man, tis sure. We are here." He points. "And Dæmons Due is here, two fortnight to the South, at a good pace."

"Well then." I look him directly in the eye. "You have answered, and truthfully, I believe. Where will you travel now?"

"My wagon?"

"You will not be getting the wagon back, but if you swear an Oath to avoid Tullamoor guardsmen, I will grant you your life," I answer in a deadly serious tone.

He nods and swears then an Oath upon his grandsons.

"Bane, travel with the coachman for a while and see that he does not happen upon any strangers."

Bane bounces back and forth and gives a short but blood curdling howl as he stares at the man.

"I suggest you make haste coachman and keep to your Oath."

He does not hesitate and heads north upon the trail. Bane sets off to the tree line and keeps pace. The coachman furtively glances in the wolf's direction often.

I head back to the camp.

17

Quill'spie

Returning to the camp, I reckon that the youngers are our first responsibility, and Finnie is sure to think so as well. Showing Moor's map
to the coachman has aided in this endeavor a great deal. He had noted we
were within a few suns travel to a towne called Quill'spie. Moor had me
place to memory a man's name in that towne as his gift to me before I had
left the homestead. He is the towne's miller, and Moor had said to look him
up if I should ever travel there and that he would be of help in whatever I
may need.

The sun has reached its highest upon my arrival back to camp, and
Finnie greets me with a tilt of her head as she glances first to the cage and
then back to me. The lads note my return as well but little Seri runs to me
and hugs me about my waist.

"Ser Drægonheart, you did not kill old Artur, did you?" she questions
me with a furled brow.

I stoop to peer directly into her eyes. "Nay, lass, I did not."

From the corner of my eye, I see Finnie's shoulders relax and a sigh
escape her lips.

"They made him do it, you know. He had grandsons younger than me."

"Yea, lass, and it is my hope that he will attend to their safety in a place far away."

With that she returns to play with the furions and the lads. The lads welcome her as the younger sister they mean to protect. Finnie has apparently shot a beaver in my absence and has already begun to prepare a high-sun meal. 'Tis time to join the camp chores and so I do. The youngers are playing a game with sticks and a small hoop they've made.

"Ho, Lilit and Jilly, can you find some tubers, onions, and carrots, mayhaps, to feed this crew?" I ask. They immediately scurry about the children and I add, "You lads, and Seri, come get a basket and follow the furions to gather what they find. Do not travel far from camp and do not be gone long. I am hungry."

Little Seri rises and pushes the boys to their assigned task. This leaves me time to discuss with Finnie what had taken place with the coachman and what I think we should do. As we prepare the meal, I fill Finnie in on my conversation with the coachman. Her face flushes with anger at the thought of the regular trafficking of children to markets in the south of Aeryth.

"We must do something about this, Arias, and informing a King who has no interest in even traveling to these reaches is no answer," she says with clenched jaw, making it clear this is very personal to her. Her knife slams home through the tendons and bone of the meat she is preparing.

"Yea, Finnie, I am thinking that very thing. But first we must bring these youngers to safety. There is a towne not but two or three suns travel from here, and it is home to a friend of my friend Moor. He has instructed me to seek out his friends if ever I am in need."

A little hope springs to her emerald eyes.

"The towne is called Quill'spie, and we can leave for it on morrow's morn."

At night, the children help us as we tear apart the cage upon the wagon, using the guardsmen's own axes and pry bar. We make a great bonfire and the boys dance around it, forgetting their recent hardships and trauma as only youngers can do, and reveling in its destruction in celebration. Seri does not celebrate with the lads, however, and seeks solace instead in Finnie's arms. Finnie, in turn, is happy to oblige with an abundance of hugs and soft warm kisses. I can see that Finnie holds thoughts of her little sister Kattalæn, and Seri, mayhaps, sees her mœther in Finnie for a while.

The dawn breaks in a chill with clouds blanketing the sun, and even the birds are late going about their morn song and business. After a bustling morn-meal, as any with youngers mind be, we organize the supplies gathered from the guardsmen. Saddles and saddlebags, weapons and cloaks, and other provisions that came with the wagon, leaving room for the three lads in back with blankets about them and Seri beside Finnie on the buckboard huddled beneath one as well. The boys tucked in under the blankets, whispering and laughing in conversation amongst themselves.

The four guardsmen's horses and Finnie's chestnut mare are tethered behind the wagon. We will sell the horses and supplies in Quill'spie as recompense for the children's losses, in hopes it will help secure them a place somehow in the community. Two of the lads, we have come to know their names as Farren and Caden, said they had an aunt and uncle that might be in some manner contacted, and hence, a place to go. Benjie and Seri, however, have no kin that they know.

Setting off, first back to the trader's byway and then east towards our destination, Finnie has become coachman with her bow and quiver aside her. I wear my pack. My Bo-staff and bow are stowed along Paints flank in rigging I had made myself for just that purpose.

The youngers are in good spirits and the sun has finally made an appearance to curb the earlier chill. Lilit and Jilly ride amongst them in the wagon in lieu of their normal vigil in front of me on Paint's back. They keep the youngers entertained on our trip to this unknown towne of Quill'spie. However, I see trepidation in Finnie's features, though I, being truthful, am looking forward to our return to civilization. We have been absent from it for more than two moons.

We spend our next night in a camp at a small stream that lies close to the trail. We eat from our provisions as we had at a short stop earlier, a little after high-sun. The children are happy to be free of the rough ride atop the wagon.

On the next morrow, after high-sun, we meet up with the great Seas-End travelway which runs from Seas End—now called Port Tullamoor, as the coachman had explained—all the way to Coffs Harbor, hundreds of leagues to the south. Once upon the travelway, we turn north towards our destination where this great travelway meets one that heads east and where we will find the towne of Quill'spie.

As we travel, we meet a merchant's train of two great wagons accompanied by two hired guardsmen, and they make little sign of acknowledgement, save for the wandering eye of one of the coachman. Mayhaps he wonders at the tethered horses and a wagon of saddlery accompanied by a motley troupe. We also pass a family's covered wagon pulled by two oxen with two horses tethered behind. A young lad stands and waves to us, and our gang enthusiastically waves back. The parents hail greetings, and we hail the same in return. It seems that Finnie is beginning to relax a bit.

Soon a mail carrier is passing us by at a trot and I hail him direct.

"Well met, carrier. Can you tell us how much further to the towne of Quill'spie?"

He reins in for a moment alongside us, taking in the unusual sight before him.

"You will reach Quill'spie afore eve-meal at your pace. You speak with the voice of one from the far east, stranger. What brings you to our part of this world?" he asks.

"Nay, I hail from south and west from here, from the foothills west out of Middenvale." I meet his gaze, confused.

"I've traveled to Middenvale and to King's Court as well. Mayhaps, you speak with your parents' tongue, who are surely from the east of the Mid Realm," he says.

"Mayhaps," I return, though I know it not to be true, but it gets me to thinking ne'er the lesser. "We thank you for your help, carrier. Good weather to you."

The carrier nods and continues on his way.

It is a funny thing that I have never noticed before now, but the carrier indeed has the right of it. My expressions of speech are indeed very different than Da. And the more I ponder, they are different from the townspeople of Middenvale as well. It is a curiosity to me now.

Sure to the carrier's advice, we have come upon the towne of Quill'spie near to time for eve-meal, and as we enter towne, we find a bustle with townsfolk, wagons, carriages, horsemen, and such. Though few wagons are headed out of towne at this time, those that do are headed mostly north or eastward. The towne itself is much larger than Middenvale, mayhaps, fourfold at the lesser end from what I can see from this vantage.

There are some stables to our right as we come into towne and not much further on to the left stands an Inn with some amount of activity about it on the front porch. I pull up to the stables and have the youngers remain in the wagon as Finnie follows me into a large barn. I hail a stable hand to care for Paint and the other tethered horses as the stableman approaches.

"Well met, stableman. Can you board our wagon and mounts with a care?"

"Aye," he says, "it will cost a silver each night for the six horses, and you can stow the wagon in the corner there. I will keep it safe and no extra charge as I have the space about the yard just now."

"For a brush down and bag for each I wager it a fair price, sir, and I'll pay for three nights in advance," I offer.

Grabbing forearms, we finish conducting our business.

"The Inn up the way appears to do a good trade."

"Aye, the Innkeep charges fair price and his wife cooks up a fine stew and fills a trencher. The ale is the best in towne as well, to my taste."

"Well then, I'll take my brood there as we have a good hunger for just such fair." He nods in response, leading the horses away back to his business now.

Finnie catches a fair number of stares from menfolk as we make our way up the street, and they, a fair amount of elbows from their lady companions. Though she needs to shed some trail dust, Finnie's short auburn locks and bright emerald eyes, along with her green elk-skin tunic and suede trousers tucked in high boots, stands out amongst the ladies in long linen dresses. Finnie, of course, feels the stares and self-consciously brushes her hands through her short hair. She is a sight to behold as she carries her bow and quiver of arrow on her back and leads little Seri by the hand.

"You two are the prettiest ladies upon the street," I say with a grin and all the sincerity I can muster. Finnie eyes me gratefully, though I can she doubts my words.

"I appear a fair bit odd to these eyes about," she says, self-consciously glancing about at the towne folk.

"I only speak the truth, Finnie," and she brightens all the more. I direct my attention to the children. "Okay lads, dust yourselves off and wash up a bit at the trough's pump with me, and let us see if we might get ourselves an eve-meal."

I lead them to the pump to cheers and jubilant bouncing all around.

"Let me pump," says little Benjie, and I laugh at the sight of him jumping up to the handle and letting his weight pull it down. We end up more wet than clean, I fear.

I, of course, carry my Bo-staff and bow with my pack ever present on my back as well. We enter the dining hall to a cacophony of sound I'd not heard in a great while. I find it rather welcoming with laughter and the chatter of conversation all about.

We lead our small group to a long table with bench seating about both sides. The sun is low to the horizon as we step into the Inn. A fire has been started in the hall's great stone fireplace. I lean my bow and staff against the end of the table, and we take a seat on the benches. Lilit and Jilly have tucked themselves inside my pack, and it lays under the table betwixt Finnie's feet and mine as she lays her bow aside and sits across from me. The bustle outside carries on inside as well. Noise, laughter, and wonderful smells welcome us.

A buxom and wide-hipped woman enters from the kitchens and makes a direct line to our table. Her eyes dart every which-a-where, assessing the goings-on about the dining hall, and directing the few serving lasses to and fro. She n'er-the-lesser makes it to our table afore we've all settled, as if on a breeze.

"What can I get for you folk?"

"We've been on the travelway a good while and when we arrived to towne, the stableman advised the Inn's matron served a most hearty trencher and the best ale in towne. So, if you will, we'd like a board with cheese and fried taters for the youngers, and I'd like to partake of that trencher with some ale. Finnie, what will you have?" I turn to her as I respond to this woman that to all appearances must be the Inn's matron.

"I'll have whatever the matron suggests this day," Finnie adds. "And an ale as well, or a house wine, if you please."

With little pomp and more circumstance, the woman responds, "Well, I am the matron stableman Pæter speaks of, and he'll get a larger portion next he comes round for his kind words. You've ordered well, lad, and for your lovely lass with the short hair and beautiful eyes, I'll serve lamb chops with baked cinnamon-n-mint apple and some roasted carrots 'n taters as well."

The drool about the corners of our mouths must be evident. I'm having to wipe mine on my sleeve.

"Ooh," sighs Finnie.

"Call me Claire if you are needing something else," This friendly woman winks and is already turning to make her way back to the kitchens.

But, before she leaves, I manage, "If the Inn has two rooms that will accommodate us for a few days, we would be grateful."

She turns back and lets her eyes wander to the youngers.

"I'll send around the Innkeep in a bit."

Two travellers are seated at the table next to ours, and as we wait on our food, they strike up a banter reminiscent of times in Middenvale at Master Bergierre's Inn. Wiping his chin and pointing a long breadroll filled with what smells of some sort of fish, the one closest to me leans towards me. He makes to swallow a great mouthful and when he can, he speaks on a wafting fish-scent mixed with onion.

"Ho, that is a magnificently carved bow you have. You wouldn't have a mind to selling it, would you?"

It is most definitely fish. It's accompanying white sauce continues to drip down to the man's plate as the potent smell continues to swirl about and up to fill my nostrils.

A tall, muscled man that I take to be a local, has taken a sudden interest in our conversation. He too has been admiring my bow from the moment we had entered.

"You have a good eye for craft, stranger. 'Twas carved for me by my Da. Nay, I could not bear to put a price on its value to me. But, as sport, I'll make a wager with you."

The tall local's eyebrows rise now, a tilt to his chin evident as his curiosity rises.

"Indeed, it is beautiful. I don't think I recognize the wood it's crafted from, but the Drægon carved about the upper and lower limbs is exquisite in its detail. What is your wager?"

"I'll wager that if you can but string my bow, I'll sell it to you for three silvers," I state and Finnie stares at me in disbelief.

"Nay don't do it, Ari," she says. "I know the worth of that bow to you!"

"I'll take the wager," the stranger declares quickly, slapping three silver on the table afore me, knowing the bow's worth to be easily ten times the wager. But I know something further. The local across the way eyes me more close, a wonder in his eye.

Locals and strangers alike turn to us all about the dining hall and a quiet radiates out from us as they watch our exchange. 'Tis a wonder that folk's hearing can be so acute a'times.

"Yea, but you have not heard my side of the wager yet."

A curious expression sweeps across the face of the local giant of a man still seated in his corner.

"If you are unable to string my bow, and I warrant it will not be an easy thing, that you will agree to pay for my humble broods' meal this eve… and two more ales asides," I state to finalize the wager.

The two men laugh aloud. Folks all about do as well.

"Tis a wager then," he says, pushing his coin further towards me.

All eyes are upon him as he rises, and he picks up my bow as I grant him permission with a sweeping gesture.

He seeks to make short work of the wager, and he is clearly an experienced bowman. He has a firm grip about the Elven-vine bow string, and he puts his foot to the bow's lower limb even as he puts pressure upon its upper limb in a standard manner to bow the weapon and accept the bowstring. He finds to his surprise that the bow gives no ground to his pressure. Sweat beads upon his brow, and his comrade just laughs aloud to see his struggle and goads him on.

A good time has passed with the man giving me the evil eye and wondering how he'd been duped. The whole dining hall is laughing heartily at the sight until the local giant stands and pounds his mug against his tabletop.

Quiet creeps across the room. The giant says in a booming voice, "I'll wager an ale that our friend with the pretty bow has indeed played the stranger for a fool and the bow cannot, by no man here, be strung." He shakes his wide billed leather hat at me.

I stand, and in a thrice, string, nock, and loose an arrow at the man standing in the corner. The arrow pierces and sweeps the man's hat from his extended hand and with a distinct thud and twang, strikes it to the wall behind him. At this, three things happen in quick succession.

First, in the silence of the dining hall, little Seri leaps to standing on the bench seat pushing her hands toward me with distress upon her face.

"Ser Drægonheart! Please don't kill the Giant!" She screams, her hands and head shaking.

After a moment, the giant man booms in laughter, and a moment later the rest of the hall explodes in renewed merriment as well. I turn to Seri and say, "As you see, little one, the giant goes unharmed, and all parties see that indeed my bow does work as intended. So be seated, and I'll see if Mãam Claire can find a pie to add to our eve-meal."

She brings her tiny hands to her mouth, then bursts into her contagious laugh aloud as well.

The Innkeep, party to the whole affair as he had just before entered the room, now proceeds to our table.

"My apologies, Master Innkeep," I say, recognizing his post.

"None necessary young Ser... Drægonheart, was it? I'll sell a great bit more ale for your display."

"The table's fee goes to my tab, Keep, as payment of my wager," offers the stranger standing to grasp my forearm as I return his silver to him.

The giant approaches behind the Innkeep with my arrow in hand and his cap back firmly atop his balding pate.

"And ale for Ser Drægonheart and his lass is on my tab for the length of their stay within your establishment, Bastèœn."

"Many thanks, stranger. Though it is I that owes you for putting a hole to your hat. Please let me introduce my troupe to you and invite you to join us for eve-meal." Pointing as I do around the table, "This is Farren and Caden, across the way there is Benjie, this is Steffænie, and the little lass here who spoke vehemently on your behalf is little Seri of golden hair. Might we know your name, sir?"

"You can call me Fafhärd, if you will. I'm the miller in towne, and I'd be delighted to join you and the lady that 'twas so passionate to save my life," and Seri grins brightly.

We enjoy our eve-meal together, with many a patron coming over to pat me on the back and congratulate me on a brilliant wager. After the strangers at the table next to us have left, I turn to Fafhärd.

"I believe we have a mutual friend, Fafhärd. Indeed, he gave me your name as a contact should I ever make it to Quill'spie."

"And who might that be lad?"

"He is my mentor and calls himself Moor."

"Ha!" he booms. "The mouser then. I know Moor well. Indeed, we traveled together for a time. He's a master of sword and sorcery." He guffaws and then he winks. "Quicker than any with the rapier or dagger, either. Any friend of Moor I call friend as well. But other than Ser Drægonheart, what might I call you?"

"If you will, call me Arias. The other is little Seri's name for me." I chuckle.

Fafhärd's 'mouser' struck me in humour as I recalled Moor's preferred manner of garment, all of grey. And indeed, he would appear small next to this mountain of a man, near in size to Da.

I lightly pull Finnie to me, whispering into her ear, "Do you think you could take the lads and Seri to the kitchens for some pie?"

Overhearing, Seri squeals with delight and Finnie whisks them away. While our little group move to the kitchens, I tell the tale of the children and Finnie to Fafhärd. The shock on his face is telling and all lighthearted banter disappears that instant.

"What is it you need of me, Arias?"

"The youngers, Fafhärd, it is all about them at the moment. Farren and Caden have kin, but we don't know exactly from where they hail, and Benjie and Seri have nobody."

"Would you mind if I say something to Bastèœn and Claire? They may be of help?"

I agree to allow him that.

A muscle in his jaw twitches. "Do you know who is behind this evil villainy, Arias?"

"Yea, I do. At least one of the villains. But this goes beyond just one corrupt Lord abusing his power. There are buyers and the users on the other end as well." I reason. "I may not be able to shut it down in all ways, but I plan to fight it where I am able, and I will punish those that I can."

"Let us speak of this again on the morrow. Will you bring the youngers to my farm?"

"Yea, I think Steffænie would like that. But first I have horses and saddlery and even a wagon to sell, in hopes that we can produce a dowry to adoptive parents," I share.

"I may be able to help with that as well. If you'll excuse me, I have people to visit and things to do. 'Til the morrow then." Fafhärd stands and when I rise with him, he brings me into a back-slapping hug, as if we are family. He then disappears into the tavern to speak with Bastèœn.

I stay and stare into the flames of the firebox. A while later, Finnie joins me. She takes my hand in hers and whispers that the lads and Seri are asleep in a room above, with the furions to keep them company. I squeeze her hand and speak in a deliberate tone.

"Finnie, I have never in my life known such anger and I don't want to lose it. I want to punish these people. What they have done to you, your family, and… and to these youngers".

"Come upstairs with me, Ari. I need you to be next to me, or I'll not be able to sleep. There will be time on the morrow for such thoughts. This night, I just need you to hold me," she answers, and I go with her, able now to let my anger fade a little.

18

Here comes the Sun

wakened by the morrow's sun, which comes upon a gentle breeze through the open window, I sit up and try to take stock of my surroundings. The swirling air billows linen curtains hung about the window and the sun touches upon the cheek of Finnie who lays beside me still fast asleep. A scent of lavender tickles my nose from somewhere. This is the deepest, softest bed I've ever in my life lay upon. Taking a deep breath, scenes float back into place in my mind. Reluctantly and slowly, so as not to disturb Finnie in her peaceful slumber, I roll from the bed and thick bedcovers. I bemoan the squeak of the floorboards as I make my way to splash some water upon my face from the wash bowl. Slipping into my tunic, trousers, and boots, I quietly pull the door to, exiting into the hallway.

I am met at the bottom of the stair by Claire and pulled into a strong, motherly hug as she whispers into my ear all the time of it, "You beautiful, beautiful man."

I stare back in wonder, when she finally releases me.

"Come, come," she says. "Ye've a little time afore morn-meal. Your beautiful missus bathed yesterday, now 'tis your turn."

175

Missus, I think to myself. And then, lavender… and then I lift my arm and bend my nose to it.

"Earthy and quite manly," chuckles Claire.

She leads me to the back and then out of the Inn proper. We walk across a flowered courtyard. Sitting high above a back building, a barrel of tremendous size, mayhaps the size of twenty of the largest oaken barrels I've ever seen, dominates the view. It is easily the height of two men the size of Da, and it has large copper piping running its height and into the top and another somewhat smaller leading from the bottom and into the building below it.

"It is a wonder. What is it?" I blurt out.

"'Tis a water tower, don't ye know?" Her eyes widen quizzically. "And the water is piped to a boiler for the laundry and the baths. Have ye no seen such a thing? Your Steffænie soaked in our lavender tub yester-eve, but I was thinking ye might be preferin' a hot shower. There now, in with ye then."

She points to an outer door which once inside, holds a hall of swinging half doors in small alcoves. As I walk its length, inside each stall is a chain with a worn oaken pull attached, and below there's a drain in the floor. I remove my garb and hang it upon a hook provided outside one of the stalls.

I enter and pull upon the chain. A large, round, copper fixture with dozens of holes and likened to a watering can that Effie used in her garden, sends hot water to hit me full aface from above. 'Tis raining upon me with a steaming shower of water. Three bar of scented soap formed with cords within them hang from pegs upon the wall, and in addition there hangs a wash linen as well. I take my time scraping and showering, soaping and showering. I smell of cinnamon and apple as I finish up.

As I exit the shower, a linen as thick as sheep's wool is there to dry myself. When I go to pull on my tunic and trousers, I find instead thick linen shirt and brown cloth trousers in their stead. My boots remain, but the dust has been beaten from them.

Leaving through the door back to the courtyard, the lads and Little Seri are coming out from another door, aside to the one I left from, their hair still damp and all with brand-new garment as well. Finnie, Lilit, and Jilly are waiting for us at the table on a veranda overlooking the courtyard.

Little Seri runs to me and hugs me about the waist. "Oh, you smell good Ser Drægonheart!"

My face flushes to think this has not been the case these past few days, and I think of sleeping next to Finnie last night and then remembering how she had smelled of lavender and honey.

The table is stacked with a meal fit for a king, and my first thought is we cannot afford to live like this for more than this sun alone. But it is irresistible ne'er the lesser. There are flat cakes smothered in rich butter and blueberry sauce, rashers of bacon, mashed taters with the smell of garlic, and eggs scrambled with garden greens and cheese. A brie, by the scent of it. A berry and melon fruit salad sits as the centerpiece of the table.

Our gang settles around the table and immediately begins to tuck in. Claire appears with a piping hot kettle of tea and another that smells of Java bean. Finnie reaches for that kettle, and I for the tea.

"I did not know we had picked an Inn that catered to simple families as royalty. We may need to seek more humble lodging, Finnie," I whisper to her so only she can hear.

She near bursts at the seams in a good-humored manner and looks to me with sparkling eyes that seem to hold a secret.

"Ari, yester-eve, after your friend Fafhärd spoke with Bastèon and Claire Bijou, the owners of this fine Inn, and while you did stare into the fire hearth for ages upon end, they came to me and offered us free food and lodging for a time. They are mighty proud that you would risk your life, and more than once, as I explained to them, for the safety of us all."

My faith in people has restored in the moment, knowing though evil and villainous actors exist in this world, also the common and everyday folk stand in the majority and win out. I will help it be so, making it my life's work if need be. I join back into the meal with a fierce hunger and start tucking in. Finnie leans in to kiss my cheek. This alone warms me to my toes.

"You have a most wonderful scent about ya this morn, Ari." I make note to myself that I shall bathe more oft, and query Claire if I might purchase one of her soaps.

As we are finishing our meal, Bastèœn Bijou comes to meet us and following him, the stableman.

"Pardon, Ser Drægonheart," says Bastèœn.

"Arias, if you please, Master Bijou,"

"Of course, and call me Bastèœn as a friend, if you will. Pæter, here, would like a word."

My heartbeat speeds up. "Is there a problem with my horses, stableman?"

"Nay...Ser. It's just that the miller, Fafhärd, has mentioned that you are in the market to part with them...the horses, I mean. I'd be willing to give fifteen silver each for the four mares and two gold and five for the stud stallion. I'd be willing to pay a stud fee for your Paint as well," says Pæter.

This morn has become all the sunnier.

"Your prices are fair, even generous, master stableman. The Chestnut is not for sale as she belongs to Steffænie here, but I will certainly part with the others at your offer and if Paint takes a fancy to a mare while you board and pasture him, I will not stand in the way of love. If his seed takes, you can pay me next I pass through your wonderful towne."

"I'll see to getting your coin then and consider your Paint's board and pasture covered in our agreement," he says after grabbing my forearm in confirmation of our agreement before leaving us.

We have finished our morn-meal and the lads are patting bloated bellies in fun when our new friend Fafhärd arrives to meet us. "Ho, Arias and Steffænie. Well met this morn."

Hugs are given all around.

"Sit a moment longer if you will," he booms and we do.

"My wife, Jænelle, and I would be honored if you two, along with the youngers, of course, would join us out to the farm this sun."

As he is speaking, Seri has climbed upon his lap and turns to face us.

"Oh, can we go Finnie, can we go? I like Master Fafhärd, the Giant, he's so funny." She laughs as she snuggles deeper into his lap. Then, over her shoulder to him, "Do you have chickens and ponies?"

"That we do, littlest one, and tiny piglets too!" Seri's eyes light up.

"Well then, it is settled, I see," say I. "Let me unload the wagon and see to the contents, and we can follow you to the farm."

"I've already taken the liberty," Fafhärd says with a throaty guffaw. "I know the Masters of the saddlery and the smithy quite well. They said they will give you a price on your wares later this eve and what they will not purchase, the tinker that serves these parts will most likely be here on the morrow and he turns little aside."

I just shake my head. "Moor has not led me astray in sending me to you Fafhärd I am in your debt, to be sure."

His shoulders slough in relief.

"Nay," his retort, "and if that bow of yours comes from where I believe it might, it is I who still owes a debt."

"My Da crafted this for me. His name was Ètœn Bard."

Fafhärd's eyes go wide and of a sudden glisten with just a hint of moisture in their lower lids.

"I knew of an Ètœn Bearheart once, and he fancied himself a Bard. I believe they are one and the same. As it was in the Inn's food hall, your pitch and wager were his selfsame, and he is the only other I've known with such a bow. But it strikes deep as you talk in a manner that says he is no longer with us," he says in a disheartened way. "I know…I *knew* Ètœn well and was ever in his debt as he saved my life not once, but twice in years long past. He was a man of the strongest honor."

With a tilt of my head in wonder at this new moniker for Da, I return,

"Bearheart. I'd like to hear your tales when you have time, for I am learning there is much more to Da's life tale than I ever knew," my voice is throaty to match my mood. Finnie notices and reaches to cover my hand with hers.

"And having met you, I see there has been more to his life's tale as well!" the great man remarks.

"Well then, let us be off to the farm. Jænelle is expecting all of you and will be disappointed if we do not arrive soon as she has baked a surprise in her oven."

"Hup," he grunts, lifting Seri over his head and planting her on his shoulders to giggles and glee.

I gather my pack, bow, and staff and meet them outside. Paint is saddled and ready and the wagon holds the lads who are seated upon bales of hay within the wagon's bed. Finnie climbs to the buckboard, and Fafhärd places Seri upon the seat next to her. Fafhärd mounts a great steed of spotted gray, near to the size of Da's Bregœ. I mount Paint, and Lilit and Jilly scurry up to their usual place on the saddle afore me. The big man eyes me, seeing the furions and eyeing the Drægon branded across my chest and chuckles as he turns his mount and leads us away to the cheers of the youngers.

By the time the morn's sun has passed halfway to its zenith, we come upon a stone bridge over a deep and swift moving stream that in the distance turns a waterwheel serving a mill. We ride into a refreshing breeze with just wispy clouds above. A large cottage and barn are set upon the farmstead with pastures that at once remind me of my own homestead. The cottage is larger and built with a second story above, and there are windows open and linen curtains of bright colors flowing in the breeze. Clearly a working farm as all manner of livestock are evident and cultivated fields can be seen leading up to the edges of forests to the north and eastern borders of the property.

As we approach the cottage, a slender woman with soft and wavy brown hair with a curl to it can be seen upon the front porch and is leaning against a thick cedar post. It is one of many holding up a large porch roof topped in copper and tinted green about its seams. Coming closer still, the lovely lady with hazel green eyes waves greets her husband and spreads her arms in opening welcome to her new guests. A small dog of gray leaps, bounds, and barks about her, and little Seri cries out in joy to see the sight. The dog bounces all the more. Having come closer now, it has what appears to be a mustache and a small beard and nearly no tail at all.

Reining in his great gray mare, Fafhärd dismounts in front of the cottage porch and unabashedly pulls the lady to him and kisses her with a passion, for more than a moment, for all to see. He then turns back to us.

"Arias and Steffænie, I would like to introduce the most intelligent and beautiful woman in all of Quill'spie, my wife Jænelle," he booms.

A flush comes over her at her husband's boast.

"'Tis an honor to meet you all. Prithee, excuse my loving husband's useless prattle and be welcome to our home," she says in a sincere tone and with the warmest smile to match her bright hazel eyes.

Finnie helps Seri to the ground and watches as she bolts forward to the small gray, bouncy creature.

"May I pet her, Mãam Jænelle?" she squeals.

"Assure!" returns Fafhärd's lovely wife.

Jilly and Lilit decide to join the fun and jump from Paint's back to scurry about the strange gray creature. Jilly lightly nips at her stubby tail and runs a bit away. The small dog gives chase only to fall victim to Lilit doing the same. The result is a hilariously fun time for all including the lads and Seri. With the youngers about their fun, Finnie and I are invited to join Fafhärd and Jænelle for a sweetened drink of lemon water in chairs arranged in the shade of the great porch on the front of the cottage.

"Fafhärd returned home yester's eve and told me the tale of the youngers and we spoke of it till nigh onto the moon setting. You see, I am a teacher of the youngers in towne and love them so, but my big lovable oaf of a husband has yet to place a baby in my belly. And 'tis not for lack of trying, I can assure," she says brazenly and brings a flush to Finnie's cheek and a wink from Fafhärd towards me.

"He claims an old war injury and ever begs for another chance," she continues very nonchalantly. "Anyway," she says a bit nervously. "If Seri and her brœther... Benjie? If they will have us, we would be honored and grateful to make them a part of our family."

Fafhärd leans toward her and places his large hand over hers.

"That is a very, very generous offer," says Finnie. "Let us see, and maybe we can discuss it with Benjie and Seri later."

She smiles and Jænelle returns the gesture.

"Also," says Fafhärd. "The tinker of whom I spoke, is very well traveled, and if he can cypher from the older lads, mayhaps we can discover where their kin live and deliver them home. And they, likewise, are welcome to share our home until then."

This is indeed good news, and I sigh in a genuine way for the welfare of the youngers. Reaching down into my pack that I had laid aside, I pull from it a purse full of coin that we had collected from the thugs we had encountered in our efforts to save the youngers.

"Please, accept this coin to help in purchasing garments and sundries of which they are in need." Turning to Finnie I say, "Finnie, this towne and these folks are good people and generous. Mayhaps the Bijous could use help. You could take the coin from the horses and start a life among these good people.".

Fire comes to Finnie's eyes. She stands.

"I will do no such thing, Ariastone Côeurdrægon Bard! Your quest to rid us of this scourge is mine first! I will see them suffer for all they have caused…and you will not turn me aside from it." There is now a steel in her voice and fists clenched at her sides.

Rising, I cup each of her shoulders and place my forehead to hers and in this caught her off guard, I think, but I am proud of this lady warrior.

"Then settle yourself, I will not ask it of you again, as I see it is in your heart as it is in mine. I only wish to keep you safe," I whisper.

"I feel safest when I am with you, Ari," her voice softens as she holds my gaze. "And you have trained me well. I would be with you as you punish and rid these hateful scum from Aeryth."

This discussion now settled, Fafhärd returns his attention to me and I him.

"Arias, we'll accept this coin, as we will send it with the brœthers when we find their kin. But know that we need no coin to help us with Seri and Benjie, as the mill has been a good venture for us and we want for naught. We will raise them as our own, so set your minds at ease."

"Steffænie, would you help me prepare for the midsun-meal for this brood? And we can leave the men to their own designs, and I would have a further word outside their hearing," Jænelle asks, beckoning her forward.

Finnie laughs with her new friend, happy to speak with a woman for a change, sure certain.

"You are a very lucky man, Fafhärd," I say, eyeing the women as they enter the cottage.

"I do believe, Arias, you are as well."

My heart gives me an extra beat.

Later, as dusk creeps up from the distant tree line, we are again sitting out on the porch and the youngers are helping Fafhärd feed the chickens and piglets a snack. A familiar warming in my heart comes upon me and I say to Finnie, "Bane is returning."

Finnie glances to me and then to Jænelle.

"Jænelle, do not be alarmed, but Bane is Arias' wolf friend, and he will not harm you or your farm animals, but be warned he is a large and fierce looking creature," warns Finnie.

Jænelle looks to Finnie, a little wide-eyed and then turns her head and stares at me in a curious manner.

"How is it you would know such a thing? I heard no howl or any un-usual sound at all. The barn animals would surely sense a creature such as you describe around the homestead."

"Bane is stealthy. More so than any mountain cat and he approaches upwind," I explain, "but he approaches openly today." I rise and step off the porch.

I nod to the tree line to the north. I look about and see that Seri senses him immediately as well.

Jænelle reflexively raises her hand to her mouth as she spies the more than formidable wolf. He lopes easily toward us, and Fafhärd glances up to see Seri running as fast as her short legs can carry her towards us as she sees that we are Bane's target.

He reaches us moments before Seri and leaps to put his paws upon my shoulders nuzzling my face. And then Seri tackles him full force, burying her face into his belly and taking him to the ground.

"Bane," she squeals and Jænelle screams out in concern. I merely laugh as Bane puts a long slobbery tongue to her cheek and rolls over for her. She attacks his belly in a tickling frenzy, and Bane gives a friendly and throaty growl all amid her effort.

Bane is back.

"Ho, Arias, you must tell us the tale of this fearsome beast with the heart of a puppy," the big man comments as Jænelle stands aside, still nervous.

"He will respond in this manner to but a handful, and Seri is a wonder. They had a special bond immediately, even as it was with Steffænie. I cannot tell you why, but our own bond is of a nature I cannot explain." I then go on to explain how we had found him.

"I've heard tales as a younger, about the Mountain Dread's, but never'd known a tale that would explain your wolf's behavior. He is a remarkable beast."

"He is fierce beyond compare but would never harm and even guards my friends with the fervor matched by my own. So fear him not," I say and reach in to rake my hand betwixt Bane's ears.

Lilit and Jilly have come to join the fun, and Seri climbs up to Bane's back to ride him like a pony as the furions nip at his paws and tail. The gray pup with a beard stays put in Jænelle's lap, a little tremor playing along its spine.

"Tis time for eve-meal," Jænelle finally says. "The stew's been a'pot long enough and the trencher bread is ready baked and still warm. What do we feed your friend, Arias?"

"No need. He will find his own dinner or has already most likely done so and he will be fine to himself out of doors. Farren, Caden, Benjie, and Seri, to the pump with you and wash up if you'll be wanting any eve-meal!" I shout to them and send them on their way.

After the meal, we explain to the youngers what our plan for them is. Seri then asks with a pout, "Mãam Jænelle and Master Fafhärd have been very good to Benjie and me, but are you leaving? Will we not see you, Bane, or Lilit and Jilly no more?"

Finnie pulls Seri to herself and kisses her forehead. "Of course, we will come and visit, and you will be living with a teacher and a master miller. We expect you will have much to show us when we return."

Seri accepts this with a squeeze about Finnie's neck as she buries her head there.

Finnie and I stay with Fafhärd and Jænelle that night and return to the Bijou Inn on the morrow's morn, having said our fare-thee-wells to the youngers. We stay another night at the Inn and sort our affairs. The third morn, having purchased further provisions, we make our way back onto the trapper's byways with a specific and vengeful purpose in mind.

We would keep our promise to Seri and see her and Benjie three more times in as many moons.

But it is with sad hearts we come each time, bringing with us more youngers and tales of death to villains. Fafhärd helps us find homes amongst the farmers of the vale for the orphans we bring that have no other kin. Fafhärd and a few others begin to patrol the byways as well, taking up arms, liberating and punishing and doing that which the Kingsmen or Lordsmen should be rightly doing.

Though folk do not know who the ultimate perpetrator of the evil was, word begins to spread of the vigilante called Drægonheart who has risen against it with great success.

19

The Lord Tullamoor

Lord Tullamoor's eagle soars across the plain before catching a sudden updraft over Goose Run River, where it rises high towards the clouds and circles for a time, surveying the landscape below. From this height, its view will include the great inland sea to the north and east and at its closest shore sits Port Tullamoor, still known as Seas End to all of Aeryth but those under Lord Tullamoor's eye. To the west and north, the great Western Range Mountains, which pick up where the Shadow Mountains leave off, dominates the horizon. In that same direction, mayhaps two leagues distant, sits Tullamoor Keep. Its view below includes the river, flowing from the western range and to the sea and a great, sparsely wooded plain spans the distance from the port city to the Keep and borders to the south by great woods.

But the eagle holds intent on other things. It collapses its wingspan about its gray and white body and dives towards the ground 50 poles below. Its eye is clearly on prey. It is a very large and majestic raptor and can easily prey upon creatures of a size the equal to a hoary fox or larger still. It is aptly named a Marshall Grey for its plumage and regal appearance. This particular bird is an especially magnificent specimen and this falconer's most prized possession.

Standing waist high to a grown man, weighing a full stone and with a wingspan equal to the height of a tall man, his favorite bird of prey will return, as it always has with a worthy prey clutched in its talons. With its mighty build, there is no need to send a falconer's squire to retrieve its prey as it can carry aloft thrice its own weight for a distance. It will lift its prey and return it to him.

Standing over the retrieved prey, the falcon will obediently wait with tufted crown ruffled high until the hunt master lops off its prey's head for tribute to the falconer, leaving the body of the creature as reward to the falcon.

The great hunting bird even now is returning from this hunt, as his close advisor, Spæctor, and the Sergeant of his personal guard troops, Kêsh as he recalls, approaches. He should remember to use the name. It will give the man a sense of worth. It would be a balance to the dressing down he is about to receive. The two have been summoned to him. His manservant had been given orders to inform them only after he had been gone a full turn of a sand-glass. He likes it that they will need to go to the trouble to find him out on the plain.

The two dismount even as Thaôs Tullamoor's falcon returns with its prey. The giant bird dropping a large creek lizard some four paces from him. The raptor snaps at its eyes as it digs its talons deeper into its neck to keep it still. Admiring the bird's conquest, the Lord thinks the lizard's tail will make a delicious eve-meal and he instructs the falconer to remove it for that purpose. Besides, eating the hunts reward would give the Lord reason to regale his dinner guests. Tullamoor grants the majestic bird the spoils, and it will not again be hooded until it eats its fill. The bird feasts first on the soft eyes of the prey, and Lord Tullamoor smiles inwardly at the sight.

He admires the beauty of this bird that is such an efficient hunter, and by extension, himself also. The eagle has cost him two strong lads and a farmer's virgin daughter, but is certainly well worth the price. After all, the four had cost him but a few Silvers and the farmers' wives as spoils for his special troops.

The falcon is clearly a champion. Its onyx eyes can distinguish the individual hairs on a fox from sixty poles high. The bird just then gives a war cry and spreads its large wings. Their deep grey plumage shines stunning against its gray spotted white breast. It is Lord Tullamoor's prized possession and as he owns much, that is high praise.

Thoughts of its original cost bring him back to the present and why he had sent for his trusted advisor and Sgt. Kêsh, the man responsible for administering shipping services of Lord Tullamoor's product through the Mid-Realm and to the far side of the Southern Reaches. And so, he turns his attention to the business at hand.

"Sgt. Kêsh," he barks, and the soldier bends to one knee and quickly rises again. "Can you explain why but one half of my shipments have made it to their destinations over the past two moons?"

"And I have lost twenty of my men in that same..." replies the Sergeant, looking past the Lord's shoulder in deference.

"Your men!?" Lord Tullamoor stomps forward to a hand's width from the soldier's ear. His breath burns the sergeant's nostrils, his spittle assaulting his ear. Tullamoor's face grows red. "I care not for the incompetent ineptitude of your fools, I care only that my product has not reached Coffs Harbor and I've lost significant coin to their failure!"

"Yes, Lord Tullamoor," he returns stiffly, his eyes to the ground now.

"And what meaning am I to take from their failure? Have they been negligent or just poorly trained?"

Sidestepping the obvious pitfall of answering such questions, the Sergeant offers instead a solution.

"We mean to turn the tables on this vigilante group that has attacked our convoys and stolen your product and have devised an ambush of our own to sort the matter, Lord," he answers, succinct and confident again, more to his nature.

"Spæctor?" Tullamoor turns to address his advisor, His voice calm and measured now.

"The plan has merit, Lord, and though it will use a great deal of resources, he should sort the issue once and for all," responds Spæctor Legermæn, the Lord's advisor.

Turning back, Thaôs Tullamoor barks, "Be off and get about it then Sergeant, and best not return to me, twice a failure."

The soldier mounts his steed and sets off at once. Again, Tullamoor turns to Spæctor.

"What of our search for this lad that the King seeks? Why have we not seen progress in that venture? I would like to be the one responsible for delivering the rogue. Kingsmen roaming over our lands searching for this lad and we bear the risk of them stumbling upon our enterprise."

"After receiving the request by carrier bird, our men were first to the homestead where the Kingsmen confronted their treasonous fellow guard. The man and the lad lived as outliers to the closest community, and the citizens there either had little knowledge or are tightlipped about what they really know. Apparently, the lad was but sixteen-year and did limited schooling in towne, and the man was said to be somewhat of an animal whisperer and did only occasional work for farmers and townsfolk," reports Spæctor.

"But, on a separate inquiry in King's Court, I've learned that this man may have been the very guard that stole away with the King's daughter near to eighteen year ago," finishes the Lord's advisor.

"Hmmm," ponders Lord Tullamoor. "Mayhaps this lad's worth is more than advertised. Let us step up our efforts to find him. If he has traveled further north than the Eastway and the Kingsmen did not find him on the road south, we should be able to find him and garner favor for ourselves in court."

"One other thing, Spæctor?" says Tullamoor. "With all of this vigilante business, is there any word of the connection betwixt me and the product?"

"Nay, Lord. We've made certain that the guards do not wear or carry any identifiable garb or weapon of Tullamoor. Even the horses carry no brand. They are from our hired corpsmen. Also, it appears all guards and coachmen have been eliminated. The reports have it that the vigilante many have named *Drægonheart* appears in townes near where the ambushes have taken place. He is well-regarded amongst the townfolk, and it is he that is responsible for the total of our losses," continues Spæcter.

"How can one man take on four or five of our men and come away without a scratch? Not once, but several times now!" growls Lord Tullamoor.

"Word has it the recovered youngers have spoken of a sky-bolt fast and seasoned warrior that wields, by different accounts, a bow, a staff, throwing blades, or a short sword. The tales grow more fantastical with each rescued brood. A man from storied tales of the King's battles of old, they say. But all call him by the same name, Drægonheart, as he wears a Drægon sigil upon his chest," responds Spæctor.

"For his sake, the Sergeant had better be sure his trap bears fruit. This vigilante has garnered too much attention. We will need to discuss alternative routes, as well, in the future," hisses Lord Tullamoor.

With that, the impeccably coiffed and garbed Lord gives his falconer orders to hood his prized bird after he has finished his meal, as he sets out back to his keep accompanied by his personal guards.

Spæctor stares after Lord Tullamoor as he rides off. He has a good life as the Lord's counsel. He'd cemented his place by recognizing him for what he really was and tutoring Tullamoor in how to gain his prize. How to subtly feed his pæder, a once revered Lord, the powdered Astor thistle, thus causing his pæder to suffer from symptoms attributed to an addled brain which the healers knew had no cure.

When the Lord's older son, Ronælt, did not return from an expedition into the Northern Reaches, Thaôs Tullamoor stepped up to rule and had done so for these past five years. Only he and Spæctor himself know that the older brœther still lives and that he is the sole occupant of the Lord's special dungeons in Tullamoor Keep. He has always been wiser and more popular and certainly the rightful heir. Thaôs finds it amusing and satisfying that he still survives in a solitary, stone, windowless pair of rooms, just below his sadistic brœther's life of excess. Spæctor remains the only one to interact with the prisoner, he himself never seeing him. He but drops raw foodstuffs down a well hole three stories deep and not wide enough for a man to climb. Stove wood and candles are granted the man as well. The rooms are well furnished and have access to fresh water for washing and disposing of his brœther's personal waste, but a most times dark and confining prison ne'er-the-lesser.

With his greed and penchant for young girls in his bed, Thaôs has been quite easy for Spæctor to bend to his whims without being the wiser. Offering a virgin, which they later turned into an enterprise, and Thaôs called bloodsport, and then arranging for his precious bird of prey, Spæctor has been able to make a plan for himself that fits his needs quite handsomely. His brethren in Kings court and he are pleased with their combined success. But this vigilante nuisance needs to be stopped and this rogue lad the King seeks offers an opportunity that shall not be squandered as well.

First and foremost, though, this '*Drægonheart*' needs to be dealt with.

Sgt. Kêsh's plan is sound but will take a good many men to execute. They know the vigilante has been attacking the shipments north and west of the towne called Quill'spie. They have somehow learned their methods and travel routes. They have backtracked from the expected check-in points along the caravan route to the south. The bodies of the guardsman and coachmen are found and personally examined by the Sergeant, himself.

Those he has found were all killed in an efficient and professional manner. The guards were killed expertly with arrows to the heart, blades to the neck and by blunt trauma to the head. Each one killed efficiently, probably dispatched with minimum engagement.

This Drægonheart is obviously a seasoned warrior with no conscience. He is either very smart or very lucky. Kêsh will assume the former.

His plan is to find a suitable spot just north of the previous attacks and make the vigilante come to him. The caravan will be as the others before it. Two guards will ride ahead of the wagon and two more will stay with it, but that will be only the visible. He has arranged for the wagon to appear to have a broken wheel and stopped along the trail. On either side of the trail, just inside the tree line, four bowmen will lie in wait. Behind a bend in the byway and just further north, four mounted swordsmen will wait until the others engage the vigilante and then they will approach from their position. Thirteen trained soldiers, including the coachman will put an end to the Lord's supply bottleneck.

Finally, as he has learned from his brœther, a Kingsman in the King's specially trained squads, there will be one more man, a trained observer. This soldier will not engage but only observe and should things go awry, the observer will report back. He has decided that the observer this time, will be himself. He has every confidence he will be returning with the vigilante's head for Lord Tullamoor.

To ensure the vigilante is engaged, he will make sure the bait will be irresistible. An infant lass and her adolescent brœther and two young sisters near ten or eleven-year. They would fetch a premium for Lord Tullamoor and with the added head of the vigilante, he will again be in the good graces of the Lord. Mayhaps even a bonus would be in order for him.

Finnie and I have established a routine with our life on the trapper's trails. But life these past suns have become sullen. We've rescued fourteen children and have dispatched twenty guardsman and coachmen in the process. Fafhärd has arranged homes for the orphans in the farms around and about Quill'spie.

Our routine is to make camp about 100 paces from the trail they are travelling. My acute hearing leaves me able to hear travel on the trail and spy if it is a slaver's wagon. These caravans happen on the byways sometimes twice in a moon cycle. We can but wonder why the countryside is not completely up in arms over such a thing. But then, we reason that few, if any, survivors are available to tell the tale and more the pity for it.

Sitting around the fire, an unease creeps and niggles about my mind on this moon's eve, and I cannot put my finger to it. Finnie remains out of sorts as well, but I know it is for other reasons. Her anger at the wrongs done to her and these children has fueled her desire to train and learn and act against the slavers, but time has begun to heal her as well. Effie's *Calming* techniques and the Chē-Song routine each morn have helped to ease her mind and turn it more each day from the need to strike back at the slavers and towards helping the victims. She speaks more openly to me and laughs easily at times, even amidst this grim work we've set ourselves about. Ofttimes, the reality of our present calling would overcome her, and she would grow sullen. She is in such a state even now; I can feel it, but I know she can also see that I am uneasy. We have grown so much closer. She feels my moods and thoughts, even as I do hers.

"What has you out of sorts, Arias?" she asks.

"I am not certain, but something is off. We have not encountered any of our evil foes in too long a while."

"But I am feeling better for the same reason. Mayhaps, they have realized that there is not the same profit their evil has bestowed before," she reasons.

"I believe you have hit upon part of it, Finnie. Mayhaps they have just recently realized that their slaves for sale have not been making it to market," I say and pause and ponder this. "But I fear they would not give up their coin so easily and they would be greatly angered at losing what they have. Mayhaps, in some manner, they have sorted where their caravans have gone missing and either changed the route or are aiming to eliminate the bottleneck. That bottleneck would be us."

Finnie shivers at the thought.

"I'll ask Bane to scout ahead of us on the morrow. My gut tells me something is awry, and both Moor and Effie preached that I should listen to my deeper instincts in all matters," I conclude, and we curl up beside each other at the fire. We have slept in such a manner now for some time. Besides the comfort of it, it stirs within me a warmth that feels right. Emotions that I know I want to explore but unsure that Finnie is ready.

Morn on the morrow has come again and we wash and eat and are ready for where the sun will lead us. I call Bane to me and the furions as well. I find myself a seat amongst the raised roots of a large oak tree. Finnie glances to me and recognizes that I am preparing to bring my body, mind, and spirit into the *Calming*.

Lowering my heartbeat, I ease my mind of all things and once again reach for the *Calming*, where my mind and spirit breathe as one and my thoughts are clear, and ideas coalesce. It also lets me reach out to Bane, and more recently, the furions as well. As I sit and absorb the *Calm*, Bane, and then the furions appear to me as kindred energies. In this state of mind, I can "ride within" Bane. I can see what he sees and experience all of his senses as my own.

I can now do the same with Lilit and Jilly. When I visit them each in turn, I can also feel the kindred spirit that they feel for each other. A very strong bond. Prior, never had I tried to accept more than one of the creatures into my *Calming* at once, but during the night I had dreamed of doing just that, and it has prompted me to try it now, this very morn.

As it happens, a number of revelations present themselves to me this sun, as destiny descends upon us once more. As my spirit-self merges with Bane, he accepts me unconditionally and then the warmth of the spirit-furions next to me in the *Calming* came. I first reach out to Jilly and she merges to my *Calming* also, and I feel Bane, Jilly, and myself joining as if one. There is no hesitation with either. And as this happens, I realize deep within me that both Bane and Jilly feel the same. Of a sudden, the second furion joins us, no thoughts on my part to initiate it. The strong natural bond between the two furions makes it happen of its own.

The four of us are now bonded as a whole. Each knowing and feeling and seeing what the others do. A bit overwhelming at the first of it, as I let myself relax back into the *Calming*, it becomes a natural sense of being. The others do not appear to have the same problem. To them it immediately becomes a most natural empathetic bond.

I bid Bane search out ahead of us along the trail, but not before the furions scurry onto his back to join him. He is large enough, and they small enough, that this has become easily possible now. Finnie would later tell me the sight of it was remarkable as Lilit and Jilly had bounded from my lap as I sat against the tree in a trance and scurried atop the Wolf. Bane then nonchalantly heads out into the woods as if this is a natural thing. As he exits the camp, he becomes a sense-heightened predator and I, along with Lilit and Jilly experience it first-hand. Bane travels half a league north of our camp, staying fifty paces from the trail and weaving through the trees. In a focused, hunting frame of mind, every step is extreme stealth and his awareness of his surroundings comes through in hyper-fine detail. To me, it is a sense of gliding silently just above the forest floor. Colors through Bane's eyes are different than through my own, and I swear that sounds come to me in colors as well. Mayhaps this is an effect of the furions' senses, as I have never experienced it with Bane afore.

We hear the two riders well in advance of seeing them as they are making no effort to ride silent as a trained scout would. Bane makes his way to the tree line abutting the trail. As he peers out, still hidden and stone still, I watch as the guardsmen scouts travel aways south along the trail, having betwixt themselves what appears to be a conspiratorial conversation. Guffaws and whispers and a snort or two amongst themselves. They have the same air about them to which we've become accustomed. Curiously, they stop near to where Bane remains hidden, and simply turn and head back north. We follow them just inside the tree line.

As we round a bend in the trail, Bane stops and remains hidden and silent. There, some 50 paces on, sits a wagon with a similar cage atop as we have seen before. Within the cage, three head... no, four heads can be seen lying about, one that of just an infant. A wagon's wheel is off on one side, but conspicuously nobody is trying to repair it. There are two additional guards at the wagon along with the coachman.

Bane's ears perk up. I hear rustling even as he does. The furions hear it as well and slip from his back. Lilit heads down the tree line on one side of the trail and Jilly scurries across the byway to do as Lilit is doing on that side. Bane retreats deeper into the woods, and my thoughts guide him to travel past the wagon guards and further up the trail.

Through the furions' eyes, the rustling now makes sense. There are two bowmen with crossbows nocked. The bolts are set at the ready but resting at their feet. One leans against the tree as the other a few paces away sits bored, whittling at the log he sits on with a small blade. Jilly comes across a similar scene on the opposite side of the trail, but with only one bowman.

It appears the actors in this play have been waiting a while.

For us, I surmise.

My attention floats back to Bane who has wound his way silently through the forest and around another bend in the trail. As he leaves sight of the wagon for a short time, he comes upon a final group of four swordsmen. These are actually seated and playing a card game of some sort, their mounts just a few paces away and loosely tethered.

So, Lord Tullamoor plans on putting an end to our work. I will make other plans. The four of us retreat towards camp, but before they arrive, I wake from the *Calming* and glance to Finnie. Though her back is turned to me, she speaks, even though I have made no sound upon waking from the *Calming*.

"The warrior returns from a hunt," she remarks, even as she tends the fire and turns away from me still.

A laugh escapes me. "How is it that you do that?"

She turns. "I believe we have become like two sides of the same coin, Ser Drægonheart. It is not only the creatures that sense you, even as you do me, I believe."

"I have news, and it is not good."

"Let's have it then." Her shoulders slump.

"They have set a trap, an ambush meant for us, I am sure. And the bastards have four children, including an infant."

A single tear leaps from her eye to her cheek, but then a determination springs to Finnie's face to accompany it.

"We can foil their plot, though it will take effort on all of our parts." Resolve sets upon wait for us. We will take advantage of the situation. Laying out my plan to Finnie, I suggest that now would be as good a time, while we know they are lax and impatient.

"We'll leave the horses here as we must travel very quietly."

Putting only what would be needed in my pack, we rise to leave out even as Bane and the furions have just returned. The five of us set out again.

Heavily overcast, the clouds are a deep greenish gray, dreary and portending a storm well in the making. A benefit to our cause, I reason.

We have carefully reached my intended spot betwixt the four rear horsemen men and the staged wagon, but unseen by either. It is near high-sun, though it remains hidden behind grumbling storm clouds. The winds have arrived ahead of the storm and the rustling of branches hide our activity amongst the trees.

We ourselves, will not wield my first weapon. Unwinding spooled Elven-vine, I send Jilly across the trail where Finnie waits, pulling one end of the tough twine. Split up across the trail from each other, Bane has led Finnie safely to her current position. I have explained what we are to do with the vine. I climb a tree and knot my end of the vine around the trunk to a height that would catch a rider upon the trail high on his person, near his neck, I hope. Finnie does the same, pulling the Elven-vine taut and unyielding and knots it at a like height on her side of the trail.

I have instructed her to approach back towards the wagon and to climb high as she is able into a thick-limbed tree, and to shoot from it—and in doing so, aid me as an archer either forward towards the wagon or back towards where the mounted swordsmen will arrive from. I then leave her and make my way back to intercept the forward riding scouts while they are well away from the wagon. Moving with furtive resolve and giving wide berth to the bowmen near the wagon ambush stage, I arrive at my destination even as a thunderclap echoes close by.

The forward scouts have paused upon the trail commenting on the weather even as they are talking crudely of their past conquests with women, which makes my mind rest easy for what I am about to do.

A mere ten paces from them, now. With all the speed and accuracy I can muster, I lay my Bo aside, nock, and loose an arrow. It finds its way into the neck of the further guard from me. My throwing blade finds the temple of the other. Both guards fall to the ground, the second silent as he falls and the first gurgling blood as he grasps for his neck. It is not a pretty scene and without another word escaping their lips, lay dead aside their spooked horses.

Running forward to them, I quickly settle their mounts. I gather and tether the horses, so that they cannot alert the others. Retrieving my weapons, I wipe them clean on the guardsman's cloaks. Finally working my way back towards the wagon, proceeding with the stealth that Moor has ingrained upon me in our training, I secret up to a bowman on my side of the trail and dispatch him with my dirk across his neck with a swift, deep pass. This is a crucial time. My noise now will expose our attack. The other bowman, but five paces away, turns towards us just as I am lowering his comrade to the ground.

"He's among us!" he shouts.

Two things happen of a sudden.

First, across the trail a scream of terror rises from the bowman's counterpart as he is attacked savagely and loudly by a huge wolf, and second, the other bowman on my side of the trail is reaching for my throwing blade protruding from his neck. I race to him and retrieve my blade, leaving him to deal with his circumstances. As quick as I am able, while chaos reigns across the trail, I run from the tree line and bound up the wagon, the armed coachman my next target. The two guardsmen at the wagon have turned to the sound of Bane tearing at the throat from their comrade. They have taken a few paces in that direction and their backs are turned to me as I bound up the wagon. I use my Bo-staff to pummel the sword-wielding coachmen in the head and neck.

He drops; dead, I think.

Glancing to the caged youngers, I turn and leap from the wagon towards the swordsmen on the other side just as they are turning back, drawn to the commotion. In midair as I leap to the ground, I see, then feel, a flash as a crossbow bolt slices through my left side at my ribs. Almost simultaneously a scream rises behind me from the caged youngers.

I fall to my knees as I land on the ground. My balance lost for a moment. A searing pain in my side.

"Oh! She's an arrow in her!" comes the scream of a young lass. "She's bleeding!"

The two swordsmen are now near upon me. They lift their swords above their heads, bringing them to ring down upon me. My mind reacts ahead of my body this time. It is normally my trained reflexes that are first to act, but my wound has been a perilous distraction. Time begins to slow as anger boils from within me as a reaction to the scream from the lass. The heavy broadswords are descending, and the intense faces of the swordsmen are as frozen images before me. In my peripheral vision to my left, two other guardsmen emerge from the bend in the trail, moving in an impossibly slow motion.

Where is Finnie? Has something happened to Finnie?

In this single moment, my reflexes are finally catching up to my mind's eye, and I swing my Bo-staff into both hands and begin to raise it in defense against the descending sword blades. The intense anger and the heartbreak at my worry for Finnie overcomes me as I rise from my knee, pushing down the burning pain in my side. I thrust forward not only the Bo-staff, but also my roiling emotions. The ends of my staff explode in blinding red and white light to match the *Drægonstones* embedded within it.

Something phenomenal is happening.

A sensation of warmth overwhelms me and that energy expells out from my person through the staff. The broadswords shatter as they make contact with the Bo and the swordsmen fly backwards five paces into the air. Bane leaps upon one and it is the man's end. My legs become boneless, and I fall to my knees, holding myself erect with the staff. The two swordsmen who have rounded the bend, having paused at the site before them, are now again running towards me.

Past them, Finnie appears with an arrow nocked upon her bow, and I sigh just to see her alive. I cannot rise nor even raise my hands. She looses the arrow. Her face twists with concern for me.

I do not rise.

I cannot rise. All strength has been drained from me.

Her arrow pierces the oncoming swordsmen through his heart and the arrow bursts partway from his chest. A breath later, its twin does the same to his comrade. As if in a fog, I shortly see Finnie run up to the wagon and choke as she peers within the cage.

"The keys."

She scrambles to the coachman's vest to find them. But I watch in a blur as she shakes her head in frustration and tears stream down her cheeks. We have won the day, but at terrible cost.

Something niggles at my brain yet again, and as I peer down the trail, I see a lone figure sitting atop his mount at the bend in the trail. All goes dark as I see Finnie nock another arrow in anger and turn.

20

Come together

J awake some minutes later to Finnie shaking me and Bane licking my chin. On their hindquarters, the furions watch. Two tear-stained faces are watching over Finnie's shoulder, and a girl of mayhaps three years is standing on her lap, arms around Finnie's neck. I shake my head once to clear my thoughts and stop the ringing in my ears. An unwise move as it has caused nausea to instantly take hold and rack my body.

"Oh, Ari, you frightened me near to death!" Finnie brushes my hair aside as I sit up.

"What happened Finnie?" I am fighting a crippling fatigue and mental fog, making speech unbearably difficult.

"She could not be saved, Ari," Finnie cries, "I tried to get into the cage to help her. I fumbled about the coachman for the keys. When I opened the bastards' cage, she was already gone." This gives me something to wrap my head around and the dizziness begins to subside.

"The arrow that struck me?" I choke out, recovering a bit more.

"We saw it go right through you and it hit Callie hard... Right here." A girl of about eight-year says, pointing at her own heart. "My sister is all bloodied...and dead."

Her face crumples and she starts sobbing, choking and gasping out syllables that I cannot understand.

"I'm so sorry about your sister." I reach out, my hand wanting to pull her to me. "I tried to save her. I tried to save you all." My throat aches for the tightness caused by the sorrow of it and guilt presses upon my chest and I weep as well.

The little lass' sobbing lessens and she can speak again. She takes my hand in both of hers. "We know. You kilt all the bad men. You and your wolf and the lady... But they still kilt my sister... Will you be well, sir? You won't die too?"

I could not help but to reach out and cup her cheek softly in my hand.

"Nay, lass. I will not die. We are all safe now."

I wonder that she can worry about my condition, having had just lost so much, for surely, as we have come to know in these cases, her further family was probably destroyed as well.

I turn to Finnie. "What happened to the Bowman that shot the lass? And the watcher...? Did you get him?"

"Ari, your furions climbed the tree that the Bowman hid in and apparently attacked him there in the branches. He fell to his death with a broken neck. And no, my arrow found the last horseman's leg, but it did not stop him from riding away."

So, others will know what happened here. Foreboding brings back my nausea to me.

"But Ari, what happened when the guards at the wagon attacked you? As I came around the bend in the trail, chasing the riders that were now on foot, your choke line worked brilliantly. There came a thundering boom as in a storm. It followed the brightest flash of white light. I feared a sky-bolt had actually struck you... And I watched, aghast, as the two swordsmen flew back from you." Finnie stares out, lost to the memory for a moment.

"Ari, when I finally reached you, I found their swords shattered and they lay on the ground a good five paces away and…they looked…broken! Their heads and arms and legs all lay in all manner and direction. They were broken, Ari."

Broken.

She keeps repeating the word as if mystified. I am as much as her.

"Yea, Finnie, it is unexplainable to me, but I believe the flash and the great force came from my Bo-staff."

Astonished to hear myself say it.

My senses returning, I reach to my side, of a sudden remembering the arrow that had killed the girl had first struck me at my ribs. My hands come away sticky with blood. But when I raise my torn tunic, I find naught but a healing, welted scar under wet and crusted blood. My wound is healing. I feel it happening within me. More of a wonder.

"The bolt-arrow struck me before it pierced the girl," I say. "But the wound is nearly healed."

I look at Finnie, quirking my head, surely not understanding the how of it.

I cannot wrap my mind around what I am saying, but know we still have a duty to these youngers and have to get them to safety as soon as we rightly can.

"Finnie, we shall pull the cage from the wagon, replace the wheel upon it, and take these youngers back to camp."

I set to work as Finnie gathers the youngers away from the carnage.

I have finished with the wheel and load the wagon with the valuables found upon the persons of the fallen guardsmen. We load the youngers into the wagon and tightly swaddle the dead sister in a bedroll. Her living sister stays by her side. I send Finnie ahead with them and the furions who snuggle about the youngers and keep them distracted from the horrors they had just witnessed.

"I shall gather and tether the horses, pull all the bodies from the trail and into the forest. I shall meet you back at the camp as fast as I might," I whisper.

Finnie nods, but I note that she appears overly fretful and sullen in a manner not like her. As she sets out on her way, a heavy shower finally reaches us from the overburdened clouds above. Warm and welcoming to me, and helping to wash away the distaste within me for this ugly business we were just about.

When I did finally meet them back at the camp, Finnie had found a way to make a fire at the edge of our lean-to which had managed to remain mostly dry. The two oldest children are fast asleep and wrapped in bedrolls tight together with Lilit and Jilly for company and comfort. Finnie has the infant girl in her arms as the littlest one refuses to leave Finnie and clings in desperation to her arm and neck. Finnie is certainly equally reluctant to let loose of the younger. We sit together, close to the fire.

"Let us bury the girl properly on the morrow's morn and let the youngers grieve for her. We will find a nice resting place."

She just nods back.

"What is it Finnie?" knowing there is something heavy on her mind.

"I've killed four men today, Ari. And I know the right of it, and do not regret it but I cannot kill any more." Finnie's voice is hoarse and strained. She sighs. "My anger and grief have finally left me, and I long for a normal life again. It feels so right to be with you, but I am torn with a longing also for life where I can heal in a safe place and give the same to a precious younger such as little Èvie here."

"Yea, I see it in your eyes, Finnie." I touch her cheek as I speak it. "Let us think on it for a day or two. It will be sunny and bright on the morrow. Let us get to know our charges and make a new plan for our destinies."

"Oh, but I know a little already. This sweet young-un is called Èvelyn, as I said. Tristan her brœther, not yet six-year, lay over with Carrie there.

Carrie's sister was called Callie, her twin, and her heart," Finnie finishes with a woeful expression.

I place a few logs upon the fire as the rain lets off and a full moon appears in the sky above. Finnie and I slip under blankets with tiny Èvie betwixt us and hold hands as she falls to sleep and eases into her dream world. I take myself into my *Calming* to sort my thoughts and emotions, from Da's death to the here and now. My Oath to his quest is weighing on me as well, willing myself to a solution for Finnie and me.

At the break to the morrow's morn, I wake to a knowing and hope I can convince Finnie in the right of it. But before I can present my thoughts on that matter specific, I think it would do all concerned well to find a place where we can banish our stresses.

I know of such a place. Hunting three suns passed, I had come across a spot that will suit us well to this end. I think it ideal. The youngers can experience the calm of the forest. There is a pond there, fed by a small waterfall. It is similar to the camp that Finnie and I had found, but in an even more secluded grotto, upon our holiday after visiting her family homestead. I will approach her with the idea. But first, this morn's sorrowful task is to lay little Callie to her final rest.

We find a beautiful spot beside a blossoming tree next to the brook just 100 paces from our camp. We ask Carrie if it would be a good place for Callie.

"It's beautiful, she will love it here," she whispers with tears running down her cheeks.

"Well then, mayhaps you, Tristan, Finnie, and little Èvelyn can gather up a basket or two of beautiful flowers to lay with her."

While they go about it, I retrieve my tools to tackle the grim task of digging a grave next to the brook and the flowering tree. Before they have time to return from their flower gathering task, I lay Callie to rest and cover her grave with river stone. When the others return, we arrange the gathered flowers upon the grave. Finnie says some words and leaves Carrie to sit by her sister for a while. We hear her speaking softly to her sister as we take leave, two sparrows hopping about a branch above the grave.

Back at camp, I approach Finnie with my thoughts.

"Finnie, on my morn hunt three suns passed, I came across a small grotto that reminded me of our holiday camp at the falls. We will not be able to reach it with the wagon, but with Paint and your Chessie and with travois that I can harness behind each. They can carry both the youngers and our camp provisions."

She smiles. "You have thought this through as you always do, Ari. I think a respite trip would be a fine idea, but what of the watcher who rode away? Will he not return and bring more guardsmen down upon us?"

"Nay. I think they made their ambush with all their available thugs and resources. It will take him near a fortnight to return to Tullamoor and back again. Mayhaps longer with the arrow you put in his leg."

"Then let us visit your pond and find some happier moments for them, as well as us," she agrees.

I pasture our claimed horses in the clearing near our camp. It is ringed on three sides with a dense underbrush made of thorn hedges. I use the wagon, piled high with the spoils of our encounter, to block the only natural game trail out of the pasture field. A small brook passes through the pasture, so the horses will have all they need for a time. My thoughts are that if some of the guardsmen's steeds wander from the pasture, it would not be an important loss. With food aplenty and like animals about, I think it likely they would not wander.

With travois to pull and three youngers to manage, it will take us the better part of our time before dusk to make it to our final trip's destination. 'Tis a bit of a challenge but we finally come upon my tiny rock and tree enclosed vale with pond and falls. A smile comes to Finnie, and the youngers yelp in fun to see and hear the falls.

The sun has dried the ground during the time it took us to make the trip. We find whisperflies aflutter on orange, yellow, and black silken wings. Songbirds chirp and cute, furry creatures skitter about the forested floor surrounding our private grotto. We unload the provisions and set about making camp. The fire started, dinner of tubers and beans soup is put to kettle. Finnie takes the youngers to the pond shallows and splashes about with them as I string our tarpen tent for shelter and gather forest straw to lay beneath our bedrolls. I return to brush down Paint and Chessie and gather some feed to them.

Looking over to our new troupe, I can see that Lilit and Jilly are up to their antics with the youngers. Finnie is laughing, something I have seldom seen this past moon. Her emerald eyes sparkle as she plays with little Èvie and Èvie's brœther Tristan. Little Carrie joins in some, but it is evident she misses her twin. My heart goes out to her and I decide I will take her with me on my foraging and trap setting routine on the morrow's morn.

After a late dinner, we all climb and sit upon a large and flat rock ledge overhanging the pond and throw pebbles at the floating lily pads. We watch as the moon shines down upon the water. I point across the pond to near the small rippling falls as I spot an otter floating on her back in the light of the moon, with two otter pups playing upon their mum's belly. Lilit and Jilly raise their heads to watch what looks to be little cousins. Èvie claps and Carrie and Tristan laugh at the fun of it.

We have made a good decision to come here for a few suns.

On our sixth sun in this quiet corner of the woods, I begin to realize that Finnie, the youngers, and I are acting as a family does. Finnie will grill up flatcakes on her cast iron pan and we'd add honey and foraged berries atop for morn-meal. We are not in a cottage about a table, but it does not seem to matter. I teach the youngers about the little forest creatures that Lilit and

Jilly would chase about. The every-sun chores of life are handled about camp.

Little Carrie continues to grieve for her lost sister and her family that has been slaughtered by her captors. The story comes in bits and pieces as she helps me in my foraging and snare baiting. She also reveals that she has an aunt, her mum's sister and her twin just as Callie had been Carrie's. She knows the name of the towne from which her family hails, and I promise I will help her find her way home to her aunt. This eases her mind. A burden seems to lift from her young shoulders in anticipation of being reunited with her true family.

For Tristan and Evie it will be a different future. At only six year, Tristan knows not of any other family than their murdered parents, which we have discovered with gentle questioning.

But our little family continues to eat and bathe together. I teach the youngers some things about the little woodland creatures around us. Lilit and Jilly have accepted them as part of our bigger family and are protective of them all.

When about, Bane certainly accepts them as part of his pack. Little Èvie attacks the wolf even as Seri had. When not upon Finnie's lap or in her arms, she is often cuddling into the thick fur of the otherwise fierce dread wolf. He licks and tends to her with the utmost care as he would his own pup.

Finnie's mind has eased as well during these past suns. I can see she has made peace with a decision of her own making. I have as well. I have brought to camp a very fat hare. When we aren't at play with the youngers, we go about preparing a most hearty stew for our late eve-meal. Laughter and smiles are the fare of the entirety of the sun and the eve-meal is a most warm and filling treat. A little later as darkness approaches, we make a large fire, and the youngers all crawled to bed, even little Èvie, and are fast asleep with Bane and the furions cuddling amongst them.

Taking Finnie's hand, I make my way to our rock ledge and spread a great woolen blanket upon it. The evening breeze is soft and very warm. The moon above shines down with a full, bright face. A myriad of stars sparkle in the night sky above as well. We sit a while next to each other, leaning into one another. My heart's rhythm beating a quicker pace.

"Finnie, will you come to the *Calming* with me?" I ask as I look deep into her mesmerizing emerald eyes.

"Do you mean like you do with Lilit and Jilly...? Or with Bane?" she queries.

I sense now that her heartbeat has risen in a chase of mine.

"Of a sort. But I think with you, if it can be done at all, it would be different. I've taught you a bit of it, as best I can, and you say you've reached an inner calm a few times. But with me, it is more, and I'd like you to experience it as well," I say, trying to express that I think she can reach a deeper experience within the *Calming*.

Finnie nods. "How do we do it, Ari?"

Thoughts and emotions swirling warm within, I grasp her hand. "Let us lay back and look up into this night sky."

And we lay back and just hold hands as we gaze upon a full moon and a myriad of twinkling stars.

I whisper after a time, "Breathe deep, and long, and slow. Try and let the *Calming* come to you. Hear the water trickle upon the rocks at the falls... Listen as the crickets and beetles sing as the night hums its sung... Feel as the night breeze washes over your arms and legs and your lovely face and tickles your skin... Keep your eyes closed now, Finnie, and let yourself experience the sensations..."

I do not need to gaze upon her. I can feel her presence and hear her slowed and steady heartbeat through our gentle touch. I reach out with my mind. But when I make contact with Finnie's spirit-self, it manifests completely different from my creature friends and is totally unexpected. I draw a quick breath and she does as well, simultaneous. Her breath in sync with my own.

With Bane, I experienced his senses in a distinct, but muted way as if a visitor upon them. Even though my senses of smell and my range of sounds were magnified, I knew that I was only experiencing but a limited portion to his senses. And with Lilit and Jilly, I could see things as they did, but their other senses were not apparent to me at all.

With Finnie, it is marvelously different. The smallest of sensations are magnified tenfold. I know it as fact that she feels this same effect. The tickling, warm breeze tingles as it rolls across my skin, our skin. Our hearts begin to beat apace with each and the other and our breathing continues in-sync as well. We both are held enthralled by the experience and to-gether our self-spirits explore our surroundings with heightened, combined senses. We do not move but reach out instead with our minds and visit upon the sounds and sights about us. The moon shines down upon us. Its features crystallize in amazing detail as do the leaves upon every tree. Even in the failing light, their leafy veins within glow in ethereal manner. The air itself becomes crisp and clear as we capture each breath. We each explore differ-ent things, but we both experience the feelings of the other. We can process them in our separate minds even as we are aware of each other's individual experience.

I listen to the trickling water as it cascades down the rocks and into the pond. I have, of a sudden, an urge to feel the coolness of the pond upon my body. Silently, so as not to disturb Finnie, I roll from our nesting rock and onto the beach to shed my garment and wade into the water. At the same time, I sense Finnie's sight and senses venture towards the slumber-ing youngers.

Even as I begin to wade into the sparkling waters, I sense Finnie's gaze fall upon little Èvie and her brœther Tristan. In that instant, I become aware that not only physical senses are shared between us, but also an emotional awareness as well. As I float in a weightlessness within the pond, I become near overwhelmed with the emotions within her—for those two youngers in particular. It is a boundless love and a desperate need to protect them at all costs. It is a deep and crushing and liberating emotion. I find that I want to accept it as my own as well. As I do, I sense in the same moment that Finnie knows that I have. She takes in a startled breath and turns to me.

Our gaze connects instantly. The smile within her glowing emerald eyes sparkles back at me and with it a deeper connection that draws her to me. Unbridled anticipation takes hold of me as she sheds her huntress tunic and trousers and crosses the few strides over the pond's sandy beach. She wades into the water. The form I see before me is no longer the bruised and battered body of a beaten lass that I needed to heal. She stands now lithe and muscled and yet soft, curved, confident, and oh, so beautiful to behold.

The sights, the sounds of our little world, begins to fade to a light hum in the background as my heartbeat lifts a pace. I can sense, nay feel, hers do the same even as her form lowers into the water. She comes floating before me so that only her soft shoulders and auburn hair and emerald eyes remain. I rise in response and anticipation to her movement towards me.

Her eyes, green as a willow's leaves in early spring, are so intoxicating to me that I cannot look away from them. She melts into my arms and her warm supple swell and softness meets my chest, my heart thumping strong just below my skin.

Her eyes draw me in even further. I breathe in the wonderful scent of her as her breath presses warm upon my face. Our lips touch in a tentative fashion, nose aside nose, and then again. The sensation reaching to our toes. This time, not so timidly. I marvel at the taste of her. A flicker of a memory appears in my mind. Fafhärd and his wife, Janælle, that he so clearly loved, kissing on the porch as we had approached.

Our first kiss. *Wanting more. The* both of us.

I cannot get enough of the taste of her, nor she, of me. Time slows and the world around us disappears and gives us this time to explore and wonder at the feeling growing ever stronger betwixt us as our mouths attempt to slowly consume the essence of each and the other.

As the cool of the water finally permeates to my notice, I lift Finnie into my arms and carry her out of the pond and into the warm, moonlit air. Even then I do not want to let go of her taste. There beams a laughter in her eyes as I bring her back to the water's edge and lay her upon the soft and mossy ground just off the beach. I lay down next to her, not wanting to be separated for even a moment.

We slowly continue our exploring ways with eager hands and lips, visiting upon each other in a quite intimate way as the warm night air begins to dry us. The *Calming* state envelopes us again as I turn around onto my back and Finnie rolls softly atop. Our hearts begin to beat as one again as our lips savor each other in soft tastes and then in warm gulps. We can feel all parts of our skin that lay flush together and softly pressed akin. My hands trail slowly down her spine and as they draw lower, Finnie's hips rise to meet them. It is as if her hips move with a mind of their own. I fondle, squeeze, kiss, and taste her. When she lowers her hips again, more than the moon and stars are aligned. In that moment, I raise to meet her and we truly become one in passion. Her warmth gliding over and engulfing me. Squeezing me in a velvet grip.

Finnie's eyes widen and then clench. A soft whimper escapes her lips as her body tightens and grows stiff. Not a breath escapes her for a long moment. She tucks her head into my neck and shoulder. Her eyelashes tickle my skin. My whole body shivers. My mind flickers in concern as I experience a sharp pain just as she feels it. A long moment passes. Her eyes open, and she stares deep within mine as her hips and body begin to move again. A soft moan escapes us both. The sharp pain, a forgotten memory.

Soft and slow movements and the feelings created become our world as time slows in the *Calming* to allow us the total sensations visiting upon our entwined persons, pressing soft, but hard, together. She and I both are consumed in awareness of the swell of her torso, as hard points of distraction amid soft swells beneath, drag up and down across our near-melded forms, bringing deep and profound tingling sensations upon her but felt by the two of us. I feel her awareness of the fullness reaching deep within her and about our coupling as she accepts and wonders at it. My sensitivity to the quiver that travels the full length and breadth of her body is igniting to me. She feels too, the twitch and ache of excitement expressed by my body in obvious and immediate response.

All about us other sounds fade, leaving only our sound. Our breath upon each other's neck and low guttural sighs and whispers of something only we can feel together. The tempo of both our emotions and our physical forms strive to an increasing pace, reaching for a *Bliss* we both somehow know awaits us. Our legs are entwined and in a glorious battle. Her thighs about mine and squeezing as if about a galloping steed as I thrust deeper into her very essence. Mine betwixt hers and pushing higher to gain ground and attempting to make the most of the sensations developing within both of us. The whole of our bodies are keeping time with the symphony and rhythm caused by our intense. impassioned game of push and pull and accompanied by the deep throaty, personal sounds of a *knowing* for one another...

We are ever reaching together for the *Bliss*. A warmth. A feeling of fullness with an itching for even more, A gripping, squeezing softness urging us on.

Heedless of the other night sounds and cascading whisper of the brook, the *Bliss* finally comes over us both, enveloping us. It begins through Finnie as a rolling cascade of small tremors and frenzied throes, emanating from our coupling and expanding to all reaches of her now soft, but tight and tense trembling form. It builds like a wave cresting and enveloping the whole of her being and reverberating through my mind as well. The intense sensations and passion urge me forward finally to an explosion of feeling from the very heart of our connection. Our *Knowing* passion becomes near, neverending as again further tremors of exploding sensation overcome Finnie in reaction to my *Bliss*. It leads again to yet even more shuttering tremors, intermixed with an intense spasm and deep-throated, guttural sighs into each other's neck as a liquid warmth spreads over our physical connection and then that same warmth spreads throughout the whole of our beings. Through all the time of it, personal sensations are experienced equally by us both through our connection in the *Calming*.

Eventually, the aftershocks and intensity subsides. We roll together and to our sides under the warm breeze and a glowing moon, neither willing to part, so we stay together in a warm but loose embrace. With small kisses, we fall into a deep slumber.

Late in the night, we wake and visit again the passion we knew earlier, this time ending in a more physical manner—akin more mayhaps to mating mare and steed but ending in the complete satisfaction to us both. But there is something else also. Both of us know that something is about to change and each fighting the need for it.

Later, we cool ourselves in our pond and never having spoken to each other throughout this night, we climb out of the water and onto our blanket upon our rock ledge. Drying and donning our garb, we sit side-by-side, her head upon my shoulder under the night's waning moon.

"Finnie, I've noticed these past few suns a change overwhelming you. One that has been coming since our encounter with Tullamoor's mercenaries and the ambush they meant to have wrought upon us."

She merely nods in assent, a tear coming to her eye.

"I've thought deeply, over these past few suns, and I feel I might have a solution and would like to tell you of it."

She lifts her head from my shoulder and looks me in the eyes. "Tell me."

I hear in her voice that she has to literally push those few words out.

I feel her heart skip a beat.

"You've been driven these past moons by grief, revenge, and indifference to the death of these villains that have placed onto you the heartbreak from the evil visited upon your family and the families of the youngers we've been able to save. But we've also seen the good in people who have taken these damaged youngers into their homes to give them a new family and new hope. I think that you would like now to feel that again for yourself. I know, through our mutual *Calming* this night, your love for little Èvie and Tristan. So, I have a proposal and an Oath to make to you," I say, and she looks to me with both a fear and a longing.

I guess at an even deeper fear she might have about me in particular, for it is the same with me.

Not wanting to delay it any longer, I tell her of my plan.

"Finnie, I have a home and friends, nay, family back in Middenvale, and a homestead aside. I would like to send you there with Èvie and Tristan to make it your own. Grayce, Argo, and Da's Effie would welcome you with open arms and help you make a home for these youngers that you've come to love so much. We've collected a fair amount of coin as bounty from Tullamoor's mercenaries and thugs. The horses will fetch a fair amount more, as well. The homestead would have the makings of all that you need to make a life without threat and strife of the life we have been living."

"But what of you, Ari? You are my dearest family—my heart. You speak as though you are not to come with us. And what of Carrie?" Tears stream down her cheeks.

Reaching up to her cheeks, I wipe away her tears with my thumbs and hold her head as I speak to her.

"And here is my Oath to go with my proposal, Finnie. I give my heart to you as well, with yesters-eve as proof to it. I will return to you and what will be our family with Tristan and Èvie after I have returned Carrie to her family and after I've dealt directly with this evil Lord Tullamoor. And finally, after I have answered to Da's quest upon me to find the Druid," I say with a sigh.

To be fair, it seems a lot.

Finnie looks at me for a long moment as she takes to her mind what I have said. Then her brow furls, and the sides of her mouth turn down. "Who is this Druid you speak of?"

I tell her that part of my story that I have not yet confided to her in all the time I have known her. I feel that mayhaps she will be angry at this revelation, but I am wrong.

"Oh, Ari, you've spent months. First saving me, then healing me, both in body and then my mind. You made my vengeance yours and have saved many youngers and dealt justice to so many evil men. You've done all of this and put aside your dying Da's wish that you seek out this Druid who offers protection for yourself against the most determined foe you could have in this land. You did this for me... Oh, Ari, I will go to your family and make peace with my life and raise sweet Èvie and Tristan... And I will wait for you," she says with a warm and soft and loving voice.

21

Getting better

The sun rises while we sit together upon our rock next to our pond. It is a place, now, that will stay indelibly etched in our memories. Our family camp begins to stir with little Èvie running on tiny legs laughing as Lilit and Jilly bound about her. She comes to our rock arms outstretched, and Finnie reaches out and pulls her up to her and into a tight hug. Tristan makes his way up as well, and I ruffle his hair and give him a tickle.

Shortly, Carrie appears with Bane at her side and asks if it is time to visit our snares and forage for the morn's meal. I can see that she has come to like this time we spend together.

"Yea, Carrie, let us do just that, and we must collect all of our devices as we will be moving on today. Back to our wagon and then on the morrow's morn we should start our journey to your aunt and uncle's homestead and reunite you with your family."

Carrie bursts into a big smile, jumps into my arms, and delivers me a strong hug. She squeals. "Really? Let's go!"

Finnie and I laugh. This is the first time we have seen Carrie show any real positive emotion since her sister died.

"Let's collect some berries and see if our snares have anything we can use for our morn-meal, Carrie. We'll have some flat cakes if we can talk Finnie into making some. We can bring the berries to sweeten them for Èvie and Tristan. What do you say?"

The little girl is bursting with a newfound energy. "Yay, yay! I saw some razziberries yesters-sun. Let's go!"

I throw my pack on and we are off to do our part. True to her word, Carrie has indeed found a patch of 'razziberries' and we fill a good sack full. We gather a good sum of nuts and some 'shrooms. Our snares bear success also.

Shortly after our morn-meal, featuring berries provided by Carrie, we pack up Chessie, Paint, and the travois with Tristan reigning over one. Provisions are in the other. Carrie and Èvie sit atop saddles in front of Finnie and I. Bane had headed out earlier, so we see nothing of him during our trip back to the wagon camp.

The forest ride is pleasant. With a warm sun and a soft breeze, Finnie teaches us a little tune-song she knew from her mum.

Oh, cat's in the cradle licking baby's spoon
Little lass pulls its tail in the gloom
"When's the sun coming mum" "Hush, l'il lassie, it'll be all too soon"
And we'll make some flatcakes then lass, we'll make some cakes then
You know we'll have some good times then

It is a catchy tune and soon we're all singing, with Èvie bouncing in time.

Arriving back to our original camp, we are pleased to find that the bounty horses are still enjoying their pasture time and have full bellies. Our time is short here as we pack all our provisions in the wagon and upon two of the horses that we had inherited from Tullamoor's men. Both the wagon and the horses will have value and to our advantage these are soldiers' horses. Harnessing and tethering them for travel is not a problem as they are accustomed to traveling in groups and formation.

The next part of the journey will be the most tedious as we need to move our troup of youngers and a compliment of ten riderless horses. The saddlery, provisions, and weapons are layered into the large caravan and covered with a canvas tarp. I have rigged a seat to carry Èvie upon the wagon's buckboard, and Tristan and Carrie ride atop the provisions in the back of the wagon. Finnie takes charge of the wagon, there being no doubt she can handle the team on our trek.

I have picked well in my selection of Finnie's chestnut mare when I had encountered and slew her captors and confiscated their bounty. Chessie had been well-trained and has become the head mare in our caravan. Harnessed and tethered, the horses follow her with no reluctance. Paint and I keep our unlikely troop on pace along the traders' trail.

"Finnie, our goal is to follow the traders' trail, and I believe we can make the greater east-west travelway before dusk and make camp there," I explain.

We've traveled together a few moons now and though usually on horse-back, we have become familiar with our life on the trails and work well as a team. Bane has not returned yet, which is just as well as the horses would be harder to handle with a huge Mountain Dread about. The furions hold court with the youngers in the wagon bed and keep them entertained as we travel. There is laughter, jumping, and play and the smile on Finnie's face does my heart good.

We make the great Five Points east-west travelway at a little bit before dusk, giving us time to set up camp just north of the travelway and safely inside the tree line.

Fire and kettle are started, and our troupe is fed and put to bed. As the sun sets, Bane makes an appearance and curls up next to Èvie and Carrie. Everyone is settled, and Finnie and I take seats next to the fire.

"Finnie, from our camp here we're just two day's travel to Quill'spie. Fafhärd can help us sell the horses and saddlery and mayhaps the weapons as well," I explain. "It will ease my mind if you are traveling without the worry of such things."

I look over at her. She can only nod as her eyes are filling with moisture. As the moon reaches high in the night sky, she and I settle close together next to the fire. Finnie nestles into my chest as I wrap my arms about her and breathe in the scent of her hair.

Our further travel to Quill'spie remains uneventful but for a few curious stares from passersby. We meet a Tinker along the way and sell him a few finger rings, dirks, cups, and pans. We then purchase from him a few pieces of linen cloth and threads as Finnie is determined to sew up some small things for Èvie.

Making towne three morns from when we reached the travelway, we settle in at the Inn after leaving the horses with the stableman. Our dear friend Claire welcomes us again. She knows what we are about and sees that we have come with three youngers this visit.

"Come, come, seat yerselves and I'll be getting you some tasty stew for you and the youngers," she belts out in a warm and heartfelt voice after taking us each in her strong arms for a welcoming hug.

"And two ales if you please, Claire, and can you find a treat for the youngers? And might we bother you to send a runner out to Fafhärd for us? We'd like to discuss things with him on the morrow's morn if he sees fit," I add.

"Aye, Ser Drægonheart." She smiles. "And I'll warm some cow's milk with crushed cocoa beans for your youngers. I've two rooms just vacant this morn that can be made up to accommodate."

"Many thanks, Claire," says Finnie as she cuddles little Èvie into her lap.

Claire offers her a sad and knowing smile as she eyes the youngers.

The midsun-meal is welcome as we had but a few travel cakes before we made our way into towne this morn. Besides the beef stew with carrots and peas in a newly baked bread trencher, Claire serves us cheeses and fresh fruits. A thoroughly wonderful meal after more than a fortnight of mostly travel foods. The ale is just as welcome, and Carrie's cocoa smile spoke well of the youngers' drinks.

Fafhärd makes an appearance after our meal, and we move to a more private table in the corner of the Inn. Claire takes Tristan and Carrie with her and leave Finnie and I to speak with the large man that we have come to call a dear friend.

"How is Janælle and little Seri and Benjie?" asks Finnie of him and his smile arises immediate and wide.

"Aye, Janælle is well and very happy to be called mum as I can see by her smile each time she hears it. Little Seri is a very clever one, and Benjie grows a finger taller each fortnight. I believe he'll grow as tall as me when he is through with it!" He beams.

We smile to hear that they are getting on so well. Finnie and I tell our most recent tale to him and again ask his aid in selling our bounty.

"Most certainly. There is a trader heading south in towne now, and I believe he will make a decent offer for much of your wares. And may I say that the little darling in your arms is quite the charmer. And what of the youngers, Arias?" This question brings us to tell him a bit of our plan.

"Fafhärd, we welcome your generous aid and thank you for all that you do. The youngers will not be in need of homes. I have promised Carrie, the older girl, that I will deliver her to her aunt and uncle, her only family now, and Finnie shall make a home for little Èvie here and her brœther Tristan as well. We cannot tell you where, as it might endanger you as well as Finnie and the youngers, for the Kingsmen may take an interest in her if they were to ever connect her to me," I state.

The big man ponders this a while. Mayhaps mulling the effect knowing too much might have on his new family.

"Arias, you may have the right of it. Though for my part alone? Well, I would help in any way I might. You and Finnie have brought a great light into my life with little Seri and Benjie, and I'll not begrudge your wishes of secrecy if it will bring some solace to you and Finnie. But King's threat or no, you two are friends deep within our hearts, and for my part, your secrets shall remain mine onto my death," he says in deep sincerity.

"Yea, Fafhärd, dear friend. And mayhaps we should tell you on your Oath that even your dear wife would not know for my fear for her safety." And so, I tell him of my plan to send Finnie, and Èvie, and Tristan back to Da's old homestead into the care of his friends. I tell to him where the homestead lies and who are my close friends there.

Over the next two suns, we are able to barter and sell all the wares and the horses and have collected a heavy purse of coin for Finnie's new life back home with Grayce. We have a new carriage for her to travel more in comfort with the youngers as well. A visit to Fafhärd's homestead is a pleasant reminder that our efforts on the trader's trails were worthy as we are well met by an exuberant Janælle and a happy Seri and Benjie.

All the youngers immediately take a liking to one another, especially Seri and Èvie. First and foremost, Seri attacks Bane. As he approaches ahead of us, she flings herself with abandon onto his neck. Lilit and Jilly leapt from our wagon and joined in the fun. The four of them romped, tumbled, and played to the laughter of all. She and Benjie approached us a few moments later as we are speaking with Fafhärd and Janælle.

"Oh, Ser Drægonheart, and Mãamel Finnie, you have come back to visit! I have a new mum and pa and it is beautiful here and Benjie has outgrown his trousers. I have my own bed and I helped mum with the pies and Benjie goes to the mill with Pa. Thank you, thank you, thank you for bringing us here!" All this while flinging herself into my arms and reaching for Finnie as well. I can see that it does Finnie's heart good to witness it all.

Our time is too short in Quill'spie. We are not anxious to leave good friends made and the normalcy of life in a setting bereft of the ugliness we have been fighting against. All about, is simple happiness of regular folk going about the standard purposes in their lives. But I seesaw a faraway look in Carrie's eyes, and I am late in delivering on my promise to her. Though having fun with the other youngers, still I can see the yearning within her. And so, after a fare-thee-well, and early morn-meal served up by Claire before her earliest guest had even awakened, Finnie and I gathered Èvie and Tristan into the new carriage, to be pulled by Chessie and provisioned by Claire with fresh foods for today and a little something more for the longer trip to Middenvale.

With dew in the grass about the carriage park in the rear of the Inn and as the sun just barely breaks from the horizon, a tearful Finnie throws herself into my arms and presses her lips into mine with a kiss of desperation.

"You come back to me, Ari," she whispers.

"On my Oath and heart, dear Finnie," I say in solemn return.

"Bane will travel with you the whole way. Though I have every confidence you can handle any situation, it will ease my mind that much more. He will return to me after your safe delivery into the arms of Grayce. Please give her, and Effie, and Argo my best regards and tell them I continue my quest," I finished, putting on a happy smile and giving her back a deep kiss of my own.

She climbs aboard the carriage, whistles to Chessie, and glances down to me with her emerald eyes to and gives me a hopeful smile. Carrie and I waved as they pulled from the Inn's yard. Bane trots along behind. I lifted Lilit and Jilly up to Paint's back, and they find their way into the deep filled saddlebags upon his hindquarters. My quiver is stowed with my bedroll and pack and my bow and staff fit into sheaths along Paint's sides. I mounted and pulled Carrie up behind me.

"Shall we be off then, Carrie?"

Carrie just hugs me hard from her seat behind me. I smiled and urged Paint on his way.

22

Here, There and Everywhere

As Finnie pulls out in her carriage from the Inn's yard, she travels north up Quill'spie's main boulevard. Looking off to her left, she sees activity in the stable yard as the lads are about their early morn chores. To her right, she can already hear the smithy's hammer to anvil as this friendly towne's folk wake to the new sun. But it isn't long before it is behind her, and she had crossed the small stream to come upon the Five-Forks travelway. She stops and turns to look back upon the towne of Quill'spie. She has visited it but a handful of times in the past two moons, but it has left a warmth in her breast as a place where Ari and she first found refuge and friends. A place where she had begun to heal from the tragedy in her life and a place that had given her hope of a better future.

Ari and she had done some fun things here, even attended a towne dance with throngs of towne folk. It is a friendly place, with laughter and every-sun conversations amongst a common folk, going about normal every-sun tasks. Youngers going to the schoolhouse. There are shops and bakeries and people discussing things in the general store. There is a barber and his wife that did the ladies' hair. Finnie's hand instinctively touches to her own head, running fingers through her own auburn locks. At one time her hair was long and her mama would comb it for her and her sister every night, and they would talk of the sun's happenings, such as what they had done, and how they felt about things.

She glances over her shoulder at the youngers that filled her heart where not long ago there lived mostly hate and vengeance. Little Èvie sits in a seat fitted to her size, fashioned like a leather sling over a wooden frame. Ari had crafted it in but a few turns of a sand-glass and it is a sturdy and safe seat, that keeps her comfortable in the bumpy carriage on a bumpy travel-way. Her brœther Tristan sits in the seat beside her, and they are both staring back at her, most likely wondering why she has stopped. Even Chessie huffs and whinnies and when Finnie looks over the side of the carriage, Bane looks up at her quizzically.

She smiles and click-clicks and gives rein to Chessie to send her on her way, turning westbound towards the mountains that shown on the map Ari had bartered with the Tinker for. He had showed her how to read one. In their travels together, he had gifted her a compass, which he had also taught her to use.

She is on the great travelway now. Chessie clip-clops forward into the breeze, taking her to a new life. In just a few moons, her life has changed so much. She used to live a simple life with her mum, and Pa, and little Kattalæn, seldom leaving their homestead where, being she was taught reading, and writing, and math's by Mum, required to do chores and help Pa sometimes about the homestead, and occasionally traveling to the village for supplies and such. Mum had taught her to cook and she was good at it.

Evil had then struck.

And then one-night, Ari had come, and it all changed. He healed her, and protected her, and fed her when she could barely raise an arm. He gave her confidence back and helped her seek vengeance upon the vile types of people who had perpetrated the cruelty upon her, and then on to others.

Finnie could take care of herself and would inflict a great deal of damage or death to any man that would attempt to do her harm. Ari had taught her well, and she became a very good and apt pupil. And through it all, he captured her heart.

Finnie's first sun on the travelway out from Quill'spie has rolled on uneventful. She had passed a few groups of three to five riders. Each nodded in greeting as they passed by. She and the youngers stopped a few times, once for a picnic meal supplied by Claire, and another time Èvie saw some wildflowers she just had to have. Finnie pulled the carriage to a halt. They all just ran about and collected the lavender wildflowers. Tristan gathered a few sunflowers as large as Èvie's face. He handed them with a bow to Èvie and some to Finnie as well.

Bane joined in the fun. Tristan and Èvie laughed and played with the great dread wolf. They were pack cubs to him. After their dalliance, they returned to the carriage and continued on their way.

Later that sun, Finnie pulls the carriage off the travelway into an open field alongside the tree line where the trees have thinned giving way to grass and pastureland. There is a small stream and she reckons it a good place to make camp for the night. She travels fifty paces off the travelway and into the tree line. Parking the carriage behind a knoll so it won't not be spotted from the roadway, she unhitches Chessie and tethers her with a long tether. That way Chessie can pasture and reach the stream for a drink at her leisure.

Finnie sets camp inside the tree line making camp the way Ari had taught her. She has the tarp-tent strung with the fire pit built, a fire going, and a kettle over it in less than a turn of a sand-glass. Marshalling the youngers to the stream, they all washed up when not watching the minnows swimming about in the shallows.

Claire's gift of a hearty chicken, green beans, and tuber soup is heated through by the time the little troupe makes it back from wash-up time.

Èvie has not yet mastered the use of eating utensils, so Finnie helps her fill her tummy with Claire's goodness stew. It has been a long sun of travel. All are tired enough to crawl into their bed rolls after a little story about the woodland creatures that Finnie recalls from a time when her Pa told them to her.

Bane quietly strolls into their bedroll area and lay betwixt Tristan and Èvie. Finnie smiles, and scratches behind his ears, and runs her fingers through his fur down the wolf's spine. She can tell he liked the attention.

She lies listening to the night sounds, which have come to be a relaxing chorus. It all is so different from nights not so long ago when those noises would drive her from her side of the fire to Ari to snuggle close to him after he fell asleep. She looks forward to being together again. Some day.

Carrie and I set out from the Inn after Claire comes out the back of the kitchen and hands a sack and a parcel up to me. She says the parchment-wrapped parcel holds two long breads that are cut and filled with meats, cheeses, tomatoes, and greens. Some thick mustard sauce is lathered on for good measure. Even after the morn-meal Claire had served us, I find my mouth watering. The sack she has filled with fruits, and taters, and mãtoes, and such. I find a place afore me for them as I have no desire to pack them in the saddlebags with Lilit and Jilly. As we are finally headed off, I whispered into Carrie's ear. We both turned and throw Claire a kiss in dramatic style. Her face turns a pleasant shade of red and we both laughed.

"Be off with ye then," she hails and chuckles as we do just that.

I spy ahead. Finnie's carriage hasnearly made the travelway, and she will soon be turning west on to it and headed towards the mountains and Middenvale. Putting that thought out of mind, my attention turns to the task at hand.

It will be a long trek for Carrie sitting atop Paint for the better part of a fortnight on the main travelway afore we make it to a towne of any significance and half a fortnight more on less traveled routes. The towne Carrie has mentioned is on Da's map and a name from Moor's memorized list associated with it, as well. There still remains a good bit of travel afore us til I can reunite her with family. The morrow's morn dawns bright, if a tad chill and dew lay upon the grass, but there is the promise of nice weather. Paint seems to almost dance to be on the byways again.

Before we departed Quill'spie entirely, I noted that the bakery has smoke rising from the chimney. I am determined to purchase a few cinnamon sweet cakes for Carrie.

"For the road-weary travelers," I announced when I had returned to Paint and a smiling Carrie.

"Oh, can we have one now?" she asks.

"We're not yet road weary. They will taste all the better for it when we are."

She puts a pout to her pretty face. I laughed.

We are finally on our way and Carrie is excited. I know her exuberance will not last. Travel on horseback is tough even for the more seasoned to it. My pack is stored betwixt the saddlebags and acts as a seat back for Carrie, and she is comfortable with this for the time it takes for the sun to reach two hands above the horizon. Lilit and Jilly slithered out of their hidey holes within the saddlebags. Carrie and the furry fitchets are able to keep each other entertained and shared cinnamon cake midmorn. The travel is uncomfortable for one of Carrie's age as she is not accustomed to riding aback a horse. To her credit, she makes no complaint to me. Just as we are about to stop for midsun-meal, we come upon a tinker on his wagon headed the way we have come.

"Hail and well met, Tinker. Have you time that we might browse your wares?" I called.

"A-sure," comes his reply, "in a little shade, mayhaps?"

There so happens to be a great Calpaca tree near to us, and it affords the perfect place to conduct a little business, as well as a great stop for our midsun-meal.

"Well met, Tinker, what might we call you, Master?" I ventured after dismounting and helping Carrie to the ground.

Afore us stands a jovial, elderly, white-haired man with a receding hairline that at one time was apt to have been full and wavy. He wears a mustache of a sort that has started to reach for his chin and he wears over-size spectacles of a sort I've never seen afore.

"Me mum, she called me Stannis Lee and that will do fine, lad," he says with a wink.

Tinker Stannis Lee proceeds to open up his wagon to us. Quite a large one, pulled by two great steeds of a breed I've never encountered before. They are monstrous large and chestnut-colored with bushy manes of white and fetlock and pastern covered in the same.

As the old tinker continues to pull open the wagon sides, exposing his wares, I query him a bit. "Master Lee, I've traveled a bit, and my Da worked with horses a good bit as well, but I must say, I've never seen a more majestic looking beast as your pull steeds."

"Assure that, lad, and ya wouldn't be likely to see any more. They're called Bonnie Dales, they are, and that there is Bonnie and t'other there is Dale,." Stan Lee says with a chuckle. "The gent I bartered with said they came from the Northern Reaches, and as he was a bit of a mountain man coming south from the mountains beyond Tullamoor Keep, I was apt to be believin' him. Some five year past now. Best trade I ever made. I don't know who did the breaking and the training of the beasts, but for what they do fer me, he musta been a talented whisperer to be sure."

"I can see you have an eye for horse flesh yerself. I've never seen a paint the like of yours," he says as he admires Paint.

"He answers to Paint." I chuckled, myself. "And 'twas my Da who had the talents.... And 'twas his own mighty war steed that was bred with a paint mare from a nomad's herd in the Nomadean desert of the Southern Reaches, or so we were told. He's a smart one himself."

I have much pride in both Paint and Da.

"Would you like to join Carrie and me for midsun-meal, Master Lee?" I offered.

"Assure, lad. You will not be catchin' me turnin' away from a meal with a traveler like unto meself nor a pretty lady like yer with! What do you call yourself, lass?" he asks the blushing Carrie.

"People call me Carrie, Master Tinker, and I think you have some wonderful things upon your wagon!" she adds excitedly.

The tinker smiles.

"And they call me Arias, Stan Lee. Mayhaps we can eat a bit before we do our business. I have some stuffed long breads—, the bread baked fresh this very morn. The Inn's matron that made them for us has stuffed them with meats, and goat cheese, and leafy greens with a mustard sauce that will have you drooling," I suggested.

He smiles a jovial smile.

I lead Paint to the tall grasses just off the travelway and near a few water puddles and pulled Claire's parcel and sack from him. I offered Paint an apple from the sack and returned to the tinker and Carrie. The tinker has pulled out a few marvelous stool seats made of wood and canvas that unfolds in a clever way. Then he does the same with a small table. I remarked on their clever design as we all gathered about the table under the shade of the Calpaca tree.

I opened my parcel, and sack of fruit, and the skin of wine I filled this morn. Lilit and Jilly make an appearance and chased each other in and out and around Carrie's legs. The tinker laughs to see the creatures.

"Ho, and what do ya call yer fitchets?" he asks.

Carrie introduces them.

"I might have a treat for them as well," he says. He gets up and opens the top of a small barrel attached to the side of his wagon.

Lilit and Jilly raised their heads and sit high on their hindquarters and take in his every move. He scoops a good couple handfuls of nuts and puts them in a tin plate. Returning to our party, he places the plate next to the furions and they do a little dance for him before they tucked into their treat.

As we eat, I keep up our conversation.

"What news have you from the north?" I query.

"I've come most recent from Seas-End, though some'll call it Port Tullamoor for the new Lord of the Keep," he says with a little sneer that I picked up on. "I've always done a brisk business there and come away from the docks with bartered wares from faraway ports. Have ya ever been?"

"Nay."

"Well, it's not as friendly as it once was. The Lord has roaming guards throughout the city now, making a nuisance of themselves. They are sayin' some of the dock waifs and strays go missing since they've been patrolling. The shop owners and market vendors are talking behind their backs. They're saying the guardsman help themselves to what they want and don't pay near enough, if at all. I was glad to be moving on this trip."

"So, this Lord Tullamoor, he's always been like this?" I wondered to him.

"Nay, he is the youngest son that's taking control after the death of the old Lord Tullamoor, a good sort he was. The rightful heir, Lord Ronælt, is gone missing. So, Lord Thaôs has taken control and rules NOT with a light hand." He has a disgusted look about him. "The new Lord spends his suns with his birds—, falconry, he calls it. Sport of Kings, he calls it. He taxes the incoming merchant vessels heavy. And the common folk pay for it with rising costs of goods. Tariffs, he calls it. They are getting angrier about it too, I'd say."

I've struck a nerve in the tinker and it helps me to understand a little more of this snake, whose head I see.

We've finished our midsun-meal, and I spy Carrie's eyes drifting over to the wagon a number of times.

"Master Tinker, what say we examine your wares and mayhaps change your mood," I suggested, and he laughs heartily.

"A-sure that, I've been running on, eh?" he says, his mood jovial again.

Carrie looks at the pretty things that tinkers keep out front on display for just that purpose. I roamed the inside of the wagon and opened the drawers along his shop's sides. I do have a purpose really and no real need of anything. I'm wasn't sure why I hailed the tinker in the first place. And then I glimpsed from the corner of my eye, something in a drawer amongst some bracelets and trinkets that I have been eyeing for Carrie. A burnished, encrusted amulet of a sort with an emerald green stone the shade of Finnie's eyes at its center. But what truly draws me to it is the embossed image on the rear of it. An etching of a Drægon not unlike Da's imagery that he had Argo place on my dirk and short sword.

As I looked up, Carrie is eyeing a floppy brimmed hat. It would be a practical thing for her in the heat of the sun on our travels. Waving a few bees away that have kept abuzz about my head, I got over to her and the tinker.

"What would you have for that lovely hat, Master Lee?" I asked as I approached and interrupted them. "And can you tell me a bit about this amulet, I'm drawn to?"

I continued as a few more bees buzzed about us, making me look up into the Calpaca tree as I know honeybees are drawn to them.

The tinker looks at the trinket I have in my hands and then back at me curiously.

"'Tis interesting that ya should pick up that piece. It has a peculiar history, it does. And now, pondering our whole meeting and all, ya know? Ya hailed me and yet ya dinit have any great desire to browse my wares," he remarks. "I'll tell you the tale of this amulet. On a rare trip into the mountains north of Tullamoor Keep and in a time where the old Lord still ruled there, I ventured towards an outpost the Northerners sometimes visited so that I might do some business with them. They call themselves Noördan, ya know."

I shake my head, because I don't. I don't even know there were folks that lived in the Northern Reaches. No one has ever told me of such a thing.

"Lord Tullamoor has an outpost there with sentries questioning all that come and go. Which are mighty few, mind ya. Just those that want to do a bit a tradin' once in a great while. Being there for just that and on this day, and making my way to a small lake aside from the outpost to make my camp as the Noördans would find me there and barter with me for goods, I knew. 'Twas where I met the man who traded me for these very same horses more recently, mind ya.... But, back to my tale.... You see, I passed an old man with two youngers afoot, and garbed a bit queer to me. I found him sitting on a stump aside a great fallen log next to a fresh-filled grave. A huge sort of a man, and he looked me eye to eye even though he was seated atop a stump. He had just planted some red poppies atop the grave and sat aside it, holding a small box. He looked up, all startled like, when I approached in my wagon." The tinker pauses, and his forehead wrinkles and his eyes go a bit wide at the memory.

"The tree he was sittin' under.... a huge Calpaca tree, very much akin to this very one we're under now—; it's a fact. He offered me some sweet honey on a bun amongst many he had sitting upon the log at his side and on a special made plate. And so, I sat with him and shared his honey and a bun. He told me a tale whilst his grandsons played about him and tried to climb the tree., tThey were both six or seven year-enders."

"In his tale, he told me his wife of sixty year had left specific instructions to bury her under that very tree near the lake as they had met there, she being from a land out past Sea's End, he said. Now this is where this tale gets a bit strange, mind ya. She told him a stranger would happen by and that he should give the stranger the box he held with that same amulet you are aholdin' now. But he remained reluctant as it had rested upon her breast for all the time he had known her and it was precious to him. Even, he said, as he knew it was precious to her. But it was what she wanted and so, not knowing me at all, he gave it up to me, not a thing asked in return," he continues his story.

Even Carrie listens close now.

"Well, I went to my wagon and shuffled things about and found two leather braided bracelets that had smaller, but like, stones as the amulet at their center. I handed them to him and told him they were for his grandsons. He just nodded, smiled, and thanked me. And here's the further mystery to it and I swear it is true, on my life. A great boom sounded over the lake, and I rose and started out to discover the cause of it. Just a moment later I turned back to the old man and he had simply vanished, and his grandsons, too. Nowhere in sight could I spy them. The stump he had sat upon lay barely visible, and the log I had just sat on was crumbled and rotted and near swallowed back into the ground. I saw no fresh grave, but in its place, a small field of red poppies." The tinker shakes his head. "Do ya know, that was near to seven year to this very sun."

"The stranger part of the tale, as if there could be a stranger part, is that when the old man put the amulet in my hands, he had said, and here's where it gets more peculiar still, 'My wife told me to tell the man I gave it to, that one day a lad would hail your wagon and find the amulet and you should trade it to him.' And I responded to the old man, 'How did she know the first stranger ya saw would be a tinker?' And then I said, 'How will I know this lad?' The old man just smiled and then clasped my hands and said, 'You will know.'"

Our eyes meet.

"So, ya see, strange as it most surely seems, I believe that amulet was meant for ye."

I chuckled but hold the thought. And as I pondered the tinker's tale, my eyes are drawn to the towering Calpaca tree and a thought comes upon me.

"Master Lee, what would you barter for a large jug of sweet honey?"

"Honey is a valuable item to me. It trades quite well, and a jug would be dear indeed," he returns.

"Find me a large pot if you will."

And he does.

Looking up, I walked around the base of the tree and smiled when I see the large hole some distance up the trunk.

"Would you have a pipe and smoke weed, perchance?"

And again, the tinker obliges.

Getting the smoke weed aflame in the pipe, I string a twine about the pot through its handles and begin climbing the Calpaca tree, making my way onto a large branch next to the hole in the trunk of the tree. I set about puffing on the pipe. The tinker and Carrie looked up to me, mouths agape as I was blowing great billows of smoke into the tree trunk. After a bit and with smoke coming back at me from the hole, I dropped the pipe back to the tinker below me and pulled the pot up to me. I then proceeded to extend my arm into the hole. I immediately find and grabbed hold of a large honeycomb. Breaking off a generous piece, I withdraw it and placed it in the pot. Using a tin cup, I gathered cupful after cupful of the leaking honeycomb within and managed to fill the pot quite full. Carefully lowering the pot to the waiting tinker, I then make my way back down the tree.

He is amazed. Lilit, and Jilly, and even Carrie are attacking my honey-covered arm. I laughed and offered it up for their feeding enjoyment.

"How will that do for you, master tinker?"

"I call it a fair trade for both the hat for the little lass and the amulet and count myself ahead by the midsun-meal ya have treated me to." He has a broad smile.

"And I have found your company quite agreeable and your tale and generosity even more so, Stan Lee. May your travels be ever safe and profitable as well. Thank you."

Carrie and I cleaned up. Carrie dons her new hat, and I pulled her up to sit afore me instead of behind for the after-sun travel. We leave the tinker as he clos up his wagon and offerse a wave for good tidings.

I think Stan Lee's tale a most mysterious story and if not true, he makes a wondrous and creative bard, in any case. I do appreciate my time with him.

23

Chere is a Place

Finnie, and little Èvie, and Tristan have been traveling close to two fortnight. She is beginning to think that Ari has sent her to the end of all Aeryth. She has not seen a living soul now for a handful of suns. The travel had been an adventure at first. She rode and cared for her new charges, her family now, and it has given Finnie hope and determination. They are near about all that is keeping her going these past few suns. Not seen her twenty-year-end as yet and she's now taken the role of mum for two youngers. She had known them not yet two moon, yet she knows a desperate love for them both. It seems a natural thing to her, and she'd be a Grizzly mum to any that would try to harm or separate her from them.

A fortnight of living out of a carriage, covered in dust from the long and earthen travelway, and spending nights off to the safety of the woods in camp, has taken toll on the youngers. She has fared little better. Finnie hopes it will not be long before they reached another sign of civilization. Her hopes are answered the very next sun.

Overjoyed at reaching a towne called Trader's Cross, she and the youngers take haven in the towne's small Inn. There, they are able to bathe and stable Chessie for a few days to rest and rejuvenate. Finnie finds the people here welcoming and the food and safe harbor as a temporary cure for the long trip on which she finds herself. In a few short moons, she has grown from a girl to a strong, confident woman—, a woman with a family that depends upon her. They spend three suns in the small towne and soon get their energy renewed and so, after the small break they find themselves on the travelway once again.

Four suns later, she finds herself in yet another small towne called Westend Towne, and Ari's map reads that she should turn south here. Great mountains filled the horizon to the west and she has never seen such a sight. They are still a great distance away and she can tell they must be massive and much grander than any tales she has heard, for she has never seen a mountain with her own eyes. No travelway heads towards them from this towne. Ari had said that nothing lay beyond these great mountains but the Endless Western Sea his Da had spoken of.

With Westend towne behind them, another five suns passes, and she has encountered not a soul on the travelway since. Trail is the word that best describes this travelway now. After the large east-west travelway she has started the journey on, this one would barely allow two wagons to pass abreast. A river flows on a line with her travel to the west of her and from time a'times she would glimpses Bane move apace with them within the tree line to the east. She is amazed at the Great Wolf. Ari had told her that the wolf would make the trip and watch over them. At the time, and though she has come to love Bane, she remained skeptical that Ari could know such a thing. But the wolf remains with them, even chasing off a bear that had made like to charge the carriage a few suns ago. He is ever present in their camp each night, watching over the youngers. She can no longer doubt the bond between Ari and his great Mountain Dread.

She has been traveling a good part of the morn, and the sun rides high in the sky. It is beautiful countryside they are traveling through. In those stretches of travelway where the trees parted, the mountains to the west are magnificent to behold. Colorful birds had alighted upon the carriage rails, curious of these human folk they see little of, most like. Great elk would pass across the way afore them, stopping to stare at the carriage and sending the youngers to oohs and aahs.

This morn, two things happened that changed her mood in as many times.

First, in the distance she can make out streams of smoke from chimneys and because she looks down into the vale in which the towne set, she can even make out the towne folk going about their business in the shops about towne. The river turns further east in front of the towne and there lies a wide stone bridge across the river leading into the village. There are wildflowers about the hillside and plain leading into this quaint towne, and it warms her heart to think she has finally reached her destination. A nervous twitch grows in her stomach knowing she is coming home, though to a place she has never visited before. But this was home for Ari and she is determined to make it her home as well. The travelway widens as she nears towne. This must be Middenvale.

The second thing she notes are the first riders she has encountered in four suns. There are three of them and the way they are riding put her on alert. She can see that they are gazing at her with intent. They were purposefully talking to each other as well, leaning from one to the other in pointed conversation. Intuition makes Finnie's stomach tighten in anticipation of a confrontation with these riders. She has become well acquainted with the 'highwaymen' term.

At her feet, she manages to string her bow, having to let go of Chessie's rein for a moment to accomplish the task. She pulls her quiver from behind the seat to the front and whispers urgently to Tristan to climb into the back of the carriage. Once there, she lifts Evie over the seat back to join him, again having to let loose of the reins to manage it.

The men approached, but keep their eyes forward, not looking her way at all. She keep her eyes forward as well, daring to hope they will just pass her by. But having fought against the slavers and thugs alongside Ari for more than two moons, her intuition tolls all alarms.

She continues a bit further when, of a sudden, the three of them come galloping from the back of the carriage. A move designed to unnerve a woman driving a carriage. One rider comes fast from the right and reins up alongside Chessie grabbing the mare's reins in front of Finnie. The two others galloped on past her on the left, going past the carriage a good fifteen paces before turning to face her. One has an ugly sneer upon his face and the other is already dropping from his saddle, short sword in hand.

Finnie has already started to move.

The man with the sneer says saying, "Come down and play with us, Sheila dear."

Before his last word is fully uttered, Finnie has risen and stands forward, one foot on the high footboard. She plants herself with arrow nocked and loosed.

Finnie's arrow finds its mark in the man's left shoulder, throwing him backwards off his horse.

The thug who have dismounted, sword in hand, turned in disbelief at the scream of pain from his comrade at arms, watching as he falls. All this distraction is to his detriment. Finnie continues forward with a great leap and runs, with bow raised, directly for him. She swings her bow down as if it is an axe and strikes must be Argo."

"And you must be a dear friend of Arias Bard," he returns with a smile to a quizzical look upon Finnie's face. "No other would be standing next to Bane in such a relaxed manner."

the sword arm of her would-be assailant. His weapon fall from his hand with an audible crack sounding from his wrist. In a move Ari had taught her, she reflexively kicks forward and down, thrusting her heel with her whole weight into the side of his knee. Another loud crack is her reward. That and a hideous scream of pain from the man.

The third attacker has moved quicker than she has expected. His footsteps are bearing down on her. A blur arrives from her left. A wild howl is followed by a heavy thud and a scream of terror. She holds the dirk she had pulled from her boot and points it to the neck of her second attacker. The third thug lies flat on his back with Bane's muzzle and bared teeth not a hand's width from his throat. He is busy soiling himself.

She sneers down at the arsehole of a soul under her blade and then over at her first victim. N who is now down on his knees looking very dizzy and swaying. He had been foolish enough to pull her arrow from his shoulder and is now near to fainting from what she can tell.

She laughs aloud and it stills the screaming that is coming from the youngers in the carriage. She lifts her foot from the chest of the thug under her and rises to her feet.

"Bane, to me," Finnie says, and the wolf slowly retreats from his victim and walks over to her, his eyes roaming from one thug to the others. After things settled a bit and their attention rivetsed to her and Bane, she says, "I'll give you three a count of thirty to be on your way. You'll leave your mounts here with me and if you aren't out of my bow's reach by my count, you should worry greatly."

To her surprise and relief, they are somehow up to the task. Just as they are limping into the tree line, a man comes galloping and reining to a stop before her. He leaps to the ground and approaches.

Finnie immediately notes that Bane makes no move to interfere.

"Are you okay, Mãamel?" he asks as he approaches, nearly breathless. "I've been watching these three from the stables as they were ushered out of towne by us. I became concerned they might cause trouble when I saw your carriage."

Finnie looks the stranger up and down as she says, "Yo They both break into laughter.

After a short round of formal introductions, Argo turns to look back towards Middenvale and then back to Finnie. She notes his pensive countenance.

"Well, Steffænie, as you are seeking Grayce, might I suggest I take you directly to her homestead?"

She does not ask his reasons, just agrees. "The horses I've taken as bounty from my attackers—, would you help me tether them to my carriage?"

She meanders over to pick up and clean her bloodied arrow. Then she returns to the carriage to further comfort the youngers.

Everything arranged, Argo takes the lead and they headed back north, away from towne. and then aways back, they turned west toward the mountains and Grayce's homestead. The ride is not too long and Grayce and Effie are sitting out under Grayce's shade tree when Argo and the carriage comes around the trail's bend and out from the tree line. They rise as they notice a much larger Bane trotting alongside the carriage. Their minds are awhirl in what this could portend.

Argo dismounts near the ladies and as Finnie is helping Tristan and little Èvie down from the carriage, he whispers to them.

"A friend of Arias."

They looked at each other for a moment and then run over to help her. Even before Finnie can introduce herself, Grayce and Effie have her in a tight hug. She beams and returns their hugs enthusiastically. Tristan and little Èvie don't wait for introductions. They are delighted to be out of the carriage and go about chasing Bane in goodhearted play.

"Well then, you must be Grayce." Finnie gazes upon the older woman. "Could this then be Ari's mentor, Effie? You would not know it, but he has said that you are the reason I live today." Grayce and Effie stared upon her in disbelief.

Finnie takes it that they are surprised that she gazes their names.

She steps back in surprise herself when they both near shouted in unison, "Ari? You call our Arias, Ari?"

They laughed aloud as Finnie's face flushes.

"Yea, you have named us sure, lass, but pray tell what should we be calling you? And if I've not missed the mark, you have quite a tale to regale us with," muses Grayce. "And your youngers, what should we call them?"

Finnie raises both her hands to her mouth, having completely forgotten to do just that, so comfortable she does feel in their presence.

"Forgive me, as I feel I know all three of you so well, I'd forgotten that I am but a complete stranger to you! My name is Steffænie, but Ari calls me Finnie, and I hope you will as well." She presents herself and the ladies each come in for another hug. "The youngers are Tristan and Èvelynn, but we call her Èvie." Èvie comes running up to Finnie.

"Please sit, Finnie, and you as well, little Èvie."

Èvie starts started toddling over and then just turns around, running back towards her brœther and Bane. A smile and a look of love fills Finnie's face.

"Argo, can you find two more seats for us while I fetch some drinks and cakes… are you hungry Finnie?"

"Oh yes, it has been a long and eventful sun," she answers. "And the excitement has left us with quite an appetite, I'm afraid."

"I'll swing the stew pot into the flame then, and it'll be heated in a turn of a sand-glass or less. When I've returned, mayhaps you can tell us a bit of your tale," says Grayce as she heads towards the cottage.

Effie and Finnie fall into the chairs and a deep sigh escapes Finnie. So good to be home among friends. Argo returns with two additional chairs and sits across from Finnie.

"Finnie, before you begin your tale, I wanted to explain a thing. You may have wondered why I brought you directly here and not into towne first. It is because there are a couple of the King's men who have been staying in towne. We believe that they're here to keep a watch out for Arias. If they find out you have seen him recently, there might be some trouble," he explains.

Finnie's pulse rises with her eyebrows, suddenly fearing her new home might not be so safe as she imagined. And then her thoughts turned to Ari's safety, hearing more, the King's serious intent.

"I do not know all of the reasons for the things you speak of as Ari just recently explained to me his quest. He did tell me that Kingsmen had murdered his Da." Finnie shudders.

"We can speak more of that later," he says as Grayce returns returning with the wineskin and a plate tall with honey cakes. The youngers, like youngers anywhere, seesaw these and run over.

Finnie begins her tale, telling first how and when she had first met Arias. The three of them looked at Finnie, aghast. There are many questions of course, and Finnie tries to answer them as best she might.

Arias' friends know she has more to tell but they can also see that Finnie and the youngers are in need of rest. All decided that they will take up the tale again later.

They talked of little things over the eve-meal, getting to know one another. Argo offers his fare-thee-wells after eve-meal and Finnie, Grayce, and Effie talked well into the night, after putting the youngers to bed.

Carrie and I traveled north on the travelway towards Sea's End at an easy pace. Carrie speaks more of her family and her life and I listened attentively.

We camped well inside the wood line each night, oft-times stopping our trek early so that I can find food as our provisions have begun to run low. Carrie is curious to learn everything I can teach her, and a strong bond continues to form betwixt us.

A fortnight into our trip, we come upon Groome, a busy cross-trail towne. I decided to stay a night or two, so that we can bathe away the dust of travel and enjoy soft beds and filling food. After a quick survey about us, we headed towards an Inn that holds promise. Inside the Inn, business is bustling and from glancing about, the patrons are satisfied with their fare. It will do quite well.

Once I can get us seated and settled, I planned to take some time to study the amulet I had received from the tinker upon the travelway. As is my custom, I wear my pack and carry my Bo-staff into the dining hall. I'd stabled Paint across the way at a large horse barn and paddock and am assured Paint will be well cared for. I'd already acquired a large room with two beds for us and this is to be our time to relax a bit before eve-meal. We are surprised to find the Inn had commissioned a minstrel to entertain the Inn guests.

While Carrie pulls her chair about to listen to the minstrel sing and play a stringed instrument, I removed my pack to find some tools to clean up the amulet. I opened my pack and the furions stealthily stayed hidden. Searching for my tool bag, I removed my Shaäcken game board and pieces to get lower into the pack. Finding the tools, I proceeded to clean the amulet. After removing the seven years of caked grime and debris covering the necklace, I see that the metal setting holding the unusually colored stone is indeed very intricate. Studying it closely, I can make out what appears to be runes of a sort, twisted within the filigree. They are not so dissimilar to the runes Da had carved into my Bo-staff. I study the runes upon it to see if perchance any are identical to those on the amulet. Though one or two are similar, none are altogether the same. Should I ever find the Druid that

Da had quested me to find, the runes are a question near to the top of my list of many.

The setting itself is attached to what appears to be braided leather. But as I examined closer, I find that it isn't leather at all. I actually cannot remember ever seeing such a material. It has the look of leather, but the heft of metal, and I can twist it in every which a way and it would springs immediately back to its original shape. It appears to be made for a small neck and even then, I know not how anyone could fit it over their head as there seems to be no opening clasp. I judged it too tight to fit over the head of the smallest younger. I placed it over my own head to confirm this and though in my hands it seems it cannot fit, when I bring it up and over, it stretches and slips easily over my head and in place about my neck—; the amulet setting itself firmly against my chest near to my heart.

A warm flush envelopes me. At first it makes me anxious, but then it overwhelms me with the euphoric feeling that it holds no danger for me. This same feeling, as a fact, reminds me of when I first grasped my Bo-staff upon the day of its gifting. I actually feel reassured that wearing the amulet is the right thing to do, and so I leave it in place.

Out of the corner of my eye, I spy another patron at the Inn has been eyeing my board-game I'd taken from my pack earlier and has risen to come over to me. Not of a mind to engage with anybody and thinking just that, of a sudden, the amulet warms upon my chest, or rather, warms deep into my torso about it. As I looked to the stranger, the man suddenly stops. His expression grows puzzled. He even scratches his head before returning to his seat and occupying himself with something else. I chuckled.

Meanwhile, the minstrel has finished his song and Carrie swings back to me and asks if we can get something to eat. I certainly am ready as well.

We are served the evening's fare—, roast fowl and smashed garlic 'n onion taters with sweet roasted carrots aside with onions and forest 'shrooms in a gravy. Carrie's eyes light up and I have to chuckle as she tucks in with a gusto.

"What, you've not enjoyed my camp food, Carrie?" I query her.

"Oh, nay, Ser. It's just that my mum and auntie would make such a meal for Callie and I," she answers. She stiffens then and sits up straighter.

Her eyes started to well up and I reached over and squeezed her hand.

"Well then Carrie, seconds for you if you'd like!"

She smiles back and says, "Oh, yes!"

After the eve-meal, the Innkeeper shows us the bathhouse and we go our separate ways to wash a fortnight of deep grit from our skin.

Finishing afore young Carrie, I awaited her outside the lady's bath-house for quite some while. She is, I'm sure, relaxing within a like bathing tub to what mine was, steamy perfumed water as it turns out and keeping her content for near the turn of a sand-glass.

She finally returns to me with a smile and a contented look about her and the scent of lavender in her hair. We decided to retire to our soft feather beds. I promised her that we can explore the towne of Groome on the mor-row's morn. We ended our day in soft beds under heavy quilted-linen blan-kets. A chill but comfortable breeze wafts in through a large window with its sashes thrown open and curtains gently waving. 'Twas a very nice sen-sation to curl up under our quilts.

We find we have slept well past the rise of the sun and deemed it fit-ting. A refreshing breeze on the morrow's morn nudges us finally awake. I treated the two of us to a huge morn's meal in the dining hall at a small cor-ner table under a window facing the travelway. We have scramblers filled with a creamy cheese and sweet red peppers, rashers of bacon, and taters skillet fried with onions and herbs. We are rubbing our bellies and laughing as I admitted my camp food cannot compare.

I donned my pack and grabbed my Bo-staff and we exited out of the Inn and onto a great travelway that the locals called a Boulevard. Great long-limbed trees are planted twenty paces apart on either side of the travelway and provided a nice shade for the walks and the travelway as well. The sounds of the towne greeted us as we walked, —Horses, and carriages, and the yells of good-hearted folk at work and play—, and the sidewalks are busy with town-folk. These are wide wooden walkways along the fronts of shops and eateries for, at the least, 500 paces down its length. There are side rues emptying onto the Boulevard from both North and South every fifty paces or so. Spying down the byways, one can see several large homes, each big enough to house five families at the least of it, it does seem.

People bustled about in carriages and there are bright-colored gown-s adorned ladies with goodmen at their arms. As we walked amongst so many others down the creaking wood sidewalks, we marveled at the shops with great glass fronts displaying the clothing and wares of their proprietors. Being a scale thrice the size of Quill'spie, Groome is the largest towne I have ever experienced. This many folk in one place busy about their lives is a wonder.

When not dodging ladies pushing carriages carrying young-uns or gaily conversing couples, I spy Carrie especially entranced by the fancy long skirts and colorful blouses displayed in shop windows. It is only then that I noticed the sad shape of her garment. Half our way down the boulevard, I pulled Carrie into one of the clothier's shops. It is not so fanciful as some and shows more practical garments in the window as well. Carrie glances up at me with a hopeful face.

Bells chimed as we entered the shop, which catches me off guard. A young woman comes out from a back room at the sound of the chimes. I looked back at the door and think it a clever device now.

"What can I help you with?" The lady beams as she puts down a spool of thread pierced with needles as if she has just finished a project in the back room.

"My charge here," I explained it as I patted Carrie on both shoulders, "is in need of some new garments."

"She most certainly is!" exclaims the shop's matron as she stares back at the pitiful shambles that is the state of Carrie's plain linen dress, torn and still caked with the dusts and grime of our trip.

"Have you been traveling a fortnight aback a horse?" she asks.

With hands upon her hips and leaning back to survey us, incredulous of the sight.

We laughed aloud and answered "yea" together. The shop mãam's eyebrows lifted at the prospect.

"And will you be traveling further in the same manner?" she further queries.

"We're going to visit my auntie," Carrie beams.

"Well then, call me Shea, kind sir and lass, and I believe I can help you out." She smiles. "I've just finished a new design of my own. 'Twas to be for my own niece, quite near to your age, as a fact. Let me show you."

Gone but a few moments, she returns with what appeared to be a long skirt in a tan linen material. She glances over Carrie, sizing her up no doubt, and goes to a shelf upon the wall and pulls out a white linen tunic as well. As I watched, she also picks up a wide leather belt and a few ribbons.

"What is it they call you, lass?"

"Carrie, Mãam," she shyly returns.

"Well, Carrie, come with me to the back-room. We will see to getting you clothed up proper." And the two started toward the back. "And you sir, pray, have a seat in the corner there for goodmen, as you wait."

As I lifted my pack from my back, my other ladies, Lilit and Jilly stick their noses out, surveying their surroundings. Just as I take my seat as proffered, Shea hurries out again and opens a drawer, secreted from it a cottony parcel, then a couple of large buttons, before slipping into the back again.

My wait extends well past the turn of a sand-glass. I heard the occasional giggle or outright laugh emitting from the doorway to the back.

Carrie and Shea come back to the front of the shop, and I marveled to see a brand-new Carrie afore me. She wears what Shea calls pantaloons. Looking like a skirt, they actually are trousers of a sort and quite suitable for travel aback a horse. She also wears a pleated white linen tunic tucked into her pantaloons and has about her waist a wide leather belt, featuring a large oval bronze buckle with a flower depicted upon its face. She is wearing a somewhat worn pair of boots, shined up, but clearly not new.

Carrie simply beams as she shows me her new garments, and my eyes are drawn to her hair, done in a single braid and laid upon her shoulder with a red ribbon tied into it. She has a like ribbon under the large collar of the tunic and it is tied into a bow in front. She runs over to me.

"Mãamel Shea even gave me bloomers to wear., I've never worn bloomers," she whispers.

I laughed. "Well, Shea, you've made Carrie into a proper young lass again, as promised! What do I owe you for your service?"

"A proper introduction for a start," says Shea with a smile.

Carrie immediately offers one. "You can call him Ser Drægonheart, Mãam,"

I take a step back and give her an astonished look.

"Where did you hear that name, Carrie?" I asked, quite puzzled.

"'Twas Seri, Ser, as you never told us your name. She told us about how you had saved her and Benji and others too, and cause of all your Drægon's and such," she says, bursting with her newfound knowledge of our escapades.

I chuckled at this news having been caught off guard with its telling.

"Seri said you made Sir Fafhärd her new papa and Mãam Janælle her mum. And I knew then you could find my auntie for me."

"Shea, call me Arias if it suits you, such long titles make me uncomfortable," I say with a hint of a smile.

She returns it with a thoughtful look. "Arias, then." We settled on some coin for Carrie's new garments, and much more reasonable than I had expected.

"One other thing, Shea, would you know where two strangers in towne might find a decent midsun-meal? And would you join us as a further thank you for your services?"

"I would," she answers. "My cousin owns a bakery just around the corner next to the park. And I would be honored to join you, Ser."

Shea closes her shop and leads us to her cousin's bakery where we shared a marvelous meal. While there, she confides to me a bit of a tale circulating about towne.

"People say there is a vigilante working about the travelways and trapper's trails, disturbing highwaymen going about their nefarious business. There have also been soldiers about towne of late and who say they are searching for this vigilante," she adds.

"What brings you to tell me such a thing, Shea?" I query.

She looks at Carrie and then back to me. Her expression softens.

"There was a sillier part of the tale as well. The tale goes that he travels with a Wolf and a pair of polecats." Her face now loses any pretense at guile.

At this, two heads poked out of my pack and stared up at her. I am not sure they liked to be called polecats.

"Some say he has done great deeds and that his cause is just," she continues. "If all the tales are true, I would count myself one in this camp."

I stared at her and wondered that tales such as this circulated in a towne like Groome, a good ways from where Finnie and I were hunting the slavers.

"Thank you again, Shea, for all your help with Carrie and even with leading us to such a good midsun-meal here. I believe that Carrie and I should be on our way soon if we are to make any distance afore the sun would set on us. She will certainly travel in style for the rest of our journey."

I leave some coin up on the table and take Carrie's hand as we headed back to the Inn and stables, Shea waving her fare-the-wells to us and Carrie returning them with an enthusiastic wave of her own. Carrie pulls on my tunic sleeve and whispers again into my ear, "She said you were a most polite and handsome goodman."

24

Morning has broken

arrie and I headed, hand in hand, back first to the Inn, and then directly to the livery stable to settle my accounts and set out as soon as possible upon Paint. Shea's warning has unnerved me, for I cyphered it to mean two things. First, that my activities with Finnie have become known, not just in Quill'spie where Finnie and I had sought aid for our rescued victims, but even so far away as Broome. It lies a full fortnight north of Quill'spie and I would not have thought that such news as that would travel so far in so short a time. Second, it has somehow brought the attention of the Kingsmen. Have they made a connection betwixt me and the activity against the slavers?

The query to myself then answers as we stepped out of the Inn, my account settled there, and as we are headed to the stables. There in front of the livery stand, stood two soldiers. One wears the colors and sigil of Lord Tullamoor, which I discovered in my dealings with the slavers, and the other wears the livery of the King. A Kingsman's special soldier's garb, as a fact. The eyes of the one in Tullamoor's colors scans across the Boulevard and fall directly to me., I feigned looking in another direction. There seems to be definite recognition in his eyes.

Seeing him move with an apparent limp, I immediately take him to be the watcher that Finnie had struck with her arrow.

Moor. Instincts.

Mayhaps, just now, he has recognized Carrie as well. The Kingsman he stands with has quite similar features and I think they could even be brœthers. They started across the Boulevard appearing to head towards the Inn, but the guardsman's attention is solely on me, I feared.

I wished with all my soul that it is not so. That he would be distracted, or though I know it could not happen, that he would forget about us completely. I feared I will be fighting these two men in the street. Let them pass us by, being all I can think, so I can get Carrie to her aunt.

My chest warms about the tinker's amulet as it had earlier. As they approached, ever closer, the guardsman stops in the middle of the travelway, nearly run down by a team and wagon, but for the swift action of his companion, pulling him aside. He stands and shakes his head, eyes blank with confusion etched upon his brow, all to the amusement of his Kingsman friend. Finally, they started back across the way again, completely ignoring both Carrie and I. They are engrossed in an animated conversation about who knows what. They walked right past us and into the Inn behind us. Reaching into my tunic, I touched the amulet hanging around my neck. It is not lost on me that this is the second time something like this has happened as I wear it.

We headed back to the travelway at a steady trot for a turn of a sandglass and no sign that we are being followed. I finally let myself relax.

Our third sun out from Broome, we are riding into a small village with a small sign posted on the trail leading into the towne. Twisted Creek, it reads. Carrie is very excited.

"Oh, Ser Drægonheart, we are here! I know this place. Carrie and I came to that store there with Papa and uncle Jed. They let us buy cinnamon sugar sticks!" Carrie exclaims.

I smiled to think she is so close to family now. "Well then, let us get a sugar stick.,"

Her eyes light up.

We entered the general store, and Carrie pulls my sleeve and whispers, "That's Master Daèton, he's quite stern."

'Twas my turn for brow to raise. Axel Daèton is the name that Moor had given me as a contact in this selfsame village. I know he resides here, as when Carrie had mentioned the name of the towne when she spoke of her aunt, I had recognized it as a name on Moore's list.

I approached the counter he stands behind and addressed him. "Axel Daèton? We have a common friend, I believe. My mentor said I should look you up if I had a need one day. He calls himself Moor."

I offered an extended arm in greeting.

A wide smile engulfs his once dour features and as he grabs my forearm in a soldier's greet, he near pulls me over the counter.

"Well met, Arias Côeurdrægon. He did indeed speak of his apprentice. Well met, lad. What tidings do you bring of the Mouser, and what need have you?" His hand is still tightly about my forearm in a grip like a bear.

I am more than a bit taken aback that he would knows me by name, but as an afterthought, I do suppose that if I know of them, Moor would undoubtedly have spoken of me to some of them.

"Well met to you as well, sir, and my need stands aside me."

"Why, it is one of the Sutter lasses." His smile melts from his face. "Where is your sister, lass? Your aunt and uncle have been sick and, in a state, over you."

"Yea, so you do indeed know her family. She knew of you and said she is especially fond of your cinnamon sugar sticks," I say seeking his attention with my eyes.

Carrie's eyes have begun to well and Axel immediately reaches into a large glass jar. He pulls a sugar stick from it and gazes back to her. Her tear receding, she leans up over the counter to accept her treat.

He pulls his work apron from his neck and yells to the back. "Rose, I'm headed out to Jed Gastôn's place, come watch the front, will you?"

"Come, Arias, and bring your friend., I'll take you to her aunt and uncle," and he is already out the front door leaving it to close with a large bang behind him. He mounts a horse he has tethered in front of his shop, and Carrie and I climbed back atop Paint and followed him out.

We traveled north from towne, mayhaps a turn of a sand-glass and at a trot the whole time. Finally, we rounded a bend and Carrie tightens her arms around me from behind, her head peeking around my arm to see. Afore us lies a large homestead with both crops, barn creatures and a large, cleared pasture. Nearest to us sits a good-sized stone home and a long low built barn. A woman of mayhaps thirty-five year tends a garden with a young lad playing in the soil next to her. I can tell that Carrie is anxious to be on the ground, so I swing her down.

No more than Carrie's toes have touched the grass and she takes off running to her aunt.

About halfway there, her aunt recognizes her, and falls to her knees, and screams. "Jed! Jed, come quick! Oh, my Carrie... my dear Carrie!"

"Auntie," Carrie cries. "Callie was kilt.... Mama and Papa were kilt, too. But I was saved."

Her aunt hugs her, sobbing. Her uncle comes running around the corner of their barn and joins his wife, falling to his knees to wrap his arms around them both.

Axel and I dismounted and standing aside, patiently observing the reunion, sad as it is. Finally, Carrie breaks away and comes to me, takes my hand, and pulls me to her aunt and uncle.

"This is Ser Drægonheart, auntie and uncle, see the Drægon on his heart?" She says as she reaches up to touch Argo's brand seared into the elk skin on my breast. "He saved us, him and Mãamel Finnie kilt all the bad men. But one of them shot Callie with an arrow and she bled too much, and she died." She sniffs. "She died. But he saved me and there were so many of them and only him and Mãamel Finnie and Bane. Bane is his wolf and he kilt one of the bad men, too."

The story just pours out from her and you can tell it is a tale she needed to tell.

Her uncle comes and grabs my arm in greeting. Carrie's aunt comes and hugs me through tears.

"If it suits," I say, "call me Arias, the youngers gave me the other name. Carrie is a special lass, Mãam."

"Call me Dẽanna, Arias, and this is my husband Jed. Please come in and speak with us," she begs and approaches Axel who says he needs to get back to the store and bids me to come see him.

Dẽanna kneels before her niece and examines her head-to-toe. "You've grown, sweet lass, since I last put eyes to you. And your garments and hair, 'tis a wonder to take in."

"Ser Drægonheart found Mãamel Shea in the big city, and she made these for me and braided my hair. I like it this way, do you?"

"Oh yes, dear, it suits you.," She pulls her back into a hug.

"Let me bring your horse around to the barn," offers Jed.

"I'll join you.; Paint can be a bit finicky with strangers," and we set out towards the barn.

Walking to the structure, Jed says, "I'll not ask you anything yet, as Dẽanna will be wont to hear all that you can say. But I will tell you that the bastards that attacked and killed Carrie's parents were as callous and evil as any in the whole of Aeryth. It could have been no uglier, what we found as we had just traveled to visit Dẽanna's sister, Carrie's mum."

"Yea, I've seen the aftermath of such a thing. I only wish I could say I have brought justice to all their killers, but alas, the murderers but kill and then steal the youngers to be traded to slavers. Those that held Carrie breathe no more, tho."

He gives a solemn nod in return.

I brushed down Paint. Lilit and Jilly make their appearances to explore the barn. Jed jumps and laughs as they squeezed out of my pack.

"So, did little Carrie speak the truth about the wolf as well?"

"Yea, I have a way with animals, like my Da," I offered.

Staying two suns with Carrie's family and when alone, I recounted to Jed and Dĕanna my tale and that of Finnie and what we had been about it these past moons. They expressed shock that such a thing could be happening and cursed the King for allowing it.

After leaving, I once again visited with Axel Daèton, to see if he can aid me more in my quest to end Tullamoor's evil business. He gives me a further contact in Sea's End to help me in my efforts. Staying but one more night with him, we speaks of Moor and to my delight he recounts a few tales of their friendship. My admiration for my mentor and coach grows in hearing them. I parted in the early morn, two suns hence as it is time to seek out Lord Tullamoor at Sea's End.

My travels were for the most part remained uneventful. Traveling the traders' trails and byways brings me to the outskirts of Sea's End from the South and East. I entered into the towne's gates there. Seas End is the largest by far of any towne I have ever visited by twenty-fold, later learning they speak of it as a *city* and not a mere towne. My senses are attacked by the sheer magnitude of it. The smell of waste and rot evident from the first. The noise makes Paint skittish and the furions burrowed deep within my saddlebags, no doubt to have the smell of the leather mask what lies about us. A fortunate breeze blows in from the sea and carries a welcome scent, though new to me. I pressed through the gates of the city, throngs of people passing in both directions, now traveling on brick and cobbled stone rues,

Axel Daèton had said that his friend owned a tavern near the docks and so I headed north towards the sea. The city, Axel had explained to me, has been built in ever-widening arcs growing wider from the center of the port which is its main business. The regal class live on the north and west side of the city. Labor and servant class lived in the low, flood prone areas to the east and where I'd entered the city. The merchant class make their homes in the southern quadrant. Fancier shops and markets lay betwixt the regal quarter and the city offices near the center of the city, but away from the docks.

I marveled at so many people doing so many different things at the same time. Street sweepers brooming debris down the stone gutters with bundles of long twigs and boughs tied to long branches to use as their trade tools. Shop owners wiping their store windows clean as others hawked wares and harkened customers in. Carts carrying fruits and vegetables rambled by me with youngers chasing after, while carriages with footmen holding good-men and ladies clip-clopped their way down tree lined avenues across the canal from me. Beyond them is a grand park with fine dressed ladies and youngers all about. Artists with canvasses set to easels sit next to the waterway on that side. On both sides, vendors with pushcarts selling food and pastries and drinks lined the banks, though on the far side they are under broad colorful umbrellas.

Axel had told me a great canal from the docks reaching fifteen furlongs to the south divides the city. Merchant and leisure castes to the west and the working caste to the east. Four great stone bridges connected the two, stretching over the canal and each are guarded on one end by Lord Tullamoor's guardsman and on the other by the city's counsel sheriffs.

Parks are scattered throughout the western and northern parts of the city whilst their equivalent spaces are used as markets and bazaars on the east end of towne.

I followed the canal, traveling on the east side of it, not sure I would be welcome on the other side. There are markets near each of the bridges.

They featured pubs and other shops that catered to the wealthy without the need for them to continue deeper into the seedier side of the city, I reckoned. It is not too long till dusk and I have a hunger and thirst, so I do not dally, thinking it better to meet with Axel's contacts here in the city as soon as possible.

Approaching the last bridge afore the inner city and docks, as directed, I turned east and into the heart of the city. The byways are made of brick here and venturing further east, they become an older cobblestone way again. I have never seen the like of it. As a fact, the experience of the city is wholly new to me and I think it a wonder. I draw stares from passersby quite often as I carry about my person and upon Paint my many weapons. Tullamoor guardsmen and the sheriffs are typically all who carry weapons within the city, though I see a few sheathed dirks aside.

Stone buildings rise as high as three stories on some corners. 'Twas dusk and they throw great shadows upon the rues. The local city folk have mostly retreated into their homes and Paint's clip-clop of hooves echoed off the stone buildings. Light is not totally gone from the byways, however. Long iron posts stand along the rue with large box lanterns sitting atop them. There are workers with long wooden poles with spouted cans attached on their top. Above reservoirs atop the iron posts are metal lantern boxes with four sides of thick glass and after the troughs are filled with oil, another worker would open one side of the glass box with yet another pole, touching a torch to each of two wicks within. The box begins to glow and shine light upon the walks and travelway.

I've reached a wide square with byways leading from it to the four compass points. What has clearly been a marketplace in sunlight is becoming now a different thing entirely. Large canopies on great poles are spread about in one corner of the square. A wide doorway to a three-story building in this same corner opens and a light encased in red glass glows from within.

Workers have carried large benches with cushions and backs out and placed them about and under the great canvas canopies. The benches are likened near to a bed. Small tables are set about them. Some are already being used by finely dressed goodmen, from west of the bridges, I'd wager. At one sit four young men and they passed a smoking tube that is attached to a tall glass bottle that bubbles with water and smoke. As each draw upon the tube, they would hold their breath in and would exhale a great cloud of smoke as from a smoke-weed pipe. They are enjoying it a great deal. Scantily clad women standing in the doorway laughed at them and beckoned them come into the red-lit interior.

In another corner men are playing at dice, laughing, and speaking crudely. From a doorway leading in from there, great chiming and ringing arises. In the third corner of the square, two great doors are open and laughter, and music, and singing is the fare of the eve.

The final corner draws my attention most. From it springs the growling of dogs and in return the cawing as from a great bird. Feathers are flying about. Hard laughter follows, and I know I will not like what I find there. Approaching, saddled atop Paint still, I gazed down upon the scene. There stands tethered to a pole, a great, white-feathered hawk of a kind I've never witnessed. It is of a tremendous size. Its plumage is speckled here and there with gold-tipped feathers and its beak is a deep gold color and tipped in onyx. One leg is rubbed raw from a leather tether and one of the great bird's wings is clearly broken, laying a kilter against its body. He sits upon a perch and guards the carcass of a large hare. It is a cruel betting game and the bird's handler holds the biggest pile of coin.

Men standing about have large dogs held on tight tethers that are drooling and in a vicious state. As I watched, wagers are be placed on whether a dog can retrieve the hare from under the raptor's guard. Dogs with fatal wounds have been pulled away and the handlers' coin pile grows larger.

I must do something to end it all.

A thought comes over me, and I sit upon Paint in a still, lowering my heartbeat and slowing my breathing., I entered my *Calming*. Reaching out with thought, or rather, I'd describe it as a *spirit-sense*, touching upon the furions, and joined them with me in the *Calming*. Pressing a thought to them, an idea, they both responded positively. Returning from the *Calming*, I dismounted. Lilit and Jilly appeared out of the saddlebags and climbed upon my shoulders. I approached the great Hawk's handler.

"Master of birds, I wish to buy your broken hawk." He scoffs, not bothering to even glance to me.

"I'll pay eight silver." He raises his eyes to me now, spying the furions.

"Master of rodents, I'll make more than that this same eve. The bird's worth three gold at the least of it, if I were willing to sell. Be gone, else my pet make a meal of one of your fitchets." His arrogance as well as his dinner's sour leftover scent wafts up to me as he rises in confrontation.

"Well then, Master of birds, I will make you a wager, as I see it is your favorite way to do business." He pause to hear more.; I wished his breath had. It stings my nose.

"I will wager even odds that my furions can do what these mighty dogs cannot. And I will cover all the coin you have in your pile of winnings."

Those watching fall silent and are now paying attention to our discourse. His arrogance presses upon him to save face, now.

"However, if I win the wager, I can purchase your broken hawk with that same pile of coin before you."

The gamesman eyes my bushy tailed furions, each smaller than the hare that the hawk guards, confident now, that he will double his take for the eve.

"It is a wager then, lad, show me your coin!"

Guffaws and mumbling arise now from the crowd.

Pulling a coin sack from my belt, I dropped it at his feet. Stooping to retrieve it, he draws the string back, weighing it and peering inside.

"Have at it then, lad." He makes grand gesture with his arm as he gives a short bow.

Having felt something when I first gazed upon the bird, I hoped, for his sake, I am not mistaken.

I slowly lowered and sit cross-legged at the bird's tether length and stared into his eyes. They are a deep golden and hold within them an intelligence akin to what I saw in Bane. Therein lay my confidence that this might work. Again, I lowered my heartbeat and breathing and let myself enter my *Calming*, slowly pushing my senses out to the people and dogs about me. I do not venture to press upon the men's minds, though I sensed each of them. But I let my *spirit-self* wash over the dogs and as I do, they all go instantly quiet. All about, the men begin to murmur. Turning my attention from the dogs, I let my mind venture towards the other presence it feels and know it at once to be the hawk. I sensed a great strength in it.

I am surprised to find the great bird's spirit-self reaching for me in return. A curiosity each to the other, as we stayed apart in a waiting game. I do not push my spirit-self but remain patient. I know he feels me there, as he physically sways upon his perch.

Finally, his curiosity gets the better of him and he opens his mind even as mine opens to him. A mutual move towards each other. Very much likened to Bane, and not being surprised or anxious, the spirit-essence of the bird recognizes me as a friend. For my part, I experienced the pain he feels in his wing and new memories that appeared to be my own of he/me soaring above valleys and peaks of mountains. In me he sees Bane, and Paint, and the furions. He gazes, in truth, my love for them and gazes their love for me as well, for there is no deception in the *Calming*. I expressed my plan in thought and he understands and bows his head as he perches.

The murmurs grow louder about us and beads of perspiration grow about the gamesman's furrowed brow.

"Well, then. Be about it, lad, or bugger off. You waste my time."

I joined with the furions again and they with the majestic bird. All proceeds well in our *Calming*. Jilly, always the first of the sisters, scurries down from my shoulder. With just a small pause, she begins to slowly move towards the dead hare on the ground in front of the great hawk. She sniffs the carcass, but let it lie. She rises up on her hindquarters and the hawk lowers his head to the furion. Jilly nuzzles about the neck and head of the mighty raptor and the bird of prey nips lightly at the furion. A group expression of awe rises from those watching.

Feeling left out, Lilit joins them. The crowd has grown now and gasped and stared in wonder. The gamesman rises to his feet in anger. I rise as well. Jilly and Lilit grabbed hold of the hare and pulled it to my feet and the crowd goes crazy. A great cheer rises among them all.

"I believe our wager is complete, master of birds," I stated and the crowd quiets to see how the man will react.

He scowls and looks about him.

"The bird is at its end., no matter." He huffs and reaches for his coin and my purse as well. He finds the point of my short sword pinning it to the cobbles.

"I believe the wager and sale was for your half of the wager only."

He gatherse the coin and the rag below it and stares into my eyes.

"Who are you, stranger, that you can do such a thing?"

I, with a gleam to my eye, say "I've a few small friends that call me Ser Drægonheart," grinning to hear myself say such a thing.

Immediately after though, I think mayhaps I had said too much.

Turning, I swing my short sword and the sharp blade slices through the bird's tether at its perch. Of a sudden, the great hawk rises to his full height and spreads his great wings, but one, not so much. And hHe gives a great cry and it echoes loudly to cause all those about us to leap back and cover their ears to keep from being deafened. People scattered about and the Gameman makes for the deepening shadows. Fearing, I think, that the raptor might take revenge upon him.

Our corner of the square empties swiftly and quiets now.

I sit back down across from the majestic and damaged hawk. A name comes to me as I do. The impression of the sharp claws piercing the hide of his prey appears in my mind and I speak, and think, his new name. *Talon, is a good name, to call you, friend.* Lilit and Jilly dragged the hare carcass over to the bird. Talon pulls it to himself and tears at its flesh.

As the bird leisurely goes about the business of eating, I pulled Effie's gifting from my pack. Unrolling the satchel, I choose an unguent and a dried and powdered Cefarous root. Using my mortar and pestle, I blended the root and the paste together. When applied, I hoped as Effie had taught me, that all sensation will leave the immediate area being treated. Unfortunately, I do not know what its true effect will be, as it is meant for use not on an animal, but a man.

In short order, Talon has finished his meal and he turns his intelligent eyes to gaze upon me. Our episode in the *Calming* has left us both with an immediate and complete trust and comfort with the other. He presents himself to me. The crowd about is gone now, as there are more interesting endeavors awaiting them on the square. There are enticing women, hallucinogenic smoke-weed, gambling or just music and dance. There remained no longer, any draw to a broken bird that does not fight mad dogs.

I placed thin gloves made of hog's intestine about my hands. Then, dipping into my mortar bowl of mixed unguent, I carefully apply the paste to the area that is clearly the broken joint in the great bird's wing. His eyes widened to my touch, but soon the salve does its work and he no longer feels the pain he'd endured for how long, I do not know.

I bring myself back into the *Calming* and added Talon's presence as well. In this state, my concentration has no bounds and I apply myself to the task at hand. Effie's and Da's and even Moor's lessons about anatomy of most people and beasts let me feel and know the problem within the bird's wing. With deft hands and precise movement, I pulled, realigned, and set back to place the dislocated bones within talon's wing. He gazes it immediately when things are righted. I hold the damaged area in a light squeeze and willed it to start healing.

I let go.

Talon attempts to spread his tremendous wings again. I marveled at his wingspan, easily as wide as I am tall with upward stretched arms. Though still in need of the healing that only time will give, Talon stands once again whole and gloriously majestic. He preens himself in pride, tentatively flapping his wings.

Hailing a passerby, I inquire after my destination, the Salty Swine Pub and Inn.

"A-sure, I know of it, Jôhan's place. It be just aways, dead reckoned yonder east," and points out from the square to the only travelway headed in that direction.

I whistled to Lilit and Jilly. They promptly bounded up my body and springs over to Paint's back as if it is inborn and not a learned response. Paint takes no notice. With my pack back over my shoulders, I nodded to Talon in a fare-thee-well manner. He just quirks his head as if to say, *what an unusual human you are*. He rises free to start his life anew. He makes a gurgling in his throat as if to say, *thank you, I'll be on my way*, but continues to sit and preen his plumage in the shadows as we set out.

I reined Paint to our left and headed out of the square, the furions' staring back at the great raptor as we go on our way.

True to the passerby's word, we have only to go a good two hundred paces off the square before encountering our destination. Light shines from the window and a large shingle hanging from chains upon a beam set over the door proclaims with no words needed that this is indeed the Salty Swine. Deftly painted on the sign, is an upright pig in a regal hat and cane.

Laughter, and aroma, and a warm light escape from the door as a patron enters and another leaves out.

Three doors down, a high stonewall with two large, open, iron gate doors on oversized wrought iron hinges as well as a sign below two great lamps, proclaims a livery stable. I settled Paint in at the stables and make my way back to the pub and Inn. Lilit and Jilly are tucked away in my pack.

The raucous laughter do not appear to have settled as I, this time, opened the door to enter. A bard sits atop a high stool upon a small stage in the far corner, waving his hands about and telling a tale to the utter delight of a goodly crowd of folk about him. He acts each part as he speaks the story... First the Lord, then a fool... then the Lord again and the crowd stares up at him and drinks great steins of ale, entranced by the bard's words, laughing at his jokes.

As for me, my stomach moans and I take a seat in the corner and across the room from the bard. My pack I simply dropped on the table aside me. I lay my bow and staff against the wall. Then I settled in. A buxomly serving lass of golden hair makes her way to me, dodging wandering hands, and slapping a few away.

Taking seat on the bench across from me, she blows a stray strand of hair from her forehead.

"What can I get you, stranger?"

"I've come some ways this sun and my stomach aches for satisfaction. If you would, a large bowl of nuts, a tall stein of your house ale, and your most hearty eve-meal, if it's not too late for the kitchens. I am surely that hungry and with a great thirst. I can see this bunch has placed a tiresome load to your sun as well. Have them fill a plate for yourself and join me? On my coin, o'course."

"Gah, I like you, stranger." She rises with a laugh and heads back to the kitchens, a bit more spring to her step.

The bard in the corner sits, still telling his tale to the continued enjoyment of his gathered minions sometime later when the fair-haired and blue-eyed server returns with two plates and two ales and a large bowl of nuts, still in their shells. She sets them on the table and to my surprise, she takes a seat on the bench across from me once again.

"The ale is on your coin as well." She laughs as she raises her stein to me.

"O'course." I raised my own stein and we lean in to clang them in a good-hearted greet. "And might I query the given name of my eve-meal guest?"

"Suzæne, but I'll answer to Susi." She surveys the bowl of nuts to see small paws reach out from my pack and snatch in a nut, then another, but says nothing.

"Shall we tuck in?"

And we do. And it is a most rewarding meal. Shredded pork piled high and soaked in a spicy sauce and cooked green beans with large chunks of salt pork as well. A large fresh bread with a huge dollop of rich butter slapped to the plate aside it. Finally, a pickle the size of… well, it is quite large. Da would have approved. The ale is heavenly, and I downed half the great stein in my first swallows. The establishment live up to its name.

But a short time later, I peered over my empty stein and clean plate and see the same in front of Susi.

"Vanna!" she yells over the din of the crowd and trailing laughter about the Bards corner. "Two more ales here."

"Aside from my hunger and thirst this night," I exclaimed while trying to hide a most aromatic belch in a deep sigh, "I came on recommendation from a good-man called Axel Daèton from Twisted Creek. I am in search of the proprietor."

Susi returns my belch, and then some. The scent of our mutual admiration for our meal rises to mingle with the already inviting atmosphere of the pub.

"That would be Jôhan over in the corner," she says throwing her thumb over her shoulder.

"He is currently entertaining those easily amused. It's what he does, so well. He is my soulmate and the reason I rise each morn!"

And she chuckles anew. But she turns and gazes at him with knowing eyes, ne'er-the-lesser for her scornful sarcasm and ridicule.

"I'll introduce you, friend of Axel Daèton.... If I can prise him from his adoring mob." And with that she rises and heads to the corner in which Jôhan holds court.

25

I am the Walrus

Susi returns with the bard, her husband, and co-proprietor of the Salty Swine. Jôhan is a bald and husky fellow with an easy way about him. As I will come to know from my time with them, he brings the clientele in and keep them drinking with his outlandish tales whilst Susi is the true backbone of the establishment. They have a remarkable cook in the kitchens as well. Brœther-to-law, and Susi's sister's husband, he can turn wild boar into a delicacy fit for royalty. Aside from the happy serving wenches who are in it for the coin, the locals come mostly for the cook's fare and stayed for the house ale with the bard as reason to do so. I can attest its worth in coin—. The food at any rate.

Knowing I've been recommended a trustworthy sort by their friend, they are both open and helpful to me. That evening, I sit and drink their ale, and eat their fine fare and tell them my tale from start to finish. They are aghast, but not wholly surprised to hear the extent of the cruelty and greed of Lord Tullamoor. They speak of increased taxes each year for the past five and the intrusive presence of Tullamoor's growing army of guardsmen about the city. Supposedly, they are there to help control the criminal element inherent to a port city the size of Sea's End, called Port

Tullamoor now by all but the old locals. They acted more to keep all aware of Tullamoor's authority.

Tales abounded of the guardsmen's cruelty and sense of providence. Oft times they take without paying and exerting excessive authority. In essence, they are thugs of the thug Lord.

I expressed my purpose in being here and though sympathetic to my intent, they advised me strongly against such a foolish venture, as it will most certain to lead to my demise. But I remained steadfast in my resolve and they are helpful, testament to their disdain for the man. As wary proprietors in the new order of things, they are very much aware of the habits of the new "guardsmen" who roamed the streets and even as Jôhan is an excellent bard, he is also a very attentive listener. He has patrons that are fond of "one upmanship" in effort oft-times to impress their compatriots of ale, and so speaks quite freely. He's heard tales from the further side of the bridges and even of the eccentricities of the Lord himself.

The information is of great use to me. I stayed with Susi and Jôhan for more than two fortnight, getting to know not only the bazaars, the wharf, the city, and its citizens, but the surrounding lands as well. I have even visited Tullamoor Keep, under cover of delivering ordered fare from the city.

Jôhan and Susi welcomed me from the start. I spend my morn-meal in conversation with Susi and quieter eves with Jôhan on opposite sides of my Schäaken board.

That morrow's morn after having first arrived, I set out to learn of the city. Donning my pack, which I seldom go anywhere without, and gathering my Bo-staff, I stepped out onto the rue. I stand a moment taking in my surroundings, which in the morn's light offers a different perspective from yester's eve. 'Tis still early as I tend to rise in a natural way to make an early start of each morn. I meet the sun to eerie effect. Quiet settles over all things. As the buildings are built tight to one another, the rue stands still mostly in shadow as the sun's fingers are not able yet to reach me on the

Inn's doorstep. It appears most of Sea's Ends' citizens in this quarter will let the sun rise a bit more before starting their day.

I wondered at a fog that creeps about the base of the buildings and conceals the cobblestone way till it is stirred by a passing wagon or cart. The furions sneak from my pack and make their way to the ground, and jumping about in the fog, eager to explore this new world that we have found ourselves in. As they do, my skin prickles and hairs on my neck raised as I feel eyes upon me. Ever aware of my senses, I take heed and searched my surroundings more closely. This brings my eyes upward, and there I find the mystery solved. For under the eaves of the dormer window placed upon the roof opposite, and giving light to some room under its rafters, I spy Talon studying me from above. I had thought that he would have flown well away from the city by now.

Though well on the mend, his wing certainly is not whole yet. I have a thought and return back into the pub and go to the kitchens. I asked Guyæm, the cook, if he has a hare unskinned as yet or mayhaps a small chicken that I can purchase. He offers one up and I returned to the travelway. With a nod, I swing the hare with a mighty toss into the air to a height near to the bird. Quick as a sky-bolt, he pounces upon the prey and pulls it back into the shadows upon the roof. Mission accomplished.

I make my way to the stables to check on Paint. They are keeping their charges well and I tell the stableman so. Whilst there, I give Paint a good brush down myself, and an apple from Guyæm, giving the stable lads a reason to stare in appreciation of my efforts.

After exiting the livery, I started my exploration. Following the receding fog upon the cobblestone way, I soon find myself at the docks and I think it a marvel. While most of the city still sleeps, the wharf has come alive and by all accounts, has been for a while. Fishermen are setting out into the sea. A myriad of boats are already out upon the waters.

I stand amazed and in awe of the sights and sounds.

'Tis my first time to gaze upon the sea. Da had told me tales o'course, but seeing it for yourself is a different thing entirely. To the east and the rising sun, there is naught but endless water. Sails of large ships and smaller skiffs stand silhouetted against the morns sky sun., A fog still floats tight to the water, but burns off, in shadowed places near to the shoreline.

I reluctantly make my way past the busy wharf and then the smaller docks and finally onto the beach—, my target. It is mostwise sandy, with great patches of seaweed washing against the shore with each wave. Familiar with the gentle lap of lake-waters against the shore, the greater crash and sometimes fury of the sea's waves are a marvel. Shells of all sorts lay everywhere. Small crabs popped from holes in the sand and skittered about. Even the beach, though likened to Moon Lake, shines different, too.

As I walked further north and west, the sounds of the workers on the docks faded slowly…. and then completely. But for the surf and gulls calling above, the world that has been pressing upon me retreats. I passed a jettee of rock and my view of the port city disappears entirely. I climbed the rock and gazed north, away from the city and its boats upon the sea. The shoreline stretches to the horizon, and to the east of it, only water as far as the eye can see. I sensed a draw from it and wondered for it. Is it just curiosity, or something more? Perhaps one day, I will find out.

Lying back upon a long, flat rock, I remembering my special place on the edge of the wood on our homestead, and another in a grotto under some falls. It is a place to capture some solace, and a time to reflect upon my life. I find myself reflecting on all that had happened since Da's murder at the hands of the Kingsmen.

The battles with the slave traders. The places I'd been to and the people I did meet. It did hit me then, that Aeryth was indeed a larger world than I ever thought possible. I pondered on the evil of men, and then, my feelings for Finnie. I reflected on Da's quest given to me and how I had been sidetracked by life itself. Da had told me once that a wise man advised him

– Life is what happens to you when you are busy making other plans – and I take a vow to myself again, that I will resume my quest once this business with Lord Tullamoor is finished. And then, I let all my thoughts drift away and just lay upon the rock, a light, refreshing breeze washing over me and the sound of waves lapping upon the shore lulls me into my *Calm.*

My solace is finally disturbed by the arrival of Lilit bounding about me. Rising up, I gazed down to the beach where Jilly feasts on a small crab. This all brings me back to the present, and I reluctantly rise to continue my survey of the city. I spy not too far off in the distance a rock just as the one I had just lay upon, and a great gray sea mammal just lying there. It has a face of long whiskers and two great curved teeth springs from its mouth. He rolls over to gaze at me. What is such a creature thinking, upon his rock?

I surprised myself that I have lingered so long and by the time I make my way back to the wharf, a midsun market has been set up. Catches from the morn from the fisherman's hulls now lay displayed on carts and tables for the city's shoppers to pick through. There, all manner of sea fare lielay in wait for shoppers, from giant crab to fish of all sorts. I spy even, a table of squirming snakelike fish that the vendor calls eel.

I take my midsun-meal in a small eatery just a block from the docks. Sitting at a table outside, I listening to the gulls and watching the city folk doing the regular chores and business in this quarter of towne. The sea's scent, along with the market's, are being tossed about on the breeze. Laughter and far-away voices mingled here, as well.

It is most likely the proprietor's wife that serves to me my stack of boiled sea-skitters, they called them, with a spicy red sauce for dipping the creatures in. First, I have to relieve them of their legs, tails, and shells as the matron instructed. I had earlier been watching a man peeling them apart with a gusto and felt it my duty to try some. Attis, she calls herself, bearing the constitution of a working lady, strong and tough, has served them up with a tall wooden mug of a delicious ale as well. I tucked into the sea critters and some savory fried fritter-cakes.

The people that bustled about me are just like any others I've seen in the other townes and villages I'd visited after leaving my homestead with Da. That is, they are until I see the guardsmen. I recognized them at once in livery I'd come to know as Tullamoor's. While eating, I have observed two pairs already. They worked in paired units and are all carrying long swords sheathed at their sides along with dirks and what looked to be batons of wood.

This third pair has a young dock waif with his hands tied behind his back and tethered to the guardsman who has his baton out, obvious for use as an incentive for the younger to mind him. The people about me stopped what they are doing and watched. The stout server scowls, but not at the unfortunate younger, and rather at the guardsman.

"You are pleased by what you see, Mãam?"

"Nay, I am not, stranger. The waifs are beggars some of times but will do honest work at the docks as well. They are the youngers of fishermen and merchant seamen what died at sea and they are just trying to make their way is all. They've been left to fend for themselves. They aren't deserving of the Lord's cruelty, sure-certain I am. It is a hard life for them. The people hereabouts don't mind giving them a hand up from time a'times and look aside if they steal a little food. But them guardsmen?" She spits. "They call the waifs a scourge and round them up when they can catch 'em. Too many have gone, never to be seen again."

She stares at the guardsmens' backs before she turns and goes about her business.

An anger rises again within me, but I let it settle for now.

And so, it goes over the next two fortnight. I learned the city well. Watching life and befriending quite a few people too, including the Mãam Chezon, Attis to me, matron at that very same eatery a block from the docks. I find her company welcome and she, mine. Her cooked seafood is very good, especially those spiced fritter cakes and sea-skitters.

Jôhan and Susi tutored me on the former Tullamoor Lord, who they had considered a good, honest and just Lord, and tell me more of his son who now resides and rules in the Keep. They explained to me how the rightful heir, the present Lord's older brœther, has never returned from a routine trip to the mountains where there remains an outpost manned by the Lord's men.

I see Talon upon the rooftop a few more days and will throw him up a hare each eve. Whereas I roamed the city in the morn hours, I spend my after-high-suns roaming the adjacent countryside and doing a bit of hunting as well. Paint is glad for the exercise. Lilit and Jilly are amazing at hunting rabbits in the grassy plains and so we bring our catches back to the Inn, offering them to chef Guy and then some to Talon. But after five suns, I see him no more.

I've appraised the Keep on my rides and the lands from Sea's End to the Keep's gates. I've yet to so much as see Lord Tullamoor at a distance and I am beginning to become discouraged in my efforts and wondering just how I can manage to bring justice to him.

Then, one day, fate steps in. In that selfsame square that I had rescued Talon from an ill fate, I happened on two guardsmen. They are leading two severely beaten youngers whose hands are tied behind them. The youngers are tethered to two large guards. They are being prodded by these guardsmen in a harsh manner with their batons. The guardsmen are clearly enjoying their duty. My ire rises to a point of recklessness and I stepped out in front of them.

"Hail, guardsmen," I say sternly. "Unhand my squires."

A small lie, but necessary to the instance. The young lads' eyes rise to me and I give a start. One bears the unique eyes of my Da! I stand stunned for a moment. I have not, since Da, seen eyes in such a hue. The other lad bears eyes a bright blue and speckled in the same gold.

"If they are your Squires, though by the look of ye, ye could not afford one squire, lesser there be two, then mayhaps we should arrest ye as well as ye would be responsible to their deeds," the guardsmen say with a guffaw and a smirk. "No matter, for these two were caught stealing and we'll be taking them to Lord Tullamoor to hear his justice. Step aside."

The two bound lads stared up to me in a pleading manner, vehemently shaking their heads.

I do not move.

The larger of the guardsmen steps towards me. He draws his longsword. We are attracting a crowd. Giving them something to see, I stepped forward and in two sky-bolt quick movements of my Bo, the large guardsmen fell. He lies flat on his back with a broken wrist and what will later be a severe headache. He is not conscious any longer to be feeling anything currently.

The other guard gives me an appraising look.

Of a sudden, the gathering crowd is parting and four more of the Lord's guardsmen, these appearing much better trained and quite tall, stepped forward. I appraised just how I can dispense with the added threat.

These guards parted as well and a nobleman walks betwixt them. At the least, he playd the part, with chin high in the air, no doubt to compensate for a…. diminutive stature. 'Tis almost comical as he steps forward, the top of his head no higher than his guards breast shoulders. What he lacks in height, however, he makes up for in attitude, especially in his garb.

The Lord prefers black. And *polished* silver.

From head to toe he wears it quite proud. Not one, but two rows of polished silver buttons adorned a quilt padded tunic in a silken black. The collars corners are enfolded in the same polished silver as well. Black suede leather trousers are a match to a cloak of the same. And silver abound. From boots with pointed toes encased in it and every cord and tie about his cloak and purse with dipped ends. Pommel end and chevrons about his wide belt, shined to sparkle. A greasy, combed back coif with a silver headpiece holding it in place. A gemless, leafy tiara, if you will. Snap. Oh, and finger rings.

"A care, Lord Tullamoor," one of his men says. "He's just laid Flæck out cold."

"I can see that, fool," comes the condescending response. He turns to me, eyes chilling and dead. "You're obviously more than what my constables expected, sir. I know not from whence you hail, but by the look about you, it is not from here. So, I will give you the benefit of not knowing our custom and law. But the facts and law are what they are. If your – squires – committed a crime in my jurisdiction they are forfeit to my justice."

He clearly likes to hear himself speak.

But then, something about his manner shifts. He casually lets his eyes wander to my chest, or rather, the sigil imprinted upon my pack's chest piece.

He recognizes who I am and what I have done to his business concerns. To be precise, I killed many of them. Things have just changed. I do not let him know that I know that he gazes.

"Lord Tullamoor," I acknowledged him and give a deep bow. "Mayhaps we can come to an arrangement."

"And what do you suggest?" Authority oozes with his every word even as his breath excretes the sour of a diet gone very wrong.

Thinking fast, mayhaps a little too fast, I presented an option that I think he might be drawn in by. I know from Susi and Jôhan that this Lord live for one thing above all others.

"I would propose a sport to decide the matter, and reparation to the man my squires apparently…" I stared directly at the guard who still holds their tether,. "…have stolen from. I plan to discipline them appropriately, I assure m'Lord. But my suggestion is that we might settle the matter with a test of honorable men. Falconry, mayhaps? I've heard tell that you fancy the sport, and rightly so."

His eyebrows rise immediately at this prospect. As I've judged, his love of the sport gives him pause to ponder my suggestion. A snicker accompanies his boast.

"Indeed… And I'll admit I find few to challenge me in this quarter."

Looking around at the crowds that have gathered, and most likely judging that he might not be able to subdue me here in the square, with what he'd heard tell of me, he turns back to me.

"I accept your offer of claim by battle, and accept your manner of dual," he says with eyes intent on me. "We have not been properly introduced, sir. What are you called and from where do you hail?"

"I am sometimes addressed as *Ser Drægonheart* by little friends, and I hail from the Shadow Mountains, some ways south of here." I give another slight bow of deference. No need for further deception on my part.

His eyebrows rise. I can hear a murmur throughout the crowd.

Mayhaps, I've taken it too far. Over confidence might some-sun be my undoing.

But no. There will be no open battle upon the square this sun. This will be a private matter.

Lord Tullamoor walks up close and whispers with sour breath and no small amount of spittle, "Two days hence, then. Halfway from here to my Keep there is a great, hundred-year-old Calpaca tree with limbs that spread near the width of this square. We shall meet there at high-sun and settle this with sport. I hope you have a bird up to the task."

The Lord's guardsmen dragged the tethered lads with them as they leave the square, sparing no cruelty about the task. The city guard begins to deal with his unconscious mate. I walked away from too much whispering at my back and thinking I have but two suns to prepare for what surely will be a trap and ambush attempt. I will need to start my counter measures tonight.

26

Why don't we do it in the Road

Having returned to the Inn and pub, I sit pondering my options and while doing so, drained a large ale. A plan starts to form in my head. Walking down to the stables, I meet with the stableman and he agrees to let me use his workshop and I get to work straight away.

Nearing to dusk, I have gathered everything I needed, but I think it best to try it at the proper location. It takes me a while to get there, but I find the tree that Lord Tullamoor had described. I sit on the ground out from beneath the tree's giant canopy and go into my *Calming*, going very deep and willing away any distractions.

Feeling for the same thread of thought I'd used the night I'd joined with Talon, I try resurrecting the thought-presence of that night and called to him. It comes upon me instantaneously. I am sitting atop a branch of a great pine with him and surveying the mountainside and valley below us. I know that he could tell exactly where I am. Thinking this, he stares off to the distance in my direction. I impressed upon him with mind pictures what I hoped he will do for me and the answer is immediate as well. He, in turn, expresses that I should wait and that he will come to me.

Then I am soaring. He is a great distance off, but I sensed that he can travel with tremendous speed. My body sits patiently, but I am not sitting at all—I am, flying now, well above any tree line. I cyphered with Talon's own sense that it is four times the height of the trees. His knowing of this translates to my own thought process so that I can discern and know the height.

The moon shines remarkably bright this night and Talon's exceptional eyesight shows the smallest details of objects and terrain below us. I've been 'aloft' with Talon but a short while and already I can see the Lord's Keep below us in the distance. We rise and fall with the natural drafts ushering up from the hills and valley below, riding the currents.

Talon no longer feels the pain of his broken wing. It has completely healed, and his full magnificence is restored.

And then, I see our destination. I spy the great tree. It lies perhaps 150 paces south of the travelway to Tullamoor's Keep and some fifty paces from a river to the south of it. The stream runs strong; I determined that any ambush will not be set up in that direction. And then I see myself, sitting solitary, head forward and unmoving.

Falling now. No, diving right towards the me on the ground. There is complete control and no distress. The spreading of our wings slows our dissent and we landed like a flutterfly in front of me. I opened my eyes and, of a sudden, I am in my own body again, but find our minds are still joined. Talon understands my thoughts perfectly and I, his. But his thoughts are rawer than mine. His are tied directly to the feelings and perceptions. Love and hate and indifference. Pride and hunger and satisfaction. And further empathy as well. His feelings are quite distinct and there is only the black and white of it. He recognizes mine that overlapped and mirrored his.... He does not bother to understand those feelings that are not akin to his own and are too foreign.

I explained the situation to him, and he understands. We practiced a little. I send him to find prey and return it to me. He immediately takes to the air and returns quite rapidly with a small possum within the grasp of his talons. I thanked him and we finally disengaged from the *Calming*. In a most regal manner, he flies off towards the moon.

I have work to do. Finding a spot near the tree's canopy on the river side, I proceeded to dig a hole, making sure to dig it waist deep and longer than I am tall. It becomes tedious work, as I must spread the soil from the hole about a great area so as not to reveal its existence. I would hope Tullamoor will not place any guardsmen on this side of the tree.

The grasses are plenty high in the field. The grass surrounding the tree's canopy stands well past my waist. I think Tullamoor is brazen enough to keep his contingent in plain view but for a few Bowman, as I imagined him to be sly, as well. After I have completed my hidey hole, I covered it with the cover I'd mostly fabricated at the stables and gathered grass and twigs and such to conceal it all the more. On the morrow's moon, I will hide myself within it if needs be.

Early morn on the day set for our meet, Talon is watching the Lord's Keep from atop a great oak not fifty paces from the Keep's gates. I am watching with him. As I had suspected, a company of four guardsmen ride out from the Cæstle grounds in the early hours. They carry crossbows on the hindquarters of their steeds. These men would need to be dealt with before the Lord's contingent arrived. They ride in tight formation, clearly well-trained. I estimated their arrival at mid-morn sun.

I will be ready.

With clearly some time separating this group from the main caravan expected to travel with Tullamoor, Talon takes flight to track the progress of these bowmen. The bowmen break from the main travelway well before they will be in sight from the tree, and they headed south into the tree line to the south of the travelway. This leaves me to wonder their purpose. Not long after, I have my answer. They exited the trees further south at the river and ride east along its bank and towards my position. They aewere doing what I had already done. They will need to keep their horses hidden if they are to be my ambush party. Likewise, I have sent Paint back east towards the city to wait, perhaps a furlong from the meet site. We keep a hawk's eye on the bowmen and I secreted myself into my hidey hole, a bit before their arrival.

Talon flies in advance of the party and lights upon an uppermost branch of the huge Calpaca tree and awaits their arrival. The furions have taken refuge in the lower branches of the tree. I listened from my hole in the ground as Talon watches from above. Arriving quietly, the bowmen dismounted and tethered their mounts near to the river. I cannot hear a word as they approached within a few paces of my hole. From above, with Talon's eyes, I can see two head west and two head east away from the tree. I will need to exit my hole before they find their positions and can look back upon mine.

Silent as the furions, I pulled myself free from my hiding place, I leave my bow, and staff, and pack behind. I followed first to the soldiers heading west, as I reasoned those going to the east will continue to spy eastward as that is the direction they expected me to arrive from. The first bowman settles to the ground on his knees, mayhaps twenty paces from the tree's canopy and turns to face east.

He is not there long.

Afore his comrade has made it another twenty paces, I silently dispatched the first, his life's blood spilling from his neck to the ground. Moor had, I realized at that moment, trained an efficient and merciless soldier.

Keeping my head below the top of the tall swaying grasses, Talon's eyes helped me to follow the second man's progress as I gained on him with every step he takes. He is dispatched as quickly as his compatriot.

Rapidly dropping into the grass, I know the final two will not go so easily. From Talon's vantage, I can see that the two to the east of the tree are already in place and they will be much trickier.

I crab-walked a few paces at a time, relying on Talon to alert me should one of the bowmen start to gaze my way. I had reasoned well, as the two guardsmen keep their attention to the east.

Having closed the gap to the third bowman, I reached for his head and neck with dirk in hand. He senses my presence. It is too late for him, but his quick yelp alerts the fourth man.

The fourth rises and turns his loaded bow towards me. I am in trouble. And then I'm not wasn't.

My furion friends have my back. One or both attacked the soldier's leg with zeal. He calls out in pain. His arm jerks skyward and his bolt follows. I am already running towards him as I loosed my throwing blade. Its point finds a home in the bowman's brain by way of his left eye. When I reached his corpse, I find myself breathing heavy and beads of sweat lay upon my forehead.

Turning to the great tree, I watched as Talon take flight. A thing of beauty onto itself, as he liftsed into the sky on what appears to be gilded wings. He heads back west towards the Keep. The first wave of ambushers has been dealt with. I do not assume the remaining force will go down so easy.

I backtracked to the bowmen and gathered their crossbows from the corpses and bring them back to the tree. I string them together with a coil of Elven-vine and throwing the other end over a high branch, I pulled them up into the canopy. Not wanting to have my early treachery discovered, I pulled each corpse further east or west and try to cover them to minimize their discovery when Lord Tullamoor arrives.

Sweaty and winded from the rigorous effort, I sit back against the trunk of the tree and seek to connect again with Talon. There is no learning curve with the great raptor. Likened to Bane now, the connection is immediate. I have a little time to recuperate. The Lord's caravan has started out from the keep and with him rides quite an entourage. Two standard-bearers actually lead his parade, each with the Lord's sigil emblazoned on a flag upon a long pole. They ride with short swords upon their belts. Next come two mounted guardsmen in fine regalia. They are followed by the Lord Tullamoor himself on a great, onyx black stallion, with polished silver buckles and needless chevrons upon his saddlery gleaming in the sun. Aside him rides his trusted advisor I judged, as Jôhan explained that the Lord seldom goes anywhere without him.

Next in line is a smaller wagon with a large cage strapped to its load board. This most probably is Tullamoor's prized bird and its handler. Behind them is a wagon handled by a single soldier. Upon the wagon sits a very large cage, with wood floor and ceiling and iron bars. The two lads I met two suns passed are resident within. It seems a squire to the Lord is present as well as a lad with no weapon rides behind Tullamoor and aside the cage wagon. Four additional guardsmen followed the wagon on horseback as well. The caravan, I judged will arrive near high-sun, as he had promised. So, it is to be a charade until the Lord gives some signal to take me down. The fore guard have left no doubt of their true purpose, had it already not been sure to my mind.

I draw some water from my water skin, sitting and pondering and refining my plan with the new information. As the time draws near to their arrival, I string my bow and determined that I would meet the Lord at a large boulder just to the north and outside the canopy of the tree. Carriage tracks lead down from the main travelway ending near to my designated spot as it appears a regular meeting site for travelers wanting to take some relief in the shade of the grand tree. In the tall grass about my chosen place, I strike a half-dozen arrows into the ground and standing straight up but hidden within the grass, in anticipation of possible need.

Before they approached over the final rise, I returned to my hidden hole and let Talon be my eyes once more. As I had anticipated, the caravan makes its way up the carriage trails track and stops in the open field in front of it. Through Talon's eyes, I seesaw Tullamoor and his counselor in animated conversation.

Whilst still in the *Calming*, I touched upon Paint's mind now and urged that he come to me swiftly. He is not but 4-5 furlong down the road to the east. It is time to meet with Lord Tullamoor and try to fulfill my Oath to end the evil trafficking that Finnie and I had been fighting against for moons now.

I spy Paint arriving at a gallop and soon heard his hooves pounding the ground as well. Tullamoor and his party turned their eyes to the east and I take the cue to rise from my hole and approached the Lord from the west, onto my predetermined spot. I have an arrow nocked in my bow in one hand and my Bo-staff in the other. The wagon with the caged lads lies to the west of the Tullamoor's group and they are the first to spy me.

I leaned my staff against the wagon and take a step towards the Lord and his counselor from their rear just as Paint comes to a halt in front of them. Confusion fills their faces.

"Well met, Lord Tullamoor," I say loudly and ten more heads turned with a start.

"I see you've come for a little sport. I arrived a bit early myself and was doing a bit of *hunting*." Tullamoor and his counselor's eyebrows rise a smidgen.

"Fat rabbits to be found in these tall grasses." I paused to silence all about. "Well then, shall we get about our sport, Lord Tullamoor?"

His face grows a fierce red. His guardsmen, to a one, reached for the pommels of their swords.

"Well met, indeed, Ser Drægonheart. That is what you call yourself, right? But where's your bird?" He smirks and his guardsmen do not relax.

Even as he says this, a tremendous cry erupts from the sky above and echoes about in a deafening tenor that has the horses go skittish and Lord Tullamoor step back in a fright.

"What evil from any hell was that?" He exclaims, peering about anxiously.

If there was no tension in the air afore, that situation is now remedied in the sweltering heat of the sun.

I realized, just then, that Talon's echoing screech in the square, when I had rescued him, was not an echoing from amongst the buildings, but from his throat alone.

As if Tullamoor's exclamation is his cue, Talon comes out of a swooping dive from high above and directly out of the sun to alight on my shoulder, his wings fully outstretched for a moment as he settles. I moved not a muscle as if the act is a most natural and expected occurrence. It must have appeared to all those gathered that he has appeared as if from thin air.

Gasps escaped from most everyone and while the mounted guardsmen fight to control their horses, Tullamoor and his counselor are gazing about furtively. They are no longer wondering if their bowmen are about as they have not made their presence known.

"This would be Talon, my entry in our little game of sport," I say, as if this was an ordinary introduction.

"'Tis the fighting bird from the square," a guardsman near shouts.

"'Tis a Mountain Echo Eagle," says one of the caged boys, and both stare out in wonderment, hands about their cage's bars.

"I've never heard of any such bird," the Lord scoffs. He looks on in amazement though, and for a moment, his only thought was to own such a feathered beast; sure-certain.

"Shall we continue Lord Tullamoor? My squires look terribly uncomfortable in your accommodations," I say in an accusing tone.

"And to that subject, is this large contingent about us for their benefit?" I query.

A sour look crosses his face. He is obviously not accustomed to being questioned or intimidated in any way.

In an effort to regain control once more, he barks out, despite being clearly a bit unnerved, "My entourage is of no concern of yours and the rules of our sport are quite simple. We send our birds out to hunt prey. The first to capture and immobilize its prey shall be declared winner. You are agreed?" His sneer and edge of voice telling me he is ever closer to a tipping point.

"O'course, shall we begin then?" I ask, showing much more confidence than I feel, considering the odds against me now.

Lord Tullamoor pulls a great leather gauntlet about his left hand and forearm and motions for his handler to bring his great Marshall falcon. The falcon, normally calm under its hood, is quite jittery. Tullamoor, frustrated at this turn of events and prideful to a fault, is determined that he will have two prizes, both the satisfaction of his Falcon's win and this arrogant, meddling peasant's painful demise. Me, the peasant in his scenario. He is determined that I will cause him no more trouble. He motions his handler to remove the bird's hood.

I watched as chaos erupts on the Lord's arm. One look at Talon and the Marshall falcon, king raptor of these skies, literally goes insane to escape its tether and take flight. Before being able to finally release its leash and free his bird, the Lord suffers deep talon strikes to his shoulder and face. His falcon rises in a panic and Talon rises with him. As they take flight, Talon screams his echoing war cry. The Lord's bird flies in another direction. Talon does not follow.

This is my time to react.

"Get this bastard," Tullamoor calls to his guards.

And I do.

As the soldiers begin to unsheathe their swords and dismount, I have already reached into my *Calming*. The arrows I'd planted earlier in the ground now become my ammunition as I pulled each in its turn and nock and loose four arrows with deadly results. Four guardsmen are down, never to rise.

About me, I become aware of the many things happening. It is unfolding as if in a time slowed to a crawl. The wagon's harnessed horses reared as the remaining four guards charged towards me from different directions. Tullamoor's counselor is pulling him from the fray.

As the wagon's horses reared and pushed back against it, the hitching buckles. The front of the wagon rises from the ground, which in turn causes the cage and its two captives to slide off its back. The wagons horses bolted forward, pulling it from the fray and causing further commotion.

At that same moment, I have dropped my bow and retrieved my staff, which had been falling away from the wagon as it rises. Two of the guards are nearly upon me when the wagon crosses betwixt them and I, pulled by the frantic horses. I tumble with purpose forward, coming up just as the wagon passes, my Bo in front of me. I come out of the roll to one knee and in a low position swinging my staff into their knees, one from the front and one from the back. The ends of my Bo are aglow.

Rising up, I use fierce strikes to their necks and jaws, hitting my marks unfailing, likened to my training in Da's barn so many times. These first two buckle and collapse to the ground, both unconscious.

Turning towards the remaining guards, the standard-bearers from Tullamoor's caravan approach more cautiously with short swords presented. At my back, Tullamoor and his advisor pull their short swords as well. I find myself surrounded by two guardsmen, Tullamoor, his evil whisperer, and the bird handler. All presenting short swords.

And then, of a sudden, there is a great howl and blur of fur as Bane flies into the Lord's advisor. The furions bound up the body of the handler and attack his face about his eyes. The distraction proves fatal to the two remaining guardsmen. In a thrice, the two are dispatched, with due prejudice.

I turn back to find Bane pinning the counselor to the ground under his forepaws with drooling and growling muzzle staring him down and the handler squealing in pain holding his mauled face as he squirms on the ground. This left only Tullamoor standing, his eyes wild in fear, frantically peering about, and his young squire, who is kneeling and out of the way of the fighting.

"Now then, Lord Tullamoor, do I have leave to bring my squires home?" I query, staring him down.

He nods his acquiescence, mayhaps thinking this nightmare is over for him.

"You there, squire," I command the younger, mayhaps a lad of thirteen-year who is sitting off to the side. "Find the keys to the cage, if you will, and free my squires."

He scrambles to the handler to retrieve the keys from his belt. The man is cradling his face and weeping.

"I find that I can no longer trust you, Lord Tullamoor. I'm going to have to ask you to place yourself in the cage. I trust you will not find it too uncomfortable."

He is steaming at the indignity of my request.

"I'll see your head on a pike," he spits, no doubt forgetting his current predicament.

"You will not be needing your weapon," I further instruct, and he drops his short sword and crawls into the cage. Unlike its previous occupants, he is even able to sit full upright.

"Squire, close the padlock if you will. And now we will see to the Lord's counselor's justice."

The man still lies under Bane's drooling muzzle, Bane's claws digging into his chest. He has soiled himself. Bane has that effect on some.

I draw my short sword and approach the man. "I can't promise it will be painless. Just as it was not painless for the many lives you've destroyed."

The man's eyes go wide as he sees his fate before him.

"Hold, hold," he wails. "It was Lord Tullamoor's doing. I have information I can give, if you spare me!"

"I am listening, snake."

"The true Lord of Tullamoor lives. Ronælt, the oldest son of the late Lord Tullamoor is imprisoned beneath the Keep!" he says, begging.

"Silence, you fool!" Tullamoor screams.

"My pæder is alive?!" screams the squire in red-faced anger. He grabs a short sword and approaches the counselor.

"Pray, still your hand a moment, lad. You are the son of Ronælt?"

"Yea, I am," he says, spitting at the counselor.

"Come hither then," and in a low voice, I continue. "I propose you escort the counselor here, back to Tullamoor Keep and find and free your pæder and let him decide the fate of this man. What say you?"

"Yea, I will do just that."

I call Bane off the counselor. I gagged him and his hands are tied behind his back.

"Handler, will you accompany the squire back to the keep and bear witness to all that has transpired here, or shall I issue justice here?" I find the torn-up man most agreeable and secure his wrists behind him. I tether their legs about the ankles, one to the other, to further discourage any attempt to flee.

The squire mounts his pony and sets the two men walking up afore him, heading back to the Keep.

After they have left and are headed down the travelway, I turned to the two rescued youngers.

"What shall I call you, lads," I query as I pull my "squires" aside.

"I am called Éshæm and my brœther here is Tœngis, Ser," the first responds.

"And what are your ages, then?" I further query.

"I've seen my fifteen-year-end and my brœther is nearing his thirteen-year-end," he answers again for the two of them.

"And from whence do you hail?"

"We are Noördans, Ser." He points north to the mountains.

"Find yourself two mounts then, Éshæm and Tœngis. There are four tethered on the other side of the tree near to the river. Bring the other two as we can use them as burden steeds. We'll set off shortly," and they hurry to gather the horses.

"And what of me?" shouts Tullamoor from the cage. As if by providence, another echoing war cry from Talon sounds just at that moment.

I looked to the sky. The golden bird of prey approaches with something quite huge, wriggling in his claws. I step back as Talon's prey is dropped from the sky and in front of the cage. A giant, hooded asp, easily three paces in length rises up and spreads its cowl and hisses loudly. It appears quite angry and more bent on revenge than on escape.

"It appears Talon has won our sporting game, Lord Tullamoor," and I walked away to his anguished cry as he scuttles to the back of the cage, drawing the attention of the great black viper.

27

NoÖrdan Wood

Leaving Lord Tullamoor to his fate, I walked back under the grand canopy of the Calpaca tree. This one has two massive, intertwined trunks that resembled a couple in an intimate embrace, and its great limbs spread outwards twenty paces in all directions. Bane and the furions are at my side. Not having to bend down anymore to scratch him behind his ears, I welcome the great wolf back. His thick coat has grown out as well. Coppery and light orange hues, some tipped in black, his fur is accented by his coppery eyes flecked in gold and with a feline look about them. He now weighs between twelve and thirteen stone at the least.

Lilit and Jilly scurry about his legs and tremendous paws and even bounded up and down his back, joyous to see him. When I had left him to be Finnie's escort, I knew he would find his way back to me. It is fortunate that it happened upon this day. I take a moment to lower the cache of crossbows, dirks, and short swords from the tree where I had saved them after collecting them from the four fallen bowmen this morn. Gathering up the blades, I leave the crossbows where they lie. I wind up the Elven-vine and replace it in my pack.

Exiting out the south side of the tree, my two 'squires' have found the

296

bowmen's horses. As I approach, they stared back at me with expressions I can only interpret as awe. Their eyes roam to Bane, the furions, and back to me several times, and they glanced up to the sky as well.

"I've gathered the weapons that will no longer be needed by their previous owners. They are yours for the taking, if you would like. We will tether these other two mares also, as burden steeds. I'd like to set out immediately. It would not be wise to remain here long, I wager." I pass out the dead bowmen's dirks. The other weapons are rolled into a bedroll and stowed upon one of the tethered mares.

As we have not discussed a clear destination, I ride north and west, following the river and then into the woods. Bane disappears, happy to be reunited, but the business of hunting and feeding is a part of life. We are, the three of us, quiet with our own thoughts for the time being. I wonder after Tullamoor's nephew and whether he will find his pæder still alive and imprisoned in some dungeon in the bowels of the Keep as the counselor had sworn. I wonder after Finnie and if her meeting of my 'family' in Middenvale will be a good thing for her and the youngers. They are all deserving of some peace and normalcy in their lives. Mine, it appears, is destined to be otherwise. I carry no further thought of Lord Tullamoor beyond the relief that his part in a vile business has come to an end.

As I ponder these things in the calm of our travel, the sun has all but fallen from the sky and dusk has overtaken us. We have left the river behind and are following a stream leading north from it, having skirted around the southside of Tullamoor Keep. Coming upon a good site for camp, I rein up Paint and turned my thoughts back to our needs.

"Time to make camp, lads. Here is as good a place as any, I reckon. I can set some snares and mayhaps we'll have some meat in the morn."

"We can set them, if you like, Ser Drægonheart. Our Da has shown us the way of such things," responds Éshæm.

Tœngis nods in agreement.

"Yea then, be about it." And I tossed them some supplies for the task that I have handy in my saddlebags.

"I'll start a fire, then." I watch as they first care for their mounts. At thirteen and fifteen-year, they have some sense about them. 'Tis amazing I was thinking, as I catch myself staring into their eyes. They so reminded me of Da. Lilit and Jilly follow them into the woods. I am left to the simple camp set-up chores that have become second nature to me.

I have strung a tarpen tent and gathered some forest floor nettles, enough for the three of us to spread beneath our bedrolls. As I am just adding more wood to the fire, the lads return with the furions dancing about their ankles. Tœngis has a string of three rabbits hanging from his shoulder.

"We have had a mighty hunger and your fitchets are adept at finding rabbit holes. Tœngis near had a blue fox 'fore it escaped into a briar but was a tad behind. We laid some snares but have dinner as well." Tœngis holds up their bounty with more than a little pride. I cannot help but recall me doing the same with Da, just three or four short years past.

Reaching into my pack, I pulled my gifting of cooking blades and splayed their leather satchel out upon a flat rock aside me.

"Well then, shall we be about preparing our eve-meal? Lilit and Jilly, could you not have found some tubers or taters or shrooms as well?" I laughed.

And to our delight, they both rise to their hindquarters and then scurry into the forest.

Éshæm and Tœngis turn their heads to follow the furions and then turn back to me with raised brows.

"Tœngis, mayhaps you could follow them to see what they find?"

He rises to jog after the two critters.

Éshæm and I take the hares away from camp and started to gut, and skin, and prep our eve-meal. We have them skewered and over the fire in short order.

Our dinner is late, but it is satisfying. Tœngis has returned with a few wild onions, and carrots, and 'shrooms which we oiled up in a small pot and serve with the open-fire roasted hares.

As the night begins to deepen, Éshæm looks across the crackling fire to me. Finally, he says, "Ser Drægonheart. My brœther and I have not rightfully thanked ye. For saving our lives and all. We surely feared they would be forfeit these past few suns. Why did ye stand for us, that first day?"

I give a somber smile.

"First, you must call me Arias, for that is my true name. And second, to answer you true, I recognized what the guardsmen that held you were about. For I have been fighting it for four moons now. You have the right of it in that your fate would not have been a good one at their hands. Though when their Lord Tullamoor appeared, it became only about him, for me. I knew him to be the head of the snake and the evil that had befallen you and many more before you. I have been intent on ending his cruel enterprise,"

"Aye," he simply says in the hearing of my explanation. "But we will be ever in your debt, in any manner of our reasoning."

"Aye," says Tœngis. His eyes peering up under his lowered brow as he pokes a stick about the campfire. His first word.

"Nay," say I. "Feel no debt, but mayhaps someday give aid to others as I did for you. Always do good for others if you can and that will satisfy any debt you feel on my part."

They nodded, and I smiled to myself. They are but two and four-year my junior, but I speak to them as Da would me. I now feel a good deal elder from when I had left the homestead.

"May I ask ye another thing, Arias?" Éshæm interrupts my thoughts.

"Yea, Éshæm, speak your mind with me."

"It is, well, my Da-Sire has all his life been a beast whisperer. He can calm and train most any beast, wild or house bred. And so, he is legend in our valley for it. But you...? You walk with a mighty wolf, we've not ever seen the likes of, and it shows deference to you as a pack Alpha, though I've never seen a beast so fierce. You have fitchets that do your bidding and you call the fiercest bird of prey, a Mountain Echo Eagle and no less, of a size even my Da-Sire could not fathom, I am sure. It is as if you but speak with them and they do your bidding. I sense even that your horse would need no bridle, as he moves as you wish without sure rein."

He pauses and I furrowed my brow and ponder what he said. I vowed not to burden Paint with a bit and bridle on the morrow.

"My Da-Sire has said that his talent is but a glimmer of an ancient mægic not seen in the world anymore. Do you carry this mægic?" His face is earnest.

"My Da, as well, was a beast whisperer of some repute," I answer. "And most beasts feel comfort about me. But these about me are of their own mind, and I do not control their behavior."

I cannot but wonder, though, about my relationship with the beasts that surround me. This is not the first time that ancient mægics were described about my connection to my beast companions. We move on to a different subject.

"Tell me of your home, so that I might help you get back there."

He glances to Tœngis and then back to me.

"There is an outpost that the Lord Tullamoor keeps and from there it is mayhaps a three-sun trip on horseback," he says, competent in this knowledge.

"Well, let us get some sleep and be off early on morrow's morn, then." I climbed into my bedroll. I am tired from this sun's activity and no little stress of it. There remains also a sense of justice done, and I hold little remorse.

Waking at sunrise from a sound sleep, I find Bane curled up at my feet with furions nestled betwixt his legs. Bane opens his eyes, even as I do and gazes up at me. I cypher that there is something different about him, aside his growth spurt. I eye him from head to tail as something keeps niggling at me; it finally registers in my brain. There about his neck, a cord is tied, and upon it, is attached a leather cylinder.

Pulling myself from the bedroll, I moved to sit atop a fallen log and motion Bane to me. Lilit and Jilly are not too happy to be disturbed from their slumber and they sneak away to curl up in the warm area left in my bedroll.

Slipping the knotted cord from about Bane's neck, I examine the leather tube. It has a tightfitting cap on one end that I manage to pry loose. Within the tube lay a rolled parchment and upon it inked a letter in Grayce's hand. I think it a brilliant way to contact me.

Dearest Arias,

Argo, Effie, and I met your wonderful friend this sun. She and the two youngers are well and safe. Though they were accosted by three would-be highwaymen at the rise just north of towne. Argo happened to be watching them as they had just been sent away by towne Council. He mounted his horse and galloped to her as he could see they were about bad business. He arrived to find that it was they, that were escaping into the forest as your friend Finnie and Bane had acquitted themselves quite well. The thugs hobbled away, one with a broken arm, another with no use of one leg, and the last with an arrow wound to his shoulder. She explained that it was just there that she had aimed and she swears it was you that had taught her how to defend herself. She kept their horses as bounty for their aggression.

She also told us her story and that of the youngers. Know that she is welcomed here as family, Arias. Though she said you offered your homestead, she will for now be staying with me. As Moor has reasoned, three Kingsmen have taken residence in towne, checking out Ètœn's homestead from time a'times. They have asked after you and have been given descriptions by

towne folk not knowing the danger it would pose you. Finnie shall be intro-
duced as my niece, come to live.

We will keep her safe. Finish your quest and return when you are one
day able. Grayce.

A twinge of a fear niggles at me, for Finnie, at the mention of the high-waymen, but smiled upon the outcome of the attack. My heart warms that Grayce and the others have accepted her as family. I stowed the leather tube within my pack, it might prove to be of worth, someday. 'Twas clearly something crafted by Argo.

I quickly build up our fire from the embers and suggested to Éshæm and Tœngis that we should tour their snares to see if we will be as lucky this morn as they had been yester's eve. One does indeed hold morn's meal, but what is most curious to me is that the snares they had placed are set exactly as Da had taught to me. Their triggers and knots are very specific in their design. Moor had once shown me snares of his own, and they were of a different sort altogether. Da had explained that Moor's method was the more common and he had learned his method from his Da and knew of no other man to set them in his fashion.

We collect our morn-meal and the remaining traps, and snare lines, and tools. We will set off again after eating.

As we prepared to go, I pay mind to what Éshæm had said yester's eve and do not bridle Paint. Surely enough, Paint has no need of them. He goes about as I think he should with never more than the slightest nudge of my knees. After our midsun break, I knot a leather strap, as a harness, about his lower neck for my own sake, to have something to hold, should the need arise.

The morn of the third sun out from our leaving, we come upon the outpost. There is some little activity as traders meet in the market's square to barter and trade their wares. I think of the tinker from whom I'd gotten my amulet that I still wear about my neck.

We dine at the outpost with coin from the sale of our bounty. The traders spy suspicious at its nature but are willing to trade, ne'er-the-lesser. In the end, we bathed in hot water, eat a heavy meal, and sleep well at the outpost Inn.

Early upon the morrow's morn, we set out through the northern gate and find ourselves from the start, riding through narrow passes, sometimes in a single file caravan. There are open valleys as well and at sun's end, we find ourselves at the shore of a crystal-clear lake and make camp there. It brings to mind the lake in the mountains where Da and I had experienced the fall of the Sky-stone when still but a seven year-ender.

Having provisioned for a few days at the outpost, we make camp and set a fire, not worrying about hunting or foraging. As we sit at the fire Éshæm speaks.

"Arias, we know this place and how to find our clan from here, but we hope that ye will join us to visit our family so that they might meet ye and call you friend as well."

"I will if you will tell me a little of your tale, as I can see that there is more than I know," I return.

"Aye then, we will. Ye would hear it in any manner when we arrive back to home," he says. "It is a simple tale and one we are not proud for."

"My brœther and I were hunting not far from here, having gone much further south than ever we had and against the rules of the clan. We woke one morn with sword points in our throats and men in the Lord's livery holding them. They took our bows, which were our most prized possessions, and then our liberty." Simply stated and I nod. "They then took us to a large warehouse down in the city and held us with other lads of a like age and some younger. They were carrying us to yet another place when you intervened on our behalf."

"Well then, mayhaps we should set watch about us this night." I whistle for Bane.

The night remains uneventful though and we continued to travel together. We make our way east and north around the lake and then Éshæm takes us into a steep pass that he calls the Wending Way and then into forested hills about it he names the Wending Wood. We travelled nonstop now as he claims it not safe to stop or camp in the Wending Wood. When I asked him why, his gaze goes blank for a moment and he does not say. A chill creeps up my back and we do not stop. Even upon the path, Bane travels close to Paint this day and the furions are quiet, but alert. Glancing to the sky, I occasionally see the circling of Talon, riding a very high current in the air above.

Come dusk, we are finally exiting the tortuous trail and the trees become sparser to reveal a grassy vale strewn with tremendous boulders scattered about us as if a mountainside had blown apart and the rubble thrown about the valley.

To the west and into a yellow-/orange sky, a great mountain ragged at its peak rises above a cloud. Below the cloud, one can see the bottom third of the mountainside. It sits stark and mostly devoid of trees and there appears to be black veins snaking their way up, reaching for the peak.

The foot of the mountain swims in black as well, any greenery ending at its base. Éshæm notes my gaze.

"Noördan folk here about call it Dæmon Mount. It is said that hundreds upon hundreds of years past a great wielder of ancient mægic summoned great, fiery dæmons from the depths of the mountains, and he split the mountain top open wide to release them unto the world in anger of some slight. The dæmons were said to breathe fire as did the drægons of lore. As they ran down the mountainside, they blackened it with their bile and the wielder saw that what he wrought was wrong, and he fought them with all his might and mægic at the foot of the mountain. In the end, he destroyed all but a few of the cleverest dæmons. But those he was able to contain by mægic in the Wending Wood that we have just traveled through. There they prey upon all and live as the fiercest beasts in all the woods. They only feed during the moon he said, but then… Well, it would be unwise to spend a night within the wood. It is named so, as once you stray from the trail, there is said to be no finding your way back. Off the Wending Way, one loses all sense of direction and but wander hopeless until one of the beasts does find you. That is the tale."

He pauses and his eyes grow pensive.

"We have an elder amongst our clan. Da-Sire says that he has thrice his years and more, but nobody knows for sure. He is revered amongst the clan as a wielder of an ancient mægic, though it is not a war mægic. He is a Seer. Folks say he sees into both the years to come and into the years long past. But we hear from him little nowadays. He is old and a bit frail and his eyes are blinded now. When he visits the here and now, with his mind, I mean, it is said to be eerie to be in the same room. When he awakens from his stupor, his eyes open and it is a shock to see, for his eyes are a sparkling deep shade of blue. When he speaks, his voice is strong and he knows without explanation, who it is that is in the room with him. They say he is both everywhere and nowhere in any moment."

"In the matter of the mountain, the great Elder at one time spoke. He said it was not an ancient mægic wielder that made the mountainside as it is, but a great swelling of fire from within the ground that did burst from the mountaintop and heave its pieces as far as where we stand. He said rivers of fire flowed like water from the mounts severed head and scorched and blackened paths to the bottom. There was night and no sun for three full cycles of the moon. The entire mountainside turned grey from the spewing fire ash and all things on the mountain died. That is what truly happened, he said… And I believe him.

"And what of the Wending Wood?" I asked.

"There is something fierce, in the woods I mean, and mayhaps some unknown mægic, but not dæmons summoned by a Mæge."

"There were ancient mægics though," Éshæm continues his telling. "According to our Elder, they exist still in the world, and will someday play a greater part again. And it is said that the old Seer shook his head in dismay in the telling. For some of the old and ancient mægics were indeed evil, and mægic will need to one day be rediscovered to do battle with it."

I pondered about what Éshæm has said. The great Elder of his village is a wonder, no doubt. As old as he was said to be? All this talk of ancient mægics, some evil, some not, did not seem to take hold in my mind, though.

"Let us set up camp, Éshæm, and I would like to hear more of your village and family, and your friends, if you care to share."

We choose a great boulder to shelter under. It leans to the west and offers a den under its overhanging eave. We still have outpost provisions and do not bother to hunt. Old wood lies about and available from strange trees that have outstretching branches that more resembled roots of a tree, but they bear fruit that Éshæm proclaims edible and we gathered some of it for our eve-meal.

Éshæm speaks of his family and village for a while and as the moon is nowhere in sight, we at the last unroll our bedrolls and take our sleep.

The morrow's morn dawns clear and crisp. We make our morn-meal of the fruit we'd gathered on yester's eve. Éshæm says that we will make his village midsun, two suns hence. I can see that he and his brœther are anxious to be home again.

To my mind, Dæmons Mount is reachable by sunset. It is a tribute to its enormous size that it appears not much larger after traveling a full sun towards it across the boulder strewn vale. Another clue lays in a herd of great elk, mayhaps 200 strong that rumbles past us in the far distance. They look the size of hares, but Éshæm assures me they are of a size near the equal to Paint and as the ground shakes even at this distance, I do believe him. By dusk we reach a pass leading north again, into the woods, and out of the vale. We camp one more night in the same valley.

Next sun, we travel among trees again and on a well-worn trail. I can hear and see bountiful wildlife in the woods we ride within and contemplate using my bow a bit. But then, as the sun has fallen half to the horizon, a mighty echoing call comes from the sky. It is a warning from Talon.

"Softly and quietly to the trees," I whisper and Bane bounds off to the north.

I take our small caravan sixty paces into the woods behind an outcropping of rock. Tethering the mounts, I leave Paint to watch over them and signaled to Éshæm and Tœngis to follow me back to the trail. I've strung my bow and set my staff to the ground next to me and we wait behind a wide tree and a wild hedgerow.

We need not have hid, for around a bend in the trail ahead, three hunters appear aside us. Éshæm and Tœngis burst through the hedge and each near attack two of the hunters and draw them into great hugs.

"Ho, Dent, Hagar, and Mag! Your hunt will yield naught with the noise you make on the trail!" Éshæm booms.

"Fates!" cries the one named Dent. "Sæmmy and Tonk!"

The friends have a lively reunion and the furions, Bane, and I step out behind them all. The brœthers look to see us do just that and their three friends turn, then all jump back at the sight of us. Well rather, at the site of the Mountain Dread Wolf staring at them with head lowered and intent in his copper eyes. Their hands, as a reflex, go to their weapons. I cross my arms and stared at them, but Lilit and Jilly fall to their backs and laughed their furion laugh. Well, a bit of a cackle actually. This has the three of them turning back at a smiling Éshæm and Tœngis. They turn back to us with eyebrows raised.

"Ye return with interesting friends, Sæmmy and Tonk. Well met, stranger. Our friends seem to have lost their tongues. Might we know your name?"

"Call me Arias, and call me friend, as I do Éshæm and Tœngis,"

Lilit and Jilly sit up on their hindquarters and watched out at this new group.

"Well met then," he says and offers his forearm in greeting. "Though if you were true friend, you'd not be addressing them in a manner only their mum would use when they are in trouble. Come to think on it, you'll most like be hearing it a lot, soon enough!"

I grab his arm and wrist in return and do the same with the others. "Mayhaps, your friends can help us with our caravan... Sæm?"

"Aye, I think they might." He grins back at me, with a nod of approval to my new moniker for him. A little more formal, a little less Mum.

We set off back to the horses. Bane disappears into the woods and our new friends relax a bit.

Our expanded troupe spends the night in a well-used cave at the bottom of a bluff alongside a meandering stream. It appears a well-worn camp and used often before. We are at the last of our provisions from the outpost and spend our time communing about the campfire that Sæm's friends have built just outside our night's abode.

On target to Sæm's estimation, we come into their homestead towne near on to the midsun following. We come off the game trails and onto a wide travelway and into a large enough towne, mayhaps the size of Quill'spie. Dust is kicked up as wagons, and carriages, and horseman travel about. It has all the familiar establishments as any towne in the Mid Realm.

Little attention is paid to us till the youngers about towne start staring at Paint's unusual markings and the furions pop up out of their home in my saddlebags and sit up upon paint's hindquarters. This sets off quite a stir amongst the youngers which in turn causes others to glance in our direction.

As we come near upon the outskirts, there before us sits a stone cottage.

A voice louder than all the others rings out.

"Tonky, Sæmmy!! By the gods, ye have made it home!" she screams and comes running as we are all dismounting.

A woman pulls the two boys into a crushing hug and her tears are flowing freely.

"Ye two have been gone nigh on two fortnight, and we were beginning to think the worst. Yer Da and cousins are still out searching for ya," she says.

"Mum, 'twas almost the worst. This is our friend, Arias, and he is the reason it is not. He is a great warrior, mum." Sæm motions me forward.

Their mum peers down at me with lifted brows. And 'twas truly down that she looks upon me as she stands more than a hand higher than me. I see that all the folk about me are unusually tall, nay huge, compared to me. I had thought the brœthers large for their ages they professed to be and now I can see the why of it.

"Well, for a mighty warrior, he's a bit small, he is. Did your mum not feed ye when ye was a young-un?" And afore I can protest, she pulls me into as tight a hug as ever I've had and whispers into my ear, "My deepest thanks for bringing them back to me." And then aloud, "Come, come, all of ye and get some warm food in ya."

She eyes me up and down for a moment and goes to her business. As she turns and waves us to the large cottage that she has been tending garden in front of, Tœngis leans into me.

"Mum's always tryin' to feed ya, she is." Mayhaps the first words I'd heard him speak.

28

Nowhere Man

"The Elder awoke seven night's past." Sæm's mum continues telling him. "He told the watcher that he wanted to see me! I never in all my years met or have spoken with the Elder."

An air of astonishment surrounds her.

We are all seated around the table in the family's stone cottage. It is warm and inviting. It has been a strange experience from the time I'd entered. The home consists of but three large rooms. There appears to be two sleeping quarters and a large room with seating about a large fireplace along one wall with a long table a-center to the room. Cupboards run along one wall near to the ceiling with plates, and bowls, and mugs neatly arranged upon it and near out of reach to me. As a fact, all things about the home are larger. I sit upon a chair that leaves my toes barely able to touch the floor. The doorways would have left two-hand's clearance even for Da, and he stood near two heads taller than me. The windows are oversized and set high in the wall that is of a height half again as high as Da would stand.

We have all but finished huge portions of roasted fowl and smashed taters in a thick, rich gravy with roast carrots. Sæm and his brœther have just treated themselves to a second generous portion to the smiles of their mum.

"Your Da and cousins have been out hunting ye two for half a fortnight, but it 'twas me the Elder wanted to see. He is a strange one, he is. Soon as I come into his room, he spoke to me. Even being blind and all, with his blue eyes not seeing but as bright as the sky and the sun, he knew who had come into his room. He said, 'Charta, fear not for yer sons, tho they have seen trials, they are safe. A young warrior, both Wolf and Eagle Master, shall deliver them back to ye seven suns hence,' he said and I teared up with hope for ye two, as I had been worried so," she says, tearing up again as she speaks.

Sæm and Tonk glanced to each other and then to me.

"Did I not tell ye, Arias? The Elder is a Seer, just as I said to ye," Sæm recalls his earlier tale to me.

"And mum, Arias indeed has a great Mountain Dread Wolf that follows him everywhere. He is a giant monster of a beast, the likes of which I've never seen. And I've seen with mine own eyes a great Mountain Echo Eagle with a wingspan greater than mine, and he flew and landed soft as a sparrow upon Arias' shoulder. Da-Sire would call it a miracle, he would!" Sæm exclaims. "The Elder calling him a great warrior is rightful, as well. He bested and killed near a dozen soldiers in the time it took in me telling this tale, with bow and staff and throwing blade."

Charta's eyes opened wide and takes a closer look at me.

"Well, then… And then the Elder, he says to me, 'Feed your sons and the stranger and on the morrow's morn, bring him to me if he will come.' And 'tis all he said to me and he took leave of us again, staring with his eyes past all that were there with me," she says, ending her tale. "Will ye stay with us tonight, Arias? Tonky can pull a cot and put it by the fire for ye."

"Surely, and I thank you for your generous hospitalities."

"Ye saved my lads, know ye will always have a place in my home," she says.

"Sæm, there's most of the sun left to us, will you show me around the village?" I asked.

"Aye, come with me then."

And we are off. As we come out of the door, I find the furions atop an eave spout above the door staring at a half-dozen youngers, and they stare back at them.

"Lilit, Jilly, would you care to join me in a tour of the towne?"

They scurry down to the water collection barrel and then up to my shoulders, trying to keep out of the reach of the youngers still about.

"We should take the horses over to the stableman, Arias, and see what coin he'll give for them. And while we are there, I can see my Sasha, she's a proud mare and my first that Da gave me to train. Then while we're there, I'll have a stable hand run for our smithy, Fenn, to see what he'll offer for your weapons. He'll be happy to have them, I'd wager," he finishes.

"It's a good plan, and I'd like to give Paint a brush down as well," I respond, and we go about gathering the four tethered mounts and Paint.

We draw eyes aplenty as the people about us wonder at the stranger amongst them now. The stables and pasture paddock are on the other side of towne and I have a chance to observe this northern towne, which few from the Mid Realm and Southern Reaches have probably ever seen. I quickly learn that the peoples of the Northern Reaches call themselves Noördan and that all those who live below the great inland sea are referred to Sûdlan or Sûdlanders. The towne is much the same as any I've seen in the Mid Realm but on a physically larger scale. Many things seem eerily familiar to me.

As we walk the horses towards the stables, it all strikes me like a sky-bolt. These people speak and have many of the same mannerisms as Da!

As a fact, I cannot recall any of my friends from Middenvale ever refer to their mœthers or pæders as Da and Mums. 'Tis always been papa or pa and mumma or mom. Not just Sæm and his family, but as a fact, all these townsfolk speak and have the mannerisms of Da. Likened to Da, they are tall and manly—, heavy built. I'd finally come to the realization that Da was Noördan. These thoughts settle back into my mind as we are approaching the stables.

"Hail, Artur, 'tis Sæmmy. Have ye a moment to do some business?" Sæm asks.

"Aye lad, just finished shoein' Edder's mare., I'll come on then," Artur calls from within the barn.

We corral the horses aside the stable barn. Artur makes his appearance. His air is every bit a stableman, likened to any I've ever met, more so somehow. He is muscled about the arms unlike any man I've ever met. He peers back at me with eyes of golden hue and alike to Da's. As a fact, about this towne alone, beyond Artur, and Éshæm, and Tœngis, there are more eyes of gold than ever I've ever noticed in all my travels.

"Artur, this here's Arias, Arias meet Artur, stableman, and beast whisperer. He's been training me in the art," Sæm says, introducing his friend.

"There's none better 'n yer Da-Sire, Sæmmy…. I heard ye had gone missing, then heard ye 'n yer brœther just come back and brought a stranger…. I'm assuming then that this is he?" queries Artur.

"Aye, Artur. And as good as Da-Sire is, Arias may be the better." Sæm claims.

"That would be a far reach, I'd reckon. And from the looks of 'im, he's a Sûdlan to boot," he says.

Sæm smiles. "Take no heed to how he says things, Arias. He's as rude to any a man."

I laughed and take no offense, of course.

"Artur, Arias rides without a bridle. Do you see his Paint? Have ye ever seen his like? And ye can see his fitchet pets, they travel every-which-a-where with him. And Artur, a Mountain Dread travels ne'er too far from him and he commands a great Echo Eagle as well."

The stableman, to his credit, does try to stifle his chuckle as he looks me over. He does glance over at Paint and the furions that presently ride upon his back.

"Well then, I'll need to take yer word for it, lad, as I see no wolf of lore, nor eagle. But about the horses, then?" He nods to them, turning to the business at hand.

"Can ye send Toby to get Fenn? Arias has some weapons and such that he might have interest in, as well?" Sæm asks and the stableman obliges us.

A turn later, we finish our business, and all are happy with the barter. I collected some coin and we are about to head out from the stables when a very tall and broad elder approaches us in the barn's training yard.

"Da-Sire," Sæm gives a yell as the man approaches. The man takes Sæm in a cross-forearm grab and shakes it firmly with affection.

"Ye've set yer mum and Da into a fright, Sæmmy, ye and yer brœther this past two fortnight. But the great Elder himself called me to him, and he told me and your mum to worry not, as ye would be back, and bring a stranger to us as well. He said he'd have an ability akin to my own, but to a much greater degree. I am to accompany him to visit with the Elder on morrow's morn, if the stranger is willing," he says, turning to me for my response.

"Call me Arias, if you have a mind to. And I'll be honored to meet with your Elder." As a fact, I carry a compulsion within me to do just that.

"I will come for ye at the sun's rise on the morrow then. But the Elder has put upon me a mighty curiosity, Arias. The Elder has said in the past that few in the Sûdland carried any gift in these times."

"Da-Sire," Sæm interrupts. "Ye would not believe what I have seen with mine own eyes. I've seen five beasts do his bidding with nary a word spoken by him. Arias, could ye, mayhaps call to a beast so Da-Sire will not think of me too boastful?"

I can sense that both Bane and Talon are not far from me. As we are at the edge of the village, I reckoned that they cannot cause too much of a stir, as few might see them. And so, I let out a great whistle. To his credit, Sæm's Da-Sire has a sense about him to be sure. For as Bane comes to us from betwixt two stone homes across from the stables, silent in his approach from the woods beyond, the man instinctively turns towards the wolf. As he does, his eyes go wide and an inherent fear battles to take control of him. Bane crosses the way and turns about at my side, never releasing the man's gaze. I do not truly know if Bane has reached his full-grown body as yet, but he weighs now near thirteen-stone and his head, when raised, stands above my waist. He is a fearsome creature near twice the size of a typical Timberwolf. His jaws and teeth could snap a grown elk's neck in but a single shake. But his eyes might just have been his most fierce feature. They are a copper, flecked in gold and their pupils are that of a cat and within them resides a clear intelligence.

Sæm's Da-Sire stands mesmerized, but his greater shock remains yet to come.

"This is Bane. I can only explain our relationship as two souls tied as one. He is no danger." I assured him.

Even as I say this, with just a whisper Talon swoops down. The sun is at his back as he softly alights upon my shoulder. The man's mouth opens in wonderment.

"A Mountain Dread and a great Mountain Echo Eagle. 'Tis not possible," he whispers to himself. As he does, the furions scurry up onto Bane's back in a playful manner. Sæm's Da-sire smiles and shakes his head in amazement, totally disarmed with the display.

"Call me Éshûr, Arias, and no further demonstration is necessary for my part," he says with a smile. "I will see you on the morrow's morn then. I believe the Elder will be pleased to speak with you."

Sæm and I headed back to his cottage. Apparently, Talon and Bane's appearance does not go unnoted after all. As we walk, 'tis like a wave before us as the townspeople whisper about to others though my creature friends have disappeared from view again. We find that the whole of the way, the stares and whispering are all about us.

As we walk, I noticed an Inn for travelers. I suggested to Sæm that he go fetch his mum and I will treat them to a dinner at the Inn. Sæm smiles and heads off and about it.

I enter the Inn as I'd entered every Inn in every towne I'd ever visited. In the many moons since I left my homestead in the hills aside Middenvale, I'd entered quite a few. Greeting me, is a cacophony of sounds and smells. I wear my pack, with Bo-staff and bow in hand, and I seek out a table in the corner facing the door. Leaving my pack and weapons to the corner, I set upon the bench and watched the Inn's clientele come and go. Many are eating a hearty fare that clearly satisfies. Whether it be a seared beef or savory roast fowl or trenchers full of a steamy stew, a standard throughout all Aeryth.

There are laughing comrades swilling ale and lasses serving them and ignoring their flirtations, but smiling and encouraging the same, as it would mean an extra copper in the end. The only difference that I can see is the scale of it all. I look the child among them—, even the serving lasses are a hand above my own height. This does not bother me at all as I know from my midsun-fest in Charta's cottage, it will mean a greater portion upon my plate and a deeper mug of ale. There is a cacophony of joyous noises and 'tis like music to my ears. It is, sure certain, a good night to be out among decent townsfolk.

Éshæm, and Tœngis, and their mum arrivedwith a joy spread upon her face. There is a sparkle in her eye. She gazes about her as they walk from the door to my table.

"My son has brought home a true goodman to be sure," she gushes. "I've not seen the inside of an Inn's dining hall near onto twenty year, Arias. Ye are so nice to invite us."

One cannot help but see that she revels in being with so many folk and hearing, and smelling, and in the whole, just experiencing the atmosphere of the Inn.

"'Twas but a simple thought to repay your earlier kindness."

I signal towards the serving lass that keeps an eye my way since a kind word I'd offered and the small extra coin that I had passed to her as she served my ale earlier.

"The lady Charta is visiting your fine establishment for the first time in many a year, Britta, it is she that cook's and cares and provides for her man and their guests with little time for reprieve. Could you bring her a tall glass of your best wine, another ale and some ciders? And Mãam Charta will be having the proprietor's finest fare this eve." I smiled at her with hopes that she will help in making Charta's experience most enjoyable. The amulet on my chest warms.

The Inn employs minstrels this night and the mood about is gay and festive. Her sons and I dance with Charta, and Britta keep our plates full and our cups as well. 'Tis a wonderful eve-fest and a long night out. The lads remark that they have not seen such a gaiety and sparkle in their mum's eyes as they'd ever recalled and vow to do it more often. I have strong feelings and a closeness akin to family with these folk. The night air is fresh, the sky shines with its myriad of stars and a sure fellowship forms among us as we shuffle through the streets back to the cottage.

A guest cot has already been arranged in the brœthers' sleep quarters for me. 'Tis plenty long enough for me. All of us settle for the night.

I wake before the sun's rise to the all-familiar smell of crushed java beans brewing. The scent takes me home to Da's kitchen. Slipping quietly from my corner cot, I make my way to the kitchens where I heard murmurs. Charta stands pouring the brew into mugs for two men at the table. One, Éshûr the elder, the other, with back to me, must be Sæm's Da and Charta's husband.

Charta's eyes climb to meet mine and she smiles. Her husband must have cyphered the cause for her smile and he rises and turns to greet me. Puzzlement crosses his face as he watches me drop my boots along with my jaw. My eyes wide as my very own Da stands afore me.

My mind starts clicking in a maddening manner, connecting tales and images from my memories of Da to the sights, and speech, and mannerisms I noted amongst Sæm and Tœngis and even the townsfolk. And even to a Tinker's tale and an amulet with unique, and it seems, mægical properties. Of a sudden, I realize I am standing afore my uncle. He reaches out to grasp me about my forearm and shakes me.

"I am Élan and we are in debt to you, Arias. One that we can never expect to repay," he says, and clearly overjoyed to be meeting me for what I have done for Sæm and Tonk.

"Excuse my expression just then, Élan, but there is more. Éshûr, have we time afore we must go to meet the great Elder?"

"Aye, he will await us in our time, Arias."

"Then I would like to sit and speak with you all a bit, if I may," a serious tone bringing about perplexed expressions.

"O'course, lad," says Élan as my heart pounds within my chest.

I go to my pack and supplies and retrieved my bow. Approaching the table, I placed it in the center. Éshûr's eyes go to it immediately and he grabs it up to examine it.

"Da crafted and gifted it to me for my seventeen-year-end. 'Twas little more than a half year past," I stated, matter of fact, despite the pumping of my heart's beat, frantic against my chest.

A bit of moisture finds its way to Éshûr's lower lids. Élan realizes the import of my words as well.

"Élan, I believe that you are my Da's brœther. You have his self-same look about you and so, as a fact I thought you were he. Charta, you are my aunt, and Éshûr, you are my Da-Sire and I truly believe this is so."

Éshûr looks to me, but then turns back to the bow in his hands.

"Ètœn was always a quick study with his hands. And it is made of Ænt-wood, as well. The fates be praised," staring back upon me in astonishment.

Élan and Charta sit silent, apparently lost for words.

"After we meet with the Elder, we will have much to discuss, it would seem." A great smile comes to my face.

"Aye," all three respond in unison. Smiles all about.

"That we will, Arias," says my *Da-Sire*.

"I've never tasted Da's roasted bean brew—, might I have a mug?" I asked and things settle to a more usual state about the table.

"O'course, nephew," says Charta with a warm smile.

A round of chuckles and tapping of mugs ensue.

My Da-Sire and I leave out to visit the great Elder shortly after. It takes a bit as he lives upon a slight rise in a small cottage surrounded by Calpaca trees outside of the village. A tall matronly woman sits upon a chair as the morn's sun casts shade under a roof and over a stoop in front of the cottage.

"He is awake and taking his brew in the kitchens," she says. "He's expecting you, o'course. Help yourselves to the cakes and there is a tea kettle for Ariastone as well."

She has not bothered to move from her seat. Her eyes, however, go to my chest and the amulet warming upon it. My brow furrow, and she smiles at me even as she raisesd an eyebrow.

"Thank you, Witchæra," Éshûr addresses her. "Yer hospitality is greatly appreciated."

And we take our leave and enter the cottage. It is not what I expected. But for a beard of white, braided in two and then braided themselves and reaching for his waistline, I would not have guessed the man carried more than 150-year. He has a bounce to his step and he glides about the kitchen and fireplace with adept movement and I would not know him blind but for the knowledge granted me earlier.

"Come in Éshûr and young Ariastone Côeurdrægon. It is a pleasure to finally meet you."

I looked to Éshûr and he back to me with a shrug. Strange words as I have just arrived midsun yester.

"Help yourself to some tea and you know your way about my kitchens, Éshûr. Be as at home and it will please me. Come to me lad, I would like to place my hands upon your face and feel your features and to know it as no longer just a vision."

I can do naught but oblige him. As he runs his fingers about my face and smiles a wide smile, I stare into his sparkling sky-blue eyes, speckled in gold. And though unseeing, I feel he stands gazing into my very essence.

Satisfied, he invites us to sit at his table, gesturing directly to it. After a weight of silence, the Elder speaks again, his smile has dissipated, and he sighs aloud.

"Ariastone Côeurdrægon, I've over many years thought on what I would say to you at this moment. As I have pondered it a great deal, and there is much I could say, it has resolved itself into few words."

I sit afore him, thoroughly confused. How has he pondered for many years what to say to me? How can he even know of me? And is there more to the tale of the amulet that hangs about my neck?

He 'looks' to the sky and slowly shakes his head, side-to-side, then returns his eyes to stare into mine, though he is blind.

"First and foremost, know that each man's fate is ruled by himself alone. This choice has always been both our burden and our gift. *You* are no different in this. *If nothing else, remember these words above all others.*" He is firm about this. His voice bespeaks his words as truth beyond a doubt.

"Great and ancient Mægics have, however, led you to be in this place at this time. To see me and hear only these same words, mayhaps. You will learn more at the end of your current quest, put to you by Ètœn of Bearheart clan. Even so, these further things I will tell to you."

We sit about his small tea table, he stirs his tea in its cup deftly, never touching the cup with his spoon, blind as he is.

"There were once in Aeryth, great Mægics. Of these, five were predominant in a people that lived in a far-away land known to none in all of Aeryth now, but there was a sixth as well. This tale begins with that. There were some Mægics also in some trees and plants and certain beasts of intelligence. These Mægics were in harmony. The Mæges that brought them to Aeryth were escaping from a land far to the south of Aeryth and across the Greater Sea. They, themselves fled Mæges that practiced the sixth of the great Mægics, but to ill end."

"Though all six Mægics are of themselves harmonious, there were some Wizærdii that sought to bend the Mægics to their will and so hold dominion over all others and hence hold sway over all Mægics. In effort to thwart this outcome, a great exodus took place by most Mæges who carried the Five other Mægics. The Mæges of the five ancient Mægics, as we know them, fled instead of fighting the power-hungry among their ranks and they sailed upon a hundred great ships north out from Destinæa and onto the shores of Aeryth. Arias, this happened twenty hundreds of years past."

I wonder how could anyone know such things.

The great Elder is silent, as if recalling what further he has to say. I take a breath as well, to worry through his words to make sense of why he would need to tell me such a tale. When he begins again, his voice steady, but holds a resolute edge.

"The Mæges that came to Aeryth were but a minority of all the peoples residing here. They had no desire to remain separate from them either. And so, over centuries that followed, their bloodlines mingled and over these many years upon years, the *knowing* of Mægic dissipated in the whole. Even still, Mægic has existed as long as history has been written. It has always existed but it's *knowing* lies deep within the few that destiny has chosen."

"The greater thinkers among them knew this to be their fate and accepted it, but they were also in fear that one day the threat from over the sea might come to Aeryth. And so, they schemed to keep their Mægics alive so as to protect Aeryth should ever the need arise. This is why I have been so excited to finally meet with you, Ariastone Côeurdrægon, for ye are Mægics heir."

"What does this even mean, Elder" His face becomes... pensive.

He pauses. He sighs. The steam in the tea kettle sets it rocking again, behind us.

Éshûr gazes at me and I just shrug and chuckle at such a farcical thought.

"O'course, you would not believe such an old and ridiculous tale and I expected nothing more," he states and chuckles himself. Let us have more tea, it is from the Isles and quite delightful. We do. And he speaks a bit more. Finally, he says,

"A new era begins with you, Ariastone. Great things will begin to happen in Aeryth again, as they once did in times lost to all but a very few. There will be peril, as well. But mayhaps not even in your life's cycle. I do not see the true time of such things."

"So, go live yer life as ye will, lad. These fears were the fears of long dead Mæges and may never come to pass. But know that ye have within ye a great living and growing ability and if ye are to learn more of it, the first step is to finish the quest set upon ye, for it will be of great aid to ye in yer life. And though it will mean nothing to ye now, mayhaps remember one other thing. When you most need it, reach into the very ether about you for it."

The Elder's serious tone lifts and he has a jovial air about him once again.

"Oh, one more thing, for the here and now. If you might humor an Elder his own mechanisms, wouldst thou take the lad Éshæm with you to visit your Druid? It is one of his fates that leaves good in this world."

He smiles and says no more. He does not wait on an answer. As a fact, his deep, bright blue eyes did then glaze over and his body eases back into his chair as I have been told mine own are apt to do when I reached into my *Calming*. Wiitchæra appears, of a sudden, at his side and takes his hand in hers. She turns to me and peers deep into my eyes and lifts her other hand to my chest and over my amulet. She sighs heavy, as one might in mourning, or having lost something precious to her.

29

Don't pass me by

The meeting with the great Elder, though an interesting lesson in ancient history, leaves me with no great revelation. This tale of great Mæges and strong mægics that were once commonplace and brought from over the Great Sea and disappeared over hundreds of years? It has little bearing on my life. His tale does mayhaps explain the unusual things that sometimes happen about me, but I am no great Mæge nor do I even know what a great Mæge might do. I have close ties with some beasts and they in turn seem to understand my needs. We protect each other as family; this gives the meaning to my life. Family.

I can fancy now that some vestiges of these Mægics might indeed still linger about, as Moor had always taught that absent all logical explanation, one must not discount what might be deemed the inconceivable. Mayhaps he's had such experiences himself.

I have no choice but to believe that the Elder carries some of this ancient Mægic himself. His age is alone a miracle. He knew of me and my quest for many years he says, and more still. He makes it a point that I know that we all carry within us a free will and choice in all things, yet he describes Mægics that have ordained that I arrive here to find him...

has indeed carried me to this village in the Northern Reaches where I have found my Da's family.

My family. This, to me, speaks most important.

Now, despite my quest and longing for Finnie, I am determined to get to know them and to tell them the tale of Da, or at least that part that I know. My quest can wait a fortnight or two.

Éshûr, my Da-Sire, and I leave the great Elder's cottage, and for all the time I stay in the village he never again wakes from his Seer's trance. Da-Sire tells me his caregivers feed him sustaining foods, but he eats as a thing of instinct with no presence of mind thought to his actions. I understand this in part, as I myself experience it at times when living within the *Calming*. His trancelike state and my *Calming* are akin to one another, sure certain.

As suns pass, I become acquainted with my newfound family and the people that are their friends and townsfolk. Sæm has asked me to train him in the skills I know. And taking my lessons with Moor as my guide, I do my best to help him in the task. He is strong and a quick study on most of the techniques I teach him. He can be a strong warrior one day if he so desires. We make an awkward Mæster and pupil mayhaps. For at fifteen-year he appears my elder. He stands taller, and his air and countenance speaks to a maturity that my own mayhaps does not.

I stay with Da-Sire Éshûr, as he has room in his cottage and it offers me time to recount my life's experiences with my Da – his son. For my part, I learn of a younger Ètœn Bearheart. At times it reminds me greatly of life with Da. As it happens, Élan is Da's elder brœther by five-year. His likeness to Da is uncanny. Though not the warrior Da was, he is skilled in the hunt and an extraordinary Bowman.

His table does never want for game food. Aunt Charta now has a taste of towne life and makes sure to visit the Inn twice a fortnight. There she does not have to cook her own meals and can enjoy the minstrels and dance.

And her sons and Élan are happy with this new side of their mœther and wife.

Towne folk have become familiar with the short stranger that carries a staff and wears a pack most everywhere he goes. I spend time at the stables with Paint and while there, find a pleasure in helping the stableman train the horses in his charge.

After the stress of the past months, my stay in this bustling trade towne helps me to see again the good in people and the value of such a peaceful life with peaceful folk. My thoughts reach to Finnie and I find a desire to spend this kind of life with her.

One sun, after more than two fortnight with my family in the Northern Reaches, my Da-Sire comes to me. How he finds me I do not know. I have traveled into the hills outside of towne. I've skirted the bluffs overlooking the valley facing east and away from the village. I had arisen early and sit peering out over the peaceful valley with an orange and violet sunrise just reaching over the far blue hazy mountains. I found a rock ledge that hangs over the edge of the bluff, high above the towne and it has become my special rock, akin to my perch back at our homestead in the foothills outside of Middenvale.

He comes upon me in silence and sits two paces behind me gazing over my shoulder at the same sunrise.

"Ètœn used to come to this very spot. He called it his pondering perch. We came to muse on the wonders of the great world beyond the horizon," he says and becomes silent for a time.

It warms to know that Da had spent time in this very spot, experiencing this same sun rise, even as I do now.

"He had always been a lad full of wanderlust. His heart ached to see the world. He held a love for all creatures and a curiosity with no bounds. I see the same in his nephew, to the fear of his Mum and Da.... We've not discussed your talk with the Elder since your day with him. But I've seen the conflict within thee, Arias, these past few suns. I recognize it for what I saw in Ètœn. I gave him his bow on this very rock perch and spoke to him of journeying out into the world."

"Did my Da ever speak with the Elder, Da-sire?

"Thinking on it, yea he did, a little afore he set out on his own, come to think."

"I did not miss it when I first arrived here, Da-Sire. There is family, and friendly folk all about. Here are all the things I miss from my homestead and with Da. As a stranger, even so, I have felt a belonging amongst my family here. There is not the cruelty and evil I have experienced on the travelways from the time I left Da next to his tree," I try to explain, scuffing my hand against the rough surface of the Pondering Perch and thinking of Da. "But amongst all that evil I have experienced, there is also innocence and good as I see here. I've saved many lives that would have otherwise been destroyed. Young lives they were, with their whole life before them yet to be lived. I was able to do good by them. Amongst all the cruelty, I found also love even still, in greatest contrast to it and side-by-side with it."

Above us, the clouds move swiftly. The sky is always changing, yet it is still sky. My life is always changing, yet I am still me.

"Here, I've found peace and contentment. Not the peaks and valleys of emotion, but the warmth and caring of an everyday life among family and friends," I say finally and fall silent.

"There is something out there that is not only about you, Arias, and you are drawn to it. You have a great empathy and the need to make wrongs in this world right again. I see it in your eyes even as I saw it in Ètœn's. His brœther is not of the same mind and that is fine too, as he has taken a fine woman as his wife and she brings forth the best in him. But Éshæm is likened to his uncle. 'Tis the reason he ventured out into the world with Tonk. But Tonk is of the same spirit as his Da and is not right for that type of adventure." Da-Sire continues, "I can see the pull of it will soon take you back and onto your quest. This is why I am here with you now. Sæmmy will go again as well. I would like you to consider letting him accompany you. You've taught him much, but he has much yet to learn and he has only just reached fifteen-year-end. Though his mum will protest in any manner, she trusts in you and will be at some ease if Sæmmy could travel aside you."

He says his piece and leaves it to me.

He has the right of it, of course. It seems my feeling and hence my heart. The time to leave and seek the Druid once more has come and as the Elder wishes it, Sæm will be at my side.

We leave out with two sun's worth of provisions and a map of the regions from the mountains to the west shores of the great inland sea. Da-Sire advised me to travel east to the sea then south along the coast to Seas End. Though the cliffs and rugged terrain about the coast keep those from the Mid Realm from venturing north, there are trails known to the Noördan to get to our destination. And so, all things settled, we are to be off. There are tears, as well as slaps upon our backs, and excitement near bursting from Sæm.

"Ye are to be squire to Arias, Éshæm," says Élan. "For your travels, he is your Mæster in all things, mind that."

"Aye, Da, I will."

Our Da-Sire approaches Sæm in the last, just before we mount.

"Sæmmy, I have something for you." Reaching around the side of the cottage, he pulls a magnificent bow and quiver and brings them to Sæm. "Use it to good purpose and it will treat you well."

Sæm's eyes widen in wonderment.

"But Da-Sire, this is your prized bow and it carries your bone within its wood. Can I even use it?" he rightfully queries.

"Come grasp it, Éshæm."

Sæm does. Grasping it about where his Da-Sire's bone lay inset within the Ænt-wood, even as mine and Da's is. Éshûr's huge hand encloses about Sæm's and by his wide-eyed expression, I can see that he is experiencing the same warm sensation reaching from head to toe that I felt within myself upon receiving my Bo-staff.

"Great thanks, Da-Sire. I'll treasure it and use it only for good purpose, on my given Oath," Sæm vows.

We mount and the furions scurry from rock to boulder to Paint's hind-quarters and sit upon my bedroll. Of a sudden, Bane trots out from behind the cottage, which happens to back to the woods. Those gathered stare in awe at the great wolf and give him a wide berth.

Finally, just as we set out, there comes a fierce echoing cry that sends Sæm's mount into a small frenzy and makes those gathered about us jump in alarm. I smile. Talon will be joining us. I am comforted. I also find I feel pleased to be moving again. Some destiny again pulls at me even as Da's quest pushes me. How much of it remains Mægic's design, I cannot say, but in the present, it will be a good day to be traveling.

A great grin envelopes Sæm's face as we finally lose sight of his homestead.

"Travelling aside me is not for the faint of heart, Sæm. Take care with that grin." But I smile myself in spite of my comments.

Sæm's Sasha, a strong mare of brown and a deeper brown of flowing mane, pulls alongside of Paint.

"Tutor me, Arias, and take me to see this world."

"I believe we will learn of it together, cousin," I say, and let Paint set his own pace. He no longer wears bridle nor rein, but still travels as I will him. Lilit and Jilly make a game of leaping from Paint to Sæm's bay. Large and strong, she pays little mind to the furions' antics.

A sun's ride still north from Seas End, we wind our way down a narrow switchback into a canyon and then through a winding crevice in the cliffs that open onto the beach. Likened to Da's Frost-Cellar, one cannot see the entrance from the beachside. Da-Sire's map has been true. In the far distance, the port city can just be made out by chimney smoke rising above the horizon.

'Tis my intention, once we reach towne, to lay low and continue on and away from the port city immediately. I am not a character that will now go unnoticed to Tullamoor guards, not with the circumstances I had left the Lord Tullamoor in. The Inn that quartered me when I had first arrived will be a good place to bed for one night only.

At a bit past dusk, we quietly enter the cobble-stone ways. I take note in surprise that the streets are not as rowdy as they were when I had first arrived near to two moon's past. As we pass through the square nearest the Inn, my surprise turns to startlement. No gambling nor whoring houses are open for business and more than a few local towne folk are still milling about. No young goodmen from the far side of the canal. The music and dance hall has survived, however. The same torch lighters are about their work, though. We watch them alight the lampposts as we continue on our way.

Finally, having stable our mounts, we arrive at the Inn. It seems a quiet night here as well. With a furtive survey about the dining hall, this seems to be a somewhat calmer lot though no fewer than what I remember before my trip north. We find Johãn, the Innkeep, just inside the dining hall, propped precariously back on a chair with its front legs in the air and his bald pate head and shoulders leaning against a wall. Several groups of patrons are still finishing their eve-meal in the hall behind him. I feel a bit bad as my Bo staff's tap on the wooden floor wakes him from a whispered snore. He quickly rises to greet us though, and he assures me that there is a room for Sæm and I.

"I should think that Susi has a bit o'stew left in the pot if you would care for a couple of trenchers."

"Oh, if she would, we would be much obliged," Sæm speaks up and I laugh. He will be a big man someday and his appetite clearly the proof of it!

"Yea, Master Johãn. Make it two, and an ale would sit well, too," I add.

He leans into me and says, "Word has spread of what happened in the fields out near Tullamoor keep, Arias. People are describing a warrior dressed with a Drægon upon his chest. There is a new Lord Tullamoor at the Keep now. The brœther and rightful Lord has returned. Things seem to be changing for the better, hereabouts, but you might not want to be showing yer sigil if you want less attention."

I glance down at my chest and nod, removing my pack and handing it to him—furions and all—to put behind the bar. I do not forsake my bow and staff, however.

Sæm and I find a corner table facing the door but still not too far away from the dwindling eve-meal crowd. Even so, more are about than in the moon past. From what can be gleaned from conversations, talk still very much continues about that event as well as the new Lord at the Keep.

We are told by Vannah, Susi's daughter and our server this eve, that new guards are about towne and the seedier actors are being driven out or laying low, not wanting to draw the attention of the new Lord Tullamoor. This explains the new air upon the square.

I have no desire to make my presence known either and suggest to Sæm that a retreat to our room after eve-meal might be wise. Sæm proceeds to quickly finish his trencher to crumbs and his order of a mountain of garlic mashers and legumes to settle the cries of his fifteen-year-end belly. I pilfer some fruit and scraps from my plate for the furions and we retire to our room, after grabbing my pack, with as little notice as possible.

I do however catch the eye of the minstrel as he packs up his citolè. There is a recognitiõn betwixt us from nights' long past, but he gives no indication he will pursue any action so we go our separate ways. Afore retiring for the night, I make arrangements for some minimal provisions to be provided by the Inn.

The remainder of the night proceeds uneventfully. We arise afore sunrise, collect our provisions from the kitchens, and head to the livery a few doors down from the Inn. Just as the sun begins to peek above the far rooftops, we mount and head out of the stableman's gate and onto the stone travelway. There we are met by a contingent of the Lord's guardsmen. Twenty horsemen stand afore us, and afore them stands the captain of the guard.

"Well met, Ser Drægonheart," his voice measured. "Tis fortunate my company and I were up early this morn. You see, my Lord Tullamoor has tasked me to keep a keen eye out for you as he is quite anxious to have a word. Report from our northern outpost indicated you'd headed north into the mountains of the Northern Reaches, and as Seas End is a logical return route, we kept vigil here for you." He wears a smile and bright eyes and speaks with authority, but respectfully.

Mayhaps, I am reading him wrong and with the armed company at his back it would be a fair assumption that I am to become his prisoner, but I do not see it in his countenance. In any manner, with Sæm to think of, a battle in these narrow ways does not bode well.

"Well then, Captain, as you seem to know me by my moniker at the least, I shall not deny any that you have said, and I guess I find myself at your mercy. I only ask that you let my companion go, as he has no part in this." Sæm glances nervously over to me.

"Ser Drægonheart, you misunderstand me. You are not to be a prisoner of any sort, but a guest of Lord Tullamoor. And your companion, if I am not mistaken, was indeed very much a part of a very unfortunate incident in the plain outside of Tullamoor Keep. As such, the Lord would also have a word with him. We are to be your honor guard, Ser, if you would so grace us," says the captain.

This is an unexpected turn of events.

"Well then, Captain. Pray, lead on," I return and pull alongside his warhorse as he turns and heads west. We travel the cobbled-stone ways and pass over the canal bridge and after a short while continue upon the travelway across the plain towards Tullamoor Keep. The situation becomes all too much for Lilit and Jilly, and they finally pop from their nests in my saddlebags and then to my lap to stare at the Captain from the front of my saddle.

"Might I know your name, Captain?" I query as we leave out of the city proper. Afore long, we have left all behind but the few cottages and farmsteads scattered about. "And I am curious, Captain, as to your source of information that has found its way to you. I do not recall many in that field that could speak of such things."

He takes his time and a few moments now to assess all that there is to observe about me. He gives a quizzical look to me as I ride Paint aside him with no bit and bridle and only the simplest rein. He chuckles at the furions. He glances about the byway to each side and then peers with intent into the sky as well and in the end, he turns his attention back to me.

"Forgive me my absent manners, Ser. My name is Captain Stone of Barrington, though Thaôs stripped me of that title for a time. I am cousin to that late Lord of Tullamoor and also the same to the present and rightful Lord Tullamoor," he begins. "There were three who recited tales of that incident. One, the advisor to the usurper, another, the bird handler for Thaôs, and the third was the son of the true Lord Tullamoor by rights and rule. Though once my squire, he was made squire to the usurper. Alas, but one other made it back from that field, and he has lost his ability to speak, from a severe injury to his neck."

"Yea, I remember the squire, Captain Stone. I left him to escort the other two back to the keep as the Lord's advisor had bartered some knowledge against his fate. Though beyond my power to grant him any reprieve, his knowledge appeared to have value and I thought it wise to let the young squire have charge of the counselor and let justice find its own way."

Capt. Stone's visage is a pensive one now. "The lad's assessment of you seems spot on, it appears to me. He has said that asides a natural ability to fight, you had an air of justice and fairness about you."

"I judged him a smart lad and he appeared quite disturbed to hear the counselor's news."

"Aye, that he is. It was he who cyphered where to watch for you, as a fact. Visiting every Inn within the city, he found where you had stayed prior to your meeting with his uncle. He took work at the stables you boarded your ponies at. He remained determined to be the one to find you... And indeed, he did. He rode to the Keep yester's-eve to deliver his message," the captain explains.

We fall silent for a while as we continue our trip to the Keep. Eventually we come upon the great tree in the open plain which had been the setting of my encounter with the old Lord Tullamoor.

The captain gazes over to the tree. "When we found my cousin, he was curled within a cage. He had shat himself and his tongue swollen in his mouth. He lay dead of a bite from a great hooded asp which still lay coiled aside him. There were a dozen of his mercenaries dead in the field about him. Carrion raptors made them easy to find."

"Twas Arias' Eagle that delivered the serpent from the sky and onto the ground afore the man," says Sæm and uncharacteristically spits on the ground. "Twas the asp's choice to bite him. I hope you did not kill the snake for its rightful decision."

"The serpent went his own way when we approached," says the Captain, appraising Sæm for a first time now. He returns his focus to me. "Do you really own such a bird of prey that could lift and carry a serpent three paces long?"

"Own? Nay," says I, "but I call one such a friend."

And as I say it, Talon swoops from ahigh and passes over our troupe from behind, screaming his echoing call and unsetting all the horses—save Paint—to momentary terrors.

When all are quiet once more, Captain Stone scans the sky and then looks back to me, a fascination in his eyes.

"The Lord's son spoke of a great wolf as well."

As he does, Bane makes an appearance, pacing us, before once again silently retreating into the tall grasses. The captain just shakes his head.

"One would be wise not to underestimate you, Ser Drægonheart." When he says this his expression is awestruck.

"Call me Arias, Captain."

As we approach the Keep, the sun has now climbed higher in a clear sky and its warmth welcomes in a soft breeze. There is a tremendous amount of activity about the Cæstle grounds. Oxen drawn carts are headed in, on trails from the fields, each loaded with produce or pulling tethered livestock. Others are beginning to head back towards towne and the way we had just come.

"They are preparing for the Harvest Moon Fest. We are celebrating the end of this harvest. The feast is on morrow's eve with the whole of the sun prior in Fest for the Keep and its village. Ah, there is the Lord Tullamoor himself," he says and points to a man helping to raise a giant scarecrow, mayhaps two-pole high, and made up in farmer's garb with sickle in large gloved hands stuffed with straw.

A cheer goes up as the pole carrying it settles into place. There are eight of the same, four aside and similar to it, lining the way up to the Keep's portcullis.

"This is the first Fest of any sort, celebrated in more than four year, as the usurper would have nothing of it," he says, obviously proud to be a part of the people's celebration.

As we come up to the group around the colossal scarecrow, Captain Stone dismounts and approaches the Lord Tullamoor. He is a tall, well-built man with a mane of light sandy-brown hair and pale skin in parts, and in others, there lay a blush of faint red in the bright sunlight. His eyes are a striking blue and are speckled with gold.

The captain leans into the Lord's ear as he speaks, Lord Tullamoor's eyes rise to me as Sæm and I dismount. With three long strides he is in front of me, grabbing my forearm in greeting and showing a sparkle in his eyes. He does the same to Sæm and then turns back to me.

"You are but a lad," he exclaims, but stares deep into my eyes, nodding, seeing more.

"Pæder, sure certain, his age belies his experience and the amazing company he keeps," says a squire, just then stepping from behind the Lord.

The furions chitter at his words. Paint cuffs the ground and echoing cries fall from high in the sky. Tullamoor's eyes open in marvel for a moment.

"My son here has told me the tale of that day, though until just now, I fancied it more than a bit to be an exaggeration," he says. "I owe you a deep debt of gratitude, Ser."

His son gives me a wide smile.

"Will you walk with me a while? I feel a great need still to spend my time out of doors. You see, I went near to five years without sunlight upon my face," the Lord explains.

"Of course, it would be my pleasure, M'Lord."

His face shines a welcoming smile. "Niklaus, see to our guests' horses and show the Noördaner to the kitchens; he looks as if he'd enjoy a healthy morn-meal."

Sæm bounces on his heels, obviously thrilled with the idea.

"Captain, mayhaps, your men can help with the wagons coming from South Village. It seems they're having some difficulty and are mired in the lowlands," the Lord suggests.

A quick bow and they too are off. This leaves Lord Tullamoor and myself alone. "Come, Arias Bard, we have some important matters to discuss."

We walk to the north and out onto a pathway through the golden fields outside the Keep.

30

A Long and Winding Road

As we walk along the path encircling Tullamoor Keep, the Lord queries me, "Arias Bard, as you can see, I know a little about you. But before we discuss that, will you tell me the tale of how you came to meet my brœther and how things turned out as they did?"

There appears no intrigue nor deception about his question and I sense no ill will towards me. So, I speak true to him. He listens intently and says nothing throughout the telling.

"Arias." He shakes his head in disgust. "I had no idea, and I am certain my pæder had not known that such a thing was happening. I am humiliated in its telling. My brœther's counselor will be questioned further, I promise you. Punishment for his involvement will be meted out to fit his crime, I can assure you, and I will do all that I can to bring his accomplices to justice as well. I will end this enterprise on my end."

He swears this with a true anger in his voice. I nod to acknowledge his sincerity. It will be a relief to be done with this chapter of my life. I take him at his word.

After a bit of silence and contemplation, he speaks again. "I've become acquainted to your circumstance because Spæcter, my late brœther's counselor, gave to me information he had in order to garner some favor for himself. He has a twisted mind that enjoys holding and giving facts and thoughts to his own greatest advantage. Of a mind with my brœther, it would seem, and to his detriment in the end... But, to my point, I was shown messages that had been received from Kings Court, to be on the lookout for a lad of your unique description. You escaped the King's justice in a small towne to the south, and you were thought to be headed north from there. There was no reason given, nor your specific crimes, but the King's description fits your quite distinctive countenance. My brœther recognized you immediately in Seas End and set about your capture, or death, to garner favor in the King's eye," he explains and pauses to judge my reaction.

I decide to tell my own full tale and that of Da. He listens intently.

"And so, you see, Lord Tullamoor, I was aware that the King was in pursuit of me for my Da's transgressions against him or some other Lord in his earlier life," I say, finishing my tale.

"Nay, lad," he responds.

And I look upon him, my expression quizzical, I am sure.

"Your words give me further pause, though. Mayhaps a slip on Spæcter's part, now that I ponder it more, and have parsed together your tale to it. You see, Spæcter said that my brœther recognized you by the sigil that you wear on your breast, though in the messages that I read from Kings Court, that specific was never mentioned."

"There is more tangled together here than first meets the eye. Aye, the King mayhaps did want Ètœn Bard's head for some treason, but it is you that is his main objective. This is quite clear from the language in his messages. My brœther wanted you for quite a different reason, though. Mayhaps, Thaôs did not make the connection, but upon reflection, Spæcter most certainly did when you met in that field."

I am taken aback.

"You say the King sought after me and not Da. How could this be?" I ask. "I have no connection with the King, but through Da."

"Mayhaps, mayhaps not. I can only relate the facts as I know them," he says. "Fear not Arias Bard, I have no intention of detaining you, nor leading Kingsmen to you. My purpose is but to give you this news. But for your interjection into our lives, I would still be sequestered by my evil and murderous brœther in a sunless room, hidden deep in the bowels of this very Keep. It is why I prefer to be discussing all of this with you in the open air, even now. My aversion to being closed within its walls is that great," the Lord continues. "This information remained known in its entirety by only my brœther and Spæcter, so be not alarmed to your exposure. And I shall keep it close to me as well. But the King has in his court a Seer and is known as one himself. So, you cannot remain here long. I would have you linger for our harvest Fest on the morrow as my guest, but I think it wise that you should move on directly on the morrow's morn after."

I signal my complete agreement. I rest back on my heels certainly more bewildered and more than ever in need of querying Da's Druid.

Unbeknownst to both the new Lord of Tullamoor and Arias, Thaôs' counselor, Spæcter, stands even then upon a rooftop eerie on the other side of the Keep. No longer detained in a cell awaiting judgement, he has just sent a currier raven on its way to Kings Court. The King's counselor will be receiving his message. He is leaving himself now, his work here has gone as far as it can. With his true identity at stake, he must move on. His jailers are unaware they've played a part in his disappearance.

Lord Tullamoor has given me revelations quite unexpected, and I see now a greater need to follow my quest for the Druid. It has been many a moon since my departure from our homestead and I have not traveled eastward towards my destination to any great advance. It seems life itself is quite a barrier in a quest.

Sæm and I stay to enjoy the harvest Fest, Sæm in greater fashion than myself, with food and lass alike. While I brood over the Lord's particulars imparted during our talks, Sæm eats, dances, and flirts with the farmers' daughters and eats more again. He has a way about him and is at home in the revelry of the sun.

Lord Ronælt has a beautiful wife and on the morrow the lady Katdollène leads us on a tour of the Keep's vineyards. She shares with us her hospitality and much wine. She makes it clear that having her husband back will keep me ever in her favor.

Lord Tullamoor has granted us passage on one of his large trading ships. One that can carry a reluctant pair of horses. The morrow's morn after harvest Fest finds us boarding the ship from the docks of Seas End and embarking, heading east to a far port called Cliffside.

The Captain of our vessel is a crusty sort who goes by the name of Poons-Eye or Poon for short. We learn he came by the name whilst he was young and a harpoons-man, working whælers in the southern seas. Whæles being the biggest creatures of the seas and hunted for their fat, flesh, and bone. Poon's skin is like leather, both in color and texture and our days aboard his trader are filled with tales of his life at sea he's undoubtedly told many a time as he has all the particulars woven seamless into his tales.

The Captain says the distance to Cliffside is near to 300 leagues, which would have meant more than two fortnight of steady travel on horseback. We make the trip in twelve suns, and that with three suns in still waters. We are working passengers and our blistered hands and sore backs are the proof of it. I have considered myself in fine strength and form, but soon realize that the rigors of a sailing vessel are of a different sort altogether. Normally unused muscles in my back and legs ache for the first few suns at sea and the use of great hemp ropes make my toughened hands blister and callous in all different places. But I learn a new skill in sailing. I learn the art of tacking, jibbing, lee, and windward. Fore, aft, starboard, and port become my life for twelve suns. We bunk in hammocks below decks with the regular crew and eat the cook's fare with them.

Poon claims Sæm's knack for figuring the winds is near unnatural. And I can monkey up the mast or catch net faster than any on his crew. He is happy to have us aboard. I eat more fish and sea life than in the whole of six moons prior and become leaner and quicker for it.

Cliffside is aptly named. The captain has us drop the mainsail to slow his vessel and upon sailing into port, we come round about a long jetty of rock, extending well out into the sea. At its farthest point, stands a stone built light tower painted in bright red and white stripes. As we round its point, a towne near the size to Seas End greets us with brightly colored stone buildings. Some appear to hang upon a steep cliff side. Upon closer examination, with the captains borrowed spyglass, we can see that after the docks and some blocks in, the travelways carry higher into the cliffside in switchbacks, wending their way to the top some couple of hundreds of paces above. When our large trader makes the point, a loud bell sounds on the docks welcoming in the ship and alerting dockhands. We make the docks to a cacophony of noises not unlike those at Seas End.

'Tis on a yellow and orange sky's morn that we make port at Cliffside Towne. Lilit and Jilly are reluctant to leave a furions' playhouse that is the ship, but Paint and Sæm's mare, Sasha, are ecstatic to be on solid ground again. They leap and bound about with the joy of it.

Capt. Poon actually hands each of us a small purse of coin as we disembark to the docks. Waving our fare-the-wells to newfound friends aboard the 'Sea Queen,' we guide the horses through the labyrinth of dockhands and gangplanks till we make the greater wharf. We put some of our coin to good use at the first Inn we find serving beef and ale—a welcome relief from seafare.

After eating our fill in the mid-morn, Sæm and I slowly make our way up the travelways to the cliff's top, reaching it a little after midsun. What we find atop the cliff is the second half of the port city and a view out to sea to be envied. What we also found are Kingsmen wandering the travelways of the towne. Too many to suit us, assure. They travel in threes, and not appearing to pay close attention to the locals, I can see they are intent in their study of the surroundings.

'Tis fortunate that our garb and faces are not their usual look. Not wearing my pack, I have taken to wearing a floppy-billed hat as protection from the Sea's strong sun. My chin carries twelve suns of whiskers and my skin is a darker hue than usual. But if they knew I rode upon a Paint? Well, that would be evidence enough for a closer inspection. A scrutiny I do not desire. I will with all my heart they do not take notice, and with a warm sensation visiting upon my chest, it appears I get my wish.

Querying among the vendors in the first open market we come across, we ask after the Shorn Rams Inn—it being on Moor's list I have memorized, along with the name of its proprietor. We have no luck in that first market. But in the second a bit of good fortune fall upon us and we find our destination without incident with the patrolling Kingsmen.

Stabling our horses in a nearby livery, I carry my pack, wrapped about my Bo-staff, and wear my cloak over my shoulders. The cloak's hood replaces my hat. No need for careless chance to haunt our movements.

We present ourselves to Dægmund Longbow, Innkeep at the Shorn Rams Inn. The phrase Moor gave me as greeting to his friends draws yet another smile and welcoming greets. Dægmund sets us up in a room to the rear and up a stair at the Inn and leads us next to a bathhouse. I guess our scent has preceded us.

Once our packs and even my Bo-staff are reluctantly hidden within our room, Sæm and I set about gathering provisions for our further trip. I seek to travel the trader's trails again, thinking it would be more out of the eye of Kingsmen on patrol. I think it insanity that such an effort is being put forth to find me. Mayhaps this effort holds some other purpose. But my gut tells me otherwise.

We find Dægmund and seat ourselves at his small table in a shadowed corner, upon our return to the Inn. Our effort in securing needed supplies shortened, as Dægmund aids us greatly in that respect. He fools about his eve-meal with his knife as he sips his ale. He doesn't bother to speak, until a low, lengthy belch greets us. With ales afore us also now, we talk quietly of what he gazes. He informs us that the Kingsmen are indeed in search of someone. After seeing my hair and eyes, he confirms that it most certainly is I that they seek.

Clanking of forks against plates and bursts of laughter surround us as Dægmund leans towards us pointing a piece of his bread trencher, sopped in a rich gravy matching the same spotting his beard. His husky voice accompanies the scent of the stew, a welcome new odor to mask his belch that is lingering still.

"They've been here in Cliffside, mind, near to half a fortnight now, to be sure, patrolling the ways and byways in groups of three. They are mostly quiet about it so as regular folk wouldn't take much notice, but they come about to the Inns and Taverns and such describing a lad with hair and eyes likened to yours. They say he goes by Drægonheart and has a Drægon emblazoned upon his chest."

It is fortunate that I have forgone wearing my pack into towne.

With each of Moor's friends I have met, I describe our relationship and they in turn recite theirs with him. In all cases, they have called him dear friend and as a fact, credit him to saving their lives. I have always known safety among them.

"Why do they say they are seeking me?"

"For serious crimes against the crown," he responds, placing his empty plate aside. Sæm looks to it with a longing.

My eyebrows lift in confusion. "I've lived my entire life in a small towne in the foothills of the Western Range and only left after Da was killed by a company of Kingsmen. How, by the fates, could I have committed crimes against the King?"

Dægmund shrugs his shoulders. "Tis indeed a mystery beyond my cyphering ability, Arias Bard."

"I'll not bring down the king's wrath upon you, Dægmund. You are at risk just quartering us here in your Inn. We will leave before the morrow's sunrise. I thank you for your aid, you have certainly risked more than need be."

He wipes his mouth and grizzled beard with his sleeve while hiding another silent belch. Sæm sighs.

"Well then, I can show you a way out of towne and to the traders' trail south that will not be watched," he suggests.

"We'll retire to our room and not expose ourselves to any others." A look of panic spreads across Sæm's face.

"I'll bring up eve-meal to your room in a bit." Relief washes over Sæm, as his belly speaks its mind.

Sæm and I climb the back stair to our room, our plan being set.

Before dawn on the morrow, we retrieve our horses and follow Dægmund through a labyrinth of alleyways to a narrow trailway and into the forest south of towne. We say our fare-thee-wells to Dægmund as he hands us a sack prepared by his wife. I swear I can hear the grumble within Sæm's stomach one more.

The moon gives way to the rise of the sun and in a clearing we find, less than a sand-glass turn into the woods, we stop and dig into the sack while sitting on a large fallen log. We find four large, salt-crusted taters wrapped in parchment and filled with chopped bacon and goat cheese, and these make for a great morn-meal. Sæm's wide grin is well warranted and we tuck in, discussing our trip as we eat.

Dægmund has informed us that the two main travelways south are being patrolled regularly now by Kingsmen. Supposedly, the King's response to citizens' complaints of highwaymen disrupting commerce. I remain sure certain they hold other orders as well.

My quest to find the Druid ends among the barrier mountains overlooking the northern straits. But by Moor's map, we will first need to travel to the city of Bladestone, which sits at the southwestern edge of the Accadian plane. It is far from the most direct route, but anything east from our current location is blocked by an unbreachable canyon. We will take the trader's trails through the forests, mountains, and vales and avoid the main travelways. This will put us heading towards Kings Court itself and into territories rife with King's soldiers and so deeper into danger to myself. I put these thoughts aside for now.

I'd given an Oath as well, to train Sæm, and so we will not rush our trip and attend to the training each day. This morn is as good as any to begin. My personal training has gone beyond that of Moor and so I marshal the techniques that have served me best these several moons, and I am determined that I will tutor Sæm in my own manner.

We start each morn in the Chĕ-Song discipline that Effie had taught me. But I add in defensive, offensive, combat skills and moves that Moor had taught me. The horses ride light as we run most suns and near all sun. Midsuns bring bow skills and practical hunting.

The horses carry our vanquished prey which becomes our daily meals. Before eve-meal we spar with Bo-staffs or walk the forest collecting herbs, plants, shrooms, and berries, and I teach Sæm some of what I know of herb lore and healing as well. When we have the chance, we swim or bath before eve-meal and after, in moonlight or by torch, I have Sæm use idle hands to craft a pack that is likened unto my own. Sleep becomes a welcome relief each night and we begin our routine afresh each morrow's morn.

'Tis tough on Sæm and being honest, it takes a few suns for my own body to adapt to the schedule. I've never let it show in front of him. To his credit, Sæm does not complain and I find he has a keen mind and needs but one lesson to learn a technique or healing salve. His memory and muscle reflex are quite remarkable. In less than a fortnight, he has mastered the mind-over-body techniques that allows him to claim hold of the *Calming*.

In Bo-staff combat, he has an intuition and the instincts that allow him to anticipate my offensive moves, even when I let my mind act inasmuch a random manner as I possibly can. He is a natural. The logical fighter who continues to hone his responses and understand the most efficient and effective strike and defense techniques. I speak of ways to assess the most dangerous man in a group attack and how we can work together if threatened together. But all would be but supposition unless we are tested and I remain determined that we will not need to test it.

Another thing I cannot teach or train him for is the effect that killing a man has on one's psyche. Mayhaps he will never need to find out. After the rush and bloodlust leaves and your body shakes, and you fight not to collapse in on yourself. The ache you feel when you see life leave your adversary in a visceral gush of blood and trauma. It stays with you despite your logical judgment telling you that you have no choice but to act as you did. I hope I will not see him experience it.

But one prepares ne'er-the-lesser for it. This, the lesson Moor and Da drummed into me over years of training. Sæm and I have been at it less than a moon. We eat well as we are both quite proficient in the hunt and take advantage. Bane has become a regular about camp and we are aware that Talon still follows our progress as well. Sæm acquits himself as one well beyond his age. This from the discerning eye of but a seventeen-year-ender, too well versed in the necessities and effects of such things.

Nearing a moon and a fortnight we come out of the hills and witness the rising smoke from chimneys that we judge to be about the towne of

Bladestone in the distance. We pass close by to cottages and farmsteads from time a'times, but avoid them. Coming across a few trappers and traders now, the first humans we see in our three fortnights abroad. We've occasionally camped with them these past few eves and speak of what they know of the city of Bladestone.

"I've just come from the city," says Castor, one such trader in premium pelts and fine cloth with a penchant for ale.

We share a skin with him at our campfire, which includes a game stew. He is pleased for the food and the company, but most-wise the ale.

"I do well in Bladestone," he tells us. "I trade in lynx and mink from the north and silken cloth from Kings Court's port, brought in from cities far to the south. The fancy folk in Bladestone pay heavy coin for both, trying to match the high folk in Kings Court."

My cousin and I both listen close, intent on hearing anything that might hold import for us. Castor takes care in his tale, til the ale loosens his tongue some.

"From here, I'll travel all the way to Seas End," he adds.

We nod and smile to keep him talking.

"I'm anxious to get there abouts with all the scuttle-speak about it," he says with a hearty belch. My wineskin is helping to loosen the atmosphere all the more now.

"Why is that?" I ask, exchanging an eye-to-eye with Sæm.

"Well, Tullamoor Keep is all the talk hereabouts, is why. I thought you coming from the north and all, you'd know of it." We stare blankly back at him.

"We've not seen anybody at all these past three fortnight on the back-trails all the way from Cliffside. We've missed some excitement?

"Aye, then, I 'spose it's possible you wouldn't 'ave heard. They say there is a new Lord there. The rightful one they're saying. His brœther has kept him prisoner in the Keep's dungeons for near on to five years, they say." He shakes his head.

"Unbelievable!" I exclaim. Sæm gives me a smirk, but remains silent. Castor is encouraged, seeing he has an eager listener now.

"But that tain't even the thing they're talking most about," Castor says. "They say some rogue vigilante done killed the first Lord Tullamoor. The usurper, that's what they're calling him. And he's did it in a grand style sure to be legend, if yer to ask me. Killed the usurper and twenty of his guardsmen by hisself... Well, not really by hisself, they say he's a sorcerer or something. He commands a pack of wolves and an eagle! O'course that's all nonsense, but that's what makes legend tales, ya know. Calling him a knight. Like a King's knight," the trader says, getting excited. "Ser Drægonheart, it is. They're singing songs and telling tales, the bards and minstrels. Troupers and gypsies are staging tales even. I heard the tale in a song, I did, in a fancy Inn, in towne." An aromatic ale belch and a further draw on my skin, accenting his story all the more.

He casts his arms about, really getting into his tale. "People in the north are calling him Drægonheart, 'cause he wears a Drægon sigil right on his chest. I may have seenpp his eye stray to mine and Sæm's packs lying against a tree, where we've left them. He kills highwaymen and rescues youngers, protects elders on the travelways. Folks say the King should be doing it, but he isn't. And the King's said to be furious and says it's the Lords' fault not keeping their travelways safe and that the rogue is a dangerous vigilante. Even has a fifty-gold piece reward on his head! For doin' what's right, if you be askin' me. I'm hoping I see him on the road, I do. But I wouldn't turn him in, mind, not me... Though a fifty-piece is mighty coin, come to think. But, Aeryth needs a hero or two, if ye were to ask me." And I reckon we have been, so we nod.

"Yea," say I, and Sæm puts in an "aye" of his own. We both hold our faces staid but a bit curious still.

I offer Castor a second helping of stew and hand the ale skin back to him. He gives a mostly toothless grin and takes my offering.

"Good stew, you make. What is that innit?" he asks.

"The last of some wild boar we were lucky to shoot a few suns back," I say smiling. "I saw from the hill as we came out of the forest at midsun that Bladestone is a walled city and there's a Keep off to the east. Looks to be a half-day's ride from the city. I've never seen a city such as that."

I'm curious to know more of the towne now—my curiosity for Drægonheart stories sated.

"Yea, it's a garrison, after all. It's Kings Court's first line to defense should there ever be an attack on the crown comin' from the north or west for that matter," Castor states. "Ye've never been, I gather. Tis a city built for that purpose. King's new troops are trained on grounds within the city. And the Keep is the watch over any force that would come from the north, like I said. The travelways bottleneck here 'n with the terrain and River as barriers. That makes it Kings Court's first defense."

He drags lines in the dirt afore him. Well acquainted with the strategy it would seem.

"Most of the King's army live 'n train here and in Lakeside. That's the King's other garrison to the South. That Garrison guards Kings Court against the Southern Reaches. Ye'll see King's soldiers were-to-ever ya turn in Bladestone. Tho most hold other jobs as well to support the towne 'n themselves." He adds, "They soldier but a fortnight each moon." I welcome the trader's information.

Sæm and I leave out of camp afore our guest has awakened on the morrow's morn. With the ale he'd consumed last eve, it may be midsun afore he wakes.

We have no choice but to visit the garrison towne, for we need provision and a better knowledge of the next phase of our trip. We need to cross the Accadian plain, a most inhospitable place, Moor had explained when we had spoken of my intended travels, so long ago now. The suns are brutally hot there a'times and the nights frigidly cold and windy with little to use as shelter or fire. I cannot help but wonder at Moor's knowledge for the whole of Aeryth.

He said it is rumored to be a great open plain with no tree for firewood. There is little water and there is said to be dangerous creatures of a like not known to the rest of Aeryth. Though accounts of such things are few, as few bother with its dangers, no gain to be had. Provisions will be needed along with advice or a guide for its crossing.

With avoiding Bladestone not an option, other plans will need to be made. Sæm and I set out to do just that, discussing as we ride side a'side. We have half a sun's time to discuss and prepare a plan if we are to enter this eve.

"We cannot just gallop into the garrison, Arias."

"Yea, I fear that I and my friends have become too recognizable. But still, we have no choice but to go. It's my hope we have at least one friend in towne. Moor's list included a name in Bladestone."

As we reach the travelway heading south into towne, we come upon a farmer returning from there with a now empty wagon. He'd run into a bit of bad luck as one of the wagon's wheel's hubs had cracked and the wheel would not hold to the axle. Sæm and I offer our help. Apprenticing to Argo bears fruit this day.

Pulling some tools from my saddlebag, Sæm and I are able to shim the hub back to the axle and attach a metal strap across the fracture to hold it together for a while. The farmer is thrilled for the help and insist we follow him home for a meal and so we do.

We arrive to his homestead and a brood of six youngers and a hard-working wife. Pulling aside Sæm, I nod towards the woods surrounding the homestead and suggest his hunting skills would be of assistance. He smiles and rides off immediately. Our new friend Alàin introduces me to his family and smiles are shared with his explanation of the circumstances. It appears he is pæder to five girls and a wee lad with large eyes of two colors and the longest eyelashes I've ever encountered. The younger is of an age to be just beginning to toddle about.

"Pleased to know your names, lassies," I says to five smiling faces as the wandering lad sets out, more interested in the farm fowl.

"You have a wonderful family, Esther," I say to Alàin's lovely wife. "Alàin, if you'll show me what you have in the barn mayhaps I can help with a more permanent fix to your wagon. I've apprenticed some with a Master Smithy."

"Much obliged, Arias. I may have some spare parts about." He returns a smile. "Esther, can we find a couple extra bowls for dinner?"

She nods o'course, but I can see a panic in her eyes. Just then Sæm returns, not a half sand-glass turn from when he'd left, and over his saddle he carries a wild boar, twice or mayhaps thrice the size of the toddling lad.

"Fates were smiling on me this sun, Arias. I found this fellow snuffling up some shrooms just inside the tree line. I gathered them up as well and some onions and herbs, too. 'Twas a veritable market in one place," he says wearing a wide and toothy grin.

An exclamation of joy escapes Alàin's wife, unbid, and her eyes sparkle.

"I would be proud to help in the kitchen, Mãam. I'm mighty handy with a knife," he says.

Esther actually laughs aloud.

"I'd be much obliged to you for your help," she says. "Taters and carrots, we've aplenty and mayhaps my girls can gather some apples about for a pie."

The girls cheer the idea and Kataleen, Leila, Jæn and the two youngers leave out immediately to find some apples from under their small orchard.

Alàin and I pull the wagon into the barn and he indeed has a few old wheels that I can use to scavenge needed parts from. By dusk, the wagon is again road worthy, and we are washed up and ready to see what Esther and Sæm have made for eve-meal. We are happy to find quite a feast awaiting us.

We come into the cottage to the scents both savory and sweet, and Esther rushes into Alàin's arms.

"Oh, Alàin, Sæm here says he is but fifteen-year, but he cooks better than me mam! He is a wonder. You've brought home people quite special this time," she exclaims.

"Well, Arias is as handy as any smithy I've known. The wagon is whole, and I'll be able to carry more crop to next market, thanks to him," Alàin says.

"Well, if it wouldn't be too much trouble, we have a small favor to ask in return," I interject.

"O'course! Let us talk whilst we eat!"

31

I'll be on my Way

Before retiring to the loft in the barn for the night Sæm and I finish butchering the wild boar that Sæm had shot yester's sun. Cutting out some bacon for morn-meal on the morrow, and more to last a few suns. we put the rest in Alàin's smoke shed for the long cook overnight.

Bringing in the horses from pasture, we brush them down and then retire to our bedrolls in the straw of the loft.

We have made plans to accompany Alàin to the market next, a few suns on. Early morn that sun finds us loading harvested crops onto Alàin's wagon and atop two additional pack beasts. We'd been busy these past couple suns helping the good folk about their farm. I took a hit in if.

Come market day next, Alàin loans us two caps of a fashion farmers here-about wear as well as some woolen cloaks. I've sewn a patch over my pack's breast sigil, and we leave our mounts and bows in Alàin's barn. Neither of us relinquish our staffs though, and Lilit and Jilly will not be left behind, to the chagrin of the girls. With the hair about my whiskered chin grown a bit longer and the cloak covering my pack, I wrap some worn leather strippings, tight about the ends of my Bo so as to cover the runes and stones. It gives a simple appearance of a walking staff or shoulder yoke for carrying bundles. We have become quite anonymous.

We do not tell Alàin our desire to remain so, and he does not ask. We say we'd help get his produce to market and will be staying in the city for a few suns before returning to his homestead. I promise Esther I'll bring some linens back with me so she can sew some dresses for her girls. She delights in this idea.

We set off mid-morn so as to make it to the farmers' market by midsun. We experience no problem getting through the gates and we unpack Alàin's wares in the market afore bidding him good-sun. We learn later that he has a remarkable day at market. I had loved Esther's pie and suggested she bake a few for Alàin to sell. She did and made a few minced boar, carrots, and onion pies as well. A local Innkeeper buys them all up for extra coin and they are thrilled. A deal then struck with the Innkeeper and of a sudden, Esher is in business.

For our tale we part with Alàin after midsun to search out Moor's contact in towne. Like his other friends, Vælen and Mavi Altorii are keepers of a pub with a few rooms to lease above. Their "Fort" tavern is known to serve mostly locals, though the occasional garrison soldier stops by as well. The Tavern lies in an out-of-the-way alley some distance from the garrison training grounds, so those Kingsmen that come are most-wise of a rank, as the working soldiers prefer to stay close to the barracks.

As we establish our credentials, Vælen's eyes widen, and he cannot help but casually glance about for eavesdroppers and Kingsmen.

"Ye've a nerve about you then, Arias Bard. There's gold coin on yer head and Kingsmen everywhere about the city, ye put yerself in harm's way coming into towne, it's a fact."

I know it would not be Vælen, nor anyone he confided in, that would turn me in for the gold.

"Yea, tis why we come to you as farmers. We will need a map of the

Accadian Plain and provisions to make the crossing. I understand there is some danger."

Vælen laughs. "Aye…there is danger *here* and *there*. There the danger is mostly the cats and other wildlings that live in the grasses. The suns are said to be hot and the nights windy and cold and full of predators. You'll find no wood for fire and precious little running water, as legend has it, though the grasses can grow as high as a man's chest. They say that nomads live deep in the plain, but those I've known of to cross into it have either left no tales of anyone met or not come back at all."

"So why did they make an attempt?" I query.

"Gems, mostly. There's tales of streams that are strewn with emeralds and rubies. A King's fortune there just for the picking. Though no one that I know can remember anyone having returned to riches. Mayhaps it is true, but I am happy here with Mavi and my lot so I'll leave such things to others."

Lilit and Jilly have kept well-hidden till now, but are bored and take to popping their heads in and out of my pack. Vælen notices, of course, and but shakes his head.

"I may be able to find a map for you, though. At least a partial map to as far as he'd gotten. And any provisions you need will not be a problem. I would suggest plenty of water and travel meats, as well. Hats with brim and heavy bedrolls and shelter tarps. They say swirling windstorms without rain are fearsome and killers in themselves. Shovels to dig in for the nights and thick canvas tarps to cover. The storms come in an instant and with little warning," Vælen explains.

"Stay a few days to gather your provisions and relax," says Mavi, his wife. "The folk are friendly hereabouts and the food is warm and good. It's what keeps us in business. That and our own bard and minstrel!"

We make that our plan. Knowing Alàin will return three suns hence, we go about gathering our needs. In the eve times after meal, I bring out my Schäaken board. There is always a challenger in the pub. I will be taken to be a local, I hope. A bard entertains there every other night. He plies his craft of tale and song for a meal and coin tips and does a good business.

But 'tis the eve before our planned departure that he gives me a shock I'll not easily forget.

"I see no Kingsman about this eve and so I'd like to sing you a tale from the north. One banned by Kings Court, but most popular for it, just the same. 'Tis a tale of some truth. It is of a lad from the mountains next to the Great Sea to the west of Aeryth." He peers about to assure himself that just the locals are in attendance this eve. Vælen and Mavi look to me and then to the crowded dining hall and then back to the bard with a nod.

He starts to play a tune on his citolè and let it penetrate the crowd a bit. Then he sings a bit of my life with his song. His voice is melodic and strong and soon the hall grows quiet, but for his tune and lyrics.

> *'Twas on a trail where first they met,*
> *where traders tread and trappers get*
> *Slavers held her in wagon cage,*
> *her brœther too with others laid*
>
> *And the far-away King held court in revelry*
> *So, he and his courtiers co'not see,*
> *He and his courtiers wo'not see*
>
> *Caged atop the wagon, family lost in villainy*
> *no hope, tears of dread, ne'er one to hear their plea*
> *Who would stop this. It was he,*
> *That fate has led...to set them free*

And the far-away King held court in revelry
And distant nobles they co'not see
And distant nobles they wo'not see

Drægonheart struck hard and fast,
with hewn staff, and bow and blade, alas
O'er thugs slain, he could, he should, and did
Deliver justice upon their heads, at last

And the wee lass wept...and cried aloud,
Oh, Ser Drægonheart, they would have sold us if allowed
But you've kilt these men and saved us now,
you've kilt these men and saved us

Yea, wee lass, I've killed these men
slavers they are, and evil's brethren,
and I wo'not let them harm thee more
Ne'er will they harm thee more

And the wee lass smiled...quite brill upon him
Oh, Ser Drægonheart
You've kilt these men and saved us now
you've kilt these men and we thank ye

And Drægonheart did sweep them up
The wee lass, her bræther, and her friends
and did carry them safely
to Quill'spee...to Quill'spee

The Kingsmen searched, and northern noble cursed
this vigilante with heart of Drægon
But townsfolk knew, his heart was true,
ne'er would'st they give him up, nay anon, nay anon

And this man, he did plea, where be the Kingsmen
...to stave off...this villainy
does the King see not the need...why does he...
but lay about in Kings Court revelry

And the wee lass laughed...finally
Oh, Ser Drægonheart, leave him be
Come dance with me,
Come dance with me

The song appears quite the hit with the crowd as they slap their knees.

Somehow, his song has affected me.

Spending a time reflecting on my many moons fighting the slave traders and seeing the damage it has done to families and the reaction among communities, I indeed cannot understand why the King does nothing to stop such villainy. I've seen, with my own eyes, scores of soldiers that could be fighting the evil of it. The evil, sure certain, runs deeper than the small part that I've alone touched upon.

I recall the comments I've heard from tinkers and towne folk. The King has not even visited the townes I had been to, not for a decade and half again. And yet he is searching for me. The son of an old soldier turned farmer. I resolve that I will one day soon, learn the reason behind it. But for now, I need to find the Druid and get back to Finnie.

Alàin will be returning to towne on the morrow's midsun. Sæm and I resolve to be ready to leave with him at morrow's eve. Mavi is approaching our table.

"It appears you've made quite a name for yourself, Arias Bard," she whispers, referring back to the minstrel.

"I know not where he came upon such a song, lady Mavi, but I'll admit there's a bit of truth in his words, and it's a shame for it, that more has not been done by our King." I take a long pull of my ale. It tastes too bitter now.

"They say that many a towne has set about policing the trails about them to stem this ugly trade. You've played a big part in their decision to do so, exposing the evil. I am proud to know you, and I pledge I will help in any way that I might," she states solemnly, gazing directly into my eyes. The Inn's sounds have faded into the background for me now.

I nod and after a moment a thought comes to me.

"There is some help I need, though not to that end, and if you are able. We have imposed upon a farmer's family before we came to towne and we mean to return there on the morrow. I promised the farmer's wife, Esther, that I would find linen to bring back to her, so that she might be able to sew garments for her five daughters. Would you know of a general store or seamstress you could send me to, so I might find some durable cloth and thread to buy and pay back her kindness?" I query.

She smiles. "And what year would these daughters be?"

"It would be—but I guess—I would say the youngest has but recently seen her six year-end and the oldest thirteen-year...? And the others somewhere betwixt?" I cypher, scratching my head.

"Well then, I believe I can help her," says Mavi with a wide smile and she explains. "I had a niece who stayed with us for near to six-year as my sister, and her man traveled to the Southern Reaches to claim an inheritance and to find work. She was but seven-year when she arrived with us and stayed till near to her thirteen-year-end. I spoiled the girl with such things and had kept them even as she grew out of them. I miss her dearly." Mavi sighs as she leads me to their rooms behind the Inn.

Entering a small chamber adjacent their personal gathering room, she opens a large chest that lies at the end of a narrow bed. Within it are neatly piled garments made especially for a young girl and under the pile more folded cloth. Also within the trunk sits a woven basket which contains all manner of tools for a seamstress.

"If you would part with these things, I will gladly pay you their worth." I reach for my coin purse.

Mavi swiftly stays my hand with hers and shakes her head.

"Please take it all as a gift, Arias," she pronounces. "Let me just say that our minstrel's song moved me deeply. As a woman who could not have young ones of my own, but for too short a blessing from my sister, I would like to see these put to use. And you've offered me such an opportunity. Take them to share with the farmer's girls and thank you for it."

I have no choice but to acquiesce and thank her yet again.

The morrow's morn finds us about the personal table of Vælen and Mavi. 'Tis piled high with pan-fried tater strippings with runny eggs sitting atop and thick rashers of bacon aside. Dark bean brew steams in front of Sæm and our hosts as I sip a hot cocoa drink, savoring every last sip. We are dressed again in our woolen cloaks and peasant caps. Mavi has bundled her gift into a great canvas bag.

The talk is easy and light, and we enjoy our newfound fellowship. We leave the Inn come midmorn and take our time wending through the streets of Bladestone, watching the folk going about their personal business. There are youngers running towards schoolhouse and shopkeepers sweeping the cobbled ways in front of their shops.

Eventually, we make it to the market square where we have left out from Alàin, two suns past. Finding him setting his produce out for sale, I am pleased to see a few pies made by his wife are included in his fare. The scent of the pies draw customers his way. Greeting him, we help him arrange his wares for sale and stay to help the full of the after high-sun and then help him pack his wagon for the trip home. We again are passengers upon his wagon and are paid no special attention by wandering soldiers nor the gate guards.

We arrive late eve to a bustling cottage of girls and Esther tending to the fire kettle and stew pot. Esther greets us affectionately and the girls all stand in a line staring up at us, expectation and hope in their eyes. Esther has apparently told them of my Oath. One cannot help but laugh. I heave the great canvas bag upon the dining table and open it up for Esther. She gasps as she removes garment after garment from the sack and nearly swoons when she sees the insides of the seamstress's basket.

I feel quite abashed as she throws herself at me and is quickly followed by her girls. They are cheering and laughing for their prize. I gaze over to Alàin, who just leans back against the fire box mantle with arms crossed upon his chest. He is certainly pleased to spy his wife so excited. He nods his gratitude towards me. I nod in return. Sometimes men do not need to speak so much.

Sæm and I spend much of the next sun preparing for our trip across the Accadian plain. Vælen, true to his word, has procured a map of sorts for us. He says it comes from a trusted friend who has made the trek across the southern length of the plain to the near foothills of the great barrier mountains, those he describes as barren of trees upon their far-off peaks. He tells Vælen that he never found the rivers of gems and is happy to be back in Bladestone after an adventure he has no intention of repeating.

We fill up great skins with water and lay them upon an old burden burro that Alàin offers us. We have accepted, but insist he take some coin as recompense. With trail food aplenty and other provisions we have gathered in the garrison towne, we say our fare-thee-wells to Alàin, Esther, and the youngers before heading out, not forgetting to brush about the bristly top of the youngest lad, l'il Lynn. It would seem Esther had not run out of names for lasses.

"We'll head due east from here, Sæm. South of the keep and past them without notice, I hope."

All continues well as we do just that. 'Tis not common at all that anyone would venture toward the plain and the guards keep their eyes to the north travelway coming from Cliffside. Two travelers with a burro draws no attention from them. Well into the late sun, we come across a little used trail leading north again. We are just about to turn upon it. But it is nearing dusk and just south of the northern way lay a pond. Thinking it would be a good place to camp before venturing into the endless tall grasses of the plain, we dismount and lead the horses to drink and pasture.

As Sæm kneels at the water's edge to scoop a drink and I head to do the same, a small sentry of four soldiers come off the path to the north, leading their mounts to do as we are, before heading back to the keep.

"Well met, travelers," the sentries lead hails to us.

"Well met, to you as well."

"Headed to Kings Court are ye?" he queries.

As I do not want anybody to know our true intent, I agree. "Yea, Ser, but we thought to make camp here for the night. We got a late start out from yon Bladestone."

He nods, but his eyes linger upon my breast for just a moment too long. I had uncovered my now famous sigil before leaving the farmstead. He smiles at me, but gives a single word and gesture to his second. The second reflexively starts to reach for his sword's pommel and the other two guardsmen come alert. Now, I recognize all of this in the blink of an eye, where another would not. But Moor and Da had trained me well, and so I am well versed in such tactics. 'Tis a tactic that I in turn have drilled into Sæm, as matter of course. We have a different ready word ourselves, but the intent results in the same alert.

"Alore, Eston. Four guardsmen come to greet us." At that Sæm casually wraps his hand firmly about his Bo-staff. They, not expecting a military move, are caught off-guard as I leap forward swinging my staff. Three bounding steps brings Sæm to my side. In a thrice, all four sentries are maimed and lying prone on the ground. My staff is poised just above the neck of the lead guard with my foot upon his wrist.

"You are the rogue vigilante they call Drægonheart," he says to me.

I smile. "Yea, Ser, but I don't believe you'll be collecting fifty gold pieces for that knowledge."

"And you said you were headed to Kings Court," he adds.

"Yea," I say, "I believe the King would like a word with me. I plan to do just that."

"Aye, he'll not care to speak with you, but rather have your tongue and your head with it, I'd wager," angered now he spits out this last.

"I would not make that wager, if I were you." I smile at him, though my demeanor does not match the smile in the least.

"Though I meant to just drop in on his highness, mayhaps you would run ahead of me and announce my impending arrival," I say and let him sit up.

He studies me, incredulous. Sæm has tied the hands of the three other guardsmen, though one lies unconscious and does not need to be restrained. Those that are still awake and have their wits learn that Sæm can tie a strong and most secure knot. And they have learned that they will be doing without their boots.

I quickly have a quiet word with Sæm and he proceeds to unsaddle the sentries' mounts. He then walks each to the pond and throws their saddles well out from shore.

"I do mean run, Ser. I will give you a sporting start. And south towards the garrison if you will," I says as I draw my bow and string it.

"You'll be needing to help your mate. So, get about it then, will you now," I state in stern rebuke.

As they lumber south, I nock an arrow. As I am about to send it to speed up their retreat, I stay my hand as Bane appears from the tall grass about ten paces from them and growls a fierce growl. They go on their way then, properly motivated. Sæm and I throw their boots into the pond with their saddles.

They will be kept travelling south and away from the keep and on a much longer trek to Bladestone. Bane keep them herded that way. Minstrels will have another verse to add to my life song.

Not sure it wise to make camp here for the night any longer, we head north along the trail, not stopping until a full moon is high in the sky. Remembering the words of caution expressed by Vælen, we finally make our camp fifteen paces off the diminishing trail, making sure to leave few traces of our passing. We take our bedrolls and curl up in the tall grasses, leaving Bane to stand watch for us this night when he returns.

As it turns, the night proves uneventful. We continue on our way north early the next morn. The next three suns are more of the same. We ride generally east and north. By early dusk on the fourth sun out from Bladestone, we ride by sun and compass only, as the grasslands stretch as far as the eye can see in all directions with no discernable feature to guide us.

It appears we are peering out upon the sea. The grasses stand higher than Paint's belly and a slight breeze makes them appear as waves upon the sea. There are never any clouds in the sky and the sun bakes our skin in the sunlight hours and bitter cold sets about us each night. We do not rush and ration our water and food.

That third night, we sit about our campsite and work on our no-idle-hands tasks. Sæm works on his pack, patterning his after my own. I pull my journal from my pack and go about filling in the events of our past fortnight. I have started to chronicle my life after Finnie had left to Middenvale. I find myself quickly filling the pages of my journal. I try to detail both the happenings and my feelings toward them. Pondering if I could have acted more positively to the situations that life has thrown upon me.

Before dark, we proceed to dig our beds into the ground. This being the method that Vælen has passed on to us before we left. The idea is meant to conserve our body heat by laying within the more constant and warmer temperature of the soil and out of the extremely chill temperatures in the air above. The stripped grasses packed within our bed holes becomes a further insulation to the cold night air.

When setting up camp, we first strap our short swords to our staffs and use them as one would harvesting sickles, slicing through the tall grass in a large circle in an effort to both give us a sense of not being hopelessly enclosed and as a practical matter as the thick bladed grass when standing upright proves sharp enough to cut through even the horse's hide. We had learned this lesson on our first sun on the plain and have to take time to fashion leather chaps for the legs of the horses and our burro.

After digging our bed holes, we line them with the grass and then cover the holes with mountain elks' skins and then again, more grass upon it as a further insulation against the cold night air. We use our canvas tarps as blankets for our horses as the night air is equally hard on them. We awaken each morn to thick frost upon our campsite. This eve ends different, however. Before dark has reached us, there comes a great echoing cry from the sky to the north some distance from us.

"I need to go to the *Calming*, Sæm. Stand guard, please," is all I say as I slip to the ground and into a seated position. The process has become second nature to me. Within a few breaths' time I find myself seeing through Talon's eyes peering down upon the landscape. In the far distance to the South I can see our camp circle and myself sitting in its center. It again comes upon me as an unsettling notion. Then, gazing directly under me (Talon), I see movement through the grasses. There appears to be five large cats, black as coal, gliding through the grass. Talon dives and lets out another echoing cry that stops the cats' progress as they leap in alarm and look to the sky in five different directions. But the lead cat finds us straight away and makes eye contact. There lives an uncontrolled wildness in its stare.

The cats are huge, each as long as I am tall and the dominant cat as long as Sæm's height—a full head above my own. The dominant turns away from Talon and continues in our camp's direction. The others follow.

I leave Talon and 'fly' back to my own self.

"Be ready, Sæm. There are five tremendous and fierce black as coal cats headed in our direction. But I want to try something."

I close my eyes once more. I can sense Sæm stare at my calm and marvel, afore turning to face the north again.

Entering the *Calming* once again, I stretch my perception forward and towards the approaching cats. This distance is not an impediment and I find them straight away. I immediately recognize the five entities... Spirit-beings. Four accept my own Spirit-essence as a friend. In the fifth lives a chaotic entity that I cannot reach. As the four slows and approaches our camp in an inquisitive and nonthreatening manner, the dominant becomes more erratic and expresses an almost rabid anger.

He bursts from the tall grass. Sæm moves into its path, bow drawn. He needs not have bothered. Even as the fierce, night-black cat erupts into sight, Bane does as well. It all happens at the speed of a Sky-bolt. Bane's mighty jaws closes on the cat's neck and his mighty claws tear into the cat's back as they toss and tear at each and the other. The hiss and screech of the great cat and the growl and howl of Bane fill the air. The great cat twists and leaps and strikes at Bane causing severe damage. But Bane gains the advantage and he does not let up. They rise on hind legs as Bane's jaws find purchase over the wild cat's neck again. A twist with the dread wolves full weight and the cat's spine and its neck are crushed. The other cats scatter back into the grasses.

The cat's body lies lifeless, with eyes staring, and Bane limps to me, even as I join with his psyche. My mind searches the biological need of the wolf. Knowing what damage has been done, I will his body to heal those areas in need, adding my 'spirit-energy' into Bane's body as well. I can actually perceive the healing happening at my will. Finally, as his greater need has passed, I fall myself into a deep sleep. I awake in my bedroll covered with blanket and insulating grass, but the heat of the sun has reached me to awaken me.

I sit up to Sæm staring at me with a lopsided smile.

"Arias, that was amazing."

"That was exhausting," I return and reach to scratch Bane's ears. Lilit and Jilly are nestled in his fur as well.

"The size of the cat...and its bloodlust—I've not seen anything it's like." A wonder fills his voice.

"The cat's mind was not right. I could not reach it. It was as if possessed. Your description of bloodlust mayhaps is closest to the mark. But, Sæm, something else happened while I was in the *Calming*," I say, pondering how to explain. "I believe I had a Seer's vision. I know no other way to explain it."

His brow raises.

"It was more "real" than any dream I've ever experienced, and I have a compulsion to act upon it."

"And what would this vision have you do?" he queries.

I gaze past him, still lost in my own thoughts.

"First, we must skin the pelt from this cat. Then we must remove its claws and teeth and put them in a small leather pouch—a coin purse, mayhaps. And finally, you must drag the carcass far from here, whilst I scrape, cure, and dry the pelts. We will stay here until it is complete."

32

Strawberry fields forever

We've spent three full suns at the camp where the cat attacked us. Having skinned the black pelt from the fierce cat, I had Sæm drag the flayed carcass half a sun back along the trail we had made to get here.

While he goes about his task, I stake the pelt upon the ground and proceed to flesh it and prepare it for my curing unguent that Da had taught me to make. I flesh the pelt once, salt it to expose any flesh I've missed, and flesh it yet again. Preparing the pelt for curing and softening a skin is time-consuming, but I always carry the powders and herbs that make the curing unguents.

Da had explained that the ingredients were a family held secret past to him from many generations of mountain men past. The paste saves days of soaking and tanning with more caustic powders and had the added benefit of being a natural waterproofing for the underside of any pelts.

As our water remains only that which we carried and that supply getting low, a long tanning process is not possible in any manner. When Sæm returns, we continue the scraping and pasting for two more suns. As we work, Lilit, Jilly, and Bane spend time observing and just lazing about our camp circle. Bane continues healing further; the furions are just bored. They take to hiding in the tall grasses when the sun becomes too hot to bear.

On the third sun, I declare the task complete. I roll up the now pliable skin and strap it to the back of my saddle. Within the pelt are the cat's longest teeth and its blade sharp claws.

"We head due north from here," I tell Sæm, "and in two sun's time we will be met by the natives of this land. When we do, Sæm, make no threatening gestures."

The next sun is again uneventful though we have to ration our water as our supply now being quite low. As I ride, I fall back into the *Calming* and travel to Talon. We fly high above and can see all manner of things. As I spy below, I see we have traveled in a light haze. A low, almost transparent cloud hangs just above the ground and grasses and continues for most of the seeable distance and extending far off to the mountains to the east and North even further. From Talon's vantage, I can indeed finally see the mountains to the east.

Flying remains still a strange phenomenon, though I grow more accustomed. Peering down upon myself and Sæm, I see that far to the north the terrain begins to change somewhat. I can even make out a few trees past the hazy cloud. We will not reach them until late on the morrow's morrow, at best.

That night we are quite lethargic, forgoing any activity after having eaten some and taking but a few sips of water. Our horses are rationed a large skin between the three as they have done the most work and are most in need. I wonder how Bane is faring. The misty haze at all times is floating in the air about us and bright red flowers are prevalent all round as well now. This last we take as a good sign, though they are a variety I am unfamiliar with.

We dig our bed holes and as I sing into it and cover myself some of the lethargy is lifted and I think it strange as I fall into a deep sleep for a second night.

I awake quite late and as I lift myself, at first, I feel quite refreshed and take in a deep breath. But as I do, I realize it turns my thoughts foggy and muddled. It dawns on me what might be happening. Taking a kerchief and wetting it with some precious water, I tie it about my head and over my nose and mouth. Immediately, my foggy thoughts dissipate, and I can think clearly once again. The lethargy is mostly gone as well.

Our horses and the burro are laying upon the ground, the three of them near to unconscious. I walk over and awaken Sæm. He does as I have done taking in a deep breath with a stretch, and I watch as his eyes glaze over and he shakes his head, as if to clear it. Smiling, I make another wet scarf and bid him tie it about his head as I have. Immediately, his eyes clear.

"What is it that has happened to us, Arias," he queries.

"Tis the haze in the air, I suspect," I answer. "And most likely a pollen emitted to the air by the flowers we have been passing through since yester's morn. Come soak some linen and I'll bring the horses about, and one at a time, place the clothes about their mouth and nostrils.

I sit down, enter the *Calming*, and first let my mind join with Paint. He barely acknowledges me. With my healing sense, I make him to sneeze and cough. As he does so, he wakes, rises, bucks, and sneezes some more, feeling the relief of a less muddled brain. Sæm does his part and fastens the wet linen about his mouth and nostrils as I will Paint to let him. After the same procedure has our steeds up and about, I go to tend to Lilit and Jilly as well. I need not have bothered. Strangely, they remain not affected in even the slightest manner.

We hasten to pack our provisions and head north again. I bid Paint set a faster pace and that alone lifts our spirits. I effortlessly meld with Talon again and watch our progress. From my vantage with Talon, I see Bane knifing his way through the tall grasses without a problem and I feel a relief in seeing it. I will do this off and on throughout the morn. Come near to midsun, on one of my trips to Talon, I spy activity in the grasses along our path. I quietly let Sæm know we are being watched.

With Talon's phenomenal eyesight, I can make out men, too many to count, disguised within the grasses and watching our progress, following behind after we'd passed. We have just lately left the haze. The red blossoming flowers are no more about us. At a point near to midsun, we come upon a depression and slow to a stop before descending the slope.

As we stop we find ourselves immediately surrounded by a score of men, shirtless and skin painted in the colors of the grasses about us, though it appears their skin carries an olive tone of coloration also. They have materialized out of the grasses and most hold blow-dart weapons to their mouths and are aimed at us.

I nonchalantly glance about at all of our assailants. Gazing one by one,into their eyes. From behind me one yelled in anger, "*Escha nay doos. Escha niche alloon. Alles gallen escher!*" (They are but two. They are not invited. Let us be rid of them!).

"*Escha estae oderleven de gassa poppei! Ka mas nos vou.*" (They have survived the poopy sea! How many have we seen do such).

"*De gassa ish nolo stalla dos autta gotta!*" (The sea is meant to keep the outlanders away!).

"*Maissa, Es nada dai.*" (And yet, it did not).

I glance between the two holding the angry discussion. I purposefully dismount Paint, carrying my staff with me. All eyes and weapons become centered upon me. Lilit and Jilly pop all the way out from my saddlebags and stand on their hindquarters, showing snarling teeth to all. I ignore the two currently arguing their points and turn to the one unarmed assailant. He wears three of a giant cat's claws on a leather strand about his neck and three deep parallel scars marks his chest. And he appears to wear both with pride.

I speak to him. "*Kassatu spassa chè?*" (What say *you*, chief?)

Silence falls throughout.

The chief's brows raise. "*Mi spasset*—well met, stranger. Will you follow me?"

His face shows no outward sign of emotion.

"Yea, well met. I am called Arias, and this is Sæm. Yes, we will follow you."

He nods and we do just that. A score of his comrades follows us, whispering amongst themselves. Sæm dismounts and catches up with me.

"How do you do these things, Arias?" he whispers.

"Tis part of my vision."

He nods, still not quite understanding, o'course. "Did you understand all that they were saying?"

"That is the strangest part of the vision Sæm. I did and I do," I respond with a quirk of my head, as if to say I don't understand how though.

We walk on for all of that sun and then camp about the open plain. The grasses are no longer as high as our chests and camp that night is a quiet affair. None of our captors speak a single word that we can tell. They eat biscuits from their tunics but offer us none. We make do with our own supplies. The next sun we resume our journey, but this sun Three Claw sets a much faster pace. We simply remount and have no trouble keeping apace. With no further conversation and but a single stop, we finally come upon two great trees of a like I have not in all my days ever seen. Their canopies stretch thirty-paces in all directions. They have an appearance akin to the Calpaca that had been so prominent in my experiences of late but stand taller and carry a much wider girth. They are more majestic and of a scale larger than the great Calpacas, and they are the ones that I spied while aloft with Talon.

We are near to sun's end as a yellow-blue sky continues receding to the west. To the east lies a ragged horizon. Mountains. Walking under these great trees and to their further sides, we arrive at the edge of a long slope as the land falls off into a great valley and across it below spreads an expansive village and a magnificent, flat as steel lake on its far side. It's still, silver blue surface, a mirror to the sky above. This village could hold many, many hundreds, I reckon.

Feeding the lake, a river that winds its way up into the mountains to the east, I imagine, and on the north side of the lake, another river spills out and continues wending its way northward around another great tree and then through farmland and farmsteads that I can clearly see from our vantage. The Accadian Plain is not a desolate place after all.

The village appears to be built of brick and stone entirely. The buildings and homes hold arched roofs of slate tiles. Though there are no hardwoods used in their construction that I can see, bamboo is in abundance as awnings and shutters. There are no horses to be seen either, but there are Llamñas, which I have seen drawings of. These are their burden beasts.

Woven bamboo shoots are used as awnings to cover the travelways and protect against the sun's heat. But as dusk arrives, these great awnings are being folded back against the structures, as they are no longer needed.

As we reach the bottom of the hill, the trail we follow becomes a cobbled-stone travelway. The townspeople upon the rues and ways begin to take note of the strangers amongst the returning huntsmen and people stare at our horses and the burro. Lilit and Jilly decide to put on a show, leaping from horse to horse and standing tall, jittering, and speaking and drawing a few chuckles along with stares in wonderment. Strangers are clearly not an everyday occurrence in this towne.

All but a few of these folks, if not blond, are of whitest hair and deep brown eyes. They are tall, and their skin carries a greenish tint over a bronze hue, and they have a look about them I have never seen before. They are very tall and lean. Their limbs work differently than our own, though they are fashioned the same. I cannot quite explain the subtle difference, but to say they move swifter and softly using no unneeded motion. Their eyes are larger than most folk I know, and their ears atop are not rounded but instead hold a soft or rounded point to them.

As we walk through the village there appear only a few whose hair remains a deep brown. All of the townfolk have a wizened air about them.

A calm and studied expression lay upon their faces. They go about their lives in an almost studious manner, and I hear no laughter. Though there are smiles in some faces, they almost seem solemn in spite of the act. 'Tis as if the smiles have died on their lips and seldom reach their eyes.

Finally, we come upon a circular structure with a hemispherical roof. The roof holds skylights open to the sky and tall and narrow slits around the side. Its sills are sloped to the ground. It is constructed of a white rough-cut marble and stone and it stands apart, brighter than any of the adjacent structures. Three Claw, the chief, proceeds up the stairs to an open doorway. I grab the bundled cat skin from Paint and climb the half-dozen stairs, leaving the horses outside. But Lilit and Jilly will not be denied entrance and scramble up behind us.

As we enter, Three Claw steps to the side and ushers us forward. Here I see the first bit of hardwood.

Ænt-wood.

Its blond and deep walnut-hued grains are intermixed in their distinctive way. It is a simple table with a thick top and the largest piece of the remarkable wood I've ever seen. In two intricately carved Ænt-wood chairs behind it sits two elders, their hair white and crow's feet prominent about their eyes. Their hair and those few wrinkles upon their faces are all that belie their age. One has the deep, dark brown eyes of every other person we have met here, but one has brilliant violet eyes that are veined in gold. She wears a brilliant violet gem about her neck and her hair lies in one long braid that circles round her neck and onto her shoulder and then down upon her breast.

They are both bare chested as most all that we meet here are, and in spite of their status as Elders, their bodies do not in any manner belie it as such. Their limbs are lean and muscled, and the lady sits tall with firm breasts and a countenance that would be the envy of a twenty-year-end lass. Their faces are of high cheekbones and holds hard squared chins as well.

They speak their own language, but I find I understand every word, and when I speak to them, I speak in their language as well. Sæm stares at me, eyes agape. But strangely, just as he learned every lesson I ever taught him in his first effort, I see that he is quickly learning this new language just upon the hearing of it.

"Well met, Mæsters," I say as I approach these elders. "I am called Arias, and this is Sæm." I introduce ourselves and give a short bow of my head.

If they are surprised that I speak their language, they do not show it.

Bright Eyes turns to Dark Eyes and says, "They both carry it, but it is remarkably strong in this one."

She has casually pointed to me with a roll of her hand.

"Is he…?" Dark Eyes asks.

"I do not know, even to us it is but legend and prophecy," responds Bright Eyes.

"My apologies for interrupting your study of the strangers in the room, but I've brought you gifts." They turn those quizzical eyes to me.

"He is so young," says Bright Eyes.

Ignoring their conversation as they ignored mine, and turning to Dark Eyes, "For you, revered Mæster, the skin of the most fierce and wild cat."

Three Claws steps forward to see.

"And for you wizened Mãam, its claws and teeth," I continue with a little bow of my head.

Three Claw unbundles the skin and searches upon it till he finds scar tissue where he expects to find it.

"'Tis THE cat, Nestör. He has killed the wildling Fury Cat!" says Three Claws, excitedly, though with a hint of disappointment, I perceive.

"Well, I can't take credit, actually, for it was Bane."

"Bane? Who is Bane? There were no others with you when you came from the Poppy Sea?" he queries.

"There most assuredly was. He is my wolf friend." And as if on a prear-ranged cue, Bane silently approaches from the shadows and stands next to me. Lilit and Jilly take the opportunity to scamper up to the tabletop and stare at the two elders.

The two heretofore stoic elders jump to their feet and step back away from the table. Three Claws steps back as well and draws his dirk.

"Fear not, he means no harm to you."

The elders again settle, but uneasily ne'er-the-lesser for it.

"Cor Dracüel," they say simultaneously, facing each other.

Dark Eyes, or Nestör, turn to me and ask, "Would you spend some time with us, lad?"

"We would like to share our history with you," Bright Eyes expounds.

"For some cool water and a warm cooked stew, I'd bathe your feet," I say with a chuckle. "And mayhaps you could introduce yourselves?" I ask more pointedly.

The two elders smile, and it reaches their eyes, both Dark and Bright.

As it turns out, Three Claws is called Lazärus. Dark Eyes' given name is Nestör, though few uses it. And Bright Eyes' gives her name as Metüshelah, but all call her Elder or Shèlah.

"I would visit with you on the morrow, if it pleases," says Metüshelah and I consent, o'course.

"Now, Lazärus will show you to food, drink and a place to rest." She bows to us.

Of a sudden, she and Mæster Nestör are as different people than we had just met moments before. A pleasant change.

Leaving the white marble meeting hall, I turn to Lazärus.

"If it is of no consequence, we would like to visit the lakeshore to bathe the horses as well as ourselves before eve-meal."

"As you wish." He smiles and leads the way. "You've made quite an impression on the great elders. Your wolf and the furions did as well!"

Bane lets out a throaty growl and Lazärus actually laughs to hear it.

After eve-meal we are shown to a long bunkhouse shared by Lazärus and three others. There are six small alcoves with beds and a central gathering area with a kitchen to one end.

"You are not married, Lazärus," I ask, and he looks at me strangely.

"Married? I have not heard that word in many a year." He muses.

I am speaking in the language of his people and the word comes naturally to my tongue, so I am confused as well.

"You do not have a wife and family?"

His eyebrows raise, and he smiles. "I understand what you're asking. Let me explain."

"I once had a wife. And I have a mœther and a pæder, and I have a brœther and a sister. The woman who was my wife lives on the other side of the village," he explains and then his brow furls up some. "Do men and women live together on the other side of the Poppy Sea?"

"But of course! How else would you raise a family?"

"But our families have long since grown, but for the few youngers by the able, every few years. Is it not so on the other side?" he asks, and I stand before him baffled. He carries a similar look.

"Husband-and-wife live their entire lives together, raising their youngers and even helping when time comes, when their sons and daughters give birth to youngers as well. Is it not the same in your village?"

Sæm, ofttimes quicker on the cyphering of such things, asks the more pertinent question.

"How many years have you, Lazärus?" He queries.

Lazärus just then removes the cord that wraps about his waist and presents it. It carries many beads. Most colored blue, a few red, and a number are painted yellow. All the villagers wear similar cords wrapped about their waists. He counts them.

"Six and five and four," he states.

"I do not understand. You have 65 year and four moons? You need a cord to remember such a thing?" I say, and he looks even more baffled.

"Arias, I believe our host means he has seen six hundreds, five tens, and four total year," Sæm says.

I laugh aloud, but immediately find neither of them laughing with me. I stare back at him.

"My cord is not the longest by far in our village alone."

"Just your red beads hold more years than Sæm and myself, combined!" I say amazed.

"But I saw youngers among those who watched us arrive. As the youngers grow to an age, there should be a sea of endless people here." I cypher quickly, doing the maths myself.

"There are but three youngers among us and we count them as miracles. We have lost five Efflæan this year alone to the fury cat whose skin you've brought us."

"But how is this possible? On the other side of your poppy sea, men seldom reach seventy year, and I have met but one who knew over one hundred year." I ponder this thought and add, "There are many, many hundreds upon hundreds of people in a single city alone, and there are tens upon tens of those townes and cities on the other side of your Poppy Sea." It is Lazärus' turn to show shock.

"Mayhaps the elder, Metüshelah will be able to explain it when you visit on the morrow." Lazarus wipes his palms against each other and announces, "I will leave you to rest."

We quickly make ourselves at home and after a few moments has passed, I turn to Sæm.

"I know not what to make of this knowledge, Sæm," I say, settling myself upon the bed, staring at the ceiling. "That such a people can live within Aeryth yet remain unknown to all. 'Tis a confounding thought, and that they can live so long. What can be their secret?"

He rubs a hand across his face. "I believe the tales we hear on the morrow might be even more incredible, Arias."

How can anything be more incredible than that?

After a large morn-meal of quail eggs scrambled amongst goat cheese and served with purple and orange routers fried with onions and herbs, Lazärus leads us to our horses. Having assured ourselves that the Llamña tenders can care for our steeds, we let Lazärus bring us back to Metüshelah and her white marble sanctuary. Two more wooden chairs are added about the table.

Here, after some initial questioning by Metüshelah, we hear a fantastical tale that I believe fully in spite of outrageous premise.

For a reason I cannot fathom, both Elders put a sacred trust in Sæm and myself. They say that for our Oath to not reveal their tale to those on the other side of the Poppy Sea, they will pass to us a history long forgotten on the other side of the veil.

"I am a Chronicler, Arias. A historian, if you like. There are three of us left from five. I carry four more blues then your new friend Lazärus." She smiles and thus reveals that Lazärus has filled them in on our conversation of the night before.

"There were five Chroniclers of a like age and ability when these Accadian Plains were first developed. As I said, three of us remain. It is our purpose to do what we are doing here today, passing knowledge of the beginning to you, who we have come to believe to be the Cor Dracüel. I will explain this further in some time, but first I would tell you my tale," she says.

We wait patiently.

"The five of us were the sons and daughters of the Destinæa expatriates as either our pæders or mœthers called themselves and specifically we are of the Lilac lineage. Our parents were one native of Aeryth and one Mæge of the wizædii. All bore eyes such as mine. And we were all barren. We could not conceive nor give seed to another. But we did have other qualities." Shèlah pauses and studies us.

Watching to determine if she can glean belief from our eyes, I think.

Satisfied, she continues, "You see, we five have total recall. I can remember those people in the room with us on that far away day in perfect detail. There were six besides us five. They all had one feature not like the others. It was their eyes. They all wore gray robes to indicate their station, for they were Mæster Wizærdii and they were three women and three men. But they all had distinctly different eyes. One woman had emerald-colored eyes of a brightest hue you could ever imagine, and her hair was a deep auburn. A man stood with them who had eyes of silver and gray. Also a man with eyes of glittering gold, and then one with eyes a deep violet in color and veined in gold, just as mine are and the other four chosen ones, as well."

I am trying to imagine all the different colored eyes she describes them.

"There was a woman with eyes of intense blue and finally a woman with eyes that had irises that were blood red. This last one, she always sat in the corner and for the two moons we spent with the Wizærdii, ne'er did she utter a single word," she says. "In the two moons we spent with these six Wizærdii, they told us tales of the land they called Destinæa, which lay six moons under sail to the south and over the Great Southern Sea. While these Wizærdii spent their time with us, others like them were busy upon the plain."

This story holds the same origin tale that I'd heard from the Elder of Sæm's home towne and so it leads me to doubt both less.

Apparently, it was then that the Poppy Sea had been first sown, in a great arc from the cliffs against the mountains to the north then across and west then south and finally east again ending against the cliffs of the mountains once more to the south. The poppies bloomed and their life essence rose above the grasses. It has been so from those first days and near to a full eon of years since. I marvel to think such a thing could be possible.

She continues, "Some animals are immune to its effects and they are predators there. They're the giant fury cats, vipers, and some badgers. Some birds of prey are immune as well. To our knowledge no man is immune to the effects and most other animals succumb to its affects. You are the first that we have known to pass through in a score of years and before that mayhaps, more than one hundred year. We natives of these lands are even more susceptible to its effects. We cannot travel even a turn of a sandglass without falling to our deaths. There have been those that have tried to burn or cut the sea, to fatal effect."

The thought of it makes me shudder, and I glance to my cousin who also appears affected as well, to think how close we had been to death.

"The other project that these ancient people worked were old mægics that they imbued upon trees, plants, and gems of many types. Some of these gems they placed in a pond at a small Falls that lies betwixt our three villages upon the plain. All villagers travel and bathe within the pond one time each year. These waters, or the gems that lay within, give us our health and longevity. Even after an eon, most citizens know not the true aspect of the pond. They know not of the short lives lived outside the Poppy Sea and think only that the waters have deep healing and spirit lifting qualities. They do, but that is just a lesser benefit. Finally, they planted the great trees with seeds they carried from Destinæa. There are but twenty in all the plains." Again, Elder Shèlah pauses the telling her tale and takes some wine.

The room waits silent for her to swallow and begin once more, but she directly addresses me, "Cor Dracüel, one of the purposes we were charged with, mayhaps is happening right now this very day. We are not sure. You see, we were told of a man that would one day come to us, and he would be likened to the teachers themselves. They said he would come to us countless suns into the future and that we should teach him of their past."

Her words remind me of the Elder I had last talked to. I cannot understand why they both think that I might be this one spoken of in their legends.

"Why would you feel this way about me, and what does this name you give me, Cor Dracüel, mean?" I query.

"They called him the Cor Dracüel or Heart of the Drægon. They had a tale for the meaning of this as well, which I will keep for another time as it is not relevant to this tale. We believe you may be this very one, finally come. You show many of the signs, if not all," she simply states.

"And what signs would these be?" I query.

She smiles at me. "First, it would be a man that could cross the Poppy Sea."

"But you said that has been done before," I counter.

"True, but others did not have your other characteristics. Do not deny that you communicate with creatures like no other, and you were able to speak to us in our own tongue, having never heard it spoken before I am sure. I suspect you have other qualities you have not expressed, as well," Metüshelah explains. Her voice softens. "Might I ask a question of you, Arias?"

"Certainly."

"Why is it you have come here?" she queries.

"My Da has set upon me a quest, even as he died, and I am trying to fulfill it," answering honestly. "I search for a Druid."

Metüshelah's eyes shine brightly at hearing this.

"You can help me find him, mayhaps?"

"We can, I believe, point you in the right direction, but it is perhaps only you that can locate him," she says, most cryptically.

33

Alænèa

One night, a little past high moon and a fortnight into our stay with the Efflæan, which is what these people call themselves, I awake to the sensation that I am being watched. Sæm and I are quartered in a long house with a half dozen other Efflæan. We each have a comfortable bed with a soft mattress stuffed tight with the hair of the Llamñas, the burden beasts of the Efflæan. This, along with a water-fowl feather pillow makes the bed the second-most comfortable I have ever slept in. It will be hard to leave the Efflæan for no other reason than this alone.

These quarters hold all men folk. It seems the men and women of the village sleep in separate long houses. With the constant snoring about me, I do not doubt the women have made a wise choice. The building is comfortable, with plenty of space for each man and his things. Each has his own wardrobe, a floor chest for personal items, I suppose, and a small table and chair. There, gathered about the stone fire pit, are tall chairs and other seating, and groups of men gather in comradery in the eves and discuss the sun's happening or play a board game similar to my Schäaken set. They welcome Sæm and myself gladly. We tell tales of the 'outside world' and they, about everyday happenings on the plains.

The embers in the fire pit located in the center of the long house still emit a soft glow in the dark and hold the slight night chill at bay. The sensation of being observed still presses upon me and my skin tingles for it. Finally, I sit up upon my bed.

Alænèa stands next to my wardrobe staring down at me with large violet eyes that glow in the dark in a calm but curious manner.

Alænèa is the wise Elder Shèlah's nèdaughter. She is the third youngest Efflæan in this village and I observe that the other folk in the village regard her in wonderment.

She returns my gaze and quirks her head in a curious manner.

"I was quite quiet and yet you awoke to my presence. The others never notice my coming and going," she says in a very matter-of-fact manner.

"I felt your gaze heavy upon me. Do you typically visit people at high moon without them aware?" I ask, remaining calm in demeanor.

"When they interest me. You and your friend are quite curious to me. You both carry an aura. Yours is particularly bright and multicolored; I've never seen such. Your friend's is a weaker violet, but still most evident," she continues, her voice still not showing emotion. "I believe that is why the Elder believes you to be the one she has been expecting."

"Aura?" I query. "I don't understand."

"The glow about you. The Elder says that it is present in those that carry mægic in their spirit-selves. The Elder, myself, and the two of you are the only Efflæan in the village that present any aura. The Elder says that only those that carry the ancient mægic have auras. Do many Efflæan from across the Poppy Sea have auras?" Her eyes widen, the first example of emotion so far.

"I don't understand this term 'aura.' I do not see a glow about me, or you, or Sæm. You say we glow different colors?" I ask, quite curious myself.

Alænèa's head does its curious quirk once more and she wrinkles her brow.

"Surely, if you carry an ancient mægic you must be able to see the glow, especially in the moonlight," she remarks. "Tis more evident in the moonlight."

Through all my travels these past many moons, I have recognized that my more 'unusual' abilities come more strongly to me while I am in the *Calming* and so I think to immerse myself into it at that moment. When first taught the technique by Effie, it would take a while to delve into my *Calm*. Now, with much practice, I can reach for it in a thrice. I do so now.

Once I attain the familiar peace of the *Calming*, I peer intensely at Alænèa. My eyes go wide! I see it. Clinging to her person like a soft, shifting, almost-transparent cloud; a beautiful glow of violet. I study myself now and see my own aura as well. As Alænèa had described, it is a moving blend of colors. This sudden awareness is quite remarkable.

"I do see them now, though I never thought to search for such a thing before."

I peer over at Sæm, sleeping but five paces away from us. He too has an aura. His is also a violet hue, though not quite so bright as Alænèa's and mixed about it a softer golden hue. Fascinating.

"If only you and the Elder in all the village have auras, why did you ask if all people from across the Poppy Sea carry such a glow?"

"It is not just the two of you, but also your beast companions, as well. The ferrets that nest in your pack and the great beast wolf that watches over you from afar. They also carry an aura," she explains.

This stirs, of a sudden, a great curiosity to me. More and more, mægics of different sorts are becoming clear to me. The world is becoming more a wonder.

"Lilit, Jilly, wake up the two of you," I whisper.

My two furion friends pop their heads up in immediate response from their nest amongst my blanket and as I study them more closely now, I see it about them as well. Theirs is a light silvery glaze about their fur, but very clear to me now. I am anxious to look upon Bane, Talon, and Paint.

"Do the beasts on the Plain not have an aura such as my friends?"

"Yes, there are a few. Especially those that we see emerging from the Poppy Sea, searching for prey upon the plain. Some of the big cats do, but not all. I've spied a few falcon and prairie kits, akin to your furions, that do as well. And the great Trees and the stones within the Life Ponds as well. Would you like to see?" she asks.

"Do you mean right now?" I stare, wondering at her.

"Yea, high moon is the best time to observe such things, o'course." She acts like it is quite a silly question. "I do not understand why everyone insists on sleeping the nights away."

"I'll just get dressed then and meet you outside," I say as she appears to be in no hurry to leave me to it. I look away then back, and she has silently disappeared.

Hurriedly splashing some water on my face, I don my garb and pack. Retrieving my staff I head out, leaving Lilit and Jilly to curl back up in my bed, it being thoroughly warmed by me to their liking. Clearly, they will not be joining us this eve.

Exiting the long house, I find Alænèa standing in wait. She carries a long bow and her quiver is laced tight to her back. There hangs also a water skin on her belt, but no other pack of any kind. Upon my arrival, she but nods, and then turns and runs north out of the village setting an impressive pace for me to follow. It sends a thrill through me and I keep to her pace. It has been moons since I have run just for the pleasure of it. I thoroughly enjoy the wind in my face.

Leaving the village behind us, Alænèa turns and sets off on a north-eastern path across the open plain. I find it a curiosity that once we pass out of the Poppy Sea, the grasses of the plain grow to a normal height again. 'Tis as if those tall grasses are a further defense against intruders to the plain. Alænèa is of a like constitution as I and exerts little effort in keeping the fast pace. Likened to the other Efflæan, I watch her as she moves in effortless, efficient strides and motions. There shines a great power and grace about it. We run for nearly two turns of a sand-glass over hill and through vales before reaching her first destination, and it is a spectacular sight to behold.

Upon rounding a line of boulders the size of the longhouse, we are gazing down into a valley with the largest tree I've ever seen in all my life. Its canopy covers an area equal to twice the size of the largest longhouse within the village, and indeed, as Alænèa had stated, there about it shines a glow in a beautiful hue of silver.

"She is said to be the 'Manna.' The Mœther of all the great Trees upon the plain. She is beautiful, is she not?" Alænèa asks.

"I've not heard any of the Efflæan speak of any tree as 'he' or 'she'. Why do you pay it such homage?"

"Come, see for yourself." She heads down the long hillside in an easy, sure pace.

I follow. We do not get there as quickly as I had judged, and the magnificent tree turns out to be much larger than I had thought it to be. The valley is deceptively larger than I had perceived as well. There being no other real point of reference and only flowing grasses as far as the eye can see. It takes us a half turn of a sand-glass to reach our destination, even at the sure and quick pace we keep.

The tremendously huge tree canopy is in truth, large enough to cover a quarter of the entire village we had started out from. And its glow, to my *Calming* sight, becomes much more intense as we near it. While under the canopy to me, the night sky's light recedes and a twilight from the tree's glow now dominates the surroundings. There almost seems an underlying hum to the glow as hairs stand on end along my arms. A stream passes nearby to the tree and many night creatures lie near to it or are drinking from it.

Peering up into the tree branches, an amazing number of beasts and birds lie within. Many are natural enemies to each other—predator and prey in any other setting—but here they are coexisting together but apart in the canopy. It is as if it is a place of truce and safety for all.

Tree rodents, snakes, great hawks, and ravens find refuge for the night here. Large cats and coyote drink from the steam together. Nearby to them, antelope do the same. All eye us as we approach but are not disturbed in our coming. Alænèa does not draw her bow, but rather she sits and gazes up into the branches.

"It is safe for all the creatures under and in her arms. I could not draw my bow if I had the greatest will, for the Mœther's will, and embrace, is so strong here," she explains.

I can 'feel' that it is true for me as well. I understand then why Alænèa calls her such. I nod in agreement.

"This is a sacred place to Efflæan and all the beasts on the plain within the borders of the Sea. We come to contemplate and rejuvenate our spirits here from time a'times, even as we soak in the Life Ponds to rejuvenate our bodies. I am restricted by the Elder from using the ponds yet, so I spend more time than most here. My mind becomes clearer, and I can gather and further my thoughts and ideas as I rest beneath her arms," she explains.

"Do the Efflæan hold the other trees in such regard? I've seen very few things made from the wood of the trees," I query.

"No, the reasons are more practical than that, I'm afraid. You see, Arias, of the outside world, there are precious few of the trees and they are the only type of tree on the plain. We fashion our few utensils and furniture from the leavings of branches that we harvest from storms that take from the trees and give to us," she explains.

"But are there not seeds from the trees that can be used to grow more trees?"

"The Efflæan have tried such things, as they know that all other plants reproduce in such a manner. But no fruit is borne of the trees and the nuts produced by the trees bear no new trees," she tutors me.

I wonder at such a thing. Scattered about me, as I sit under the canopy, lies many large 'acorns' that have apparently fallen from the Manna. Some are quite different from the rest.

"But what of these?" I ask, lifting one from the ground. "The ones that have an aura as the Manna does."

Alænèa's brow furrows and she does that now characteristic quirk/turn of her head that she does.

"And when I place it in my palm next to another that does not glow with the aura, they become warm and the glow surrounds them both, you see?" I explain and reach out to show her the two 'acorns' side by side in my hand.

"Arias, I do NOT see that. I believe the Elder is right. You bring knowledge and mægic that we do not possess." She looks to me in wonderment.

I gather up a half dozen of each, the acorns with aura and a like amount without and put them into my pack.

"Shall we continue our exploring?" she asks but does not bother to listen for my response.

She has already turned and is headed North at a run. I rise and follow with a like pace, invigorated to be doing what always makes me feel free back at the homestead with Da.

We run for what I judge to be about three turns of a sand-glass this time. As we go, I catch a glimpse now and again of Bane pacing us and he indeed carries a distinct aura about him as Alænèa had described. How have I not seen this afore? I do not need to force my spirit to the *Calming* to see the auras anymore. My mind has learned the trick of them, and they are evident to me in even a normal state.

Of a sudden, we burst through into a huge clearing, devoid of vegetation but for a mossy growth upon the ground. Far off, and in the center of the clearing, stands three monolithic obelisks of stone. They are near to thrice my height and in their center lies a boulder flattened on its top that rises near to my height. As I gaze around the clearing, many white stones the size of my fist lie about and emit an aura of silver. These stones define the edge of the clearing with no tall grasses encroaching within this grand circle. They are like tiny moons to me, they glow so. More remarkably, the ends of my Bo-staff glow in their presence. Alænèa does not seem to be aware.

"This is the Council Rock. The Sudefflæan and Nordefflæan elders meet in council here twice in a year's time to discuss matters of importance to all Efflæan. They then bring their decisions back to the villages, both North and South," she says. "There are times when the whole of the Efflæan peoples will gather for the most important matters."

A predawn glow upon the eastern horizon begins spreading now and as it does, the stones glow dissipate with it. Alænèa makes no comment, and I take it to mean that it is not apparent to her.

"Let us have our morn-meal, Arias, and we can head back. My NèeMã will no doubt be expecting you to meet with her again."

She reaches under her tunic and produces two biscuits wrapped in broad leaves. "Travel cakes," she explains and hands me one. "You'll find they will give an energy to you, and they are quite filling despite their size."

She offers me one.

"Thank you," I say. "I thought you would be hunting for our meal, as you have brought your bow."

"I carry it everywhere as my tutors have taught me and I am quite adept, I assure you. But to cook up a meal would be time consuming, and as I said, the Elder will wish to speak with you this morn."

We finish our cakes and wash them down with water from our skins. My energy level indeed grows after consuming our small meal. Alænèa rises and starts off back south to the village at a swift pace, and I join her at a matching run. We arrive back at the fountain in the village square and say our fare-thee-wells. She suggests we continue our night forays and I readily agreed, as this first trip has served to pique my interest a great bit.

I meet the Elders again that morn and continue my history lessons, both of the Efflæans and a little more of the Destinæans, as the Elders call them. We will stay amongst the Efflæan for more than three moons and time seems to not exist here but in mine and Sæm's minds.

After our first trip to the great Manna tree, I take time to find a proper place not far from the lake and proceed to plant two of the 'acorns' I had brought back with me, pairing one with an aura with one that had none. I am anxious to see if my theory about them proves true.

Alænèa and I continue our forays about the plain in nights to come, for lesser periods, allowing me some time for sleep. We take a longer trip as well and run the entire circumference of the plain at the edge of the Poppy Sea over the next fortnight, and we visit with the Nordefflæan in their main village for a time. We are invited to join the wandering patrols on hunts, as that is another of their duties, bringing back antelope and other beasts as food for the villages.

While I spend my time with Alænèa, Sæm spends his time learning about the Efflæan as well. They welcome him and his questions. He becomes part of the village in his own way. And so, it happens that on the same day that Alænèa is showing me the life ponds, some villagers arrive with Sæm as well.

Alænèa and I have been running again the night prior. We start by visiting the foothills of the Barrier mountains to the east of the great Accadian lake and observe there, where the river the Efflæan called Esper flows from the mountains and into the plain. We eventually cross the river from the south side to the north, using an elven-vine rope bridge shaped in a 'V' with a sturdy woven rope as its foot bridge and two guide ropes strung to the base rope every pace or so. The Efflæan have strung it between two Cliffsides. The Poppy Sea runs up to the river from both north and south, and the river runs deep, rough, and strong through it, a natural barrier to escaping through the poppies by navigating the river. A fall would be perilous in the lesser and most likely fatal. Alænèa springs upon it with the dexterity of a lemura I'd seen in the Northern Reaches and runs its length with the speed of a hunting plains cat. I follow at my own pace.

Coming off the bridge, we then run north and west for some time and come finally to what Alænèa calls the Life Ponds near about to dawn's break. I am amazed at the sight as we come upon them. A glow about them permeates the grotto of rock that they lie within. There are three small ponds, each mayhaps ten paces across. Large flat boulders surround them. They hold crystal clear waters that have a shimmering emerald glow. The ponds appear to be bottomless with a dark blue shadow developing deep within. The emerald glow emanates from stones of the same color embedded into cracks along the sides of the stone ponds below the surface of the water.

Alænèa explains that the Efflæan travel to the ponds in their birth season each year and add then a bead to their mosha belt. They then immerse themselves and partake of the benefits of the waters. They camp upon the plain and visit with old friends and talk of the seasons past. Though she has never entered the pond waters, her Coming is this very year, and she is excited to experience them.

"The waters are said to rejuvenate both body and spirit and fill one with a euphoria that lasts a full moon," she explains. "Your mind becomes most clear after each visit and you can see a pathway through the coming seasons."

"And when is your season, Alænèa? When will you immerse yourself in the ponds?" I ask.

She smiles excitedly, her eyes bright. "It is why I have waited so long to bring you here, Arias. The season of my Coming is now. NèeMã is to meet me this very morn's sunrise and be with me. My birth mœther will also be present." Anticipation clearly grows within her voice. "Will you join me in the ponds this day?"

"Is it allowed? I am not Efflæan," I ask.

"But certainly, you are! And your friend Sæm will be invited as well. The elders and your friend should be here in only a short while," she explains.

"Then I will be honored to join you." I smile.

Even as I say this to her, a group of travelers came over a rise from the south and west. There are at least two dozen in a caravan with pack Llamñas burdened with supplies. Walking at the head of the procession, I can make out the Elders with walking staffs ahand. Shèlah appears to get on just fine for a woman who has seen near to ten hundreds of her own birth seasons. By her side walks a tall Efflæan woman with long dark hair, which is a rarity here. Her hair is braided in the same manner as Shèlah, and laying on her shoulder to one side. Though Alænèa assures me she wears a mosha belt showing four hundreds of years, she moves with the ease and grace of a woman of forty-year, and Alænèa tells me she is her birth mœther. Sæm walks in the front of the troupe as well. An honored guest at fifteen-year.

The ponds lie near another of the great Trees. Its branches gently wave and its leaves whisper-chatter in a light morn breeze. The caravan winds its way and finally comes to a halt beneath the tree's canopy. The accompanying contingent of Efflæan begin to build camp just to the outside of the furthest boughs of the tree, erecting several tents, tables, and fire pits. We join in the labor and after completing camp, we meet the Elders over mornmeal. Sæm joins us as well. Alænèa is beaming.

The Coming of an Efflæan is a festive affair. As it might be as many as thirty or forty years that a new younger is born into the village and another fifteen-year before the Coming ceremony, much is made of them. Dancing, singing, and great ballads are chant in melodious a cappella troupes of Efflæan. One group sings across the camp space to another and them answering in turn. A single gorgeous voice sings a verse or two to compliment the troupe's song. Pairs are dancing in great flowing grace about the spaces in camp to a pair of stringed instruments similar to those I'd seen bards and minstrels use in many an Inn amongst my travels. Alænèa appears near bursting with the joy of it.

We have learned that the majority of the Efflæan living now on the Accadian plain are at least 600-years-old. Some have died of accidents or fallen prey to the predator beasts, but a new conception and birth among them prove rare, and Alænèa being only the third in as many decades born to the Sudefflæan.

Her 'Coming' to the Life Ponds therefore is an event visited by this large group of Efflæan. It would be erroneous, but then not, to say these are her 'family,' but they are those that mayhaps care most for her, these few short years since her birth.

When it comes time for the 'Coming,' all the Efflæan present gather near the ponds. The Elder speaks a few words, and they are light hearted, not solemn in any way. She then bids everyone to lay aside their garb and step up to the ponds. Sæm and I seem a bit too self-aware at first but relax as all are preparing likewise. All about the three ponds, the Efflæan step up to the edge, we do as well. Alænèa appears as if from nowhere, step up be-tween both Sæm and I. She takes one hand from each of us tightly in hers, and boldly steps forward and into the pond; we follow in step with her.

I expect a shock of chill from the water, like the lake we bathed in aside the village. Instead, a warmth and a weightlessness envelopes me as we enter the deep pond waters. I slowly sink and am immersed in a deep *Calming* to which I feel very familiar and comfortable with. I become in-stantly aware of my connection with Alænèa and to my other side, Sæm. I feel her comfort with me and I feel... a devotion from Sæm. This last comes as a bit of a shock, but I do not betray myself to it and instead accept it and return the feeling in kind.

Time slows, but my mind races on. I know from delving into my *Calming* that the flow of time and all my coming thoughts will fit into the breath I've pulled in before plunging into this pond. I recall in detail my life with Da and all that happened the day I lost him. I relive our experiences and then my mind takes me further back and liken to the time I opened my true mœther's box, I experience more memories of her. I know them to be real memories. I recall playing in the courtyard of a Keep with a large dog and a Lynx, an odd combination, I think Just a toddler. Next, I find myself reliving my long trip upon Da's great warhorse.

Finnie then bursts into my consciousness like a Sky-bolt. My experiences of the past several moons rolls in front of my eyes. An echoing cry comes at me from several directions. Jilly and Lilit are playfully nipping at my toes. Next comes Alænèa and the Efflæan Elder with the mountains in the backdrop.

And then, back a measure of time once more. I am spinning around to endless books in a great library of the same Keep. An older gentleman with bright silver eyes is kneeling afore me speaking silent, earnest words to me. I am now a five-year, I know this, even as I know my name. I am experiencing a true memory. The face of the older gentleman is morphed into the face and body of my mãmere, I recall her instantly now. She, too, speaks to me in earnest silence, for no sound comes from her speaking lips. She then smiles and hugs me tight. A moment later I am gazing into a stranger's face, but not a stranger. I mean, I sense that I know him, and he has a warm regard for me in his golden and sky-blue eyes. He too speaks silently to me in earnest, but somehow, I know a living manner. Real words I now long to know but cannot recall.

I come to the present consciousness holding both Alænèa's and Sæm's hands. They are staring at me through the emerald glow in the waters of the pond surrounding us. Floating about me. Waiting on me. As if to a cue, the three of us kick our feet in unison, turning our faces skyward as we rise, finally breaking the pond's surface and taking in deep breaths.

About us, all the others have already climbed from the ponds. A few are holding to the rock shelves at the pond's edge and are staring intently back at us three. The Elder sits with her legs dangling like a younger in the pond also looking to us, her face contemplative. Of a sudden, people standing at the ponds rock shelf part, and Bane comes to the water's edge. A few paces from him, the furions scurry to the edge as well, and then raise onto their hindquarters. Finally, an almost deafening cry comes echoing from the sky and Talon alights on a boulder above the stone deck of the pond, opposite to Bane. The Efflæan gasps at these happenings. Alænèa bursts in a laugh of joy, immediately drawing attention back to her. A warmth and an energy envelopes me. The silver auras of my creature friends are shown in sharp contrast now, against the emerald glow emanating from the pond. The auras about Sæm and the Elder and Alænèa nearly hum in their brilliance. It all must have meaning, and the time has come, as destiny bears down upon me, to get answers from the Druid. If indeed, he holds them.

34

The Deep Wood

The next sun in the village, after immersion in the Life Ponds, I find myself sitting across from the Elder. "I'll be leaving you soon Elder, though, I'd like to return at your leave," I say finally, after sitting across from her for some time silently.

She acknowledges my admission with a knowing nod.

"I have a good bit more to pass on to you, Arias. We've barely discussed our history with the Destinæans, and there is more to explain to you of their intent. But perhaps you're not quite ready to hear it. You said that your quest leads you to the Druid of Esper Keep," she relents.

My brow raises at her mention of the Druid.

"You speak as if you know of him, yet though I've told you of my quest, you've not mentioned that you knew of such a man," I say, a bit accusing.

"I know of him. Indeed, I have met him. We call him a deep friend of the Plain. But I have my mandate as well. I thought to entice you to stay with us so that I might impart this knowledge on to you because, after these many hundreds of years, I believe you to be the one that it is meant for." She continues ignoring the accusation in my voice and only just seems to notice my raised brow again. "But now I can see that there is more you need to learn before you are ready to hear the whole of my tale."

I wait.

I wait more.

Time passes.

Finally, she says, "I cannot tell you the way specifically to his Keep, as no Efflæan of the Plain has been there, but I can send you to the general vicinity. We once were able to get two of our brethren up the Esper River and through the Poppy Sea and into the mountains in an effort to contact him. They never found the Keep, but *he* found *them* in dire condition and wrought with ailment and near to death. He healed them and returned them by way of the river and once more he came to the aid of the Plain, saving the Æntae."

She has piqued my curiosity now. For so many moons this Druid has been just a name to go with the quest. Here, now sitting afore, somebody that actually knows of him, calling him friend. I deem it wise to learn something of this Druid.

"Elder, I would like to know this tale, as it might give me a glimpse to a clue to why my Da has sent me to find him. Please tell me," I entreat of her. "What are the Æntae, and how did he save them?"

"I will tell you this tale then, before you leave us, so you will know how the Druid saved the most important part of life upon the plain. It is also appropriate as it is a story related to beginning of our life on the Plains and one that you should know," she acknowledges, more to herself, I think.

"The tale goes to a distant time, some twenty hundreds of seasons past, and twice that to the tale of these Æntae that we hold sacred and live among. You see, Arias, the Ænts are the name of the great trees that survive here on the plain," she says.

"Ænts! The trees!" I gasp and hold up my staff before me. "My Bo-staff, bow, and Schäaken board are fashioned from Ænt-wood. But Da told me that the Ænts were extinct from all of Aeryth."

"And that mayhaps be the truth outside of the Poppy Sea, and it would have been here as well, had it not been for the Druid of Esper," she says. A studied look plays upon her face.

"Twenty-hundred seasons," I then say. "That is five hundred years past. So, the Druid is of a like age as the Efflæan?"

"Of a like age, yes, but there was one before him in my time. And as I said this tale goes to the origin of the Efflæan tribes of the Plains," she re-iterates. "In the age that the Council of Mæges established the Plain within the Poppy Sea, and even then Æntae were already a special tree. You see, Arias, the Mæges and Wizærdii came to Aeryth an eon afore my birth. And in that time, many mægics were made commonplace and a great help to the peoples of Aeryth."

She pauses to take a long drink whilst studying me before continuing. "But that tale is for another time — when you return. We Efflæan were always a peaceful people living in the Deep Wood of the mountains further to the north of the Plains. Living in peace with woodland creatures apart from the greater world about us. We were the perfect people for the Mæge Council's purpose as we were used to living apart from others and were little known even then to the other peoples of Aeryth. But they needed to protect us and the knowledge they wanted to keep, knowing their time in Aeryth was growing shorter with each passing decade."

"And 'tis so, when they established the Accadian Plains, they used the Æntae as our communication with the world outside of the Poppy Sea, and in particular to our previous home in the Deep Wood. You see, with the Mæge's ancient mægic placed within the Æntae, one could stand beneath the great Manna upon the plain and hold counsel with those under her sister tree in the Deep Wood. My brœther then was the Deep Wood Sjaman," the elder says gazing off past me. "In the beginning, the plain had not been anything but scrub trees, bamboo, and Efflæan fruit vine which we had cultivated within our tribes for generations untold."

Another thought strikes a memory within me. The Efflæan fruit vine is, of a fact, the Elven-vine that Da hunted for and cherished when he found a batch on his mountain forays. We never bothered to harvest its fruit, as Da said it must remain to reseed and replenish the grove and thus sustain it. But, here on the plains, the vine and fruit are very plentiful and even a staple in the Efflæan's diet.

"We insisted our new settlements would need trees. The Mæges planted score upon score of Æntae about the plain and along the shores of the Esper and the lakes, and many more about the Life Ponds and Counsel Rock. They were a species most strong, robust, and plentiful in the Northern Reaches where the Mægii first settled and some few were already known to us Efflæan to the north of the Mid-Realm. We could hold counsel, my brœther and I, through the Manna, once each moon until the Scourge." She gazes past me once more and pauses her tale for a while, taking a long sip from her wine from a Ænt-wood goblet. "This is why we sent for the Druid. The Æntae began dying, against all our efforts to save them. At that same time, I stopped receiving any response from my brœther. We could not make the Ænt reproduce and we feared we would lose all of our trees."

I adjust my position, for the tale measurs a long one, and take my own sip of ale, engrossed in her words.

"The Druid came and he solved the riddle and stopped the scourge. We owe him our very existence, I fear. But still, though he halted the further demise of the trees, they did not grow anew and we were left with only our existing population of Æntae, mayhaps one in a hundred of what they once were. We are very careful with our resource now," she explains.

My wonder at their care with the trees is clarified. I ponder this tale for a bit and then ask the elder a question. "Elder, during the scourge, were other plants or wildlife affected as well?"

She reflects on my query for a while before she answers, "We once had a type of small boar that died out about that time, I believe. And the burrowing rodents as well. I remember because they were of a number too great to count, and I would find myself stumbling into the burrowings that littered the plains. They were a nuisance, and then they were gone. I recall noting to others that we received a small blessing that came with the great disaster that was the scourge of the Æntae. Why would you ask such a question?"

"I beg pardon, but one more query before I answer. Alænèa has shown me the auras that exist about myself, Sæm, herself, and you. She also showed me that there are some creatures that also carry the auras. My question, did these rodents carry auras?"

"Yea, they did. What does this mean to you?" Her face looks puzzled.

"Are you aware that flying insects such as bees carry life's essence from plant to plant and thus plants may multiply?"

She shakes her head. This is one of those many lessons I have learned from Effie and I explain this to the elder. She is clearly fascinated at this new knowledge and her face brightens immensely. It is likely seldom she learns new things about her small world.

"And in a like manner, some rodents might store the nuts or seeds of the tree for a meal later and may inadvertently be doing the same thing if they are buried and hidden away."

The elder nods in understanding. "So, you are saying the scourge of these rodents, and I do remember they took great glee in dancing among the branches of the Æntae, stopped the spreading and growth of new Ænt trees. But we took the nuts ourselves and planted them, as we knew it to be the way and cycle of life with plants and trees. I do not understand why it would work for rodents and not for us."

I smile.

"I believe I may have that answer as well, and I've started an experiment to test my theory." I explain my discovery that I perceived auras about some acorns and these, put tight together next to those that did not glow, have resulted in an aura expanded to include both. "So, you see, the rodents would store many acorns together in their stash and some would bind and produce a new tree."

This thought astounds the elder.

"I have collected a great number of both into sacks and are keeping them by my berth in the longhouse. I will show you where I've buried the first two by the lake and should my theory prove true, you should have enough to start a small grove again," I say. "The one thing that is important though. I do not believe that Alænèa can see this aura, and you may not either. On my trips about all the plains with Alænèa, I've noted that only the great Manna appears to produce the acorns with aura and they may be but one in 100 under her canopy."

"Arias, this is a great service you've done for us and I thank you!" She rises, grabbing me about shoulders. Her eyes are glassy with moisture and I feel a great pride that I can help.

Four suns hence, Sæm and I express our fare-thee-wells. Sæm especially has heavy heart in leaving, but he will not let me leave without him. We have become quite fond of Alænèa and she us, I believe. We gather our packs and weapons. I mount Paint, and he, Sasha. They have not forgotten the feel of our weights upon them, though it has been some time since carrying us last. Only Alænèa has tried to mount and ride Paint during our stay, though I offer any Efflæan a chance, and she does not favor riding a second time. And so, they have been free of burden the entire time we stayed in the village.

My plan is to head north and east as I want to visit the Council Rock. The stones there carrying auras still hold my curiosity. And so, I desire to study them more.

From there, we will travel further north and cross the Poppy Sea, then on through the Deep Wood that the Efflæan elders have mapped out in detail. Though their information is as old as dirt and Roger, the mountains and passes known to them are not likely to have changed in all that time. The map indicates the large area that is likely to hold Esper Keep. With the information found in my mœther's box, I can only hope to find my way from there.

By midsun, we are approaching the clearing about the Council Rock. Across the open grassy plain, the towering obelisks surrounding the stone are evident from a great distance away. Just as before, as soon as we reach the perimeter of the clearing, the glow from the white stones becomes evident. I ask Sæm if he can see the aura about them, but he says he cannot. I tutor him in searching for the auras while in his *Calming*, and he has been able to see a slight glow about Alænèa, himself, and a greater one about me, but could see nothing about the furions or any other creature and so it does not surprise me.

It fascinates me that these stones appear to somehow keep the grass at bay, allowing only a moss to cover the ground from where they lay in concentric circles about the Council Rock. I dismount, lift a stone, and study it. But other than the glow and its absence of color, it appears as any other stone. I ask Sæm to describe the ones I hold up to him. He shrugs and names it simply a very nondescript stone like any other that lay about us in the clearing. My eyebrows raise. Sæm sees the stone as nothing more than any other stone. He does not see that it glows a faint white and as I handle it and study it more closely, I see that it really does not even resemble the random shape of a stone, but is actually a smooth, nearly perfectly shaped oblong disc.

Experimenting, I take the stone into the grasses with me and toss it a pace in front of me. Immediately, the tall grasses recede from around the stone. Or rather, it recedes forward from the narrowed end of the stone about fifty paces in the direction I had tossed it. Remarkable. But when I travel the distance cleared by the stone and turn gazing back, after a while the grasses begin to reappear. It is as if the stones are meant to clear a space only in front of them. If I place a second stone and aim it back in the other direction, the effect becomes a permanent one. Lifting the stone again, grasses return over the course of a slow count. Where have the grasses gone, and how can they return intact?

Regarding my experiments, Sæm queries, "Arias, how is it that you can make such a thing to happen? Ye are truly possessed of mægics!"

"Nay, Sæm, this is not I but the stones that have been possessed of some mægic. But mægic I believe it is, ne'er-the-lesser," I return. "I have now, most certainly, come to believe mægic of sorts are a part of Aeryth."

I then toss three of the stone together in front of me. 'Tis not fifty paces that are cleared of the tall grasses ahead of us. As far as my eyes can see the grasses have receded.

Returning to the Council Rock clearing, indeed, all the stones along the perimeter face inward, but many about the clearing pointed in all directions, and hence, keeping the circle about the Council Rock clear at all times and for all time.

I carry the stones to the Council Rock and sit studying them, pondering my many experiences since I have left my homestead in the foothills far to the west. Sæm pulls out midsun meal. We eat fresh bread, spiced and smoked meats and cheese made of Llamña's milk. We eat under a warm sun and a fresh, soft breeze. 'Tis delicious. And as we eat, I realize that I have truly accepted that mægic truly does live in this world and mayhaps lives within me. It then decide to embrace the reality of it and somehow learn more of it.

Would the Druid have these answers?

Ever studying the stone, there is another thing about it. Assuming it is a stone, it initially appears and weighs in my hand like a stone. But focusing on it, I find that it no longer has the weight of a stone with its apparent size. This boggles my mind. In "reality,' it has only the weight of a pebble more than a stone. A lesson then, mægic can act against one's sense of reality and cause illusions to more than just one sense.

There are countless numbers of the stones about, and so I say to Sæm that I intend to collect a goodly number of them. He just shrugs not seeing any purpose. But I have in mind a certain further experiment that I want to try with them. And so, I spend the turn of a sand-glass collecting and storing a great number of the stones in a sack.

"Let us be gone now, Sæm, as I would make one other stop before dusk," I say, settling my stack of the curious stones upon Paint over my saddlebags and behind my saddle.

Near on to dusk, we reach my next destination. The great Manna Ænt tree. 'Tis the largest tree I have ever encountered. An enormous Ænt. Here, I search the ground for a few more acorns that carry an aura and a few that are whole but carry no aura. I toss them in my sack with the stones.

"Sæm, let us make camp here for the night. I'd like to sleep upon one of the great branches up in the canopy where the creatures feel so safe and comfortable."

He just gives me a quizzical look as it is just one more of my eccentricities this sun.

"I think I'll remain on the ground."

Mayhaps, his growing, long and lanky body would be best suited to that.

Thus, we make our bedrolls for the night. I find a wide, very secure berth betwixt two wide branches that crosses mayhaps four pole up into the canopy. A large cat with eyes that shine bright in the tree's twilight glow, stares at me as I settle. But it does not give me any pause, as I know the spell the tree has cast upon the creatures about and among her boughs. My belief in mægic is ever growing stronger these days. I quickly find my *Calming* and fall off into dreams.

I fall into a deep sleep this night. My only dream – of the tree itself. But it is different in some manner. There are a myriad of forest sounds, the like of which I've certainly not heard since we have last left the trader's trails and well before entering the plain at Bladestone Keep. I also spy among the branches, woodland creatures that do not inhabit these plains. There are marvelously colored birds as well and I spy a lemur. This is not the Plains Manna I see about me. The dream passes into the further night. I wake quite refreshed in my hammock and bedroll. The sun breaks over the grassy hills in a blue cloudless sky to the east.

We make our morn-meal of the Efflæan travel cakes and take a quick bathing in the deep, cool stream. We are off again soon enough. I have no other place I want to visit and so we head just west of due north sighting our path to what we perceive to be the end of the barrier mountains to our east. Near to sunset, two suns hence, we can make out the Nordefflæan village well to our west. But I have no plans of stopping. Sæm and I have gotten into our old easy pattern of travel. He speaks of what he has learned of the plains ways, and I speak of my visits with the Elder and my trips with Alænèa. Sæm's interest lies in these tales most.

On our fifth sun out from the great Ænt, we come upon the Poppy Sea and make camp here. It is a bustling campsite to be sure. Bane has joined us for the night and even Talon makes an appearance with an earsplitting and echoing war cry. He drops a hefty woodland creature at our feet, clearly a contribution to our eve-meal. Lilit and Jilly are frantic with excitement for the reunion of our full group as well. This will be our departing point for travel into the unknown once more, the last time being when we had entered into the plain from the south. The Elder told of a pathway into the Deep Wood and the landmarks we should look for along the way. But first, we will need to traverse the Poppy Sea. Before we start our trek into the Poppy Sea, I have a few things I intend to try. But it will need to wait for morrow's morn. We bed down for the night.

With sun rise on the morrow's morn and after our meal, I proceed to try my experiment. Tossing three stone in front of me and into the Poppy Sea, I look on and smile. Just like at the Council Rock, the tall grasses and poppies alike have disappeared from sight. There lies before us a clear pathway, mayhaps two paces wide that extends to the edge of my sight, mayhaps near to 800 paces into the Poppy Sea. A parting of the sea, as it were.

"The stones from Council Rock, I should have cyphered such a plan," Sæm says, eyes sparkling in delight of my idea.

"I've still a few years of wizærdry on you, friend." I jest. "Come, I'd like to plant a couple of the Ænt trees on either side of this pathway. Retrieving the acorns from the sack, we dig holes to plant them fifteen paces to the east and then west of the pathway.

"I've decided to call them 'Waystones.' But do you remember the strange property they exhibit? The path will open before us, but when we've traveled the path, it will eventually close behind," I explain. "If enough stones are not brought to place in the other direction, one could not see to return upon the same route. I believe I may have enough to see us across, but little more. I will leave a parchment explaining this to the Elder. I believe he will be excited to learn this. We will leave it with a marker for a hunting party to find. After that we will be off into the next leg of my quest."

Sæm nods to my reasoning. "He will indeed, Arias. The Efflæan will be able to return to their ancestral home in the Deep Wood if they so desire. This is a good thing you have done for them."

"I hope," I say thinking just that, wondering what will come of this development.

We make good time and do not dally to let the poppies affect us. Thus, we are able to cross the 'sea,' traveling throughout the night by the light of the full moon. By the dusk on the following sun, we come out of the sea and immediately into a great forest. As I had suspected would be the case, there remain but a few of the Waystones left in my sack. We plant two more

Ænt tree acorns on this side of the sea, just as we had upon the other end. With little left of the sunlight we continue on for but a short while, finally setting camp amongst the most ordinary looking trees, something we have not seen in many a fortnight. Something that does not exist upon the plain.

We go about setting a few snares as it has become too dark to be hunting with our bows. Wildlife and plant life are equally plentiful in the area and the furions come back to camp with their dinner. The familiar sounds of forest beasts and bugs permeate the air and is comfortable to us. We are quite wary from our single file trek across the 'sea' and setting Bane the task of watching over camp, Sæm and I both lie down for some much-needed sleep.

35

Ænt Manna of the Deep Wood

We wake to the full moon and the sound of a piercing yell and a mountain cat's responding cry of the hunt. Immediately, both Sæm and I rise from our rolls, grabbing our bows and a few arrows from our quivers, running towards the scream. I enter my *Calming* to assess and pinpoint where the sounds are coming from. Even as the no-longer-quiet of the forest night rings in our ears, a cacophony of wildlife proclaims their presences, the hunting cat's growl becoming as clear as a bell to my now heightened senses.

Springing first into an opening where I know the cat is waiting, Sæm draws the attention of a large tawny cat high in the branches, diverting its eyes for a moment from its intended prey. It lies poised on a thick branch overhead with forepaws extended and claws protruding and piercing the bark of the tree limb. It continues stalking its prey. Its hindquarters are raised and tail low, ready to pounce upon...

Alænèa!

She stands upon the wide branch of an adjacent tree with her back against the trunk and a blade in her hand.

I take all of this in during but a fraction of a moment. Her bow and quiver lay at the base of the tree, no doubt having fallen from her reach when the cat startled her awake. And in the moment that the great cat's attention has been drawn to Sæm, I halt, plant my feet, and nock an arrow into my bow. The next moment sees the cat's awareness return to its prey, dismissing our distraction, as hindquarters release the spring of its taut body. My arrow is loosed in the same instant.

The cat's body continues its flight towards Alænèa even as the arrow pierces its heart. Life leaves the cat. Its body continues its lethal trajectory and hits our friend hard onto her breast, even as her blade enters the cat's neck.

The great cat's momentum slams Alænèa hard into the tree's trunk. The dead weight of the large cat's body pulls itself towards the ground, and a thrice later, Alænèa's inert unconscious body falls also.

Fortunately, Sæm is now there to catch her. I join him. We carry her away and set her down, her back against a tree. She wakens in a daze, staring up at us a few moments later.

"Amazing meeting you here, on this very night in this fine forest, so far from the village," I say, smiling down at her with Sæm peering at her from next to me, his expression a bit more dire.

"It is indeed a fine forest. The first I've ever seen in all of my life. And I believe I have you to thank for that as well." A smile breaks out upon her face. "I suppose I have some explaining to do."

"Join us at our camp and let us get some sleep after all this excitement. It's been a long, sleepless journey here, so mayhaps the morrow's morn will be better suited for your tale."

She seems thankful for the reprieve.

Sæm lifts her to her feet as I gather her pack and bow. Lilit, Jilly, and Bane have joined us now. As the furions dance about Alænèa's feet. Bane wanders over to the cat to confirm that it will no longer be a problem. I retrieve my arrow and her blade from the cat, and our group heads back to our camp.

Upon returning to the camp, Sæm adds some wood to the embers in our small fire and stokes it to flame again. We spread our bedrolls about the fire and arrange ourselves.

"Are you feeling well Alænèa? You took quite a hit from the cat?" Sæm queries.

"I'll be fine, but I think I'll sleep through this night and not wander about in the moonlight," she responds.

"Bane will keep watch and we will be safe. Let us all sleep and we'll discuss things in morn's light." I tuck into my own bedroll.

The forest canopy is thick, and the sunrise does not immediately rouse us from our much-needed slumber. The sleepless, two-sun trip across the Poppy Sea has taken its toll on all three of us, and Alænèa's brush with the great cat, even more so on her. A gentle breeze and cool air on the forest floor holds us snug in our bedrolls. The whisper-chatter of the leaves above creates a white noise that accompanies late dreams. Being first to rise, I have a pot of water boiling in a new fire when the others wake. I have crushed some brew beans and fill a small filter sack and toss it into the pot. Mugs of the hot morn brew bring us to our senses as we sit and drink about the fire.

"Alænèa, you promised us the tale this morn. I believe Sæm and I are anxious to hear it." I prod and at first she does naught but take a serious interest in her mug.

We wait patiently. Finally, she raises her head and speaks clearly.

"It started the day of my 'Coming.' I found the clarity that the elder said I would in the Life Ponds. And in the clarity, I saw it my destiny to reach past the Plains to find my true self. You had decided to leave us, and I knew that I must leave with you. I also knew that the Elder would not approve of such a thing, so I did what needed doing. I am sorry for the deception, but I am not sorry for my choice," she says with a stern conviction.

Both Sæm and I chortle in mirth and Alænèa takes offense and stands with an anger I've not seen in her before.

I raise my hands as if to fend off an attack. "Do not take offense, we are not laughing at you or your choice of destiny. We are finding amusement in the Elder's miscalculation of your guile and determination."

"Aye, Alænèa," says Sæm. "The Elder took us aside to say that you would approach us with a request to join with us. We are dumbfound that we did not need to deter you of the effort."

She sits back down and looks upon us both.

"The Elder expected it then... You will not take me back?"

"Nay, we will not. You survived the crossing and so we cannot return now without putting your life at great risk. So, we have now become traveling companions. I do not dislike this fate," I state. Sæm nods, and her violet eyes brighten brilliantly.

"I swear you will not regret this decision, Arias Côeurdrægon!" she adds.

"Well then, traveling companions." I exhale and gaze about at my friends assembled, man, Efflæan, and creature alike. "We have a good way to go to find this Druid of Esper, as the Elder has named him, and we have a beautiful pathway through these great woods to follow, so I say let us pack up and be gone and about it."

Alænèa will not join either Sæm nor I upon our horses but says that she would rather explore beyond our path, as she has never experienced the forest before in all of her life. The Elder Efflæan of the village had spoken fondly of memories they held dear in their hearts about great trees and abundant wildlife in the forests of their youth. They would sometimes lament and wish they could but take their final rest among the forests of their memories. But their words did not match the splendor and discovery that she can now experience. She disappears for half the sun and returns with tales of her discoveries and eve-meal tied over her shoulder.

I and the furions teach her to hunt for tubers, roots, and forest berries that are edible as well. I show her herbs that grow wild and shrooms that take a practiced eye to find. She proves adept at all of it. And in the evenings, I show her the ways of the camp cook. Travel through the Deep Wood remains mostly pleasant. There are dangerous creatures in this world as well though, and we travel alert and with care to avoid the largest venomous vipers I've ever encountered and arachnae the size of our heads that have rodents of equal size spun into cocoons and hanging like sides of beef in a butcher's larder in webs as thick and strong as Elven-vine.

We find the river that the Elder had drawn upon the map and are following it deep into the wood. We travel east and south, then ever towards the great mountains to the east again. There is a southern spur to these mountains that on the map trails so far south as to be in the sight of Kings Court. Our destination is to the east of this wall of mountains though, and so we will follow the river east through the mountains and past its source to the land that lies beyond. Then we will head north again to the valley that is home to the Druid.

At the end of a fortnight, we find ourselves deep in the forest with little light filtering to us on the forest floor, guided only by my compass now. Going is slow and we walk as the way is often twisted and hard to navigate on horseback. We chance upon a great tree the like I do not know. It has grand branches that climb and circle about the massive trunk and if there were twice our number we could not have stretched and locked hands around it. Wagering that it stands taller above its neighbors, we make a game of climbing to its top branches in a race so that we might spy about us and to get our general bearings.

Lilit and Jilly join in and the challenge is on. Alænèa is light and quick, but my longer arms and legs win the day but for the furions. We burst through the surrounding treetops with fresh air and sunlight to greet us. Surveying the ocean of waves brought on by breezes flowing over the treetops, I can see that we are indeed at the zenith of the most magnificent tree that stands easily five of my height above all the others – save one. In the distance stands another much taller and wider than even the one we cling to. What is more, I can see that it is an Ænt, mayhaps a twin to the Manna that sits upon the Accadian plains. I know immediately it must be our next goal.

"Do you see it, Sæm and Alænèa?"

"Aye, Arias," comes the quick reply from both.

"Let us fix a bearing to it," as I take out my compass and do just that. "If it is of a size to its twin on the plain, I judge that we should make it there by sunset. I see from here that it has an aura akin to her sister."

At first our travel is a tough go towards it, but we meet up with an old and overgrown track that heads in the right direction and we begin to make better time. Not too far off in my travel time estimate, we arrive just after sunset. In the last, her ghostly silver aura guides us in after the sun has set.

This tree is truly of a kind with the Mœther of the plains. We arrive to a menagerie of this forest's creatures, in harmony with each other under her canopy. We are confident we will sleep easy this night.

Setting up camp, we eat some fruit for an eve-meal and sit about a small fire just within the canopy of the great tree and in casual conversation. A lull and quiet sets about us. Alænèa is tending to Lilit and Jilly with pets and combing their deep fur with fingernails and they to her with chin kisses and earlobe nibbles. Sæm at the moment sits leaning his back against his saddle and bedroll, twisting a leather wristlet and staring out into the darkness. It carries a stone that our small firelight catches and coaxes a sparkle from. I think it very much likens to the gem in my tinker's amulet, which has me in turn, trying to cypher a thought about its finding which niggles at my brain. Alas, Alænèa pulls us both back to the here and now.

"Arias," she queries, "Tell me how you came to name Lilit and Jilly. Your creature friends all seem to have names clear to their character and origin, save these two. I feel there must be a curious tale to it. Otherwise, I would expect their names to be Fitchet 1 and Fitchet 2!" She jokes, and I laugh aloud in return.

"Your jest is near to truth Alænèa... They were for a while simply called pup 1 and pup 2! But their present names do have tales to them," and poking a stick into the fire, I lean back against my saddle and tell the stories.

"Lilit's name came from Da in a manner, and from one of his tales at the least. She is the 'Big Sister' and the 'Warrior Queen' of the pair and has always been. She is the first to sit up straight and tall on her hindquarters and stand guard and watch. This is what prompted me to name her so. Da once told me of just such a character. He said it was a tale told to him by his Da-sire, who in turn said it came down through generations from his Da-sire's Da-sire and most likely further back. The tale went that when once on a trading journey to the far south, his ancestor met a troupe numbering a score of the tallest women, and only women, garbed as soldiers and riding horses at least the size of his great warhorse, Bregœ. The leader of this group sat tall and straight in her saddle and had a most fierce countenance, carrying on her back a great bow and quiver and with a great pummeled longsword hanging at her side. She introduced her companions and named herself 'Lilit.' They met and camped together on the shores of a small lake and under a great Calpaca tree."

"Ho, Arias," Sæm exclaims. "We are surely cousins, as I've heard this same tale from Da-sire! They camped and visited for a ha'fortnight and when the women warriors left, the youngest and smallest among them stayed. She was called Wee'cha and our greatest Da-sire married her, and she was said to know ancient mægic."

"Yea, Sæm, that was the rest of the tale as I was told it by Da," I respond as a warmth envelopes me in knowing I have a greater family.

"Well, then, it seems Lilit comes by her name with a strong history and has a role to live up to. So, from what great figure does Jilly fashion her character?

I chuckle.

"Da would ofttimes make my favorite morn-meal. Flatcakes. He would stack them high and atop he'd first place a great splatter of fresh cream butter. Even as it started to melt and drizzle down the sides of the stack, he'd place atop a large scoop of berry preserves. Lilit's little sister would always stand tall on the tabletop and stare as he did this. As we jostled the table while we seated ourselves, the berry heap would jiggle and jilly… And Jilly's body would do the same in anticipation and glee. We have ever and since called berry preserves Jilly. Oh, and her as well!"

This sets us all to chuckles and as Jilly sits up and stares about at us, Lilit falls over on her back and chitter-giggles as well.

Later, we each find a space that is comfortable to us so as to find some sleep.

For me, I decide to spend this night as I had spent the final night at the plains Manna—in her arms. After having arranged myself in a hammock I had rigged for sleeping in the great tree, I settle and bring myself to my *Calming*. It is a wonderment to experience all the spirit-essences that I sense about me. All are at peace and in their own version of *Calming*, I think. There are cats and fierce wolf-badgers and a myriad of birds. There are rodents and snakes. I even sense a family of lemur and wonder if they are the same that I felt when I lay within the Plains Ænt Manna. Here are natural enemies, many of them, but at peace in this tree.

Though to feel this unusual group about me is interesting and quite re-markable, I have other intent. Elder Shèlah had said that she communicated with her brœther whilst they were both within the embrace of the great Æntae. It is this that I mean to attempt. Alænèa had said that most nights, there is at the least one Efflæan that visits and spends nights within the canopy of the Manna upon the plain. My hopes lie in this thought.

Reaching into the *Calming*, I send my thoughts to the Great Plains' Manna. I know her and I know right away that I have found her. The wild-life here in my dream are different than those surrounding me in this great tree. I search with my spirit-self with the help of the Manna and, after a time I am successful to an extent. There is an Efflæan bedded for the night under the canopy. I can actually see him in my mind's eye. It has a 'dream-like' quality and at the first, he does not respond to me in his sleep.

I recognize the man as a Llamña herdsman I had spent some little time with amongst his animals at the lakes edge. Knowing he does then know me, I continue in my attempts to contact him. From Elder Shèlah's tale of speaking to her brœther within the great tree, I surmise that it was in a dreamlike state that they spoke one to the other.

And so I persist in willing myself to be in front of the herdsman's eyes. He is stirring in his sleep but does not recognize nor take notice of me. An idea pops into my head. I meld with Bane and then I present ourselves to him. This makes him take note in a big way. The man yelps and near wakes from his dreamscape. But he recognizes me and in his thought presence his eyes go wide.

"Chaka. I am speaking to you from the twin to the Manna in the Deep Wood that Shèlah knew of old. Will you take a message to her for me?" I think to him, and I see that he understands.

I explain that Alænèa now travels safely with us. I express that the Ænt tree is well and that there is no longer evidence of her brœther's tribe that they left behind in the Wood.

He understands. I know that he will deliver the message to the Elder. I fall off into other dreams afterwards and sleep a long and deep sleep. I find that mægic is an exhausting affair.

As the morrow's morn dawns upon us, we wake to the beasts leaving the Ænt's protection and going on their way.

36

Imagine

As the morrow's morn dawns upon us, we wake to the beasts leaving the Ænt's protection and going on their way. We take our time packing up our camp, first having made a small morn-meal with those leftover provisions we have in our packs and saddlebags. As we sit about, I tell Sæm and Alænèa of my experience within the great Ænt at yester-eve's high moon. They are in awe that one can communicate through the trees.

We start off wading across a large stream that passes near to the great Manna of this Deep Wood. On the other side, we quickly find a game trail that follows the stream before heading due east towards the mountains once again. The way climbs steadily for the next few suns as the forest starts to dwindle about us.

We are seeing more of the sky these suns and as fish and game are readily available to us, along with wild growing root vegetables, herbs, and shrooms, camp life becomes quite comfortable. We set camp each eve and take our time about it. We are two suns out from the great Ænt and free of any time constraints. Our routine from the trip down the trader's trails out of Cliffside resumes, and we show Alænèa our ways and she easily adapts to them.

Sæm and I find ourselves discussing our travels again and our more recent stay upon the Accadian Plain. As Alænèa explores and discovers the forests in this new world about her, she joins in with many queries and tales of her own. I find I have many more questions than I had when I first left out of my homestead in the mountains outside of Middenvale and hope the Druid will have the answers I seek.

I miss Finnie immensely along with my friends back in Middenvale, but I have gained new friends along this last portion of my trip as well. It's taken several moons to get this far and I now hold a strong need within me to discover the answers to my questions. We are getting close to my journey's end I sense, mayhaps within a few suns. Each eve I brush down Paint and play a bit with the furions. Bane joins us in camp. Most eves I see Talon perched atop high trees next to our camp. My thoughts reach back to what I have accomplished these past many moons and know that Da would be proud of me.

We awake a bit before dawn, this sun to a clear and brisk morn, deep in the shadows of both the wood and the mountains. I have another vision during the night where an old man with a long, white beard held tight with braided leather circulets under his chin and again at his chest, awaits me on a stone bridge—knowing that I am coming.

So, in knowing he is waiting, we set off into the mountains upon a trail that wends through the mountains passes. The path is clearly marked and so we make good time, but we walk as though there is no great rush. We continue this way, winding about through the mountains for the next five suns. On the sixth sun we enter a forest on the other side of the range in mere foothills to the great rocky heights left behind. And throughout the sun we spend traveling game trails leading us further north and east. As dusk approaches we come to the end of the woodland pass and peer out before us unto a great valley with a single mountain not too far to the east. Only silhouettes in the deepening gloom of sunset.

We make our camp just inside the tree line and head towards the mountain on the morrow's morn. We reach the area that Elder Shèlah had thought that we are most likely to find the Druid's Keep. Off to the north of us, as the quiet of the coming night envelopes us, we can hear the sounds of a faraway surf breaking against the shore. Alænèa becomes excited and quite beside herself to think that we are near to the great Sea that Sæm and I had spoken to her about.

We wake the next morn just before sunrise, looking east out from the trees and seeing the lonely mountain as a silhouette sets a glow in the new sun's orange sky. In the light of the sun we can see that we sit atop a rise that overlooks down an incredibly expansive valley where a stream snakes far from the South and then north past us to the sounds of the far-off surf that we heard upon yester's eve.

The valley afore us is a sea of tall high grasses, but unlike the Plains, this sea of grasses breaks upon huge outcroppings of boulders and small copses of trees and both likened to islands. A northern breeze from the real sea bathes us in a silky warmth, even as it whispers through the tree's leaves and branches above. We have a leisurely and filling morn-meal and as the others are breaking down the camp, I walk to the edge of the tree-line once more and gaze down upon the vale. This time as I look long and hard, I spy a stone bridge off in the distance and upon the bridge stands a figure that brings back with clarity my dream from just afore we had entered the mountain trail. I quickly speak to the others, don my pack, and take my Bo-staff to me. I bid the others to hold back a while as I want to approach the man alone—the Druid I somehow know, and speak a few words to him first.

As I stride down into the valley headed directly for the stone bridge and the man standing atop it, I look back behind him and see in the brightening sun a remarkable Keep perched tight against the lone mountainside. It has two tremendous spires, and below them are walls encircling a large village as in a great hug. I continue my walk with long strides heading directly toward the figure on the stone bridge.

As I approach further, I can see that he is staring straight towards me and even at this distance, mayhaps 100-paces out now, I can see his distinct silver-grey eyes as clear as a hawk sees the tale of the field mouse he's tracking.

The tall man wears a dark grey cloak and has a long beard just as I saw in my dream. His beard hair is braided in two parts and is held together with leather woven circulets, one below his chin and the second at his chest with small bells hanging from each. His thick and wavy, shoulder length white hair flows about him in the wind. He leans lightly on an oaken staff, the height of my own Bo-staff. He appears to be waiting for me specifically. It is as if he has been waiting all morn for me to appear out of the tree line from a particular trail, though I have traveled no true path but only game trails to reach that point. And so, as not to disappoint him, I walk out from the tree line across the grassy vale and towards him as he expected, I presume.

As I finally approach the bridge, I stand in the roadway at its foot.

"Well met, stranger. I have come to speak with the Druid that is said to reside at this Keep. Do you know of him?" I ask, staring into the eyes of the Elder before me.

He tilts his head in a quizzical fashion, his eyes gleeming and a smile spreading across his face as he first glances back over his shoulder and then turning back to stare unabashed into my eyes.

"Well met indeed, lad. I know of him... As a fact, I am he," returns this old and mysterious man. "Tell me, lad, do you actually see my Keep behind me?"

I think this strange, because of course I can see something as big as his Keep against the mountain wall. And so, I nod with a wondering look back at him because of it.

"Well then, I'll need to work on my wards some more." He shakes his head and leaves me wondering what this can mean.

I take a further step forward and with a slight bow, I reply, "Mæster, well met indeed then, for I was sent on a quest by my Da to meet and speak with you. I've traveled for near to ten moons from the far west on this specific quest and hope that you will hear me."

"And who might your Da be, lad?" he queries.

"He was called Ètœn Bard, Mæster. An ex-soldier of the realm and someone of your acquaintance, I believe."

The old man's chin twists and the corners of his mouth turn down as he quietly ponders the meaning of this news.

"I knew an Ètœn Bearheart. He had sworn an Oath and was set to a task by me twelve-year and some moons ago. He was a giant of a man and an ex-soldier of the realm as you say," the Druid acknowledges.

"Yea, that would be my Da, then."

"You say you've traveled far from the west. Have you managed this feat entirely alone? And your garb and sigil are peculiar. I've not seen any such like it that I can recall. Is it of a make they employ in your faraway home, and what Lord flies a Drægon sigil, pray tell, lad?" He is almost jovial in his query.

I, in return, react a bit harsh mayhaps, as I think everything about this man quite peculiar, and the fact that he continues to refer to me as a mere lad—a younger—after all I have seen and experienced. Further, I will reach my eighteen-year-end in just two moons' time and so, looking square at him I reply, "Nay, I've not traveled alone, and would be further obliged if you would use my name,. You may call me Arias."

This elicits a truly hearty guffaw from the man in grey, but he makes a slight bow towards me. "But, if you have not come alone, where are your companions?"

And as if on cue, the two rascals within my pack emerge and climb about my shoulders.

"Ha," the Druid exclaims with bushy eyebrows lifted. "Your furions would be strange companions indeed! They're usually a creature not found to have any contact with humankind and are quite rare here in the Middle Realm. And yet, they appear quite fond of you."

I then whistle my special whistle to call upon Talon. The Druid bends and covers his ears in pain and I am set aback to see such a thing. No man has ever been able to hear the sound of my whistle.

"You heard my call?" I query of him.

"Indeed, I did, lad – er, Arias, pardon," he says bowing to me. "I have excellent hearing, thank you."

He lifts his hands from his ears.

Talon cries his echoing war cry in return and the Druid's eyes go directly to him as he plunges towards us. The Druid takes a half step back as Talon's great wings spread wide and catches the air as he floats a moment above us, afore alighting upon my shoulder as Lilit scurries down from it. He has healed, o'course, and grown since we started our trek together. His wingspan is as wide as my arms outstretched and reaching and then some. He is a very formidable raptor and the Druid's eyes widened and sparkled as he settles upon my right shoulder. Jilly jumps to the top of my head and nuzzles Talon's beak, and Talon returns the gesture.

"Ha! Well met indeed. You travel with special companions, there is no doubt. A Noördan mountain hawk, an Echo Eagle, if I am not mistaken?" The Druid laughs with delight. "And have you any more traveling companions I should meet? Your hawk has been hovering about my Keep for two sun's past. I see it was a sign of your imminent arrival."

He looks deep into my eyes in questioning wonder.

I give another call and Paint comes in a galloping thunder and Bane arrives silently from the grasses at the Druid's back. Paint arrives to a halt at my left with a proud whinny and huff. Bane suddenly circles in front of the Druid, and he tightens his grip on his staff and steps back to stare at Bane in total surprise. Bane gazes at the Druid and paces twice in front of him, never taking his eyes off the old man. But he does not growl and all he gives is a noncommittal huff afore circling about me to lie at my feet on my right.

"Well, now we have a larger than normal Paint from the Southern Reaches and a true to life Mountain Dread, thought to be gone from these parts of Aeryth. Could your mighty steed be of a bloodline with Ètœn Bearheart's mighty warhorse? Yes, I believe so. Ètœn has surely requited himself masterfully. You are traveling in quite peculiar company, young Arias," the Druid whispers as he takes in the spectacle afore him.

"They are my friends, Mæster, and yes, we met and traveled together on a quest to find you. I mean to know why Da has sent me here, if you will."

But my troupe has not finished arriving quite yet and I can hear as Sæm and Alænèa arrive from behind me, Sasha, tethered and walking behind Sæm. They are casually discussing something or another and approach as if joining friends for an eve together. The Druid at this point is beside himself and his smile reaches from ear to ear.

"Well," says the Druid in a sober way. "I apologize regarding my comment as to your status, though at *my* age, it was a simple error of judgment. You are truly not just any lad. Indeed, you are a man to be reckoned with, I dare say, and I see that Ètœn Bearheart has kept his Oath to your mœther."

I just stare back at him and wonder at his calm appraisal of me and my companions.

"He has also imparted his love and mastery of creatures, I see, or mayhaps even more so, he's brought your own talent to the surface in a greater way than I could ever have suspected," he continues. "If you'll do an Elder one last favor? I've admired your staff since you've approached, might I have a look at it?"

He appears totally in every ease with my troupe about me.

And so, I hand my Bo-staff to him as he hands his to me, so that he can better examine mine.

"Ænt-wood, to be sure" he proclaims, "and I suspect that Ètœn had a hand in its crafting. A remarkable piece this is. And is this 'Drægon's tooth,' and Drægon's fire to its other end?"

I nod.

"And the runes are totally appropriate, but I am aghast that Ètœn would know that!"

The bone in the staff's center that appeared as a glistening piece of ivory has caught his eye, and he remarks on it as well.

He grabs my Bo-staff about its center and with the quickness and surety more akin to a man of thirty-year, he raises it to the sky and blinding white light bursts from the Dragon's tooth and a hot red glow emanates from the Dragon's Firestone. I stare in amazement to see such a thing as a warm rush engulfs me and instantly draws my hand towards the Bo.

The Druid laughs aloud in delight and returns my Bo-staff to me.

"And are there any more surprises?" he asks as his eyes turn to Sæm and Alænèa.

"I have no provisions for a Noördan Mountain Echo Eagle nor a Mountain Dread, but you and your other companions I can accommodate. I have gone by many names over many a year and across many lands, but pray, call me Èschereon, Arias. Èschereon they call me here-abouts," states the Druid in a most sincere manner. He then turns and simply walks back towards his Keep, not bothering to see if I am following.

"But Èschereon, Ser Druid, I would have at the least a word now as to why I was sent to find you... Who am I that the King hunts me? My mãmere sent me away and mægic flows within me?" I ask, near pleading.

"Come, you must be hungry after your travels, and then we shall speak of your mœther and pæder and the truth of your bloodlines and mayhaps of your destiny." He turns to peer back to me, but for a moment and he says in quite a grand fashion.

"You, Arias Côeurdrægon, are an Enigma."

Summit of Seven

A muted orange, fringed in red, still fills half the darkening evening sky under spreading fingers of billowing cumulus. Their underbellies glow in those same fiery hues with the failing sun. In my mind's eye, the glowing clouds can surely be mistaken for rising plumes of smoke. Defended by the fiery clouds, the inky sky above is beginning to push the sunset towards the horizon. Still, the entire far skyline seems ablaze and screaming of a different time altogether. A chill breeze, contrasting the scene, washes over me even as it did on that similar day. The colourful twilight sky is setting the valley's thick forest, behind its huge lake... *afire*. Finding myself taking a moment, I reflect further upon the memory. Why not? It is, after all, quite significant to this very eve. Those of smaller minds in this land called *Aeryth* are of little consequence. And those of any consequence are more the more under the thrall of *my* council, ever as we have schemed.

I am called Mensæ now, a name worthy of my talents.

Leaning into the railing on the third-story balcony of my room at this hunter's lodge, every detail of that night long ago on a distant shore materializes crystal clear within my memory. Ruminating, I find myself peering back over that bay of Esperance, its city of that same name is burning in the distance. Notwithstanding that it had been quite memorable, my mind can relive it in complete clarity and detail. One of many traits that make me special, as it does all my compatriots here at this otherwise deserted mountain lodge…on this mid-winter's eve.

This land called Aeryth, was new to me then, those forty years past, having first set foot upon its shore, that very eve. Though *that* night, the burning sky from north to south was indeed and verily aflame. Looking east, I witnessed raging fires, not a sunset. On the left horizon, fires engulfed the structures within the city itself, set afire by our army of orcæn troops even as they were forced to retreat back to the sea and into the few hundreds of giant galleys, they had arrived to Aeryth upon. But more than the city itself was ignited and burning that night.

To my right upon the open sea, all of the ships of our armada lay ablaze as well. For while Prince Aegèas, from the Mid Realm and heir apparent to the throne in Kings Court, had driven our invading forces back to the sea, his fleet of every imaginable type of sea vessel and 1,000 strong swept through our anchored fleet of 300. Having sailed in from the north and the harbour at Kings Court and every harbour betwixt there and Esperance, they rained fury and devastation down upon our elite galleons with torch arrows and flaming spears from ballistae. Small barrels of oil were set afire and catapulted from their rag-tag decks and onto our more majestic fleet, as they sailed swiftly through the anchored warships on a stiff breeze. Our invasion from across the Southern Sea was turned back that night, and our armies were utterly vanquished.

I smile to myself. Aegèas became a hero that sun and would soon rise to the throne over all of Aeryth. But the invaders were not entirely vanquished. As a fact, the true and more powerful nemesis had made it successfully to shore unnoticed and we are now meeting at this very lodge, discussing our successes and plans of further conquest. As the advisor and seer to the now seated King of Aeryth, I am also the governor to this council. I have come far and accomplished much since that night. I take my roles seriously– king's advisor, council governor, and seer to the crown. Though a true seer,

I am not. But as close advisor to the king, my chambers in the cæstle at Kings Court are adjacent to the king's, and with such proximity to Aegèas, my mind mægic allows me to intercept the king's *sight* and claim it as my own, denying the king his very own mægic and cementing my place as advisor and seer to the king.

Those convening here, like myself, are wielders of this same ancient mægic. It has become clear to us that our particular form of mægic is mostly unknown and never practiced in Aeryth. Our successes have been easier for this fact. But, though muted to history, 'tis indeed that mæge elders, Source-Sayers, escaping from the Wizærdii of this art, is what had brought the practice of mægic to Aeryth more than three millennia ago. And now, for these past forty years, our stronger, dominant mægic is now taking seed in the courts, keeps, and mountain lairs throughout Aeryth.

Our council, meeting this week at the lodge, is made up of seven mægi. We carry a specific mandate set down by the Three Eye Council, who in turn sit as the extreme rulers over all of Destinæa and, as they see it, the whole of the world.

In theory, my council of seven are under the thumb of the Three. But practically speaking, we are separated by a great sea. A sea that took three months for we and the orcæn invaders to cross, losing a third of our force to watery graves upon the journey. And then we, all seven I dare say, also have individual ambitions. We are loyal to the Three, of course, as to not be means a torture worse than death by many fold. But we will be given leeway if the result will benefit the Three in the end. We are ones of a mind to take full advantage of such a gift.

Our mission originally conceived, to find at the least the Druidæ and even more to our benefit would be to find the Elders, Source-Sayers who wielded the other five ancient mægics to full effect. Few in Destinæa know this story, me being one that does.

Though sure there is more to the tale, I understand the Three feel that the five other ancient mægics were stolen from them and are rightfully theirs. And with these other mægics once again under their sway, the entire vast world, and indeed the heavens above will be under their exclusive dominion. The Three already hold complete reign over all that they survey, and when my council has accomplished our goals, they will rule all Aeryth as well. We have been sent by the Three across the great Northern Sea with a trained army, just as similar groups had been dispatched in centuries past to the other three corners of the compass. south, east, and west out of Destineae. Separate councils, each made up of eight acolytes, had been sent searching after the stolen mægics. Each expanded the empire but without finding and regaining that which the Three seeks most. When these other mægics were not found upon the land in the other corners, it was cyphered that the traitorous Source-Sayers must have travelled north across the sea.

I and the others were tutored long and thorough in our art, gained through strong bloodlines. A vast army of orcæn were bred for the sole purpose of undertaking our charged mission. Though this army was destroyed, we eight acolytes, of course, survived. We are the true mission in any case. We have been mostly successful in our charge over these past four decades, though the Three do not know it yet and will not for some time. But time is a commodity of which the council has plenty and even more so the Three. After all, the Three have been searching for three millennia, a century more will not matter.

Finding any of the Elders holding the true mægic has not happened yet. But the council knows that mægic exists in Aeryth and then so must the trail to the Druidæ and then further to the Elders. I believe that I have even encountered one of the Druidæ and I am eager to pursue it. In the meantime, the council continues expanding its control over Aeryth, each member in a position of power over great numbers and increasing more every year.

The Druidæ are the answer, and I can feel we are on the verge of a breakthrough. The Three have said that the Druidæ are the keepers of the knowledge and mayhaps even on a par in the Arts as myself and my compatriots. But for some reason, the ancient mægics that I was tutored about are only displayed in small ways around Aeryth. Could this land be only a steppingstone to the Elders of the Mægic, or is their mægic only being hidden further or deeper in some spot here in Aeryth not yet discovered by this council? Mayhaps this is an effort to thwart us, the Elders knowing that someday the Three would find them and exert their right.

Some recent happenings are encouraging though. Word from Spæctre in Tullamoor speaks of a boy that controls beasts and holds another mægic in his staff while disrupting his business and killing his agents wholesale. I intend to discuss it further with Spæctre on the morrow when we convene. Further, this boy might be the offspring of the king's daughter. The same daughter that was spirited away by the man that I believe to be one of the Druidæ disguised as the lass' mentor. That effort foiled even more plans that the council had set in motion. These Druidæ may be more aware than I thought, working in ways similar to our own.

The council had schemed to have a king's courtesan from a wealthy royal family murder the king's wife and then be exposed for it, thereby killing two birds with the one stone, as the saying goes. Discrediting a royal family that has the king's ear–oft times opposing my counsel to the king–and opening an avenue by which the king's daughter would be betrothed to a council ally family, thereby solidifying more future control by the council. This mentor stole the girl away before a wedding could be consummated, setting back our plans for a time.

Capturing this lad who clearly displays one of the ancient mægics and mayhaps has a connection to a member of the Druidæ will become an imperative for me and the council. We are here to discuss this as well as other pressing matters.

These further thoughts of the council pull me back to the here and now and why I have convened the others here at the mountain lodge the king has just recently frequented. We are meeting away from any prying eyes at a time the lodge would normally be closed for the season. Each of the original eight acolytes will be present save one who has vanished into the Northern Reaches two decades afore. I cannot help but wonder, due to recent events, if the Druidæ are somehow responsible for that disappearance as well.

Looking out over this unique horizon, I recall the night we boarded the skiff to shore from our command vessel. Compared to the other ships of the orcæn fleet it had truly been a luxury craft that suffered no hardship in the three full moons it took to cross to this land. Each of the eight had our own bodyguards and servants to attend us. And over those last seven suns of battle, while the armies fought ashore, we eight entertained, in our fashion, a like number of well-to-do citizens gathered up in forays by our personal bodyguards. We used our specific mind mægic to learn the language and ways of our 'guests.'

On that last night, our guests were arrayed on deck with the obvious success of their homeland in evidence as they saw many of the invading ships afire behind them, flames licking the horizon. They could not be helped but to be encouraged. I surveyed each of them...seven men in various lordly attire and a woman in the obvious finery of her station at court. It was, even so, the way of life back in Destinæa.

"Eyes forward, if you please." I struck a loud and commanding voice to swing their attention.

A tall, lean, and obviously brave man with a noble bearing stepped forward and addressed me.

"I see your fortunes have turned somewhat, Master Mensæ sir. Mayhaps I can act as an emissary to strike a truce between our armies," he said.

"There will be no truce...sir. All of you, disrobe, now!" My curt return.

Our guests looked about at each and the other, a fear finally setting in at the gravity of their situation. All went quiet for a moment–the only sounds the rigging clanging against the gunwales and the waves lapping against the hull. They had been lulled into a mistaken sense of security as they had dined and drank in luxury as civilized 'guests' of their captors. I knew what they were thinking. Their situation would be remedied with ransom or favor of a sort as their station would typically warrant. It was what civilized enemies did amongst nobles, after all. But now, swords could be heard being drawn, and chuckles heard from the ugly orcæn guards. Our *guests* remained cowardly and compliant. In their time aboard, the noble lady had commented in private that these 'orcs' seemed to be an unfortunate cross in bloodlines betwixt a strong lean stock of man and a toothy, large-eared lesser being, and she could not truly disguise her disgust. What manner of men would even attempt such vile experiments with bloodlines? We would. They were pale with black beady eyes and a curve to their spine. Drawn faces housed large, toothy mouths and overly large and pointed ears tucked flat to the sides of their heads. Yet they were, strong and fearsome looking to be sure, and subservient and knowing their place.

Each of the council stood across from their own individual 'guest' of like build and stature. Mine carrying the look of a well raised academic. Each of the guests were now beginning to undress, resignation and fear in their movement. Mayhaps we would but toss them overboard and leave them to swim to shore, I read my guest's thought. The noble lady, however, refused.

"I will do no such thing!" she screamed in defiance. Anger boiling there with a bit of panic creeping into her voice.

Her host, Maya, the only woman among us eight, nonchalantly addressed her.

"Then my guards will help you, though they are known to get a bit handsy." Maya smiled and her guard attendants chuckled ever louder.

A guard moved forward from behind her and placed a hand on the lady's shoulder. She gasped and stepped away from his grasp, and reluctantly started to disrobe. She had managed to turn all eyes to her.

I eyed Maya closely, as did the other council mægi. It is seldom that a woman advances to such a level in Destinæa's crown city elite. She would need to be tougher than any man and ambitious, extremely talented, and smart as well. I, of course, know that Maya is just such a mæge. She has aligned herself recently with Chalmæn. An inspired move on her part, as Chalmæn is ambitious and of like mind. A powerful ally.

The noble lady, I never bothered to learn her proper name, shook and in near hysterics, finally finished. Maya's guards grabbed up her clothes immediately. All the guards on deck stared brazenly at her nakedness, openly licking their lips. I watched as Maya approached her and put a calming hand to her forearm. Then with a sky bolt fast move, ran a knife across her exposed neck, quickly stepping back to avoid the bloody body collapsing to the deck. Maya's eyes seemed to sparkle as she looked at each of the mægi in turn. The guards shuffled and groaned at their loss.

While the 'guests' stood in shock, Mensæ nodded and each of them found a similar fate at the hands of the guards behind them. Little struggle amongst them as they were still in shock at what had just transpired. I could not help but smile at Maya's guile, sending a message to her compatriots that she was not one to be trifled with...and just maybe with a little mercy with a quick death to the noble lady. *Mayhaps*, that was in my mind only.

We eight quickly donned our new apparel and climbed down into the waiting skiff tethered alongside the ship. The captain had orders to sail immediately back to Destineae to inform the Three of all that had happened. I gazed back with intent from the bow of the skiff as six others rowed, and Maya stood at the rudder. He could see looking over her shoulder in the distance the fate of their ship.

"Mensæ, what is it you see?" Maya queries me across the sound of oars rhythmically rattling in their iron brackets.

"Alas, the captain will not be able to fulfill his last order."

Once on shore, there was little discussion amongst we eight. Pushing the skiff back into the waves, having set it afire, we quickly gathered what little we had brought with us. Our plans had been laid in detail on the journey over, assuming we would find what we were looking for. We would travel out from our landing spot and assimilate into Aeryth society. Once gaining a foothold, we would then start our search and further work according to the direction of the council of Three. We would meet back two years hence to this same location to take our first council. That was near to four decades ago.

I step from the balcony as well as the memory and back into my rooms, pulling the glass-framed balcony doors tight against the cool night air. I am taking my eve-meal alone and the table is already set as one of the lodge's help sets down a steaming bowl of soup. I smile at her and place an extra coin on the table next to her as she finishes placing the meal out on the small table. The lodge has a small working crew, gathered specifically to cater to their unexpected guests and their off-season stay.

She smiles at her luck to be making coin this time of year.

Glossary of Names

Ètœn: *Ee* - tuhn
Steffænie: *Steff* - uh - nee
Kattalæn: *Kat*-ta-lehn
Aegèas: Ay- *Gee*- us
Èglæsèa: Ee- *Gless*- ee- uh
Adrèæn: Ay- *Dree*- uhn
Aeglèsia: Ay- *Glee*- sea- uh
Alænèa: Ah-La-*NAY*-ah
Escher: *Esh*- er
Mensæ: *Mehn*- Say
Bastèœn: *Bass*- chee- un
Jænelle: Jann- *Elle*
Fafhärd: *Faf*- herd
Éshæm: *Esh*- umm
Sæm: Sam
Tœngis: *Tong*- kiss
Ronælt: *Ron*- uhlt
Katdollène: Kat- *Doll*- een
Èschereon: Ee-*Cher*-ee-on

Any others: read them as you see them!

www.ingramcontent.com/pod-product-compliance
Lightning Source LLC
Chambersburg PA
CBHW072253020726
47501CB00002B/252